Hazim

By Ammar Al Naaimi

Cover Art by Mohammed Al Attar, @Mimoon_art

Printed in India

ISBN
978-99969-99-14-7

Also By The Author

Sarim
Majan Chronicles

The Story So Far

*This is a recap of Sarim

Mishal Al Balushi was ten years old when he first met demons. A jinni (of a type called Amour) climbed into his mind, giving him strange powers. However, it is always whispering terrible remarks in his mind.

An old man approached Mishal five years later, claiming to be able to save him. This old man was **Shayib Ghalib**, who helped Mishal unlock his ability to ignite fire from his hand. After defeating the Amour, Mishal joined **Sarim, the Public Authority for Anti Jinn Operations**, where he joined team seven and met **Ahlam Al Hatmi** and **Eman Al Lawati**. During the first mission, Mishal fails to save a little girl called **Khadija**, and vows to grow stronger.

After training and many more missions, Mishal appears to be getting better. He also learns that a boy with a 'heart of fire' has been prophecized to save Oman, and meets the ultimate exorcist **Asaad Al Nabhani**.

Mishal and Ahlam appear to be falling for one another. However, they're attacked by a strange man during a mission and Ahlam dies. The man, **Julanda**, says that he was sent here to kill Mishal because of the prophecy.

Mishal goes off to train alone in a cave in Qurayyat under an eccentric man while Asaad waits. They hear that Al Julanda is trying to summon ancient jinn to use them as tools with a group called Bani Safi. After some time, Mishal rejoins Sarim and they go to attack Al Julanda and his group of sorcerers. They defeat Al Julanda, after which Shayib Ghalib decides to retire, Mishal is promoted to team leader, and Asaad becomes a Shayib.

Prologue

Ali Al Marzooqi sat feeling sorry for himself in the cafeteria of Sarim, the Public Authority for Anti-Jinn Operations, where Omanis became exorcists and worked to protect the country from jinn, wizards, and the astral dangers of the world.

Ali's team leader, Musab, was leader of Team 16 of Sarim, but he didn't appear very glorious in that moment. Musab stood furiously in front of Ali, trying to convince him to read a book.

"It's going to make learning ruh manipulation easier for you!" Musab argued, pulling out a new-looking copy of what appeared to be an old tome called *Al Sharih.*

Ali sighed. "Boss, I failed Thanawiya last year; how am I meant to memorize ten types of jinn, as well as types of visual, geometric, spell-based, *and* imagination ruh skills?"

Musab brought his hands up to Ali's throat as if he was going to strangle him. "Boy, nothing else is *working!* You have some potential for wind manipulation, but if you can't control the power of your soul - your ruh, then how are you going to fight any jinn? Even a Mughayab can beat you!"

Ali weakly said, "Maybe I can support the rest of you from the sidelines?"

"My performance review is coming up, and I'm not failing it just because you haven't learned any spells in your first quarter working here!"

Musab continued hissing angrily even as Ali sighed, then loosened and retied his Msar around his head in an effort to discourage more nagging.

The cafeteria grew louder as a group of three exorcists came from the other side. One of them was a tall, lean man with a square mustache framing his lips and a brown backpack slung over both shoulders. He walked with military precision while talking to the second man, a handsome-looking man with an impeccable beard and a smug air of confidence. Both wore dishdashas.

The third man - a boy, really - looked to be Ali's age, but he towered over him. His biceps bulged through his standard dark fatigues. The boy had an air of primal physicality, even as he looked with kind eyes throughout the cafeteria.

Ali noticed Musab following his eyes towards the trio. "Who are these guys?" Ali asked.

Musab's face lit up with triumph. "That's Team 14, only two ranks ahead of us. But see that kid? That's Mishal Al Balushi. He's a couple of years younger than you."

Ali sucked his breath in surprise. "Really? He's a giant."

"Exactly. It takes *dedication* to succeed in Sarim, not special powers. Mishal uses an in-born fire power, a bit like yours. He was a weakling when he got here, and failed his first mission. But six months ago, he took down the leader of Bani Safi all by himself."

Ali focused his attention on the trio's mannerisms. While the two others chatted, the boy walked with an air of introspection, as if he was deeply thinking about something.

A short man was walking in the trio's path, not paying attention. After a few more steps, the short man would trip over the leg of a chair and crash to the floor in front of them. Ali thought about warning the man, calling out to his attention the cahir. However, Ali knew the man wouldn't know what he meant, and that he would fall anyway. *It's too late,* Ali thought to himself. *It's not a big deal, just let him trip over the chair.*

Suddenly, Mishal's face snapped to attention. His eyes scoured the room, and identified the man walking towards them. Mishal moved subtly in front of the other two and quietly moved the chair out of the short man's way, preventing him from tripping. It was a quick, graceful movement. Nobody noticed it at all save for Ali.

"...Ali, Ali, are you listening?" Musab said, and Ali snapped to attention, realizing he'd been staring at Mishal for the past few seconds.

"Oh, sorry," Ali said. He looked back at the trio, feeling as if he didn't want to stay still. "Can I have the book now please?" he asked, putting a hand out to receive his copy of Al Sharih.

Musab frowned in bemusement, but he happily handed the book over. Ali vowed to pour over the book and to grow stronger to be more like Mishal Al Balushi. Kind, thoughtful, confidant, accomplished, powerful, and brave in all things.

Chapter One

Mishal Al Balushi was a bundle of anxiety that was trying its very best. At sixteen years old, he was discovering that anxious hearts can find comfort in a number of different things. Comfort is granted by the kind words of loved ones. It can be derived from a pleasant experience or a meal. It can even be extracted somehow from sitting in a small café in Al Adhaiba, noticing a nervous man with a big mustache, and giving him your attention to distract yourself from your own troubles.

"You look worried," Mishal said to the man with the big mustache: former corporal, Salim Al Ghafri.

"Of course I look worried, boss," Salim replied, running a hand over his unshaven face. "Did you hear what this idiot said?" he added, pointing at the other man who was sitting with them at the cafe. Suddenly, Salim's eyes widened as he appeared to realize that he had just offended a superior. "Oh, I'm so sorry, sir!" he added with a salute to the second man.

The second man was handsome enough for two of the girls in this café to turn around and start eyeing him. He had a slim *khaizranah* - a white cane - slung over one shoulder wherever he went. And he appeared to be thoroughly enjoying Salim's flustered attitude, as well as the attention in general.

"You've gotten so cruel that you'd say this to me?" the man said to Salim in a fake hurt voice, the small beginnings of a grin playing along the edge of his lips.

This was Asaad Al Nabhani, the ultimate exorcist of Sarim. *He's a cocky bully is what he is, guilt-tripping Salim,* Mishal thought to himself. "Stop it," he said out loud to Asaad.

Asaad ignored Mishal. "I've been working on protecting and guiding you since you joined Sarim, six months ago. Of all things, you *question* me? I thought the military had more discipline."

Salim looked down, seeming properly chastised. "I-I'm sorry sir! The thing is, I don't see how what we're doing is a good idea."

Asaad's handsome smile turned ever so slightly feral. He moved forward in his seat on the comfortable sofa and pointed at Salim. "You, my older-than-usual subordinate, are an exorcist in training. I chose this assignment because I know for a fact that it will aid in your growth."

"Hiding our powers in a busy café, during day-time, will make me stronger?" Salim asked in a half-whisper. Mishal could practically see the man's eyes glinting with the promise of hope.

It wouldn't, Mishal knew, but he stayed quiet.

"Of course. That's why I decided on this plan," Asaad Al Nabhani said, pointing to himself in a showman's gesture.

Salim's eyes spawned stars of wonder. "I'm sorry I ever doubted you, Shayib Asaad!"

Mishal harrumphed, interrupting the conversation between Salim and Asaad. The latter man gave him a cautionary stare. Mishal ignored it. "So the reason you chose this timing is because of Salim's growth," Mishal said while pretending to look at the busy café around them. "It has nothing to do with the fact that you forgot to tell me about the mission last week, and that the Shayib council has a meeting today where you might get chewed out for neglecting another mission, leading to you rushing said mission, and thus bringing us out here in the afternoon instead of at night?"

Asaad coughed even as Salim's reverant eyes turned disdainful. "You didn't have to say that in front of him," he accused, making Mishal laugh.

Even as a Shayib, Asaad Al Nabhani will never change, he thought. Asaad was the ultimate exorcist, powerful enough to rival entire teams by himself. As such, Asaad was cocky, lazy, selfish, and razor-focused on appearances.

The sun shone in Oman with such intensity that even the ever-present sparrows took refuge beneath the shade of the trees planted along the side of the road. The sun cast faint glimmers over the interior of the busy coffeeshop, lighting everything up with an ethereal haze impossible to find anywhere else in the world. The peaceful haze made it so that the café appeared to be the most unlikely place and time for an exorcism.

Mishal Al Balushi, Salim Al Ghafri, and Asaad Al Nabhani were part of Sarim, the Public Authority for Anti-Jinn Operations. The purpose of today's excursion with Salim was to exorcise a minor jinni, which had been causing a disturbance during moonless nights. Due to the lacklustre attitude of Asaad, their supervisor Shayib, Mishal's team hadn't heard about the mission until Asaad burst into Mishal's office earlier that day and yelled at him to "Gather the team and come right now, or I swear to God-".

Mishal sighed. Working with a manager as chaotic as Asaad was hell.

At Asaad's direction, Salim opened his backpack and pulled out a small flashlight. Around this he tied a match using a thread. He flicked the switch and the light from the flashlight burst out directly upwards, painting the ceiling in a bright yellow glow.

Mishal sent ruh, the power of his soul, into his eyes as Salim worked. The ruh entered his eyes and illuminated the world, showing Mishal ruh everywhere. Now, he could see how Salim was controlling the ruh in his own body using small, precise bursts which traveled from his body into the magical flashlight, turning on its peculiar effect.

Salim pointed the flashlight directly in Mishal's eye, making him gasp as he was blinded by the light. "Agh!"

"Sorry boss, this is necessary if we're going to work while everyone's here," Salim said, repeating the gesture again with Asaad, who tutted but showed no other reaction to being exposed to the violent light. Finally, Salim turned off the light. "It's done." Mishal glanced around. The two girls who had been looking over at Asaad somehow seemed to ignore him now, as if he wasn't even there anymore. One of the girls looked in Mishal's direction, but her eyes slide off his face like oil on water. He and his surroundings were now unnoticable to non-magical eyes.

"Well done," Mishal said to Salim, always keen to let his subordinate feel appreciated. He felt like Salim needed these words. The ex-corporal still lived by the rules of the military. Worse still, Salim felt insecure, Mishal knew, because his ruh vessel was smaller than most exorcists, giving him less raw power than most. "Now, are you ready to summon the creature?"

"Yes sir," Salim said, moving to get something else out of his pack, but Asaad stopped him. The man's eyes grew intense Mishal felt the air in the room grow heavier. It became like a blanket, pushing down on their surroundings slowly but surely with the buildup of ruh, the inherent power of the soul.

"Asaad?" Mishal asked.

"I need to protect the onlookers, just in case." Asaad said with a grunt. "The jinni this time's a weakling. Level E at best, but…"

"Just in case."

Asaad nodded, a bead of sweat coming down his forehead from the indirect heat of the sun. "The entire purpose of Sarim is to protect humans. It's why we usually keep our work out of the vicinity of humans or take missions during the night. I know you're nervous being in a crowded café, Mishal, invisibility spell or not. But never forget who I am," he added with a sigh and a grin. Something *expanded,* and suddenly the café around them sounded muffled.

Mishal stared at Asaad Al Nabhani in hesitant admiration. The lunatic had created a defensive barrier around them, sealing them off from the rest of the café. Normally, such a barrier required two exorcists chanting in unison for minutes. And Asaad had done it alone in the blink of an eye. "Of course, A'bbath," he said, using the special codename Shayib Asaad held. Pandamonium. The most powerful agent in the history of Sarim, the youngest hero to ever be promoted to Shayib.

Mishal had recently observed that power first-hand. He had seen Asaad sitting atop a mountain of jinn he'd single-handedly destroyed. A'bbath was a fitting name for such overwhelming chaos.

"Gah, I hate that nickname," Asaad muttered sullenly. "They should've given me a cooler one. Now, we're ready. Salim, are you ready to pull the jinni to us?"

Salim saluted and Asaad turned to Mishal again, leaning back to sip his coffee. "You ready, prophecy boy?" he said with a grin.

“Oh, hush,” Mishal groaned, recalling with embarrassment the time the entirety of Sarim had thought Mishal was fated to protect or doom Oman, all thanks to an old prophecy. Only Asaad had dismissed the idea.

Salim reached into his backpack and now pulled out a long piece of old-looking wire, followed by a hook and a fishing weight. Asaad gaped. “You’re kidding me, right?”

Salim laughed. “We’re fishing for a jinni, aren’t we?” Next, he began to breathe heavily, summoning his meager stock of ruh and pushing it into the magical tool using a special pattern.

Asaad nodded. “Team captain?” he asked.

Mishal caught Salim’s eye, seeing a glimmer of nervousness there. “You did a good job,” he reassured his new recruit. “It’ll be fine, go on.”

“Thank you, sir,” Salim replied, unable to hide a shy smile. He pushed more of his ruh into the tool. Mishal sent ruh to his own eyes and began to see the flow of power more clearly, a small trickle flowing in a very particular geometric pattern which went through Salim’s hands into the fishing line, making the hook glow with small water element and binding element glyphs. A weak hum began to sound, and Salim’s hands shook, as if a fish eas pulling on the hook. “It’s on the line,” Salim said, excitement lacing his voice as he leaned forward. “The jinni should be here in a minute.”

“You’re ready, Mishal?” Asaad asked. Mishal didn’t reply, simply nodding to Asaad as he waited, his hands clenched. Slowly, Salim pulled and let the line loose in alternate rhythms, grunting, until finally a small, shaking voice rang out.

“No, no!” it yelped, “There’s still a mess to make, pranks to play, lives to ruin!”

And with that, a tiny Zaa’ij appeared, its leg caught on the hook of Salim’s line. The Zaa’ij looked like a small fat man, about the size of a finger, with long claws and yellow eyes. It was pulled across the table, small claws scraping on the glass, which splashed like water, and it affixed a hateful gaze on Asaad Al Nabhani. “You, monster!” it shrieked. “Traitor, liar, threat to us all!”

"Yeah, yeah," Asaad said. He often got this response from jinn, Mishal had noticed. "You could've lived, you know, if you'd kept the pranks small. You do know you led a child onto running traffic yesterday, right?"

"It was just a joke!" the imp pleaded, turning its eyes to Mishal. "I wouldn't have let the cars *hit* her!"

"Sorry," Mishal said, finding himself meaning it. Despite the fact that this was a weak jinni, it had more intellect than most he'd encountered. Most jinn weren't very smart. It told him that the jinni was close to graduating from being a standard Zaa'ij, and would soon become a unique jinn with its own personality. This one, in particular, would start killing humans soon.

Somebody needs to do what has to be done, Mishal thought to himself. *We protect Oman from the astral dangers of the world, even if the jinn don't look too dangerous.*

Mishal let the ruh surge through him, causing a bright flame to burst from his hand.

This was Mishal's power, the only skill he knew. While Salim could use all six elements of ruh, Mishal could only use flame.

The Zaa'ij's eyes turned towards Asaad. "And *you,* destroyer. Don't think all jinn are afraid of you!" it threatened. "One day, you'll meet your match!"

Mishal grabbed the jinni softly in his fiery hand, instructing his blaze to be as painless as possible. He burnt the little imp from existence, trying to shut out its quick yelp.

When it was over, a small pile of ash was left on the table, as well as a wide scorch mark, which stretched through the center of the table. This piece of furniture would need to be thrown away. Mishal grimaced.

Asaad looked at the scorch mark, then glanced around at the other occupants of the café. None of them could see a thing, thanks to Salim's magic, but as soon as the invisibility spell wore off... "How about we just leave our money here and walk out?" Asaad asked sheepishly. "I'd rather not deal with the café management right now."

Chapter Two

Mishal rode in the passenger seat as Asaad drove him and Salim back to the Sarim headquarters. The Sultan Qaboos highway rolled past, yellow lines whizzing by Asaad's white Dodge Charger. The small white dashes on the road quickly blurred into one another, becoming a continuous line that pointed from one end of Muscat to the next. Confident, bright, clear.

Mishal smiled to himself. They'd managed to get the mission done. Later, he would arrange with the admin department to have an anonymous donation sent to the café, replacing the scorched table with a new one. He wondered how to find the manager's number to arrange things properly.

"So, how does your first mission without the child feel?" Asaad asked, moving to turn down the volume on the radio. Salim sat quietly in the back, listening with a grim frown. He and Salwa, a little girl, had been assigned as new recruits to Mishal's team around six months ago.

"Oh, err..." Mishal considered the question, trying to find the right words. "Here's the thing: Salwa is a great kid. She listens and she has talent. But she's ten. What if she gets hurt?" he added, glancing sideways at Asaad's perfect beard. The man was a stereotypical Muscat male in every way: Relaxed, cocky, perfectly dressed and always with a perfume lying about somewhere in his messy car. It was hard to believe that Asaad was actually a Shayib, an advisor assigned to a team of Sarim exorcists to help ensure their safety.

More importantly, Asaad Al Nabhani was the ultimate exorcist.

Asaad sighed. "Mishal, Sarim has long taken in exorcists as young as eight years old. She's a child, but don't forget that she's a powerful healer as well. Leaving her on the sidelines is an insult."

"I did *not* leave her on the sidelines," Mishal protested weakly. "She has a parent-teacher meeting today."

"U-huh, I see."

"...You don't sound very convinced," Mishal grumbled, causing Asaad to laugh. He overtook another car, a fancy-looking Land Cruiser with a two-number plate.

"I'm not, but let's avoid starting an argument now, I'm starving." Asaad glanced at Salim, who was frozen as stiff as a board in the back seat. "I have a feeling you'll do the right thing on your own. You're better at that than I am."

"What, doing the right thing?"

Asaad snapped his finger. "Exactly." He turned the music back on, only to be met with the voice of Talal Al Shahri on Oman FM.

'So that was *I've Been Working for the Weekend*. It does feel like that sometimes, doesn't it?' The man continued talking, giving in a few witty one liners, then shifted to the next song, a Rock tune.

The music began blaring, going in a strong, fast beat which stole Mishal's own breath. He recognized that song. Mishal's heart clenched as he stared at the radio monitor, which displayed the song name. The music slowed down to a crawl, becoming a single, deep tone that filled Mishal's ears. All he could see was the monitor, with the song name on it. *Another One Bites the Dust.*

Asaad looked at the radio sadly. "Oh man, that was one of Ahlam's favourites."

Mishal turned the radio off. Asaad said nothing, and Salim seemed to shrink back into himself in the back seat. Mishal could feel his recruit's confusion: Salim Al Ghafri had joined in too late. He didn't know who Ahlam was. Mishal, for his part, had never mentioned her.

The three exorcists watched the streets flicker by. They passed next to the mountains - sliced apart to make way for civilization and modern roads - and finally they reached a large, square, dust-brown building which almost seemed to absorb the afternoon sunlight. A black sign on the front read: *Ministry of Education Auditorium.*

Asaad parked outside the building and they got out of the car, Salim retrieving his backpack of magical tools. They walked to the front of the building, ignoring the giant main door, and entering via a small, inconspicuous side door on the right. Inside, a tight, seemingly unremarkable corridor greeted them, along with flickering ceiling lights and a floor of porcelain. Asaad walked a few steps forward, to the only ceramic piece in the floor which wasn't perfect. This piece was cracked, leaving a strange indentation on the floor. Asaad brandished his white cane and inserted it into the hole in the ground with an audible click.

"Alright, guys," he said, the first time he'd spoken in fifteen minutes. "Congratulations on a job well done."

Mishal held Asaad back for a moment. "Make sure you update the Sarim app."

Asaad fidgeted, then groaned. "Fine, fine. Gosh, you're as bad as the Council of Shayibs sometimes."

Asaad twisted his cane, and a part of the wall disappeared, giving way to a pristine corridor of pure white: Luxurious white marble, snow-colored walls, and powerful lights illuminating the area. This was the base of Sarim, which was officially established late in the 20th century but which had been created long before then. This was the base out of which Oman recruited, trained, and sent out agents with the explicit goal of protecting humans from harmful jinn. The Public Authority which, a year ago, had sent a Shayib to help Mishal overcome possession by a jinni and then offered him a job.

"I miss Shayib Ghalib," Mishal said.

Asaad sniffed. "Hey, I'm not that bad!"

"No, no, it's just that-"

Asaad interrupted Mishal with a waving hand. "I know, he was an interesting sort of guy. Amazing listener. Maybe we can go visit him in his retirement place. You know," he added darkly, "if he hasn't died yet!"

"Was Shayib Ghalib that good of a leader?" Salim asked, even as Mishal smacked Asaad's shoulder for daring to joke about Shayib Ghalib dying.

Oh God, Mishal thought to himself in a bright panic. His eyes glanced over to Asaad. *How do I explain, without making Asaad feel bad?* "He was… interesting," Mishal replied, memories coming back. He found a nervous smile playing on his face. "He was always either grinning, yelling, or pranking someone. But he cared about people, and he loved life. He was the one who helped me with my possession, you know," he said. "Shayib Ghalib helped all of us, back at Team 7. Me, Eman, and…" All three of them.

Mishal remembered the day when he first met his team, a year ago, right in this very spot. Remembered Eman's kindness as she explained things to him and urged Shayib Ghalib not to send him on missions too early. He remembered the other girl too. Ahlam Al Hatmi.

Mishal could almost see her in front of him now, a recollection in the lamplight with her gold-tinged eyes and those silly rock band shirts of hers, urging him to keep up with her wild, confident power. Their mutual trust had run deep. "He helped all of us," Mishal added wistfully. Asaad looked at him sideways but said nothing.

Now, it was a year later. Eman was now the team leader for team 10, just as Mishal had been promoted to lead Team 14. Shayib Ghalib had retired, relaxing in a farm in Al Dakhiliyah and taking care of his shop of magical favors, and Ahlam Al Hatmi was buried a few floors beneath Sarim.

As they walked down the path, Mishal completely absorbed in his memories, Asaad suddenly stopped and sniffed. "Wait a minute," he murmured, seeming suddenly tense.

"What's going on?" Mishal asked. Salim hung back a few feet behind, messing with his phone.

Asaad tutted, then said, "Something smells wrong."

"Excuse me?"

"I said what I said, okay?" Asaad replied, now visibly annoyed. "I'm going to go ahead to the Shayib Council. You can, I dunno, rest or something? Brief the kid about the mission, whenever she gets dropped back to base," he added, pushing forward darkly, his dishdasha fluttering with the speed of his gait.

"And train her, Mishal! I will smack you if she hasn't improved by next month!"

"Yeah, yeah," Mishal grumbled while Salim saluted. Mishal turned to the ex-corporal and smiled, noticing the man's heavy-looking backpack still strung on his shoulders. "First thing first," he said, "How about you put your backpack somewhere?"

Salim shrugged easily, bumping the backpack up and down on his shoulders. "It's fine, sir. At the military academy we were used to carrying a backpack weighing 20kg and carrying it while we ran. This is nothing." A proud smile spread across his face.

Mishal slowly and deliberately pinched the bridge of his nose. He could feel a slight headache coming on. "Salim, do you need your backpack right now?"

Salim paused. "Uh, no sir."

"Is it going to inconvenience you to go to your room, which is… on this same floor, if I remember right?"

"Not at all, sir."

"Backpack. Your room. And stop calling me sir."

"Yes, sir," Salim replied, causing Mishal to roll his eyes even as the older man walked off, pulling ahead easily with his longer stride. Dealing with Salim was always a struggle.

Salim al Ghafri was twenty years Mishal's senior, which had initially made the teenager nervous. He'd worried that Salim would walk all over him, or maybe yell at him. Thankfully, Mishal actually faced the opposite problem: Salim was a soldier to the bone, itching to treat Mishal like a superior. Mishal sometimes caught Salim randomly standing at attention near him, especially around the Sarim cafeteria. Worse still, Salim seemed to find it difficult to do things on his own. Lastly, Salim seemed hell-bent on proving himself, even when there was nothing to prove.

Mishal walked along to the end of the corridor, where he was met by Sarim's core structure: A massive abyss, apparently carved into the rocky heart of the ground, crowned by a giant sapphire-blue gem which hovered in the air. As Mishal watched, Arabic writing appeared on the gem, reading, *Welcome, Mishal Al Balushi, Team leader of Team 14.* Below the hovering gem, a metal staircase spiralled down and down along the rock, with exits leading into the different floors of Sarim.

A rumbling sound came from Mishal's stomach, making him blush slightly, and he headed down to floor two where the cafeteria waited. Various agents waved or nodded a hello at him, some shaking his hand and asking after his family (who had no idea that Mishal had become an exorcist). The greetings went by in a flurry, but they left a warm imprint in Mishal's chest as he walked down, feet clanging softly on the metal steps, taking out his iPhone with the sword-shaped keychain he'd hoped to one day gift to Ahlam.

Mishal entered the loud, bustling cafeteria, a white hall with small buffets on either side of the room, striped with long benches and tables for Sarim agents to eat at. Focused as he was on the phone, he meandered towards an empty bench and sat down, going into the yellow-tinged Sarim app on his phone.

Mishal al Balushi, B-ranked agent, his profile on the app read. *Team 14, Rank E. Successful missions: 37.*

Mishal clicked into a different tab and began to file a summary report, thanking the heavens that the app had been developed. Normally, such work would be taken care of by the Shayib. However, Asaad wouldn't be caught dead with paperwork in his hand, and so Mishal kept things going from the shadows - at least until Sarim found a permanent solution for his boss's procrastination.

Low-ranked jinn exorcism. Two agents. No injuries. Minor property damage. Quickly, he began to write the details. As he did, the events of the past twenty-four hours ran through his head.

Time limit. Asaad shouting at them at eleven in the evening, after training. Salim's disappointed face when Mishal told him that maybe Salwa should stay at home this time. *She had school, didn't she?* Mishal had said, to defend himself. Al Adhaiba, Muscat, in the middle of the morning, with a long line of cars ahead of them, people going to work and yawning in the traffic as they listened to the radio. The café, with its fleeting customers laughing, the décor looking soothing. How Salim summoned the jinni. The Zaa'ij's screams, and its pitiable threats to Asaad.

The jinni was exorcised promptly under the supervision of Shayib Asaad Al Nabhani.

There. With the report filed, Mishal relaxed, ignoring the red tab which informed him about his teammates' progress and training. He was worried about them.

Mishal had a powerful urge to protect his loved ones from this bone-breaking world. His team fell within the category of loved ones, each with their own issues. Salim was a soldier full of bravado with a small ruh vessel. And Salwa was only ten.

"Rough day, huh?" a voice asked, causing Mishal to jump. He looked to the side to see a bearded gentleman in a simple dishdasha. The man's hair was startlingly long and soft, spreading almost like wings under a messy turban. His eyes were jet-black and kind, surrounded by dark circles, over a straight nose and a small smile. One of his sleeves was raised, showing off a scar that ran along his forearm. Just as Mishal was about to shake the man's hand, the man coughed suddenly, covering his mouth, and Mishal pretended he'd only been reaching for a bottle of water. "Sorry, I didn't mean to startle you," he said. "It's just odd for someone to sit right in front of me for a full two minutes without saying anything."

"Y-you were here the whole time?" Mishal asked, feeling heat rush up through his face. His heart fell with the promise that he had completely messed up. "Oh gosh, I'm so so sorry! Were you waiting for anyone? Oh lord! I, uh, I'm Mishal Al Balushi."

The man seemed a bit surprised. "*The* Mishal Al Balushi? Saviour of the fight against Bani Al Safi? I heard you took out the leader all by yourself!"

Now, the heat filled Mishal's face. "I-it was nothing!"

The man's eyes widened in surprise. "I can't tell if you're being humble or arrogant! Hahah, it's alright, don't worry about it. So, are you so overworked that you can't enjoy a meal in peace?" he asked.

The teenager fumbled for a response. "I, well, I like my job, I guess," he said, tripping over his words.

"Well, it's good that you like the work. Sarim's important for the very fabric of the country. Just do be careful," He added, standing up slowly. "Too many people get absorbed in the fights, like with that Shayib of yours."

"Asaad?"

"Asaad Al Nabhani, the prodigy. He lives for the fight, that one. And for good reason. He's remarkable, wouldn't you say?"

Mishal fidgeted. "He's a bit over the top, I guess."

"Hahah! In strength and in personality. Anyhow, be careful of fighting too much, and of the paperwork, hahah! Good luck out there, Mishal," he added with a friendly tap on the table, then walked away from Mishal's table. The youth sat in place, watching the man disappear into the crowd.

Mishal al Balushi and Asaad al Nabhani had started off on the wrong foot, about six months ago. Asaad's power had translated into a mountain of cockiness. He stood atop that peak, surveying the ants beneath him, and Mishal had hated it. Hell, Asaad had beaten Mishal unconscious once. However, Mishal now respected Asaad's cockiness, as well as his capacity for kindness. The two of them had grieved together, fought together, and laughed together.

As Mishal sat at the table, thinking, Salim walked into the line of his vision, holding the hand of a small girl with her hair braided a double braid - held in place by butterfly pins. Mishal couldn't help but stifle a laugh when he saw the two of them together. Salim practically looked like Salwa's father, if you neglected his bushy eyebrows and the obvious difference in the shape of the nose. Mishal got off the chair and went down to one knee. "Hi Salwa, was the parent-teacher conference good?" he asked.

She nodded, hesitating for a moment before removing her hand from Salim's and taking a step forward. "They said I'm the best, so Dad finally decided to get me an iPhone!"

Mishal blinked in surprise, then looked up at Salim. "Really?" he asked, still speaking to Salwa but keeping his eyes on the ex-corporal. Salim, for his part, looked absolutely horrified.

"Yeah; it's so I stop using my parents' phone for Tiktok."

"Tik-tok?" Salim asked, his mouth tripping over the unfamiliar word. He slapped a hand over his face. "Oh lord, I'll to have to learn what that means, won't I?"

Mishal laughed as Salwa huffed and pulled Salim to the cafeteria line. Mishal watched her point out a box of cereal. The ex-military man shook his head, saying something and then pointing at his bicep. She pointed again, insistent, and he gave up. A minute or so later they returned, Salwa carrying a bowl of chocolate and peanut-butter cereal and Salim hefting a massive portion of Mandi with chicken breasts piled atop it. "You don't want to eat anything, sir?" he asked.

Mishal shook his head. He'd grown more muscular over the past year, a necessity considering how physical his power was, but he still only really ate when he needed to. He made a mental note to make sure the cafeteria was always stocked with chocolate and peanut-butter cereal. "So, I suppose your mom wants to meet with me again soon?" he asked Salwa.

The girl's eyes widened. "How did you know?"

Mishal shrugged. It's Se*ptember, schools are just getting started; I'm sure they want to know how Sarim's going to ensure their daughter has a proper education while dealing with missions. I'll schedule a talk with her tomorrow.* "It's the same for me, you know," he said.

"You're still in school?" she asked, with astonishment.

Mishal chuckled. "Do I look that old?" he asked.

Salim gave Mishal a sideways look. "Honestly, boss, even I forget your age sometimes. Never met a teenager with this much good sense in my life." He shuddered. "When I was your age, I was constantly stealin- uh," he interrupted himself as Salwa looked at him. "I would, erm, nevermind," he added, then clamped his mouth shut even as Salwa begged him to finish what he'd said. Behind his back, he mimed a steering wheel at Mishal, indicating he used to steal his father's car. Mishal raised an amused eyebrow at that but said nothing.

"I've always been a little old for my age, I guess," Mishal said.

"What does that mean?" Salwa asked.

"It means he's reliable!" Salim exclaimed, then pointed at her. "It means he always finishes his cereal quickly. Come on now, quick quick!"

"I'm not a baby!"

"Finish the cereal and prove it!"

Mishal leaned back peacefully and watched the two of them argue, marvelling once again at how quickly Salwa had taken to Salim. They'd only been in the same team for a few months, and already she treated him like a goofy uncle.

Good, he thought to himself. He imagined Salim and Salwa being like this forever. He wished he could bottle the scene and keep it with him in a drawer in his room at Sarim, or even at his home in Al Khoudh. He promised himself to protect Salim and Salwa from danger.

Suddenly, Mishal froze in place as an intense feeling took over his body, giving him goosebumps. The air turned electric with pure, unbridled power. Around him, he heard the more sensitive Sarim agents also stop in place, and a woman facing him literally dropped her knife, her face aghast. Ruh swirled around the cafeteria, drawn to something.

Mishal turned and saw the source of the feeling walk into the cafeteria and make a beeline for him. Asaad walked straight, forcing the people in his path to scramble out of the way. Ruh crackled in his footsteps, and Mishal could see pure anger reflected in the Shayib's face. His khaizranah twitched in his hand as if he were itching for a chance to hit somebody, anybody, with it.

Mishal sent ruh to his eyes instantly to improve his magical eyesight and caught a glimpse of Asaad's power: It shifted constantly around him like a black cloud interspersed with stars. It was space, with its infinite possibilities. In the center, Mishal could see patterns of glowing reds and greens, a supernova in the midst of an explosion in space. To see ruh was to see something of a person's magic, as well as their mood.

At this moment, Asaad was dangerous.

“Kid, come with me,” Asaad hissed. Mishal stood up without preamble, making his chair screech. He gave a reassuring nod to his terrified teammates. Asaad turned on his heels and walked right out, ignoring the rest of the team. Mishal’s heart beat faster. Asaad hadn’t called him *kid* in months. “What’s going on?” he asked as they filed out of the cafeteria and ensuing corridor.

“Remember when I said I smelled something wrong as we came in?” Asaad spat behind his shoulder. “I was right.” He cursed. They kept walking, with Mishal confused as he followed at Asaad’s heels.

At the abyss, Asaad surprised Mishal by taking the metal staircase down instead of up, his footsteps unusually loud. His dishdasha fluttered eerily long, as if held up by the sheer thickness of the space-like ruh drifting off his body. Whenever a Sarim employre crossed them in the pathways, Mishal would wave them away before they could spark Asaad’s wrath.

Mishal gulped, wondering at what could have made Asaad so angry. He’d only ever seen him this way once. On the first occasion, Asaad had tortured a Sarim agent-turned spy by splitting his body into many segments.

“Tell me what’s wrong!” Mishal asked with insistance, turning Asaad by the sleeve to face him. The Shayib’s glare made Mishal want to take a step back. For a second or two, Asaad’s anger flashed across his hazel-colored eyes, but then that furious light dimmed. He took three, slow breaths. Mishal noticed the air grow noticeably lighter.

“It was my mother,” Asaad said slowly. “That sickening smell I told you about when we first stepped into the building? It was my mother’s ruh. My mother is here to meet with the CEO of Sarim.”

Mishal found himself lost for words, and his hands let go of Asaad’s sleeve. They continued down the stairs. Asaad’s mother, nicknamed the Witch of Calamity, was the leader of a rogue group of sorcerers called Nasr. As far as Mishal knew, the mysterious woman was on Sarim’s most-wanted list, along with Butcher, Shalmazar, and Mohsin Al Naaimi. She was supposed to be attacked and captured on sight.

What had she been thinking, waltzing into Sarim? And to meet the *CEO*, of all things?

The marble of the first floor disappeared, replaced by the older ceramics of the second floor, where one could find the training halls and small offices. Then the third floor of the higher-level training halls, lined with loose cobblestones and lamps, came and went. Mishal noticed the door of the maze-like library, where he liked to spend time alone.

The building morphed into a more ancient version of itself as they passed by the prayer hall and the graveyard, where Ahlam's grave lay. Here Mishal's heart tightened, but he forced himself to move on after Asaad. Finally, the metal stairs gave way gave way to caves, hewn out of the ancient rock. The dark tunnels were damp and moss-ridden, but Asaad walked through them confidently. He chose the right path, revealed only to Shayibs and advisors of Sarim, to avoid triggering the multitudes of mechanical and magical traps which protected the inner chambers of Sarim. Mishal followed nervously, conscious of every step, listening for a click or a growl, until finally the two of them stood outside an ancient door, on which Mishal saw faded etchings of smiling faces.

Asaad knocked three times, and was rewarded with a response from a voice as coarse and old as desert sands. "Enter, my boy."

"Are you sure?" Mishal asked Asaad. He was worried about Asaad. Though older than Mishal by about four years, Asaad had the penchant of doing whatever he liked - regardless of consequences. His emotions rode him like a storm, which could be very bad indeed when dealing with the CEO of Sarim.

"Don't worry," Asaad said, "I'm just here to talk."

Mishal nodded, reminding himself of the facts. No matter what lay beyond the door, they would be okay. Nothing was dangerous to Asaad Al Nabhani. Besides, the CEO liked him.

They opened the door.

Chapter Three

Inside Mishal saw an office carved completely out of the cave rock: An office of stone, chairs of ore, and even a little rock-hewn pen-holder. Around him, everything was colored a majestic assortment of browns, rust-reds, and blue-greens. Someone had even carved the semblance of windows into the office - though, of course, the red-brown panels would never open. The air smelled of bukhoor, coming out of a large frankincense-holder in the corner. Mishal noticed that some pieces of furniture were more detailed than others. The two guest chairs, for example? Those had been exquisitely carved, so much so that they appeared like petrified chairs. The desk, however, was basic at best.

In the midst of the room, Mishal noticed a few other colors. The white of a dishdasha, a light-brown of hands. He looked up at the face of the CEO of Sarim, a man who appeared almost older than the cave around him. The man sat on his chair on the other side of the desk as if it were a floor, lifting his feet up to curl under him, with his beard on his lap and his sandals lying on the floor.

The old man was staring at Asaad, and Mishal couldn't honestly tell if the CEO had seen them or if he was looking at nothing.

Asaad sniffed then growled. "Yeah, she came here alright. So?" he spat. "Is the she-demon dead?"

Mishal's stomach clenched. What was this *idiot* doing?

The old man chuckled softly. "Asaad Al Nabhani, I have half a mind to slap you for talking about your mother that way."

Asaad grinned, ignoring Mishal's horrified look. "And the other half knows I'm right. So, *is* she dead?"

"No, my boy. When Atheer breathes her last, I can promise that you'll be able to feel it in your heart. I see you brought our youngest team leader here with you," he remarked, leaning forward to train his eyes on Mishal.

Suddenly, Mishal took a step back. The old man seemed to expand, stretching higher and higher into the ceiling, until he was like a giant leaning down to look at Mishal. His eyes were wide pools of white, sunken into wrinkles the size of ravines. Power radiated from him in every direction. "Oh?" the old man said, voice booming across the corners of the world and coming back to crash into Mishal's ears like waves. "It seems you've grown more perceptive since I saw you last, child. No need to fear, little one, I'll do you no harm," he said, and Mishal blinked to see that the ancient man hadn't expanded at all. In fact, he still sat exactly where he'd been, watching him. What Mishal had seen was only the CEO's presence.

Asaad stepped quietly between them. "You're scaring him," he admonished, the cocky tone leaving his voice for once.

"And you're protecting him," the CEO replied, sounding slightly surprised. "Has Abbath made a new friend?"

"W-what? N-no! Wait," Asaad hastily said, waving his hands aggressively. "It's more like a, uh, you know, a pet!"

"Excuse me?" Mishal asked.

"Never mind that! Anyway, what did Mom want?" Asaad said to the CEO, then turned and hissed to Mishal, "We can talk about this later!"

"A *pet*?"

"Later!"

The CEO cleared his throat politely, causing them both to look at him. "It appears that Atheer's network of spies has grown more competent, with her recent freedom from the meddlings of Bani Safi. She came to tell me about a threat."

Asaad's mouth hung open. "And you let her go?"

"She came under a *salfa*, Asaad. A promise of non-violence. One I willingly signed just this year. I am not one to break such pacts."

"I can't trust her, old man."

"But I *can*," the CEO said, a faint glimmer of ruh shining through the deep wells of his eyes. Just then, Mishal noticed the ruh steaming softly off Asaad's skin as well. Mishal gulped, took a step back, and dried his palms on his dishdasha. Asaad and the

CEO stood there quietly, each of them holding off their power in a stand-off of wills. Mishal grabbed Asaad's shoulder in warning.

Asaad started, then withdrew his magic, saying, "Yeah, well. That's your mistake to make. My mother has never made a pact with anyone unless it benefited her more than it did them. Anyway, what was the threat, that she had to come all the way here just to tell you about it?"

For a long time, the old man sat silently as if in thought. Eventually, however, he put out his hand. Ruh burst from his palm in a long, soft stream. Mishal's eyes widened in surprise, observing the hypnotic patterns as the magic wove around itself, thickening until it became completely visible. Then it unfurled, the patterns dancing and strengthening into vivid shapes as the old man told a story, of all things.

"A long time ago," he said "Long before tall Adam was born into this world, out of clay, jinn roamed the earth in earnest. They varied in temperament, lifespan, and power. However, the jinn also had their own many varied kings and tribe-chiefs. These chiefs are nowadays sealed far beyond the reach of our world."

Mishal turned to watch the ruh dancing around the room, morphing into the shapes of figures running through a forest, cowering in terror, and then being driven off elsewhere. Asaad, too, appeared captivated with the golden ruh swirling about him. However, he shrugged off his amazement and said, "Common facts."

"True. Now, let me stress that the chieftains of jinn cannot appear in our world. Under normal circumstances, they can barely even affect our human world unless a sahir creates a spell dependent on their magic - with the proper tools. A question, young Mishal," he added, pointing his finger like a weapon into the middle of Mishal's chest. "What does a powerful jinni require to enter our world?"

"A human vessel," Mishal said automatically, reaching with his mind to pluck the information out of one of the jinn books he'd read in the library in Level Three of Sarim. "One powerful enough to withstand the jinni's ruh. If the human is too weak, he or she would simply break. If the human is too strong, then he or she would overcome the jinni."

"Precisely. So far, all of this is old information," the old man said. "Now, to the real news: Atheer has let it be known that it's ripe time for a jinni chieftain to awaken. This is nothing like the threat we faced from Bani Al Safi last year. We know next to nothing about the jinni which is to arrive, nor about how it intends to break through. Atheer shares our concern that we will be put in terrible danger if this jinni is released. And so, she came to tell me what she knows and to propose that each of our two organizations attempt to stop the jinni separately."

"Wait," Mishal interrupted. "But we just said that summoning a jinni needs a powerful vessel…" he trailed off, eyes sidling off to where Asaad stood very quietly, lips pursed, eyes furious.

And suddenly, Mishal understood. "Asaad is the vessel?"

"Hopefully it won't come to that," the CEO said quietly. "You are like a son to Sarim, Asaad. We hope to stop this eldritch horror before it actually attempts to arrive to this world. In a best-case scenario, this will all be background noise."

"It will not have me," Asaad promised. "I'll bury whoever tries it. And don't even think about trying put me in a cage, or else I'll take you down first of all."

The CEO sighed. "I know you will, Asaad. I told Atheer as much. She had been suggesting that we give you to her for, ah, custody."

"Absolutely *not*."

"Did you think I'd agree to it?" the CEO said. "Never forget, Asaad Al Nabhani, that you're one of us. She may be your mother, but you are not her son. This was the deal you made with Ghalib, I believe. Sarim takes care of its own, even if some our colleagues have… more pragmatic thoughts. For now, I'll urge you to take care of yourself and to report anything suspicious to me."

Asaad hesitated then nodded, pulling Mishal with him out of the room. The teenager could still hear him muttering darkly.

"Should've just killed her, honestly… Wants to protect me, she does, eh? I'll show them all."

Surprisingly, Asaad sounded happy.

Chapter Four

Mishal was filing the paperwork to compensate the owners of the café, where he'd destroyed a table earlier that day, when his phone dinged. When he looked at it, he saw that there was a new mission available on the Sarim app. *It's E level, something about a single Hussais near Al Mouj. This might be a good chance to involve Salim and Salwa in a mission.*

Mishal clicked accept on the mission, claiming it before anyone else could; especially Musab Al Aisary from Team 16. Mishal messaged Salim, and fifteen minutes later the two of them stood outside the Sarim building, basking in the sunlight. It was winter, and so the breeze came in salty and cold from Muttrah.

"Sir, I'm ready to go whenever you are," Salim said, his feet shifting in excitement. "We're going to pick up Salwa first, right?"

"Definitely," Mishal replied. He was messaging Salwa's father at that moment. Both of her parents had been admins in Sarim at some point, before leaving the organization, and had immediately come to Sarim when their daughter healed a kitten which had been accidentally run over by a car, as so often happens in Oman.Salim drove Mishal all the way to Al Hail, where Salwa lived, and the two of them waited as the door opened and two figures popped out of the front gate. Salwa's father walked with his daughter to the car, where Mishal and Salim immediately stepped out to shake his hand.

"We'll keep her safe, sir," Mishal promised, certain that he could see worry in the man's eyes.

Salwa's father gave him a confused look. "Oh? Yeah, of course. I've got no concerns there."

"Oh?" Mishal asked.

"She needs to learn how to control her powers, and this is the best way to do it," the man replied. "To be honest, I always wished I had powers, so it's good to see her enjoying this." The man leaned down into a fighting pose, squaring off against Salwa. "How do you stand?" he asked her.

"Like this," she replied, mimicking his pose.

"Great, and if you get hurt?"

"I won't forget to heal myself!"

The two shared an airheaded laugh, after which Salwa climbed into the car. She had her head into pigtails, held together by butterfly pins.

Mishal marvled at the man's cool-headedness. The three agents got into the car, and Salwa immediately began chattering about a new game on Roblox. Mishal was able to follow some of her monologue as she chattered in the back seat, sitting with her elbows lodged squarely like pins in Mishal's and Salim's seats, respectively. "And then, um, Haneen actually scammed him, and we took his Petzy because he was so rude!"

Salim's eyes squinted into razor-sharp points. "Where does this guy live?" he asked, his eyebrows furrowed.

Mishal laughed at Salim's serious expression. "He doesn't live in *Oman*. Or at least, probably not."

"Good for him, else I would show him a thing or two!"

Salwa started laughing maniacally. By then, the two of them were in Al Hail. The dirt around the roads turned into sand, with patches of weeds growing here and there. Soon, Salim's car reached the roundabout which signalled the official start of Al Hail beach.

"Where's the place?" he asked.

"Thankfully it's out of the way," Mishal replied. "Just park here." It was the afternoon, meaning that as soon as Mishal's feet left the car, he was able to feel the heat radiating off the interlock beneath him. Nobody was on the beach. "Salwa," he said, "the sand is going to be very hot, and you won't be able to step on it. How about you wait in the car?"

Salwa's eyes turned into a shocked expression. "I'm an *exorcist!"* she hissed. "It's not going to be too hot for me!"

"The sand is really going to burn though!" Mishal argued, even though he could tell it was futile. *She's way too excited about this mission, I won't be able to convince her to stay here. How can I compromise?*

Mishal noticed a bisat in the back of Salim's car. "Oh, there's a bisat Salwa can stand on to protect her feet. Salim, can you and Salwa get set up on the bisat near the sea?"

Off to the side, Mishal saw a man standing solitary at the edge of the interlock bricks, at the cement barrier before the sand started. Mishal walked over to the man, leaving Salim and Salwa to get set up. He could hear Salim and Salwa cluttering behind him. "Hi," Mishal said to the man, feeling slightly nervous.

The man turned around with a smile. "I'm impressed. How did you know I was a Sarim scout?"

Mishal shrugged. He could sense the man's eyes on them from the moment they'd arrived. Besides, it didn't make sense for anyone to be at the beach when it was this hot out. "You're sure it's an E-level?"

The man nodded. "I checked it myself. A water Hussais, out that way."

Good, at least nobody's in real danger today. The whole reason why Mishal wanted to exorcise E-level jinn was to expose Salim and Salwa slowly to this world, free from unforeseen dangers. It wouldn't do for the jinni to be more dangerous than expected.

Mishal thanked the man and walked away, to where Salim and Salwa were now sitting on the bisat. "That way," Mishal told them, and helped carry the bisat, while Salim carried Salwa to the correct spot.

The ocean stretched farther than the eye could see. Its blue sparkled in the sun, begging the exorcists to come forward and enjoy a splash. Seagulls floated in the wind, looking like kites. Mishal stepped forward, bidding Salim to stay closer to Salwa. "What tools do you have with you?" he asked Salim.

Salim showed Mishal a Khanjar. It was a sharqiya-style dagger, with a wooden handle which curved like a determined frown. Mishal sent ruh to his eyes, and noted with satisfaction that the dagger had a slight covering of magical force around it. *Well done.*

"Sir, who was the guy you spoke to just now?" Salim asked.

"It was a Sarim scout," Mishal replied. He noticed the way Salim's frown deepened at that revelation. Salim had vehemently rejected joining the scouts, even though they had invited him due to his military training coupled with his small amount of ruh. "You don't think of them as real agents."

Salim tutted. "They're fine and all, but they're not protecting people."

Mishal disagreed, but he didn't see the point of pressing the issue at the moment. Instead, he led his team forward, instructing them as he walked. "Stay close together. As always, I need you, Salim, to observe and protect Salwa. Salwa, I need you to heal Salim and me if anything goes wrong. I'll take the front."

"Can't I be in front today?" Salwa asked from behind him. "It's a weak one today!"

"You don't have any fighting techniques," Mishal replied over his shoulder. They were now up to their chests in the water. Salim had taken Salwa over his shoulder. "Okay, we're almost there," Mishal said.

And then he saw it.

Mermaids are described in legends as wonderous creatures, beautiful as they are dangerous. They lure men to their death through song and laughter, then drag them into the darkness of ocean deep. In truth, water Hussais looked nothing like the mermaids of legand. This creature floated in the water like a plastic bag, its bulbous glassy eyes staring at Mishal. Its teeth were sharp, and its webbed hands reached in their direction, promising not slumber, but a sharp release from life.

"Ew!" Salwa hissed, pulling back instinctively from the creature - even as she sat atop Salim's shoulder. Salim, for his part, gave Mishal a grim look and raised his hand with the dagger. "Do you want me to take care of it?" he asked Mishal.

"Not with Salwa on your shoulder," Mishal replied. He thought for a quick moment. *Oof, he's really excited about fighting this jinni. I should have thought more about our positions. Maybe we can take the jinni on together? As long as I'm in front, it won't be too dangerous.* "Let's go for it together."

Mishal and Salim stepped forward, causing the water Hussais to step back as if in annoyance. It leaned forward, its hands reaching for something. Mishal could see its eyes going from him to Salim and Salwa, as if the jinni was evaluating something.

The jinni raised its webbed hand and twisted it, and Salim shouted from behind Mishal. "Ooof!"

Mishal looked, only to see Salim diving under the water, holding Salwa aloft above the water with both hands, even while still clutching the dagger. Bubbles rose up to the surface. Salwa, for her credit, kept her eyes focused on the jinni. Her hands were up in a fighting pose. "Come at me!" she shouted.

Idiot, it's a water Hussais - it must have controlled the water to make Salim lose his footing, Mishal thought to himself. He stepped towards Salwa, only to see her eyes widen as she looked at something behind him. Too late, he realized his mistake as a hand clamped on his foot. He was yanked from his place, and Mishal was dragged under the surface.

Chapter Five

Mishal couldn't stop cursing at himself as he was dragged underwater, like so many sailors in the history of Oman. *Stupid, stupid, stupid!*

The whoosh of the water seemed to echo the rhythm of Mishal's thoughts. He sped through the water like a torpedo, the impact making his body ache and the salt stinging his eyes. Above him, the sunlight went through the water to paint it a light blue. Below him was darkness and sand. He could feel the vice-like grip of the water Hussais on his ankle, threatening to break his leg and leave him here to drown.

Thankfully, Mishal was an inborn type, with a focus on physical power. He sent his fire throughout his body, strengthening it against the Hussais's grip as well as the speed with which he was dragged through the water. Mishal tried to send fire to his hands, but it immediately went out in the ocean, instantaneously boiling a small amount of water around his hands.

I need to figure out something else, Mishal thought to himself with another curse. Already his lungs burned with the need for air. If the Hussais succeeded in pulling him into the depths, then he would die. Mishal increased the intensity of his fire, focusing on his legs. The fire went out immediately, as before, but not before it raised the temperature of his skin.

The hand around Mishal's ankle let go. He heard a bubbling, sharp scream, and something kicked him in the stomach. Mishal tried to grab the Hussais, but it easily slipped out from his reach and swam away, its webbed feet making it go twice as fast as any human.

Mishal's heart fell as he realized that the Hussais had decided to leave him here. It was speeding back in the direction of the beach, where Salim and Salwa were.

It would take him around forty seconds to reach them. Would they last that long?

Angry, Mishal kicked off behind the jinni. He pushed ruh into his legs and arms, strengthening them and making him swim faster towards his teammates. Mishal ignored the burning in his lungs. *If only I could hit it from far away,* he furiously thought, even though he realized that he wouldn't be able to send his flickering fire into the distance.

Another thirty seconds to reach them.

Finally, he saw them. Two shapes above him were coming closer, clashing. Mishal could make out the closer of the two figures as the Hussais, meaning that the second was Salim, with Salwa hopefully still on his shoulder. The Hussais was swimming around Salim in quick, deliberate circles. It darted in and out of his range, and Mishal panicked. He was still about twenty seconds away. Even if he reached them, his fire went out as soon as he ignited it. He hadn't expected to be at this much of a disadvantage in a E-level mission.

Focus, Mishal. Being scared won't help you now. What do you need to do?

An idea blasted through Mishal's frustration at that point. Back when he first started training at Sarim, Ahlam and Eman had urged him to think of creative ways to use his fire, rather than simply burning his hands and holding onto creatures. Similarly, Ustaath Ismail - who was a strange exile in Qurayyat - had said the same after Ahlam's death.

In fact, during one of his conversations with Ustaath Ismail, Mishal had brought up the example of using fire to make water evaporate. Now, Mishal stopped swimming and stood floating in the water, mentally preparing himself. He put out his hands in front of him, as if holding an invisible ball. His ruh ignited between his hands, a fire burning and extinguishing within the blink of an eye. Mishal growled silently, pushing more power until a small, glowing fire appeared between his hands. He squeezed the fire, willing it to grow hotter, hotter, and steam rose from his hands in a giant spout.

The steam bubbles rose through the water, bursting between the two figures, disrupting their fight and hopefully giving Salim the time he needed to run away. Mishal made as much steam as he could, and then swam up with all the speed he could muster. The glowing surface came closer, and closer, welcoming him back to the land of humanity.

One second left.

Mishal burst through the surface with a massive gasp, filling his lungs and opening his eyes wide against the sting. In front of him was the Hussais, bleeding profusely from many cuts. On the other side was Salim, his magical dagger in his hands. His shoulder also bled from where the Hussais had bit him. Salwa sat atop Salim's shoulder still. Her hands were on his bleeding shoulder, and Mishal saw that she was healing him.

"Sir! We're so glad you're okay!" Salim said.

Without wasting any time, he raised his hand in the air and filled his fist with fresh, white-hot fire. The Hussais barely had time to react before a massive, fiery punch took off its head.

"Great job!" Mishal said, putting on a brave front as he saw his two teammates safe. In the back of his mind, he was still cursing himself.

Chapter Six

About an hour later, Salwa finished healing Salim. The Hussais had taken a quick bite out of his shoulder, using its speed to dodge his first dagger strikes. When Mishal's steam interrupted the fight, it gave Salim the cover he needed to fight effectively.

The three of them sat on the bisat, in front of sea, each holding a bottle of water. Mishal sipped his water slowly, savoring how sweet it tasted in comparison with the sea droplets still on his lips. He looked out into the ocean - massive, unknown, inviting. "Why didn't you two run?" he asked quietly.

Salwa stiffened. "I would never run from a weak jinni like that one!" she announced. "Isn't that right, Salim?"

Salim took the time to consider the question. "We were able to handle it."

"Only because I came back in time," Mishal replied. "The point of the steam was to buy you time to run."

"If we ran, it would have just come after us. Besides, you saw how it could control water. I read in *Al Sharih* that water Hussais could use water like whips, to drag their victims to them."

"I was slowing it down. You could have just gone and taken Salwa to safety," Mishal said.

"It didn't even cross my mind, sir," Salim replied. "Not with you gone in the depths. I wasn't going to leave you behind." For once, Salim's eyes were defiant. As much as Mishal hated the man's answer, he couldn't fault him.

"Well, I'm glad you're safe," Mishal said, dropping the issue. "You did fine work with that dagger."

Salwa jumped up and down, high-fiving Salim. "Did you see how I healed him?" she asked.

Mishal laughed. "Just like a princess."

Later, as they drove back home and Salwa hugged her father, Mishal replayed the mission in his mind, casting in light the weaknesses of each of his teammates.

Mishal should have found a way to attack the jinni from a distance. Salim had too much bravado. He should have taken Salwa and left Mishal behind. Instead, he'd tried to stand his ground and fight. Salim's ruh was too weak, and his control over his tools incomplete. Salwa's healing was too slow to be practical in a life-threatning situation.

They're not ready for another mission anytime soon, Mishal thought.

Chapter Seven

Mishal woke up late that Friday, feeling a yawn starting at the corner of his mouth then expanding until it stretched across his face. He lay on his bed for a long time. The sunlight leaped through the windows of his room, attacking his eyelids, but Mishal simply turned away from the window, burying his head into his pillow with a satisfied groan. He could hear his sister's music pounding through the wall.

Friday mornings were a special thing in Oman. They lacked the pure, blanket-cuddling laziness of Saturdays but, in its stead, Fridays offered the gentle excitement of a spiritual routine. Mishal would get up reasonably late, lounge about for a couple of hours, shower, trim his nails, and dress in his finest while his mother bathed the house (and him) in frankincense. Mishal would put on the woody, familiar perfume of oud and go step out with his father to the house of Allah.

Well, at least Mishal felt that way. He had the sneaking suspicion that, unlike him, most teenagers in Oman went about Fridays with a mixture of trepidation and boredom.

"Safaa?" Mishal's mother shouted, cutting his contemplation. "Safaa, you morally deprived girl, you're listening to music on a Friday morning?"

"Moooom," he heard his sister yell back through the walls. "It's just BTS, wallah!"

"Astaghfirullah!"

Mishal groaned, still feeling the half-warm, half-cold embrace of the pillow. The air conditioner on the wall, an ancient model from General, roared loudly as it cooled his room, but even its best attempts couldn't drown out the shouting match between mother and daughter. Safaa's tone had risen in pitch as she pleaded, until she sounded like a whistle. Mishal's mother…Well, his mother was recounting some of the horrors of hell, which Mishal thought was a bit of a low blow in this context.

Mishal rose from his bed to make for the bathroom, then paused. He could hear the desperation in his sister's tone. And to be honest, she had the right in this fight. Mishal wondered for a moment about what he could do to support his sister. Mishal walked to the door and opened it. "Mom?" he shouted with his head poking through the doorway.

"Wallah, I will beat you with- yes?" Mom's voice came back, its threat interrupted.

"Sorry, what's for breakfast?" he asked, with a hint of a smile on his face. If he knew his mother, this was exactly the sort of question which would get her sidetracked.

"Dangu, with a side of olives and cheese!" Mother shouted back. "Oh, wait, I forgot to put the olives on the table. Ya rabbi!" He saw Mom rush through the corridor in front of him in a red laisu, her argument with Safaa forgotten. Mishal smiled to himself and ducked back into the room. He brushed his teeth, electing to shower later, and checked his phone. Mishal found a message from Eman al Lawati, leader of Team 10 of Sarim.

Joint training tomorrow, she'd written. *Are you up for it*?

Mishal pondered. He'd been hesitant in joining training sessions with mixed team members so far. The idea of trying to socialize with new people made something prickle inside of him. His anxiety would flare, as it often did.

What if I say something stupid in front of Salim and Salwa? Mishal thought to himself, rubbing his neck. Besides, he wasn't sure the two of them were ready. Salim's ruh vessel was small and he found it difficult to recall any useful spells, so he focused on using his tools. Salwa's healing was far too slow to be practical.

Mishal looked at himself in the mirror, noting the bags under his eyes, facing the fear apparent in his visage. *What if they fail?*

Still, Salim and Salwa were looking forward to meeting other teams. *I can stomach a little anxiety, as long as the two of them have fun.*

Sure, he typed back with a number of smiley faces, then sent an invitation via WhatsApp to Salim, as well as Salwa's mother. By the time he made it down the stairs for breakfast, his phone dinged twice, indicating both Salim and Salwa had accepted the proposal.

I'm busy cleaning, so we'll tell Salim to bring her, Salwa's mother added. Mishal acknowledged the response and sighed. It was still nine AM, but he already felt exhausted. Something about talking to people drained him instantly, leaving him dry inside.

Mishal continued his way down the stairs, to where his father sat on the floor on a mat of old newspapers, eating his breakfast. Mishal hesitated, then walked into the room.

"Al Salam Alaikum," he said.

Father kept his eyes glued on his plate. "Wa Alaikum Il Salam," he replied. Mishal sat down quietly on the other side of the makeshift floormat and ate, a simple meal of daal and bread - expertly made.

“I have some special classes tomorrow,” he slowly said.

“Hmm,” his father replied. “Do you need someone to drop you off?”

“No, they’ll pick me up.”

“Umhm.” His father checked his phone, squinting. “Scholarships really are amazing, aren’t they? Keep working hard.”

Mishal smiled on the outside, even as his stomach clenched. *Lying is the scariest thing in the world,* he thought, even as he supposed it must come naturally to some people.

Mishal had been lying to his parents since he joined Sarim. He’d fabricated a story about a special government scholarship program for gifted students, which occurred in the evenings after school. Around February, he’d even brought an enchanted letter to help convince them to allow him to go on special training with Ustaath Ismael, an odd hermit living inside oceanic cliff in Qurayyat. Now, Mishal’s lies were becoming increasingly challenging to maintain. School teachers might call his parents if he skipped classes for morning missions. Worse still, Mishal now received a tidy sum of money as a team leader in Sarim. So far, he’d been supporting his parents by leaving small bills behind on the kitchen counter and hoping that his parents would think *they* forgot it.

There has to be a better way to give them cash. Think, Mishal...

After breakfast Mishal headed to the bathroom to shower. Once done, he stepped out and stood in front of the mirror. Mishal let soft tendrils of fire spread across his body in small chains, evaporating away the water. He hadn't used a towel in months, one of the perks of being a fire-type exorcist, with an excess of ruh.

Mishal stood staring at his reflection in the mirror. On the inside of his thumb, he could see the small chain-shaped scar. Since he was ten, an Aamur, a type of jinni that possessed people's minds, had been living in his head. At fifteen years old, Mishal had confronted the jinni - with help from Shayib Ghalib - and he'd won. After the fight, Shayib Ghalib had sealed the jinni, and Mishal found this chain-shaped scar on the inside of his thumb.

Back then, Mishal had been scrawny. Now? Mishal's shoulders bulged like armor, giving him a menacing look when paired with his bushy eyebrows and the bags under his eyes. Hell, Mishal didn't *look* like he was shy. He looked like the kind of guy others would be intimidated by. *Chin up, it's going to be fine,* he said to himself. To distract himself, Mishal thought of how his sister's Maths grades were lagging recently. He could probably lend her some of his old notes, couldn't he?

Two hours later, Mishal was dressed in his finest dishdasha, a Kumma to match, and had put on an array of cheap perfumes as well as a small dab from the one good bottle of oud his parents kept in their room. He stepped out of the house at almost twelve, making his way to the massive mosque which dominated the neighborhood view.

Inside, the mosque smelled of bukhoor. Waves of cold slammed into Mishal's skin from the massive air conditioning units. Hundreds of people filled the mosque, either sitting on the giant red carpet or praying. Their different outfits made for a patchwork of color which contrasted with the white and gold of the mosque walls, the Quranic calligraphy on the walls, and the giant chandelier which hung from the center. The sight, familiar now after years frequenting the mosque, filled Mishal with a sense of peace. Something inside of him hushed, as if paying homage.

As he entered the mosque, dodging around people here and there, Mishal saw a solitary man stand in the front row and step up to the microphone.

"Allahu Akbar, Allahu Akbar," the man began, his voice carrying through the entire neighborhood. As he finished each sentence of the Athan, a soft hum filled the mosque as people repeated his words to themselves. At the end of the Athan, almost everyone stood, praying two rak'aas before dropping back to their seats. Mishal followed suit, knowing that the speech would begin soon.

At exactly quarter past twelve, a bearded man - dressed in a white turban and wearing a black cloak over his dishdasha - climbed the steps of a raised dais that waited in the front of the mosque. "Al Salam Alaikum wa Rahmat Allah," he said.

"Wa Alaikum il Salam," Mishal repeated with the rest of the people. The Mua'thin repeated the call of prayers, and the Imam, the man in charge of this mosque, launched into his Friday speech. His voice had an odd set of inflections, and he used complex words. He tried to make each of his sentences rhyme.

"And so, as I tell myself to raise my spirit to do good in this world, and so do we all, we must also take care in how we raise the next generation, for them to grow straight as a blessed tree, healthy and…" he said, causing Mishal to immediately lose interest.

Oh, this week it's about raising kids, he thought to himself. He'd heard variations of this speech a hundred times before: watch your kids, tell them about the righteous path, do not allow them to stray. Honestly, it wasn't like the Imam gave any concrete information, and many of the topics felt similar. So Mishal's finger strayed to the soft red carpet under his feet and he began to trace shapes absentmindedly, the Imam forgotten. This wasn't the kind of advice he needed. He probably won't have children until he was forty or something.

Mishal pondered over and over again what to do with Salwa and Salim. The girl, sunny and bright, was talented and highly attached to Salim. Everyone could tell that Mishal was shielding Salwa from the front lines in various ways, from scheduling missions while she was at school, to keeping her in the car, and a variety of other tricks. It didn't feel fair, but Mishal was only doing it out of fear.

Maybe the training session would be good for her. That way, she wouldn't need to go on a mission this week.

When he looked down, Mishal realized he had drawn a simple stick drawing. He'd drawn himself, Salim, and Salwa standing together. They looked happy.

That Friday flew by quickly, and Mishal found sleep difficult to come by, same as always. When he awoke, he had bags under his eyes, giving him a puffy look. He showered quickly then stood outside his front door, yawning more than usual. He was the only one out on the street at six AM. Being here, all alone, filled Mishal with a sense of wonder.

It felt nice to be the only person in existence. The air, the trees, the very earth belonged to him. It was nice to be embraced by a moment of utter silence.

Salim's car rounded the corner and Mishal snapped out of his state of bliss. He waved politely.

The car, a 2008 model Mitsubishi Lancer, was outfitted with wings on the back like an EVO, but Mishal knew it only boasted the normal four cylinders. Its paint was a cross of ash-gray with a hint of silver buried within the embers. As Mishal stood there, the car ground to an unsteady halt, shuddering with exhaustion. Salwa stepped out from the passenger-side seat.

"You get in here, Mishal, because you're the older one," she said.

"Don't you want to sit there with Salim? You can control the music."

The girl paused, then firmly shook her head. "No; Mom said older people sit in the front, kids in the back. Not that I'm a kid, though! Just - I'm younger than you, so you sit there!"

Mishal smiled to himself as he obliged the girl, getting in the passenger seat next to Salim. "Good morning," he said.

"It's the morning of flowers, of sunlight, of a gentle breeze," Salim hummed. His eyes were wide, his beard trimmed, and he'd filled the car with the scent of perfumes. As Mishal tried to take stock of this surprising level of good mood for the usually somber man, Salim hit the button on his car radio. The display read *Fairuz morning songs.*

"So, you're a morning kind of person?" Mishal asked as they drove out into the highway. He had to raise his voice to be heard over the tunes of Fairuz, a beacon of classical singing. Mishal and Salim rarely went on early morning missions, certainly never with Salwa, and so he found this side of the man unfamiliar but refreshing.

"Morning?" Salim asked with a laugh. "Sir, do you know what my schedule was like back when I joined the police academy?"

"Err, busy?"

"They woke us up at around three AM. We had to jog to Fajer prayer. I'd get so tired I would fall asleep in the middle of sujood!" he added, causing Mishal to sputter with laughter.

"It's only ten seconds!"

"Best ten-second sleep I ever had, boss!"

"Did you sleep after Fajar prayer?" Salwa asked, leaning up from the maroon-colored back seats to join in the conversation. "My dad, he always wakes up for Fajer but then sleeps afterwards."

"Oh no, then it was off to drills. Every single day, little girl. So, what I'm saying, boss, is six AM isn't early; not by a long shot!"

Salim continued to intermittently tell them stories, ranging from the time someone got kicked out for hiding a phone in the ceiling vents, to nostalgic tales about the blisters on Salim's palms after he finished the customary afternoon pushups. Mishal leaned back in his seat, soothed by the stories, as the sun competed against the car AC, one trying to warm his skin and the other to cool it. He marveled at Salim's easy speaking pace. The man went quiet for short stretches, then launched into another story to entertain Salwa. This power, Mishal had never managed. Silence unnerved him, but speaking terrified him. *It's always better to be quiet,* he thought to himself. *That way, you can never say the wrong thing.*

Mishal looked in the mirror behind him during one of Salim's quiet stretches. He could see Salwa sagging in the back seat, her head lolling. Mishal smirked for a second, imagining what would happen if Salim went into one of his loud stories right now. Mishal tapped Salim on the shoulder.

"Yes sir?" Salim asked, startled.

Mishal raised a finger to his lips, then gestured behind them. A small crease formed between Salim's eyebrows. "What, are my stories too boring?" he grumbled in a whisper, but went quiet and turned on more of Fairuz's songs on the radio.

Soon, the group reached the front entrance of Sarim, where they opened the secret panel door using Mishal's work card. Inside, the magnificent gem pulsated in slow welcome. Mishal's phone dinged once more with a message from Eman. *We're downstairs on floor two, basic training room one.*

Mishal nodded to himself and said, "Guys, we're going down one floor. It's the basic level training areas."

"Not the hard ones?" Salwa asked, pouting.

"Not the hard ones," Mishal replied with a small smile. The light next to him flickered, mimicking the fluttering of his heart. He was relieved that they'd be in the easier training halls. *It's too early in the morning for a proper workout.*

Down below, Mishal came to the lower-rank training halls. These were easier than the other training areas which team leaders and B-rank teams used. Mishal keenly remembered the bruises from the training dummies in the rooms. "Here, it's this one," he said, pointing to a smooth, modern-looking door.

On the other side, Mishal found five teams of three: Eman Al Lawati stood in the far corner, leading her team into warm-up stretches while giving them small points of advice. She looked up with one hand wrapped around her body and smiled warmly. "Mishal, it's been too long!"

"Only two weeks," he replied, smiling back in spite of himself. "Still going around giving advice to people all the time?" he asked.

"It's my job, isn't it?"

"Sure is. Guys, you know Eman's team," he said as Salwa sprinted past him and towards the youngest team member of Team 10, a boy who was two years her senior and sported a nose which looked as if it'd been broken multiple times in the past. The boy's almost purple eyes were set in an owl-like scowl, which disappeared as soon as he saw Salwa.

"Hi!" the boy said, his voice loudly carrying across the hall, causing everybody around them to whirl around and stare. A grim-faced figure broke off from their place by the wall and stepped forward.

"I didn't know he was coming," the man said, kissing his teeth in irritation. "Are we in a training session or a show-off competition? Should I get my nice-looking sandals?"

"Yazeed," Mishal said, his heart leaping to his mouth as it always did during verbal confrontations. *Maybe I can avoid the unpleasantness,* he thought. "How are you? And Team 9?"

"Fine, fine, it's just a rough day, it looks like," Yazeed replied, barely holding in his contempt. He looked like a goat, with a narrow face ending in a spear-like beard. "One comes to these things hoping to get some sort of benefit out of it, you know? You want everyone who shows up to have the same standards, to be on the same *level.*"

The young boy from Eman's team stepped forward. "We're all good here!" he enthusiastically blurted out, causing Yazeed to laugh out loud.

"You're a child. I worry for your education. With her as your boss," Yazeed said, pointing at Eman. "I don't think you had any fight training to begin with."

"I don't *need* training!" the boy announced defensively, stepping forward. Mishal could see Yazeed's brick-hard eyes tighten at the motion. Mishal's hand shot out and grabbed the boy's shoulder quickly, pulling him back.

Yazeed looked from the boy to Mishal. When their eyes met, Mishal glimpsed distaste lurking within Yazeed's narrow eyes. The man turned and walked away, grumbling to himself. The young boy from Eman's team struggled in vain against Mishal's strong grip until he whirled the boy around, bending down to look at him properly.

"Laith, right?" he asked.

"Yes!" the boy replied, a hand shooting out to shake Mishal's hand in a businesslike manner. "Thank you for helping out here, sir, but there's no need. I don't let anybody talk trash about our team; team leader or no team leader."

Mishal brought a hand to his own cheek in surprise. When he'd seen the boy before, Laith had been just as shy as Salwa. Now, he'd seemed to overcome that tameness and then some. The boy's grimace reminded Mishal of mountain cats. Mishal looked to Eman, not knowing how to deal with the situation. *Laith is too young. There's no need for him to find out why Yazeed dislikes Eman and me.*

Eman sighed and stepped forward, coming up behind Laith. Without saying anything, she poked him in the back of the head, causing the boy to yelp and spin around to face her. He rubbed the back of his head furiously.

"What was that for?" the boy practically screamed.

"For being a little baby!" Eman said. "I thought you said you wanted to protect me, no?"

"I w-*will* protect you!"

"Then I need you close to your team, not picking fights with whoever shows up calling you short!"

"I… You don't understand!" Laith said, then windmilled backwards when Eman raised her perfectly trimmed fingernails to smack him again. "Ok, fine, fine! I'm coming."

"Good," she replied, coming down to his level. "Laith, you're a strong man. I just need you to stay close to us, ok? There's no need to constantly go out to prove yourself."

Laith mumbled something and Eman gave him a little pat on the shoulder, drawing him away and back towards her team.

Mishal, as always, marveled at Eman's artistic skills for mending feelings and uplifting spirits. As always, Eman was the first person Mishal associated with the phrase, 'a good person'.

Meanwhile, Mishal still wasn't able to convince Salim to stop calling him 'sir'.

Eman walked to the center of the room, drawing attention to herself, and cleared her throat loudly to emphasize the point. "Alright, everyone!" she announced, adjusting her ocean-blue hijab over her silken gold hair. "I think it's time to start our first joint team training session!"

The crowd gathered, some grinning, some looking as pensive as Mishal felt. When everyone stood in an interested semi-circle around Eman, the girl smiled with the warmth of daylight. "First of all, thank you for being here."

"You're welcome," someone said.

"The purpose of this series of training sessions is for us to learn more about each other's strengths and weaknesses. Each of us is good at something different, so competing in a *friendly* way," Eman said this last part pointedly, staring at a trio of women Mishal didn't recognize, "should help us get some pointers. Now, the Shayibs helped me draft this list of teams," she added, pulling out a rolled-up piece of parchment. Eman walked over to the nearest wall and stuck the parchment up using tape. It detailed a list of teams. "Step one: We do a rotating session of team matches against each other. Team one fights against team two, team three against team four, and team five sits out to wait for its turn. This way, one team is always going to be waiting. Alright?"

Everyone nodded. Mishal took a look at the piece of parchment, noting that his team was team three. Team four was... Eman's team.

"Everyone settle back into your spot!" Eman said, drawing her team aside to a corner of the training hall. Mishal grumbled to himself as he did the same, ushering Salwa across the ceramic floor in front of him. Salim walked behind, already starting to pull out tools from his overlarge brown backpack. "The little one is a physical fighter, yes boss?" he asked.

“Yes, but I don’t exactly know what kind of combat he uses,” Mishal whispered back. “And I honestly have no idea what the third member of their team does. I’ll be in front, and you two watch for their attacks. Is that alright?”

Salim hesitated, then said, “Yes, sir.” He held a small black object, like a raisin, held between two fingers. This he placed in his pocket. “I hope we don’t hold you back.”

“Of course not,” Mishal answered quickly. “You two are the valuable ones.”

“Uh huh,” Salim replied, his eyebrows furrowing.

“It’s true!” Mishal said, sensing Salim’s growing frustration with himself. “All I can do is make fire and punch things, while you have three magical tools, and spells to boot.”

“Spells I mess up half the time,” Salim replied.

Mishal ignored Salim’s interruption. “Besides, I need you to analyze what they’re doing, you’re great at that.”

Salim took a deep breath, then nodded. “Ustatha Eman,” he announced, “is your team ready to start?”

“Don’t call me that,” she replied with a flowery smile. Mishal noticed that she’d also drawn out her trademark forest-green bead bracelet out from under her long shirt and wrapped it over the fabric, so that it hung visibly on her wrist. “All teams, ready?” she asked.

The door creaked then and Mishal looked over at the entrance to see that spectators had begun to file in. Some of them leaned against the wall, others squatted down on the floor, and some sat on benches. Their eyes glittered with hungry interest, hoping to gauge the current skills of the participating teams. Mishal noted the bearded man he’d seen in the cafeteria, standing to the side. The man caught Mishal watching and smiled brightly. Asaad was also there, standing with an air of power that repelled those around him. A grin filled his face. “Ay, my team’s going to kill you, Eman,” Asaad announced to the room in general. Immediately, Mishal could almost feel a cloud of ill-will towards them grow. He groaned.

Mishal turned around to see Eman's team in formation, with the boy leaning in forward as if ready for a fight. Behind him stood Eman, with the third woman, who appeared older, hanging in the back.

Salim leaped back to his position, pulling the small black bead from his pocket and drawing Salwa in closer to him. Mishal stepped forwards, getting the full attention of his three opponents.

Team 14's formation was simple and consistent: Mishal punched while Salim analyzed and kept Salwa safe, even when she widened her already large eyes and begged for a fight.

Now, both teams were ready. Mishal's vision sharpened, ruh filled his body, and a fire sprang to life inside of his heart.

"And… start!" Eman announced.

Chapter Eight

Laith jumped in without hesitation. His mouth opened to reveal a feral snarl. Mishal hastily sent ruh to his eyes, filling his sight with magical truths. Laith's legs were covered in magic, and as he began to recite an incantation the magic swirled around and around, like a miniature hurricane. The boy leaped forward, his purple eyes shifting like violent winds.

Ah, wind magic, Mishal thought, even as he summoned his own magic to his feet. Experimenting, Mishal kicked out with his leg to send fire surging out in a half-circle. Even before the fire appeared, Laith's eyes widened and he leaped into the air, speaking a complicated incantation. The boy sent out a gust of wind to propel himself forward. He flew spinning across the room, landing in a faraway corner with his eyes wide with surprise.

"You don't use spells!" Laith accused Mishal, pointing an angry finger. "That's *cheating*!"

Mishal declined to reply, instead sending fire to his legs and leaping forward. Laith appeared to panic, jumping backwards even as Mishal adjusted his strength, then punched forward lightly, catching the kid in the jaw. However, rather than fall down, Laith instead grinned and aimed a roundhouse kick at Mishal's legs.

What? How did he not get knocked out by that?

Mishal leaped back, then came back in with an elbow strike, which connected properly with Laith's midsection. Again, Laith didn't fall down. Something felt off about the contact of the strike, so Mishal sent more fire to his arms and punched one more time. The punch connected cleanly with Laith's temple, sending him back a few steps. However, the boy didn't appear to be phased by the solid hit.

"What, are you holding back?" he asked.

"Boss!" Salim called from behind Mishal. Mishal turned to see Salim holding his Sharqiya-style dagger, trying his best to fend off a giant white lion, which sported an emerald mane as well as snake's head instead of a tail. This was Eman's beast, Sahib, alongside which Mishal had fought countless times. However, this time Sahib was their enemy.

As Sahib scratched towards Salim, forcing the man backwards, Mishal felt a pang in his chest. For an instant, his throat went tight, his chest constricted in a gasp.

What if Sahib hurts Salim?

Ignoring Laith for now, Mishal ran forward, spraying out fire towards the beast.

The lion reared backwards, roaring. It whirled around, facing Mishal with eyes full of jade.

"Salim!" Mishal called. "Pull it towards me!"

"Sir?" Salim asked, perplexed. "I can keep it back!"

"Don't fight it, send it to me!" Mishal shouted, louder than he'd intended.

Salim saluted quickly at the order and pulled out another tool, the fishing line he usually used to draw in jinn. However, this time Salim threw the line expertly towards the lion, which struck the line away with its snow-white paw.

"It's still focused on you!" Mishal hissed, already crouching down in preparation. Mishal stabilized his feet, gathering fire to his fist. Mishal's fire always responded to his emotions, a power which he'd spent months learning to control. Now, the fire shone red with anger, then blue with fear, then white as he accepted the fight as inevitable. He was with comrades. He would protect them with all his strength. "Quick, before Laith gets here!"

"Any minute now," Salim replied, pulling back the line and presenting the fishing hook, which now had a small coating of lion's blood on it.

"I'm ready!" Mishal said. His muscles ached with the force of the fire gathering in his fist. Laith was running towards him, flying through the air.

Salim pulled the line. Suddenly, the giant white lion hurled into the air as if yanked by a giant rope, coming directly towards Mishal. Its snake-tail swished, hissing. For a second, Mishal's eyes locked with Sahib's cat eyes.

"Sorry, buddy," Mishal said.

Mishal threw out the punch, aiming it at the lion's chest.

"No!" Laith shouted, flying across the air towards them.

A massive explosion rocked the lion, which broke apart into a hundred emerald beads. The beads dissipated into the air, leaving only a faint green glow. On the other side of the explosion, Eman fell to her knees with exhaustion.

Mishal took a step forward towards Eman, then stopped. "Do you surrender?" he asked.

"Yeah!" Eman panted, raising a hand to the air. "Team 14 wins this match!"

Chapter Nine

Mishal smiled to himself as Salim leaned down to high-five Salwa. She returned the high-five, though her expression looked upset.

"I didn't even do anything!" she complained.

"Aww," Salim said with a laugh. "I'll try to get hurt next time so you can heal me!"

In the background and all around, flashes of magic burst and raged, Sarim employees flew across the room in heated spirits. One person, in particular, stood out: She stood with feet steadied defiantly apart, shooting giant glowing arrows from a crossbow held against her hips. Clangs and shouts echoed across the room, along with grins, laughs, and grimaces.

Mishal walked across the marble floor to Eman; she was getting up slowly off the floor with help from Laith, whose lips quivered softly. The third member of their team, the quiet woman, stood a few feet away with a worried expression on her face. Laith whirled around to face Mishal. "You ran away from me!" he accused.

"I beat you down three times," Mishal replied, confused. "What, did you want me to keep going?"

"Of course!" the boy replied, purple eyes glittering with indignation.

"But-"

"Don't mind Laith," Eman interrupted, yanking the boy back by his collar. A sigh escaped her, but then she smiled. "You did good, Mishal. It looks like our strategy works better for jinn than it does for people."

Mishal felt his confusion deepen, dropping his thoughts into an abyss. "What do you mean, strategy? Your third team member didn't seem to be doing much."

"I mean that our third member… Suad, say hi," she added, pointing towards the woman, who nodded politely but said nothing, "wasn't just standing around. She was the whole reason you couldn't damage Laith with your fire."

Mishal recalled the odd way Laith kept standing up despite the blows, as if the blows hadn't even touched. "Ah," he said. "Defense."

"A skin-thin barrier, to be exact."

"Yeah, there's no *way* you could've hurt me!" Laith jumped up to say with a whoop, even with Eman's hand still around his collar.

Not knowing what to say, Mishal played along. "You're right," he said, hoping to take some of the edge off Laith's animosity. "That defense sure is something. I couldn't have broken it."

"Not without getting *serious*," Eman said with a laugh, ignoring Laith's stare of utter indignation. "Well, I'll go off to the side now; you rest until the next round."

"What do you mean?" Laith piped up, face turning from Eman to Mishal. "Hey, what does she mean, *serious*?"

Mishal shrugged in embarrassment. He could sense in his bones that the boy wouldn't take well to finding out the truth about Mishal's power.

Mishal's fire responded to his emotions. His blue and red flames were far less potent than the black and white blazes, which appeared during periods of extreme hate or acceptance. Mishal's white and black flames could have obliterated Suad's barriers, most likely, but such emotions were not meant for training.

Instead of saying anything to Laith, Mishal turned back to Salim and Salwa, then glimpsed someone coming up towards them. It was Asaad Al Nabhani, their Shayib, walking casually through the mayhem of the battle around them. As Mishal watched, a beam of swirling energy whizzed towards Asaad. Without pausing, the Shayib raised a hand and let the magic crash against him, stopping it in place. "Eh," he said apologetically to the teams that were fighting. They in turn only stared at him.

"Sir," Salim said to Asaad, giving him a salute. Asaad responded with a quick nod.

"Mishal, come with me," he urged, adjusting his razor-straight Kumma. As always, Asaad cut a handsome figure in his dishdasha - even though he refused to wear a turban, as was customary for the male Shayibs. He said the Kumma had more style.

"Alright," Mishal replied, feeling apprehensive. He didn't like the slight frown on Asaad's face. "Salim, were you alright during that last fight?"

Salim laughed. "I didn't do anything."

Mishal paused, noticing the way Salim's feet shifted. He wasn't happy about his performance during the last fight. "Hey, keeping Sahib at bay is no easy feat. That creature could easily qualify as a C-level Jinni."

Asaad led Mishal to a drinking fountain, at the far wall of the hall. His steps were sure, but this time he kept away from the battling teams. As Mishal watched, he could see one of the contestants reciting a spell. The woman's hand slowly transformed as she spoke, growing scales and fangs. She lashed out against her opponent, hissing.

At the water fountain, Mishal used his hand to cup water from the freezing stream and drink it. "Yeah?" he asked.

"You won the fight just now. As the leader, that was your job and I won't chastise you for it," Asaad said.

"I can sense a 'but' coming."

Asaad smiled. "Kid, tell me what you did right and what you did wrong during the fight."

"What we did wrong?" Mishal asked in confusion. "We held back their advance party: Laith. After pushing him aside, we dealt with Eman's lion. I think we did well. Was it wrong to focus on the lion?" Uncomfortably, Mishal replayed a previous conversation with Asaad. "Is it because I still haven't found a way to attack from a distance?"

"No, no," Asaad said, the frown returning to his angled face. He leaned back against the wall, scratching at his perfect beard, which had been trimmed to a point at the corners like daggers. "I don't think you know what just happened. *You* dealt with the little boy. *You* beat the lion. Salim was containing it, but you jumped in anyway."

"Salim is a tool user, with a single dagger; he isn't equipped to fight."

"He isn't equipped to fight *yet*," Asaad corrected. "And he won't be, if you keep jumping in every time he raises his knife."

"There's no need for that; he has more important tasks!" Mishal objected. Why didn't Asaad see that there was more to being an exorcist than just fighting?

Asaad sighed, leaning back to twirl his white Shayib's cane. "That aside, what did the little girl do? Did Salwa add *anything* to the team during the fight?"

"She's a healer," Mishal retorted, feeling heat spread through his cheeks. He felt like he was being yelled at, like a child. His voice must have risen, since he saw Asaad raised his strong eyebrows. Pushing the feelings aside, Mishal repeated, "Salwa is a healer. There's no need for a healer to heal, if no one gets hurt."

"Kid, look behind you. Can you see what the other teams are doing?"

Mishal turned and looked. "They're fighting battles."

"As a team. They're coordinated. Meanwhile, instead of finishing Laith, you ran away from him and attacked the lion. You could have let Salim deal with the beast, and instead taken care of Laith and Suad. Heck, you could have gone for Eman. Instead, you decided to take everything on your shoulders. I have a question for you, Mishal," Asaad leaned in close, almost whispering in Mishal's ears. A shadow fell over his face, his hand clamped over Mishal's shoulder. The fights all around them sounded subdued, far away. It was just Mishal and Asaad now. "What if Laith had gone for Salwa instead?"

Mishal felt his stomach drop. "I would have turned back to stop him."

"…I see. Well," Asaad said, taking off his Kumma just long enough to run a hand through his straight hair and then put it back on. "I've said my piece. Let's see how well you do on the next match."

By then, the last of the teams - Team 16, with Musab and the new guy - had finished their fight. Musab stood in the center of the ring, exhausted, and raised his hands in celebration.

“Yes, yes,” Eman said as she clapped her hands twice. Mishal snickered as he saw the exasperation on her face, “very impressive, Musab; now, shake hands with the other team and thank them for a good match. We’re all colleagues here!”

The winners of the past matches stayed on their stretch of the large training hall, while the losers rotated one place to the right. Mishal made his way back to his team, where Salim and Salwa were arguing about something. “What’s the next match?” Salwa asked when she saw Mishal.

Mishal tried to put on the best smile he could, despite Asaad’s earlier beratement. “I checked the last matchup,” he said.

“You’re so reliable, boss,” Salim said with admiration.

Mishal laughed. *If only he knew that I was too scared* not *to check on our competition.* “Team 5 won the last match, so we should be up against them. Eman said that they’re good people, but I didn’t have time to find out more.”

Mishal soon stood on the mat, with Salim and Salwa behind him, and found himself facing a team of three eerie women. The three looked alike, like distorted reflections of one another. The tallest held a short, stout black rod in her hand. Mishal stared at the hand, which was translucent enough to reveal green veins beneath the skin. The woman’s lips were full and glistening, completely unlike that sickly hand clutching the black rod.

“Erm?” Salim asked. “Is this quite alright for Salwa?”

“I don’t like it…” Salwa muttered, leaning behind her team member. “That lady is scary.”

The woman cocked her head, staring right over Mishal’s shoulder to regard Salwa with claw-sharp eyes. “You know, my hearing becomes quite impressive after I’ve fed, child. Also, I get a little *testy* when I’m insulted. Salima, Halima, that little girl in the back is our target.”

“Yes, Aalima,” the two others replied. Now, Mishal’s eyes ventured to the other two women. The woman on the left, who was more rotund than the others, wore lipstick deeper than the night sky. Something about her mouth held Mishal’s eyes in captivity, like a mouse encountering a predator. The last woman, who was short but wide-shouldered, wore something that looked like a traditional Omani Dara'aa, a thick golden chain, over her chest. She crouched down in preparation even as Eman stood up to the side, raising a hand and surveying the combatants.

"She's just a girl," Mishal said to the women, trying to calm the situation down. His three opponents felt less like friendly opponents and more akin to true jinn. They felt *feral.*

"So were we, a long time ago," the rotund woman, Salima, said, smiling. As her lips parted, Mishal noted one, long fang poking out from her mouth.

A thousand Western movies flitted through his mind. Movies about pale-faced strangers who drank blood and turned into bats.

There's no way, Mishal thought to himself. He turned to look at Eman, hoping to squeeze in a question.

"Start!" Eman shouted.

Aalima turned away from Mishal, Salim, and Salwa, hiding behind her thicker sister, Salima. Instead of appearing on the other side, she simply stayed there. Mishal made a mental note of the woman's position as he sprinted forward, sending fire to his legs to increase his speed. He zoomed across the marble floor, floating like an ice-skater, heading straight for the woman with the dark lipstick.

"Boss, wait!" Salim shouted, but Mishal ignored him while running straight toward Salima. Something about this fight felt urgent. She smiled at him now, her ruh coiling in geometric shapes mirroring black clouds around her. Instead of punching or kicking, she leaned forward and breathed.

A gust of thick smoke erupted from the woman's chalk-black lips, roiling outwards. Mishal ran straight into the inky cloud and accidentally inhaled a large gulp of sulphurous smoke.

Mishal immediately began to cough, feeling something take root in his throat and rise up to his head like scratching fingers. He could hear Salima laughing from somewhere outside the thick cloud. "We have a minute," she announced to her sisters, and her voice rang painfully in Mishal's mind. He couldn't summon his ruh, it felt like he could barely think. "Time to take care of the weak ones."

"Stop," he croaked, his panic rising. These weren't contestants, he knew now. Given the chance, they were certainly willing to kill or maim his teammates. He could hear them battling against Salim, the ex-soldier's futile cries echoing across the ring even as flashes of light danced across the ring outside the black cloud. Salwa shouted for Salim to help her, the girl's voice like cracked glass.

These women were going to kill his teammates. Mishal's throat constricted with deep-seeded fear, rooted in his deep memories. Memories of Ahlam, of her smile, of her laugh, of the day she stepped towards death in his stead.

Smiles, protection, death. Smiles, protection, death. That's what his life was. People smiled, people protected, then people died.

This stops now.

A shout ripped itself from Mishal's throat. Fire burned through his fear, catching his heart like a coal. He could sense heat everywhere. His panic had subsided, replaced by something which had always been a part of him: hate.

Hate coursed through his body, leeching from his heart to his shoulders and his hands. Mishal breathed out, feeling coal-black fire coming out from his mouth, from his hands, from his legs. The smoke burned away, leaving only floating ashes and black fire.

If these people had done anything to Salim and Salwa... *I'll kill them.*

Mishal looked up, ready to destroy, and froze.

Salwa stood only meters away, held in place by the tall woman while the two others restrained Salim. Nobody had been harmed. All five exorcists were looking at Mishal with horror etched on their faces, even Salim and Salwa. As he watched, Mishal noticed Asaad running forward, an angry look on his face.

"What the *hell* do you think you're doing," the Shayib hissed, pointing at Mishal's black fire, "bringing that thing out here?"

"I-"

“Stand down, now!” Asaad ordered, “this is a *friendly* match.”

Mishal gaped, looking from Salwa to Aalima, who hastily removed her hand from the Salwa’s wrist and waved to show she held no ill-will. The woman was looking at him as if he was a demon. Asaad had brandished his cane, ready to protect everyone in the room from Mishal.

Now, the participants from the other teams were looking too, watching Mishal’s black flame with a mixture of curiosity and disgust. None of them were killing each other. Things were fine.

He’d only panicked.

Mishal breathed out, extinguishing his black flame with difficulty. His heart still hammered in his chest. “I’m sorry,” he said, the words escaping his lips with difficulty. He tried to mould his face into a smile somehow. “I think your team won this match.”

Chapter Ten

Minutes later, Salim and Salwa were getting looked over for bruises by some of Sarim's healers. The healers all wore white coats, and hijabs or hats, standing out from the black sweatpants and sweatshirt uniform that most Sarim agents donned when working. These healers were part of a special team which rarely went into battle proper. Mishal wished offhandedly that Salwa would agree to join the healer squads. However, she vehemently refused each time he'd brought it up. Salwa's parents, who used to work as Sarim admins long ago, agreed, saying their daughter would grow up to be a fine agent.

Mishal sat against the wall a few meters away. A towel hung over his head, hiding his face from the onlookers. He wished to find some source of emotional support. Instead, he only had the towel and the wall and they would have to suffice for now.

Footsteps approached from the side, and Mishal saw a long shadow slide under the bright overhead lights. He could tell the shadow apart by the powerful way it moved.

"Asaad, I don't think I can handle being scolded at the moment," Mishal said calmly. He wasn't looking for pity. He was only telling the truth.

Asaad paused, then leaned on the wall next to Mishal. The youth could see Asaad's sandals, an expensive dark blue leather affair from some brand he didn't recognize. "You know what thing Shayib Ghalib did that always surprised me the most?" he asked.

Mishal thought about it, smiling to himself as he pondered the question. "When he cared."

"When he cared," Asaad echoed, a grin sliding easily into his voice. "He cared so much, and in turn I cared about him too. He never pushed too hard, nor pulled too far. I never could figure out how a man could make fun of me so much, and then still care so seriously. And he listened."

Mishal laughed. His voice traveled crystal-clear through the air, even with his face hidden under the towel. For a blissful moment, Mishal felt like he and Asaad were alone, leaning there on that little empty stretch of wall, one standing, one sitting. "You know, Asaad, I'm not over Ahlam's death yet. It creeps up on me sometimes when I least expect it."

"Like a damn monster," Asaad said in agreement. "I'm not over it either, buddy."

"No?" Mishal asked in surprise, looking up so that his towel fell off his head and plopped onto the floor. Above him, Asaad stood against the wall in sharp contrast, looking almost too real.

Asaad sighed. "She was one of the few people in here who weren't scared of me, at first," he said. "Her, the CEO, and Shayib Ghalib. I loved her like a sister."

"It's better now, it really is. But when I saw that woman holding Salwa there, do you know what I saw?"

"No."

"I saw Ahlam getting stabbed by Julanda in a cave in Bahla, with the moonlight hanging over them. I see his black cane, and I see her confused look, like she didn't quite believe that she was dead. My lungs stop working, pools gather on my hands, and I stop seeing the world around me."

Mishal noticed Salim and Salwa coming back, the older soldier pausing slightly as he caught sight of Mishal and Asaad. Mishal could tell that Salim wanted to come over, maybe crack a joke. Mishal slowly, gently, shook his head. *Don't come yet.* "I think I realized something during this last fight."

"What do you mean?"

Mishal thought about how to formulate his next words. "I thought that Salim isn't ready to fight because his ruh vessel is small; he can only handle a few weak tools at the moment, and he's unable to remember spells well enough to use them in battle. I thought that Salwa isn't ready to fight because she has too much ruh, which runs wild. Because she's young. Because her healing is too slow to be practical in a fight."

"All of these are valid points," Asaad mused. "What are you saying?"

"The real problem is that *I'm* immature, and I keep interfering with their growth because I worry that they'll get hurt. It's not them who's not ready, it's me."

Asaad frowned. "Mishal, it's not a crime to want people to stay safe."

"I can't lead these two if I still get flashbacks of Ahlam every time one of them comes across a Mughayab," Mishal snapped.

The youth's blood was pumping, his heart felt empty, but he knew this was the right thing to do, even if it made him feel terrible to yell at Asaad.

Asaad dropped his hands in silence, examining Mishal's face. "You're serious," he said.

"Can we figure something out, boss?" Mishal asked.

When Asaad left, Mishal sat by himself for a time. The other teams continued their matches, though he noticed that the teams that had consistently won earlier were beginning to show fatigue. Sweat covered the marble, and he noticed team members often shifting positions. One team in particular caught his eye. The leader, who kept his hair long under a Dhofari Msar, kept making hand gestures, which caused his team to constantly change formations in obviously predetermined patterns. None of the members of *that* team were exhausted, though none of them appeared particularly powerful. That was Team 6, Mishal remembered. They'd been fighting together for years.

"You surprise me," someone said in a clear voice next to Mishal. He flinched, only to see the stranger he'd met in the cafeteria earlier. The man's long hair seemed to almost shine in the light.

"I'm sorry, I didn't hear you come closer," Mishal said.

The man laughed. "That's alright, there's a commotion going on right about now," he added, gesturing towards the combatants. Eman raised her hand then, halting all the matches. The last stray magical bolt whizzed across the air, and someone dropped a sword clattering to the ground.

"Finally!" Mishal heard someone gasp, and he laughed quietly. The stranger joined him.

“Are you here as one of the judges?” Mishal asked the man. A number of people had been recruited to the training session, tasked with finding information about each team’s weak point as well as to designate future training partners to address these issues. Today’s session was only the first part of Eman’s training camp, after all. At the end of the year, it might even change the team rankings.

The man shook his head. “I’ve never been all that good of a teacher. I’m better at encouraging people,” he said, then added, “You know, that black flame of yours is impressive. Hate, I suppose?”

Mishal stiffened. He knew everyone had seen the black flame, yet he’d assumed no-one would gather its significance. Mishal’s magic was directly related to his emotions. Hate gave his flames an everlasting fury. The black flame was a determined one, never letting go after it began burning someone. “I suppose others might think it’s impressive,” he answered truthfully. “I don’t like it.”

The man shrugged. “Emotions are valuable things, Mishal. You only hate because you want to protect. I think your hate is admirable, in a roundabout sort of way.” These words were followed by the swoosh of soft footsteps, and soon the man left the room.

After a few uneasy moments, Mishal stood up as well. He had a lot to work on. “Eman!” he called, “I need to talk to you, please!”

Chapter Eleven

It turned out HR was not well-equipped to handle team leaders who resigned of their own accord. Mishal walked knocked on the doors of the HR department on the 15th of November, 2019 with a mixture of hope and apprehension.

"Come on in," a female voice called out from the other side. Mishal opened the door to see a female employee he recognized. The tired-looking woman had been here on Mishal's very first day at Sarim, when he first met Ahlam and Eman. Her bored expression brightened slightly when she saw him. "Assim's furious with you," she said.

Mishal gulped. "Sorry about that."

"It's fine, he's usually furious. Can you wait a minute until you're called?"

Orange lights lit the office, going well with a 70's style thick carpet which covered the floor. On the other side of the office Assim's door waited, closed so he could have peace. Paperwork littered two rich-brown desks, although a third desk lay empty. "I don't remember seeing this desk here before," Mishal commented, feeling awkward at the stretching of silence between him and the woman, whose name he couldn't remember.

"We're getting a new intern soon," she said. "She's here to help out with a few processes. Good job on keeping up with the paperwork for Salwa and Salim, by the way."

"Oh, thank you," Mishal replied.

"The day we found out Asaad would get a team, Assim practically threw a tantrum. But it's good to see someone in Team 14 has a sense of responsibility."

Mishal smiled sadly. The woman's words meant she didn't know what he was here to talk with Assim about.

Something slammed into the door, making Mishal and the receptionist jump. "Oh, that's a sign from him that you can come in," she said.

Mishal thanked the woman and stood up. He thought about asking her for her name, but… *It's been too long, it's rude to ask now,* he thought to himself.

Mishal knocked on Assim's door. "Come in," a gruff voice replied. Mishal opened the door to see a large office which mixed ceramic flooring and metal frames. The right wall had four windows, which overlooked the Sarim crystal and the pit. Blue light flowed in, illuminating the angry-looking face of Assim.

"You're out of your mind," Assim said before Mishal could speak. He pointed a ringed finger at an empty spot in his otherwise messy desk.

On the empty spot lay a letter in Mishal's neat handwriting, where he requested to be allowed to step down as leader of Team 14. He'd also asked for Salim and Salwa to be taken off the exorcist force. Salim was to be absorbed into the Scouts, while Salwa was to become a healer.

"I think it's the best option for us all," Mishal replied.

"You don't get to make decisions for other people," Assim said flatly, causing Mishal's hackles to rise.

"But sir-"

"No buts! What do you think being an exorcist means? It takes extraordinary skills, skills these two recruits have."

"Salim's ruh vessel is too small for him to become a fighter!"

"He'll learn to use his ruh better then! And the kid is only ten, she'll grow and might lead a team of her own in the future."

"What if they get hurt?" Mishal demanded, his voice rising.

"Then we heal them."

"What if they die?"

Now Assim paused. The crystal outside the windows hovered slowly, warping the blue light on his worried face. "After Ahlam Al Hatmi died, you never took proper time off, did you?" he asked. "No, of course not. Bani Safi were at our throats, and you were preoccupied with prophecy and revenge."

"…What are you saying?" Mishal asked.

"Consider this your time off," Assim said, hunting for his desktop keyboard. He began typing, then made a series of short, intricate gestures in the air and snapped his finger. A pen flew up from his desk into the air, then whizzed past Mishal and out the door. A printer began whirring. A few seconds later, the pen flew back with a piece of paper clipped onto it. Mishal marveled at the man's control of his ruh.

"Sir, I don't understand."

"In your letter, you mentioned three things," Assim said, putting up three fingers. "First, you said that Salim Al Ghafri's ruh is too weak, and that he would excel as a scout. Second, you said that Salwa, the child, is too young and heals too slowly, and that she would be a fantastic healer. Lastly, you said that you yourself are immature, and should not be allowed to lead a team," here, Assim paused. "Is that right?"

"Yes sir."

"Well, thank you for letting us know about these issues. But we're ignoring your suggestions."

"What!"

"You are hereby sentenced to work independently with Asaad Al Nabhani, with no team to support you. Salim and Salwa will be absorbed into other teams. Upon occasion, you will be grouped together to test your teamwork. Once we decide you're ready, the team can be put together again."

Mishal didn't know how to respond. "B-but this way they'll still be in danger!" he protested.

"You want to protect them?" Assim replied, a sly grin forming on his face.

"Of course!"

"Then I suggest you improve your teamwork and…" Assim glanced down at the letter as if to purposefully make Mishal angry, "*immaturity* real quick. Give them space to get stronger, and whenever you see them, treat them like teammates instead of civilians. Now, get out of my office."

Chapter Twelve

Mishal woke up early the next Sunday. The sun had just started its long crawl up the night sky, and so Mishal could see the world bisected in two. The top of the world still had the dark tinge of promised dreams, while the bottom was colored in the yawning orange of optimism. He took in his first cognizant breath of the day, wondering if this morning would bring him good or ill. For a fleeting moment he felt optimistic, like things would be alright in the end. Then he remembered that Ahlam was dead. No matter how much he tried to make up for it, she would still be dead.

Something had been done to Mishal and the pain would linger between his ribs. He sighed, reminding himself that the person who'd been wronged wasn't him. Ahlam was the one who died, not he. He had no right to make her death about how he felt. But, God, she'd been stolen from their lives. Although the pain had dulled with the passing months, it returned occasionally - like a smudged imprint. Was this how widowers felt? Like a victim trying to go on, even though a chapter of their life had been taken?

The youth sighed. "Asbahna wa Asbaha il mulk lilah." *We awaken and the kingdom awakens for Allah.* He should go pray. He should live his life. "It's better now," he said. "I loved her, and it hurts and that's only to be expected."

He had other problems now.

Mishal got up and performed his ablution, then prayed the morning prayer on the green prayer mat in his room. The room had multiple praying mats, their soft thickness bringing him comfort when he lay his forehead against them. In fact, the particular mats in his room had been blessed by a sheikh before his parents presented them to him years ago, saying that *these* mats were special and would help with his possession.

The special prayer mats had not helped. Instead, Shayib Ghalib had forced Mishal to confront his jinni about a year ago. The humor of it all, the fact that an eccentric old man had helped more than the sheikhs, made Mishal smile.

Mishal missed Shayib Ghalib, especially after yesterday.

Salim and Salwa had been furious with him, after hearing about their transfer to other teams. Salim, in particular, had refused to even sit and discuss it with Mishal.

It was now Thursday: Two days after Mishal had been informed of the HR department's decision, via a bone-white piece of paper stamped with the Sarim logo name. Mishal had been avoiding Salim and Salwa, feeling miserable. Everything had gone wrong and his hopes of protecting them had gone up in smoke.

Mishal was sitting in an office on the second floor of Sarim. This office was left empty for the most part, due to the fact that it had bad ventilation. Mishal often went there to think in solitude.

A hesitant shuffle greeted Mishal as soon as exited the office door. When he turned, Salim was there.

"Salim," Mishal said. Salim was silent, but his expression already said everything for him. Hurt filled his face. "I'm sorry," Mishal said.

"Now I get it," Salim said. "I always wondered why you kept us away from missions. We were slowing you down!"

"That's not what happened!" Mishal said.

Salim pulled out a piece of paper and began reading aloud from it. As he did, Mishal's stomach dropped. "'Salim Al Ghafri's ruh vessel is well below the average for exorcists,'" he spit out. "'He is unable to take full advantage of his tools. He is currently facing difficulties memorizing spells for audible incantations, as well as patterns for imaginative spellwork. He tries hard and has exceptional bravery, but may be better suited to being a scout than an exorcist.' *You're* the one who keeps suggesting the scouts, so the rest has to be from you too!"

Mishal felt his insides twist at the way Salim read the report. "Salim, the issue is *me*. I'm not ready to help you and Salwa improve."

Salim gave Mishal an incredulous look. He whipped around and walked away. "Salim, it's not-" Mishal had called after him, but Salim away through the corridor, almost running over another exorcist in his path.

Now, Mishal sighed. *It's not what?* He thought to himself. *Not his fault? That doesn't matter. The guy feels like I betrayed him.* Salwa's parents had started ignoring Mishal's WhatsApp messages, after the transfer came through from HR. He knew that he needed to make things right, but the thought of confronting Salim and Salwa again filled him with terror.

Besides... Mishal really *wasn't* ready to lead the team. Weren't things better, just like this? It might be better to allow his teammates to hate him, and to go their own way.

Would Shayib Ghalib, Mishal's grinning old teacher, approve of Mishal's decision, he wondered?

Mishal dressed for school and picked up his bag, heavily laden with books he wasn't sure whether he'd need or not. The bag pulled on his shoulder, feeling as if it were begging him to rest, but Mishal moved on down the quiet flight of stairs. Mother had made breakfast and left the kitchen, and so he found a ready-made egg sandwich waiting for him on the table. Mishal opened the fridge door, pulling out a bottle of Eagle brand hot sauce, and poured a few dollops into his sandwich. Its tangy heat seemed to wake him up, and the youth walked out the short distance away to his school.

Like most public structures in Oman, Mishal's school was built out of brown cement - made to stand the test of time. Bars had been put outside the windows to discourage students jumping out the building, in their eternal quest to skip school, and some of the bars had broken over the years, making the school look a little bit like an abandoned jail.

Mishal couldn't help worrying about Asaad, despite how strong he knew the Shayib was. Just a few days earlier, the CEO had warned Asaad that there might be a jinni trying to possess him. Since then, Mishal had noticed Asaad's irritation rising. The man barely even seemed to seek attention anymore, and instead he walked around Sarim with an annoyed look on his face. Still, Mishal couldn't imagine a jinni actually successfully taking over Asaad's body, and so he tried to forget about the danger.

Mishal barely felt the school day pass by, and he felt as if the school barely noticed his passing either. Most kids kept away from him, and he wasn't sure why. However, he didn't really mind.

Mishal sat at his table pondering these questions when the bell for the end of school rang. He absentmindedly stood up, ignoring the rush of students towards the door, and began to slowly close his notebooks.

"Boy," a voice crackled sharply through the room, catching Mishal's attention. He looked away from his notebooks and towards the front table, where their teacher sat with a tired look on his face. It couldn't be easy, taking care of over thirty teenagers at one time, Mishal concluded.

"Yes, sir?" Mishal asked, putting the notebooks in his bag and taking the cumbersome thing with him to the front of the classroom, standing now just feet shy of the teacher.

"You're getting big, I hope you're not using those needles," the teacher said, leaning forward in his chair and motioning towards his own veins. His eyes practically glimmered with suspicion. "Needles break your organs, you hear?"

Mishal bit down his startled laugh, saying, "Yes, sir, no, of course not sir."

"Also, you don't pay much attention in class," the teacher added, stroking a cloud-like beard which floated down his jaw and neck, missing his lips entirely. "But I can see you taking notes."

The words caused Mishal to panic, worried that he'd offended the man. "I, oh no sir, the class is very interesting an-"

"Nonesense, boy, I can tell!" the man said. "Are you actually taking notes?"

Mishal went quiet. His toes fidgeted in his sandals. No matter how many jinn he fought, he could never stand offending people. "Yes sir."

"Where from? You're not listening to me."

"I... well, sir," Mishal mumbled, "I study the day before and I sort of revise during the class."

The teacher's hand slipped off the table and he almost fell off the chair into the ground. At first, he was cynical, but after taking a look at Mishal's notes and verifying the truth of his words for himself, the man relented and leaned over his desk in interest. "What's your name, boy?"

"Mishal."

"Full name!" He snapped.

"Mishal Azhar Said Al Balushi, sir!"

"Hmmm... Well, if you're studying, then that's all I need to know. We'll see from the quizzes whether your studying works."

Mishal nodded, turning around and leaving the class in a rush. Who knew you could avoid trouble with your teachers if you just spoke reasonably with them? He had all but had forgotten about the teacher by the time he was out of the gates. It was already quarter to three, and he needed to hurry for work.

Fifteen minutes later, Mishal stood by a white sign under the sun, kicking rocks away from the road. He checked the sign, which said the bus would be there at three PM. He looked at his phone, which informed him it was only one minute away.

Mishal kicked a few more rocks, walking around and around the long stretch of gravel and dirt which separated the houses from the road. He checked his watch again. Two minutes past. He sighed and unbuttoned his dishdasha, feeling sweat dripping down his neck. The stones around him appeared to welcome the heat of the afternoon sun, absorbing it lovingly before emitting it outward in a furious haze.

"Why does Oman have to have this kind of weather?" Mishal muttered, checking his phone once more. It was now nine minutes past. However, this time he also found a message from Asaad, which simply read: *out for some business, a replacement will have details about today's paperwork.*

No mission today? Mishal asked, but his boss offered no reply. As far as Mishal could tell, Asaad hadn't even received the WhatsApp message.

Finally, the large red bus came whirring down the corner, driving with a certain air of professionalism mixed with a sense of urgency. Mishal got in, showed the driver his month ticket, and sat down, grateful for the refreshing breath of air conditioning coming down the vents at the top of the bus.

At around 3:45, the bus stopped at the Qurum Natural Park, which almost looked like its own country instead of being a part of Muscat. Trees, Mishal thought that couldn't grow locally, poked out from behind the large fence of the park, and flowers sent forth a waft of intoxicating scents. To the side he could see at least seven different driving instructors sitting together under the shade, arguing about politics. He saw a Mercedes, parked to one side of the parking lot, with a man lounging on the driver's seat. Mishal walked up to the car, causing the man to glance towards him. Radio sounds, probably the news, blared out even through the car's window. Mishal didn't recognize the man and so pulled out his phone, opening the Sarim app to flash his agent ID towards the man.

"Can I please get a lift to HQ?" he asked.

The man smiled. "Sure thing, agent 398," he said. "Do you have a name?"

"Mishal al Balushi, brother."

"Oh, you're *that* kid." the man asked as Mishal got into the passenger side and buckled on his belt. "Oh, you're a belt sort of guy?"

Mishal grimaced, saying, "Sorry, just being careful. I'm sure you're a great driver."

The man lowered the radio volume. "What's it like working with Abbath? He still as bad as the rumors?"

"What are the rumors?" Mishal asked, feigning ignorance. This was a question he'd gotten constantly over the past months, ever since he was shifted into the same team as Asaad Al Nabhani.

"Arrogant, sees himself as the king of the world," the man replied. "He's the strongest and knows it." The car pulled into Qurum roundabout, taking a left into the short winding road through the mountains which lead to Ruwi's bustling finance district.

"He's not too bad," Mishal said. This answer appeared not to please the driver, and he spent the next minute in contemplative silence while they drove towards the Sarim building and Mishal got out. He could see many yellow and white buses, and a throng of children between ten and twelve years old milled about the area, their voices growing in volume by the moment. It appeared that an event was about to begin here, in the sand-colored building under which Sarim hid. "Thank you for driving me today," Mishal said. He banged the door closed, annoyed with the driver's assumptions about Asaad Al Nabhani.

The children around were a sea of white, shifting over and over. Among them, Mishal saw one dark blip. An agent stood waving at him from near Sarim's entrance. Mishal walked over to her, trying not to get swallowed by the wave of children, and said, "Hello, Mishal Al Balushi reporting."

"Agent Mishal," the woman said, nodding in recognition. Some of the older boys around were gaping at her openly, and she took a step back into the shadows. "There's a replacement for Shayib Asaad who'll be giving you the work briefing for today. Please report to the third floor underground to meet him."

Mishal bid the woman goodbye and walked into Sarim's hidden entrance, passing through the wall and into the blissful white silence of the public authority. At the end of the hall, he found more agents going about their work. Three floors down, the marble gave way to semi-cracked porcelain and bricks, and Mishal walked through the corridors, dodging agents and employees, until he reached the shared office spaces.

Sarim agents hated the paperwork areas even more than the training areas, the labyrinths, or even the monster pits. Mishal took a deep breath as he entered.

Here, sharp white fluorescent lighting filled the area. The room was a giant hall, with row upon row of white desks separated by plastic shades. AC units labored in full force, trying to cool down heads heating from the piles upon piles of papers scattered over every desk. A thick carpet covered the floor, muffling most sounds.

Some agents worked in silence, laboring over word documents, typewriters, and pen and paper forms. Others chatted to one another softly, trying to avoid the eye of the dark-haired supervisor glaring from a massive stone-gray desk at the head of the room, sitting about a meter higher than everyone else.

The woman in the head of the corridor tutted. She looked like an ancient judge from legends, here to divide people and to deliver them their fate.

Mishal saw one agent grappling with an imp he'd previously captured but seemed to be struggling with.

"Come with me quietly," the man hissed.

"Never, you worm-fingered, lazy-eyed damnable human!" the imp screamed.

"Stop that!" the woman at the head of the hall snapped, waving her pen. The man and the imp both gasped, then promptly passed out onto the desk. The occupants of the room continued working while exchanging worried glances

Mishal put his bag down. "Al Salam Alaikum," he said to the room at large.

"Wa alaikum Il Salam," the fifty or so occupants of the office space replied back, in a soft hum. No further conversation was needed, it seemed.

The supervisor snapped her finger angrily from the head of the room, catching Mishal's eyes. She adjusted a fist-sized stamp in her hand, motioning for him to come to her. Mishal walked slowly, the sound of his footsteps absorbed by the thick carpet. "Yes ma'am?" he asked.

"You're Al Balushi, right? Sign here, phone number here," she said in a business-like tone that never rose above a whisper. Her face, however, spoke volumes. It threatened to break him, if he so much as stepped an inch outside the lines in this place. Mishal gulped as he signed the papers she presented to him.

"Where do I sit?" he asked.

"Row five," she said, pointing towards a row labeled with a large, black number. "Seat three. And, boy," she added. "Asaad Al Nabhani has left a mountain of work." She gripped her pen so hard that her hand shook.

Mishal gulped again. "If I don't do it, then nobody will." Although Mishal said that, in his mind he knew the truth. *If I don't take up the burden, it will fall on the shoulders of another.*

The woman's hands loosened over the pen. Her eyes glittered. "I'm glad *someone* in that team has a sense of responsibility."

He padded to his desk, a small cubicle which appeared to overflow with papers and was marked with the number fourteen. Paperwork obscured the grey top of the desk, spilling from desk drawers, tumbling over the desktop mouse, and even scattering over the carpet. A small platform to the side was labeled 'Completed Paperwork'. This platform was the only empty area of the desk.

Mishal growled, then rubbed over his face in preemptive exhaustion. The mere sight of this mountain was enough to almost break his will. But Mishal looked behind him, where the woman was still looking at him with admiration, as if gazing at a soldier marching headlong into battle.

Fine, let's waste a day of our life, I guess.

Work crawled forward with the sickening monotony of impending doom. Boredom filled each minute as Mishal signed papers, corrected dates Asaad had mislabeled, and glanced at his phone periodically to check for missing descriptions. Each time he looked at the phone, he couldn't help but notice how little time had passed. His neck cramped and uncramped, people came and left, and Mishal sat in place, feeling his eyelids grow heavier with every breath of air he inhaled.

Slowly, the pile of paperwork in front of him began to organize into neat squares. The 'completed' paperwork platform began to fill, then disappear. One second Mishal looked down, then the next he looked up and saw that the pile had shrunk. He noticed a small magic circle inscribed on the platform, which caused the paper to be transported elsewhere.

Finally, Mishal began to feel a headache slowly thumping behind his eyes and stood up abruptly. He noticed that the employees to his right and left had changed for others. The supervisor at the front of the room glared around, disapproval flowing off her in palpable waves. However, when her eyes met his, the woman's lips twitched as if attempting to summon a smile. She nodded at him in respect, like a fellow warrior. *I don't know if this makes me feel better or worse.*

Mishal went out of the room, rubbing his exhausted eyes. If only Salim was still part of the team, they could have split this labor.

He made his way to the cafeteria on the second floor, pausing when he noted how empty the place looked, drained out of occupants. Mishal glanced at his phone, seeing the hour had shifted to six PM when he wasn't looking. He flinched. He would be late returning home; his parents would begin wondering where he was.

"Ah, friend," he heard a voice say, and Mishal turned to see the man with the long hair. He appeared to be looking at a notebook.

Mishal waved. "Uh, hello." He felt curious about the man's name, but it was too late for that. If you don't know someone's name the first two times you speak, how could you possibly ask them for it later? Mishal would probably wait until the man mentioned it himself or, well, until someone else said. "You're staying here this late?"

"Oh, the things I do, my friend," the man said with a dramatic wave of the head. "I barely feel time anymore. One second, it's morning; the next, the sun has set."

"Sounds like you're a busy man," Mishal said, stepping to leave the cafeteria. "I need to go home. My parents will be worried."

"They sound like a handful. Anyhow," the man said, "take a sandwich before you leave," he added, pointing at a row of shwarmas basking under the light of the heating lamps. "I'll take care of the bill, just take it and go."

Mishal hesitated, but then grabbed a warm sandwich and left, thanking the man. He ran to the training halls, worried about the time, and paused in the hallway when he heard gasping and shouting coming from behind one of the doors.

"Go *faster,* Salim!" Someone was yelling. It sounded like Shayib Basil. "Your magic is all about how *quickly* you construct the spells. Use minimal ruh, draw faster. Support your leader even before he knows the support is needed! Now, give me a blinding spell; you have fifteen seconds!"

Salim's muffled grunt came from behind the door. Mishal smiled to himself, knowing that Salim's military training was preventing him from complaining.

"Do you have a moment?" a voice called. Mishal turned to see Eman looking at him with cool eyes.

Chapter Thirteen

Eman led Mishal through the corridors until the two of them stopped next to one of the reading areas. Eman opened the door, then closed it promptly and leaned against the door. "Shayib Hashil is here," she said by way of apology. "I like my boss well enough, but now is *not* the time to see him. How about a meeting room?"

Nervous thoughts spun around Mishal's mind. What did she want to talk to him about? *It must be serious, or else she wouldn't make it so formal. Oh no, it's going to be about Salim and Salwa. I just know it.*

Minutes later, Mishal found himself in the meeting room he often used to get away from people. Despite being a modern-looking place, it had an old-school gas light, which Eman now tried to light.

"Wait, let me help you," Mishal said, using his ruh to a start a small flame in his finger. He opened the lid and used his fire to start the wick, before closing the lid again and turning the gas on. It irked him somewhat that Eman also knew about this place. "Do you come here often?" he asked.

"No, but you do," Eman replied with a shrug. "I thought since it works well enough for you, we might as well use it."

Wow, she really did train as a spy. "What did you want to talk to me about?"

A slow, exhausted sigh escaped Eman. The orange glow flickered across her face, setting her blue eyes on fire. "About how you made a huge mistake."

Mishal's heart sputtered in a sudden angry fire. "What?" he asked.

"I hear Salim's devastated, and Salwa's parents don't know how to explain to her that she's not weak."

"Who told you that?" Mishal asked.

"Laith," she replied. "You pushed your teammates aside, instead of bringing them closer."

"That's not what happened. I was trying to protect them."

"By getting them to stop being exorcists?"

"Yes!" Mishal practically shouted. He hated how this all made him feel. "I already feel terrible, I don't need you to make me feel even worse."

I'm not good enough to be by their side.

Eman's eyes widened. "That's not what I'm trying to do!"

Mishal wasn't listening. "You have a teenager with wind incantations, and a woman who can protect people with barriers. And most importantly, you're able to be with them, to guide them and train them. You're smart, confident, strong, calculating, planning, and kind."

Everything I do is wrong. I'm just a musclehead who got promoted because I'm good at hitting things hard.

"Mishal, you're taking this too literally."

"On *my* side, I don't even know how to talk to my team. I'm worried sick that I'll somehow mess up and get them hurt. Or worse yet, *killed.*" He was now standing over her, practically shouting. "They're better off without me," he said, his inner voice and outer voice uniting.

Eman's face looked practically sculpted in the orange light, from how quietly she sat. Mishal could feel the storm coming. "Let's go on a mission together," she said suddenly.

"Huh?"

"You and me," Eman added. "I have just the thing. You won't even need to fight. But I think it'll be a nice change for you."

Chapter Fourteen

The weather that September was confusing. The sun alternated between blasting concentrated heat, and calming down just enough to usher in a nice cool breeze. That day, Mishal and Eman were travelling in a Sarim transportation vehicle, through the Muscat Expressway, then out in the path through Fanja, Bidbid, and Nizwa.

The destination? Bahla.

The Wilayat of Bahla in Al Dakhiliya was often thought of as the jinn hotspot of Oman. The reasoning was based on silly superstition, as far as Mishal could tell from his reading in the tome of *Al Sharih,* but as with anything concerning jinn, superstition gave rise to reality. The more people believed a certain thing, the more specs of their ruh would detach and clump together. These specs of ruh would eventually gather strongly enough to turn into a basic jinni. Thus, since people *believed* that there were jinn in Bahla, Bahla had more jinn than most other Wilayats.

Besides, Mishal thought to himself as he watched the mountains roll by through the rear seat windows. *Some of the myths are true.*

"You'll be handling the talking, right?" he asked nervously. He was angry with her, on account of their previous talk, but he tried to put that aside for now.

"Sure," Eman said. "I don't know what the issue is, to begin with. The sheikh has been peaceful for generations."

About sixty kilometers northwest from Bahla, there sat a village called Mawil. Mishal had never heard of this village, until today, but apparently it was famous.

Soon, the Sarim agent stopped the car near a mosque in Mawil. "Will you be alright here?" she asked.

"No worries," Eman replied, smiling politely. The woman drove off around the corner, leaving a trail of dust leading back to Bahla proper.

“So, who is this sheikh we’re supposed to meet?” Mishal asked, already feeling nervous.

“Over here,” Eman said. A group of sad-looking older men were staring at the two of them, each with a curious expression on his face. Before they could say anything, Eman led Mishal quickly away. “They wouldn’t want to talk to me anyway,” Eman said. Mishal followed, understanding that older conservative men would probably find it scandalous if a strange women came up to them and asked them questions. Mishal could do it, but… the mere thought of walking up to Bahla strangers and talking with them sent shivers down his spine. *Salim would’ve found it easy to talk with these guys.*

“We are told from our ancestors that a long time ago, in the village was a girl of beauty unmatched. She caught the night in the waves of her hair, and she had the eyes of a deer and a laugh like the evening rain. The girl was loved by all, and respected her elders, and could make bread faster than any other girl in the neighborhood.”

“Wow, sounds like a catch,” Mishal said sarcastically, still annoyed.

Eman continued walking, leading Mishal off the beaten path and alongside a dried up falaj. “Stop it, Mishal. Anyhow… One day, the girl went missing. The villagefolk looked for her among the farmlands, and in the depths of the wadi, but they could find no trace of her. Finally, when her father prayed for the girl in the middle of the night, a jinni appeared to him. ‘I am sorry, but I was smitten by your girl and have taken her to our village inside the caves. She has agreed to stay, and I am happy to greet you as my father-in-law.’”

Here, Mishal paused with his foot halfway towards a rock. “The jinni married the girl?” he asked.

“It happens, but at least - this time - it was with her consent. You’d be surprised at how rare that is, even among humans.”

Mishal paused for a second, but the serious look on Eman’s face discouraged him from breaching that particular subject. They were now hopping from boulder to boulder. Mishal checked both sides to make sure no one was watching, then sent ruh to his legs to jump across a particularly large chasm. Eman similarly touched her green bracelet and summoned Sahib, then allowed him to carry her across the gap and onto the next boulder. "So, what happened later?"

"As compensation, the jinn's Sheikh Waddhah offered their protection to the humans of the area, along with a stipulation that they would share the boons of the falaj. On some days, the falaj dries up. That is when the jinn use its water. When it flows, it is the humans' turn. Furthermore, the falaj water always arrives if the humans require it for an urgent need, such as a fire. This is a deal that Sarim continues to mediate between the jinn and humans. The falaj never dries up completely, even when there have been years without rain."

Now, Eman and Mishal reached large cave in the mountain. Mishal noticed a chasm at the foot of the cave, which looked almost like a small lake. "Until now?" he guessed.

Eman nodded. "It has been three months since the villagers have seen a single drop. We are here to investigate, and to negotiate with the jinn. Come, let's go."

Up ahead, the mouth of the cave beckoned. Mishal could hear a soft sound coming from it, like a hum. He gulped, then followed Eman into the darkness.

Chapter Fifteen

Mishal and Eman ventured into the cave, the sunlight streaming in from behind them to illuminate the multi-colored wadi rock. Soon, however, the path inside began to weave right and left. The darkness grew. Mishal sent a small wick of fire through his thumb, giving off just enough light to show them the path.

"Keep your light soft," Eman whispered. "I don't know why the falaj dried up, but it can't be good news."

Mishal began contemplating the possibilities, as the two of them ventured deeper into the colorful caves. They didn't know the path forward, meaning they were just going based on gut instinct. The caves were filled with thick ruh, masking any distinct sense Mishal would've otherwise gleaned. *If Salim were here, he would've been able to use his compass to tell us where to go,* Mishal mused. He wondered where Salim was. If he was training with Team 16, then things were probably okay. But what if he were with Team 4?

Anything but Team 4, they're always out on dangerous missions. Besides, Shayib Jamal doesn't like Asaad so he's bound to punish Salim.

Mishal heard Eman stop suddenly behind him. "What's wrong?" he asked, snapping back into attention. He looked back to see Eman standing framed in the firelight, her chubby face pouting. Behind her stood a figure in strange grey clothes, holding a dagger to her neck.

"We didn't pay enough attention, I guess," Eman said.

"What are you doing here?" the figure said. "It's just as the man said - you have no honor!" she raised her dagger, aiming to stab Eman.

Mishal readied himself to strike. He would leap in, block the dagger strike at the wrist, then use his fire to punch the figure in the stomach.

“No, stop!” Eman said, halting Mishal in his track. He stared at her calm face. Eman moved one of her hands subtly in a gesture. *Wait.*

The figure threatening Eman chuckled, thinking the plea had been for her. She leaned closer into the light, revealing ocean-blue hair and small curved horns. Mishal had never seen a jinni like this one before. “Why should I wait?” she asked.

“We’re only here to talk,” Eman replied. “Sheikh Waddah promised, long ago, that the falaj could be split evenly. What went wrong?”

The woman’s face turned smoother than the rock behind her. “You dare ask me that, after you attacked one of our own? Using pesky borrowed magic, no less?”

“We don’t borrow magic from jinn,” Mishal replied before he could stop himself. He paused, worrying that he had crossed a line.

Eman gave Mishal a reassuring smile. “We’re from Sarim. My name is Eman Al Lawati, and that is Mishal Al Balushi. Put the dagger down and let’s talk.”

The jinni hesitated, then did as Eman had asked. “Fine, but I’m taking you straight to the Sheikh.” The jinni led them through the beautiful caves, which spread out over Mishal’s head like a canopy. He could hear the song of running water somewhere, almost out of earshot, but the rock under his feet remained dry. He leaned in towards Eman. “What do you think the issue is?”

Eman’s brows furrowed. “If it’s what I’m expecting, then it’s an issue. Ma’am,” she added, raising her voice to catch the attention of the jinni. “Do you know who attacked your clan member?”

The jinni tutted. “You speak with the Sheikh, not with me.”

“Well, I see. Won’t you even give me your name, at least? You’ve heard ours.”

The woman’s expression softened. “My name is Ghaitha.” She led them to a hole which fell endlessly downwards into the darkness. Had Mishal not been led to this hole, he would not have been able to find it. “Let’s jump here; the Sheikh is downstairs.”

Eman pulled Sahib from her bracelet, then climbed on the white lion's back and jumped down with a whoop. Mishal hesitated, looking into the darkness, but then he looked at Ghaitha. Despite her gruff attitude, she struck him as the honest type. Mishal spread fire into his legs and jumped after Eman.

Finally, after walking through three more caves, the trio stopped at a massive hall. "Finally!" Eman said, gasping from the exertion. Mishal grinned at the dramatic way she threw her hand over her face.

"Who is this?" a voice called. Mishal peered into the darkness, and gasped.

The figure was nine feet tall, even sitting down against the cave wall with its legs crossed. Its blue hair and beard covered most of its old body, save for bright blue eyes that looked purer than fresh-running water.

Ghaitha went to her knees. "Sheikh Waddhah, I have captured intruders."

Eman, to Mishal's surprise, also went to her knees. Before Mishal could protest, Eman grabbed him by the collar and tugged him to the floor beside her. "Be respectful, this is a long-lived," she hissed, then added, "Sheikh Waddah! What is your news?"

The massive figure rumbled, and Mishal realized that Sheikh Waddhah was chuckling. "This is the first time in a while that I have seen munashada by a girl."

"I am the daughter of these lands," Eman replied in a soft, light tone. "Do you have news?"

"No news to ask of in the land of Dunn," Sheikh Waddah replied. "What of you, daughter? How is your people?"

"They suffer no injustice, Sheikh. There is nothing but good," Eman replied dutifully. Mishal almost laughed at the ridiculous exchange, but he recognized it as standard Omani etiquette. Had the Sheikh immediately told them his troubles, it would bring dishonor upon him by signalling desperation. "Now, sheikh - I hear that you are beset by a traitor."

“A human,” Sheikh Waddah replied gravely. “This human has attacked one of ours - and has used the power of another jinn to do so. I cannot recognize the power he wields.”

“Surely there is no magic beyond your knowledge,” Eman replied. Mishal glanced at the blonde girl, surprised. *Did she change her accent? She sounds like she’s from Al Dakhiliyah.*

The sheikh pursed his lips and scratched his face, dislodging some small animals from his beard. “I’ve never seen magic like that. It was like the night incarnate. The victim, Gaitha’s sister, lies gravely wounded in her bed. We fear she is not long for this world.”

“Why did this happen?” Mishal asked, causing everyone to look at him. He squirmed at all the looks, but resolved to continue. “I can understand someone using dark magic. But why attack you?”

Gaitha stepped forward. “Maitha had been away for a few days, deep in reconnaissance. I’m assuming that she had come across something that our enemies didn’t want her to know.”

“Didn’t she say anything to you?” Eman asked.

“Not that I remember,” Ghaitha said.

“In all cases,” Sheikh Waddhah added, “Maitha is a precious friend, as well as a skilled jinni. She and Ghaitha together built Bahla wall in a single night, using the water of the falaj. I cannot think she would be defeated, unless…” the figure paused. Mishal looked up, only to see the old jinni’s massive eyes spreading wide and glowing like twin blue moons. He was looking at something directly behind Mishal. “Who are you?”

Darkness fell over the cave instantly, blinding Mishal.

Chapter Sixteen

Mishal fell to his knees in an attempt to move himself out of harm's way. "Down!" he shouted in the blinding night.

Eman fell down next to Mishal, her hand clamping on his shoulder. "Mishal, your fire."

Someone could use the light to attack us.

Ghaitha shouted and Mishal heard someone running away from them. Still, he could not see anything in the darkness.

"Mishal!" Eman urged.

Mishal cursed himself and sent ruh to his hands, bringing a solitary blaze to life. He braced himself for an attack, but none came. Eman's face was illuminated by the flickering fire, giving her a shadowy look.

"Where is Ghaitha?" Sheikh Wadhah's voice boomed. Mishal could hear a rumbling threat in the jinni's voice.

"This way! Come to the right cave and -aargh!" Ghaitha's yelp startled Mishal. He began running in the direction he felt the voice had come from, with Eman following. A calmness came over him as they traversed the dark caves. Now, he knew that there was an enemy they could fight. This gave him comfort. Talking to strangers, navigating through strange caves and seeking out sources of ruh? These were challenging activities, for greater minds than his.

Mishal and Eman reached the mouth of a large cave to see Ghaitha lying on a large boulder, holding her bow up to ward off a warped figure which stood in front of her. It was an old man with a long beard, but behind him a tall shadow spread over the walls, grinning hideously.

"It can attack from anywhere!" Ghaitha said, gasping with the pain of an open wound on her shoulder.

But punching wizards is something I can do quite well, Mishal thought to himself. However, when he made to step forward, a hand stopped him.

"I'm in front," Eman said.

"But-"

"Shush, I'm not some nine-year old you can over-protect," Eman cut him off. She walked towards the old man, putting both hands out and starting to hop in place. "Come on," she urged him, not even summoning Sahib.

The old man's head turned sideways, and the shadow behind him mimicked the movement. *Wait, that's not right,* Mishal thought to himself. *The shadow moved first. It's is in control here. The old man, he's being possessed.*

"The wizards said Sarim would come soon," the old man said in his normal voice. However, he crouched like an animal. "But a woman? How the world has changed, in our years of waiting."

Eman groaned. "It had to be a sexist, huh."

The old man ran forwards, jumping from boulder to boulder with unnatural speed. Eman leaped back, but Mishal knew it would be only a matter of time until she was caught. As an inborn type, she had limited access to spells. Her only real skill was summoning Sahib.

Eman dodged twice, pulling backwards. Mishal noticed her leg land precariously close to a rock, which would lead her to trip.

"Watch out!" he shouted, but it was too late.

Eman's foot struck the rock, causing her balance to falter. The old man laughed in delight. The shadow *detached* itself from him, and slid across the wall, then jumped out behind Eman. Its long claws reached out for her.

"No!" Mishal shouted.

Eman raised her hand defensively, and Mishal noticed that her green bracelet was glowing. Inside the green beads, he saw a set of feline eyes watching the shadow with predatory anticipation.

Sahib's paw reached out from inside the bracelet and blocked the jinni's attack. Black shadow and white lion locked together, each growling. The old man's look of joy disappeared. "No!" he pouted. "That's not fair!"

"Mishal, now!" Eman urged.

Mishal sent ruh throughout his body, filling himself with fire. He shot from his spot like a cannon, heading right for the shadow.

His fist burned right through the shadow. The old man screamed, then fell like a puppet which had had its strings cut off.

Everything went quiet for a moment, then Eman raised both hands in the air. "We're *beasts!*" she said with a wild laugh.

Despite his best efforts, Mishal laughed with her before going forward to help Ghaitha.

Chapter Seventeen

Eman turned off the phone with a sigh. "Sarim's support services say they'll take around three hours to get here."

Mishal glanced over at Ghaitha, who had a big smile on her face despite the blood dripping down her shoulder and splattering onto the colorful cave rock. "Do you think you'll be okay until then?"

"Oh, sure; as long as Maitha's attacker is gone, everything else will take care of itself."

Despite Ghaitha's assurances, Mishal couldn't help but feel a stab of guilt. The muscles of her shoulder had ripped from the sharpness of the jinni's attack. Over time, her smiles would turn into grimaces. *Salwa could mend this injury in half an hour.*

The jinni had been heading in the direction of Maitha's rooms, Mishal and Eman discovered. Inside the room, Maitha lay on a bed of rock, her blue hair covered in sweat from the jinni's poisoned attack. "Why did it want her dead in the first place?" Mishal asked Eman quietly.

"I don't understand either," she whispered back to him. "But I've never seen a darkness Hussais in the years since I started helping out in Sarim. This jinni is something I'm unfamiliar with."

Mishal considered this, running the scenarios in his mind. The jinni had been right behind him, Eman, and Ghaitha. If not for Sheikh Waddhah, the jinni may have been able to sneak in and out without notice, killing Maitha and erasing any presence of its existence. "I think it didn't want anyone to even know it was in this village," he reasoned.

Eman's blue eyes glittered with understanding. "It might not be the only one. There could be other wizards like the old man, scattered across Oman, and they didn't want anyone to find out about them."

"Sarim definitely needs to know about them," Mishal said. Every year a number of new jinn types were uncovered or came back from obscurity. Still, this was his first time being part of such a discovery. "Do you want to walk around the village?" he asked.

In response she only smiled.

Dunn village was a hidden haven for water elemental jinn from the kin of Sheikh waddah. The entire village sat within a cave, which was fed by a five-foot waterfall. At the foot of the waterfall, an oasis of date palm trees, grape vines and Raihan shrubs surrounded a lake. Children played amidst the ever-present trickle of water.

Mishal and Eman walked around the village, talking to various residents with blue hair, who'd grown wary of humans on account of Maitha's injuries.

Ghaitha had spread the word that Miwal village was innocent, and that Sheikh Waddah would share the falaj with the humans once more. Still, Mishal saw the villagers shying away from Eman's attempts to make conversation. The jinn villagers were isolated to begin with, and could not feel comfortable with two humans walking in their midst.

"I think it's best if we just go, and let the Sarim healers take care of this," he whispered to Eman, who gave him an appreciative nod even as she sipped from a strange but delicious vegetable soup which Ghaitha had given her.

"I'll need to visit this place again," Eman said. "It's so peaceful. But for now, you're right. The village is not ready to speak with Sarim."

A few minutes later, Mishal and Eman stood in front of Sheikh Waddhah.

"Thank you for rescuing my clan members," the old man boomed from where he still sat cross-legged against the wall.

"Are you willing to reconsider the decision to close the falaj to the humans?" Eman asked.

The giant considered Eman's proposition, then slowly began to move to the side. From behind him, a big crack in the wall poured pure water to the floor. The water flowed past Mishal and Eman, disappearing through another wall and presumably to the falaj.

“That’s it?” Mishal asked incredulously. “You were physically blocking it by sitting here?”

The old jinni’s laughter rolled like a wave. “Not everything needs complicated spellwork.”

Mishal and Eman left the cave, coming back the way they’d come. As they walked through the tent-like caves, Mishal contemplated the things he’d felt on this mission. More than anything, he felt frustrated. Salim would have been needed to talk to the villagers, and to negotiate with Sheikh Waddah. Mishal didn’t have the ability to see the strange darkness jinni. Eman had come up with a great plan to fight the jinni, which Mishal had almost ruined. Salwa would have been a great addition in this mission, since she could’ve offered her skills to heal Maitha and Ghaitha.

Mishal remembered Eman’s words during the fight.

Shush, I’m not some nine-year old you can over-protect.

“Earlier you called me over-protective. Does it count as over-protecting when I’m crippled by the fear that someone might get hurt?” Mishal asked, his voice echoing. “I care about them. I can’t let them get in harm’s way.”

They were almost out of the caves now, and Eman turned with the sun behind her. Mishal sometimes couldn’t tell which of the two was brigher. “Sure… but there’s a thing called trust. I’m not sure if you noticed this, but Sheikh Waddhah didn’t move when the jinni ran off. He let *us* go after it. Same with Ghaitha.”

“You’re right,” Mishal said, remembering the old jinni’s reaction.

“He knew we would handle it, but he was close enough to help if things went wrong. Right now, you’re nowhere near Salim and Salwa.”

“And they’re still going on missions, going God-knows-where,” Mishal said, mulling things over. The longer he thought, the more he knew what to do. “Eman, I’m still not ready to lead my team, but…”

“But?”

"But I need to get them back. If they're going on missions anyway," he said, his heart beating faster and faster. "Then they need me by their side, where I can help if something goes wrong."

"But at some point, you'll need to trust them to take of things on their own. If you really want what's best for them, I mean."

Idiot, a voice in the corner of his mind urged. *You're weak, selfish, scared. There are a thousand people in Sarim more qualified than you to protect Salim and Salwa.*

"They need me, and I need them as well," Mishal said, shaking away the incessant voice. "I belong by their side. I'll train, and I'll make sure I'm ready when the time comes," Mishal growled. He stomped off through the mouth of the cave.

"Now you're talking like a wolf!" Eman said. "You're going to need to convince them, though. Laith says Salwa's deleted your number from her dad's phone."

Mishal groaned as he realized how much work still needed to be done. He had to train, grow more reliable, then convince Salim and Salwa to take him back as their team leader. It was an uphill road, and their trust had to be earned. Still, Mishal promised himself to try.

Now, the youth's thoughts went to the darkness jinni. The jinni had possessed the old man, he realized. It had been a terrifying sight.

The CEO had said there was a jinni hoping to possess Asaad, too. If it succeeded, would Asaad become like the old man? A doll on strings, with no will of its own?

I can't let that happen.

Chapter Eighteen

Seven books and scores of old tomes and scrolls lay splayed out in front of Mishal in Sarim's library in level 3. The faint orange glow of lanterns illuminated them.

Mishal glared at the scrolls for a long time, trying to figure out the common thread. Behind him, a Sarim scout coughed from a different table. Mishal could tell she wanted him to take more care with the old scrolls while researching. However, he was too upset to tidy up at the moment.

Mishal had come here intent on researching two topics, and both of them turned out to be dead ends.

There were too many ancient demons sealed away beyond the veil of this world. Each of them had a different object, a different level of power, and various different weaknesses and methods of binding. Some were sealed away so long ago, during the glory days of ruh powers, that even their sealing methods had faded into obscurity.

How am I supposed to know how to help Asaad when I can't even tell which jinni is hunting him? Mishal thought to himself. Maybe, after all, this task was beyond him.

Mishal got up and turned to the scout. "Sorry," he said, "I'll clear up now."

The woman's eyes softened a bit. "Let me know if you need help putting everything in its place." When Mishal said no, the woman went back to her books, looking content.

Mishal returned the scrolls and books to their shelves. He paused at the final shelf, with the last book in his hand. Old emotions of anger swelled within him.

This book was the second topic of his research today. It was newer than the scrolls, and contained information about the current most-wanted jinn, almost like a more advanced version of *Al Sharih.*

Mishal had the book open to a specific page. *Shalmazar the Life-Thief,* the heading read.

Just seeing the name filled Mishal with rage. He had first encountered Shalmazar during his first mission in Sarim.

The terrible mission had taken him to Saham, where a young child called Khadija had been taken over by a jinni. The jinni had summoned Mugayabs which killed everyone in the neighborhood. Finally with her life force spent, Khadija had died in Mishal's arms. She had, however, provided him with the name Shalmazar.

Shalmazar is considered an S level threat. He is at least hundreds of years old, and preys upon young children giften in ruh. He chooses children who are abused in their life and carry strong negative emotions. Shalmazar offers them liberation and revenge.

Liar, Mishal thought.

However, liberation in his eyes includes forcefully opening up their powers and flooding them with dark spells, unleashing deadly Mughayabs in an area proportional to their talent. Often, the neighborhood becomes the scene of a massacre. When the task is completed, Shalmazar absorbs all of the child's life force and leaves their body. The child dies soon thereafter.

Signs of Shalmazar's possession:

- *Many Powerful Mughayab*
- *Widespeared scenes of Death*
- *A child on the brink of death, often mumbling a twisted version of the common lullaby 'Lu Lu, Lu Lu, Lu Lu Bah'. The most common version is below*

Lu Lu Lu Lu Lu Lu Bah *Lu Lu Lu Lu Lu Lu Bah* *Wil Ghali Ma Yiskhabeh*	لولولولولولو به لولولولولولو به والغالي ما يصخابه
Il Shar Yiruh Wa Ba'dain Yioud *Sabeen Sana Wa Badain Tmut*	الشر يروح وبعدين يعود سبعين سنة وانت تموت

Shalmazar is a threat when he is within a child. However, his true power appears in the intermittent periods between feeding. Having fed on thousands of children in the past few hundred years, this jinni is a force to be reckoned with.

If encountered, run unless you have a Shayib within your team.

Mishal wiped a helpless tear from his eye and angrily shoved the book back into place.

One day, he vowed.

Chapter Nineteen

The last three months of 2019 gusted through like a warm ocean breeze. Mishal went to his classes in the morning, largely ignored by students and teachers alike. He caused little trouble, aside from one unfortunate incident where he pushed off a bully who'd thought him easy prey. The bully flew across the school courtyard and gave Mishal an incredulous stare. Thereafter, Mishal caught glimpses of the boy during the morning assembly, but they never spoke again.

The teachers at school found Mishal satisfactory enough. The boy had a strange air about him, they remarked to one another during conversations. It felt like he was much older than he let on.

"He looks at you like he's already lived a lifetime and knows there's more to come," one of them told the others, over a cup of overly sweet milk tea.

"The boy has bags under his eyes," the other remarked, while gesturing to mimic fat bags drooping from his face. "I don't know if he sleeps."

The oldest teacher in the group harrumphed, while scrolling through a never-ending list of WhatsApp messages and videos. He remarked, "Must be those video games."

"Well, his marks are alright, so it doesn't matter," the first teacher remarked. The others agreed that a too-quiet student with high averages was a good problem to have. They moved on to other topics, such as how unbearably hot the year had been.

On most days, Mishal headed out of school directly towards his place of employment at Sarim. Normally, a Sarim agent would be waiting at the bus stop. However, other days forced Mishal onto the swaying red Mwasalat bus, towards the city. He sat there, surrounded mostly by expatriate workers, enjoying the sights of the city as street after street came by, revealing lush trees, barren rocks, and an ever-present ocean.

Twice a week or so, a mission would come up. Mishal and Asaad would venture out on these missions alone. Mishal tried not to think about his two team members. Was Salwa eating properly, without Salim or Mishal to goad her? Did Salim's training partners push him too far? Such thoughts stormed into Mishal's mind while he tried to catch up to the ever-widening expanse of documents which Shayib Asaad had mislabeled.

The missions Mishal and Asaad went on together ranged from imp exterminations in Ruwi, to convincing a relatively harmless jinni to leave an older woman's body.

"Another E-level mission?" Asaad complained one day, glancing down at his phone. "Management knows you can handle a B-level mission alone, if it's a pure fight."

"I guess they don't want me fighting alone," Mishal replied with a shrug. They were seated in Asaad's Dodge Charger, parked outside a rikhal bread café. "I hope Salim and Salwa are okay," Mishal said, fishing for information about his old teammates.

Asaad groaned, then ordered an egg bread for Mishal and a honey-soaked one for himself. Salim had been avoiding Mishal recently. Salwa was quite clearly angry with him. *I'm going to need to give them some time,* Mishal thought to himself. Asaad wasn't going to make things easier, by passing information back to him.

The scent of honey danced through the air, brighter than the orange of Muscat during the late afternoon. "Mishal, do you read the news?" Assad asked, suddenly.

"Not really," Mishal replied. "Why?"

"Just some worrisome stuff," Asaad replied, going quiet. "I've been digging, ever since you told me about that mission of yours in Bahla. I suspected to hear about more such cases, but there's nothing."

Chapter Twenty

Asaad continued to be only half-present most of the time, despite the looming pressure of the end of year performance appraisal. Asaad would disappear for days at a time, going on wild hunts for information about the jinni the CEO had warned him about, the jinni that was apparently hoping to possess Asaad. Each fruitless chase culminated in him returning to Sarim infuriated, his beard longer than usual, his clothes dusted with dirt. The man would burst into the building to greet Mishal, then cast gazes around the corridors.

"Anything new?" Mishal would ask him.

"Later, later!" Asaad snapped every time, running off to shower and shave before anyone could see his unkempt state. When he returned, beard properly trimmed and lavished in fine oils, he would sit next to Mishal and say, "Nothing. Nobody knows a thing about a jinni or cult aiming for me. I have no clues whatsoever. I don't even have a name." Mishal often tried to do his own research in the Sarim library, or to provide the names of informants, but nothing seemed to help Asaad.

One day, Mishal sat in the library of floor three of Sarim, pouring over a tome of old jinn stories. Colorful tapestries hung upon the walls, and a soft buzz came from a kerosine lamp which sat on a table.

And when I looked upon the flesh of my blood, he was not himself. The jinni had taken over him in full, the text read. It was written in a flowing hand. *I called upon what power I could and struck the boulder of old, dropping my boy into the mountain rocks. Then I closed the rock behind me, and bathed it in my tears. Thus was the punishment for allowing himself to be taken over by jinn, and for attacking his father, and for his foolish pride.*

But who was it who was punished? He or I? Does my mastery of ruh mean anything, if I was unable to protect the boy I once held in my hands?

Emotion welled unbidden in Mishal's heart, and he wiped a stray tear from his face.

“I always hated that story,” an exhausted voice called. Mishal glanced up from the book to see Asaad, in one of his foul moods. Something, however, looked worse.

“Did you get *hit?*” Mishal asked, in astonishment. He’d never seen Asaad visibly injured, but now a bruise crossed the man’s face.

“You don’t learn anything about ancient jinn without getting into a scuffle or two. I should freshen up on my Mutaqah martial arts,” Asaad said.

Mishal wanted to ask Asaad what Mutaqah was, but he felt a rush of embarrassment flow through himself at his ignorance and decided against it.

Asaad sighed. “I want you to look into ancient binding rituals spells. Maybe one of these old spells could be used to track down the jinni that’s after me. Focus on the older ones, from before we figured out intricate spellwork. I bet this happened far enough in the past that most ruh practitioners were still in-born types, using their instincts, rather than external types.”

Around December, Mishal’s phone dinged with a notification. *Update on Teammate Training,* the notification read. Mishal was lying on his back in his room, as he often did when not working. He checked the notification, frowning at what he saw.

Salwa had become able to heal her own injuries without crying, the notification read. Her store of ruh was growing at an impressive pace, and trainers were confident.

Mishal threw the phone aside, fuming. They were putting Salwa in the way of injuries? What was Salim going through? Was the man also hurt? Salim’s store of ruh was much smaller than other agents. This was why Salim relied on tools, and it was a clear disadvantage. What if he were hurt because he ran out of ruh at a critical moment? What if he was injured, or scarred, or killed?

You’re being unreasonable, Mishal said to himself. He stared angrily at the blank ceiling above him, frantically filling the empty space with imagined scenes of Salim and Salwa getting injured.

His heart and head were conflicted, and so Mishal let his heart win.

The youth threw a hoodie over his head and stormed out the house, passing by his father as he watered the jasmine shrubs.

"Did you study?" dad said without any real conviction in his voice.

"Yes, Dad, thank you. How are you?" Mishal replied, still angry. He continued the conversation as well as he could, hiding his emotions behind a façade.

Mishal told himself that there was no need to overreact to the notification. Still, he climbed into a Mwasalat bus and traveled through Muscat, to the Sarim building. After checking the training schedules, Mishal found himself leaning behind a wall, sneaking a peak at Salwa's training regimen.

Salwa was doing well. She hopped from place to place on the smooth floor, dodging practice magical shots from her training partner, Halimah.

"Great!" the woman said, weaving ruh in an intricate pattern around her hands. "A healer's first duty is to keep herself alive. Dodge, look around, and heal yourself. Your secondary role should be as an analyst."

"Yes!" Salwa whooped as she jumped over a magical stream of darkness.

Another stream of darkness rushed through the room. Salwa jumped again, the plastic butterflies in her pigtails flopping. Salwa crashed to the floor, almost causing Mishal to jump out from his hiding spot. "Ow!"

"It's okay!" Halimah soothed, running over to Salwa. "It's not a big wound. Heal yourself, and take a five-minute break."

Mishal's hands shook from where he stood, but he did nothing to intervene. He could Salwa smiling through the pain. She was doing well, he noted. *She wouldn't have been able to dodge this well a month or two ago.*

"Kid?" Mishal heard behind him. He spun around in shock, spluttering when he saw Asaad Al Nabhani standing there, leaning on his Khaizaranah with both hands. Asaad had a disbelieving smile frozen on his face. "You are *not* sitting around spying on your former teammates!"

"No!" Mishal lied, his face burning hot. "I was just passing around."

"You're lying with a straight face!" Asaad said. He grabbed Mishal by the shoulder and pulled him out the room before Salwa could notice anything. "We've talked about this before: you need to prove you're able to trust the team before they fully come back. Besides, you haven't even apologized yet."

For a long time, Mishal said nothing. "Can you at least let them know that Salim is more of a visual learner? And Salwa has a habit of not focusing her ruh enough on one body part when she heals. Also, she doesn't eat enough."

Asaad took Mishal into a nearby office, then sat on a rolling chair and said, "Fine, I'll tell their supervisors, but don't let them catch you spying. For now, you need to go on missions solo. Also, don't forget what I told you about finding a way to shoot your flames long-distance. A team leader shouldn't be limited to punching things."

"It's not that easy," Mishal complained, rolling his big shoulders.

Asaad made a dismissive noise. "You figured out how to make defensive walls with fire. Why not throw the fire?"

Mishal didn't know how to respond to that, so he nodded - even though the image of him chucking a fireball through the air felt silly.

Asaad smiled to himself in satisfaction. "So, you'll go on a few more missions?"

"You're right," Mishal replied, wiping his face nervously. "I need to keep my mind off their training."

"Well, good," Asaad replied. "I've got something fun in mind for you."

Chapter Twenty-One

A glorious sunset was taking place over the Wilayat of Manah in Al Dakhilya when Mishal and Asaad walked into Manah proper. They'd parked in the empty area near Sur Manah and were now sitting in a small coffee shop, contemplating how to initiate this mission.

"So, recap," Asaad commanded.

"There have been complaints of a jinni appearing at night, at around two AM near Al Bilad street, the old hara. We only have one witness."

"Has he given Sarim all the information we need?" Asaad asked.

Mishal gulped. There was a checklist of information that Sarim tried to receive, before executing any mission. The goal was to rank the jinni properly, discover its abilities, and when it was most likely to appear among other things. "Not yet," he said, dreading the idea of talking to a witness. Any form of new social interaction caused fear to slam into Mishal's stomach. "Do we need all of this?" he asked.

Normally, Sarim scouts would take care of the interviews and reconnessaince. Unfortunately, the agents assigned to this spot of Al Dakhiliyah had not been available.

Asaad tutted at Mishal. "Sixteen years old and still afraid of talking to strangers; what is this new generation coming to?"

"Plenty of teenagers are sociable!" Mishal said, bitterness spreading through him along with an angry burning sensation. "Besides, you're no good with strangers either!"

"Excuse me?" Asaad asked.

"Salim's good at it," Mishal went on, "and Eman can *really* get people talking, but whenever you talk to witnesses they just badmouth you!"

For a long moment, Asaad didn't say anything. Mishal paused, staring at the man's bright gaze. Had he gone too far? "Can't argue with that," Asaad finally replied, casting his gaze out over the street. "Eman's off on a spying mission; hear she's supposed to bring down a jinni cult in Al Dhahirah, single-handedly. Salim's training, and you're not supposed to interfere with that. So, what do you suggest?"

Finally, Mishal relented. He messaged the man back and forth, and finally blew out a happy sigh. The man appeared shy and preferred voice notes. The gist was that he'd been walking down an abandoned road at two AM, when he began to hear a noise behind him. Every time he turned around, he saw nothing. The man had begun to run, and had heard something behind him.

"I swear," the final voice note said, "I swear that when I turned around there was a woman, white like bone, with long hair and fangs. I ran and began reciting the Quran as loud as I could."

"That can't be right," Asaad said, exchanging a glance with Mishal. "Keep going."

The man had then reached his house and closed the gate behind him. Something had crashed into it. The man immediately ran into his room and hid under the blanket till the morning. At nine AM, he looked back out and saw the mark of a hand on the gate of the house.

Mishal shivered as he reached the last of the man's messages. "Thank you, sheikhs, you are the crown upon my head. Thank you for taking care of this."

"Well?" Asaad asked, his eyebrows pushing high into his forehead with surprise. "Do you recognize the jinni he's talking about?"

Mishal nodded, and took a sip of his sweet tea while he thought. On the second floor of Sarim, there was a library - used by Sarim agents to research jinn. Mishal had read about this one. "He's describing a Sariyya," Mishal responded quietly.

"Exactly," Asaad replied. The coffee shop's sign lights flickered over him, casting his face in intermittent shadow. "They hunt laborers who leave the workplace too late, too exhausted to pay attention to their surroundings."

"Sariyya are not supposed to exist anymore," Mishal replied.

Asaad sipped his karak. "Do you think the guy is lying?"

“He sounds too scared to be a liar,” Mishal said with a quick shake of his head. “What do you think we should do now?”

Asaad smiled a wicked smile that made Mishal shiver. “I think you haven’t been working hard enough.”

Mishal frowned as he realized what his Shayib meant. He was about to become bait.

*****

The plan was simple: Lure the jinni in, then destroy it. However, luring a Sariyya meant doing overtime work, as the jinni only hunted workers and farmhands who came home too late. To that end, Asaad had Mishal log in to the Sarim app and write extra reports on their previous missions.

“After you’re done with ours, take a look at Eman’s mission logs. I can give you access.”

“Is she *that* good?” Mishal said, feeling slightly frustrated. Eman was a dear friend, but Mishal’s pride still stung from the occurrences of the joint training sessions.

Asaad raised two fingers. “Oh, she’s an excellent team player,” he replied, lowering one finger. “However, even when she’s alone, Eman is a phenomenal spy. She’s a natural at sneaking around and going undercover. Apparently, she brought down two minor cults recently.” Asaad brought down the second finger, then made to leave. “Anyhow, I need you to keep working on my, uh,” he coughed, “correspondenses until two or three AM, then you should take a stroll around the neighborhoods.”

Mishal gaped as his Shayib walked away, disappearing into the darkness. *He wants me to do his paperwork again? Seriously, how irresponsible could one man be?* Mishal thought to himself. Angrily, he began to go through mission logs and write reports. However, sooner or later he began to fall into a steady rhythm of typing, reading, and approving.

The moon was high now, casting an additional glow to compliment the streetlamps and the light from the flickering coffee shop sign. People came and went through the streets, always greeting each other and chatting. Their laughter lulled Mishal into a deeper relaxation. In the distance, he could hear two women arguing about how to set WhatsApp settings to avoid showing read messages. In the distance, children played with a ball.

This town seemed closer-knit than Al Khoudh, where Mishal had grown up. He wondered if he could one day live somewhere like this.

By two AM, Mishal was the only one in the streets. Two hours earlier, the coffee shop had closed, and Mishal had continued working - perched atop a short wall. Manah went to bed earlier than Muscat, and barely any sounds could be heard in the neighborhood. Mishal put his phone back in his pocket and leaped off the wall, landing on the street quietly. He walked down the street, heading nowhere in particular but appearing to walk with purpose. He kept his strides long and quick. *Tap, tap, tap.* It was only Mishal and the street, just him and the tapping of his feet, mixing in with the glow of the occasional streetlamp and the damp smell of the farmlands in the distance.

Tap, tap, tap, Mishal's feet said.

Slap, slap, slap, a second set of feet replied.

Mishal froze, and both sounds immediately stopped. Now, the street was tensely silent; as if the world was holding its breath. He turned slowly, and saw nothing behind him, save for a long, narrow road lit by the orange streetlamps. Again, Mishal began to walk. *Tap, tap, tap.*

Slap, slap, slap.

Mishal whirled behind, moving quickly, and glimpsed a pale, tall figure, dressed in a dirty sheet. The figure was about to hide, but saw that Mishal had noticed it.

"Youuuuuu…" the figure growled. It was a tall gangly woman, with long black hair and hate-filled eyes. Her skin was the color of paper. "You're mine!"

Mishal prepared himself, sending fire to his hands. The Sariyya jumped forward, swinging an arm in a long punch. Mishal dodged the fist, then gagged at the strong stench of blood and gore wafting off the jinni.

The jinni punched again, then again. The fists whistled over Mishal's head each time he dodged. This jinni was physically strong. He remembered what the witness had said- that the jinni's hand had caused an imprint on the iron gate. If one of its punches hit Mishal, he'd go down.

"Need help?" A voice called out. Mishal looked to the side, where Asaad stood atop a clay house, his figure framed by the white moon.

"No, I can handle it!" Mishal snapped.

Suddenly, however, the jinni paused. "It's you," she said, her eyes wide. "The vessel!"

Mishal stiffened. "What are you saying?" he asked the jinni, voice climbing in vume. "Why did you call him a vessel?"

"Silence!" the Sariyya hissed. She punched at Mishal again, but her eyes were on Asaad, who looked down at her coldly.

Mishal's mind whirred. Why did the Sariyya say that phrase? Was she related to Asaad's possession in some way?

In the second that Mishal's mind grew occupied, he saw the Sariyya's expression shift to one of triumph. Instead of swinging at him, she leaped towards the clay house above which Asaad stood. Her hands pulled back in a punch.

If she hit it, the people living inside would be in danger.

Without thinking, Mishal jumped between the jinni and the house. The punch struck his midsection with the force of a truck, and he heard something cracking inside of him. Blood filled his mouth with a metallic taste.

The jinni grinned at him. Mishal grinned back, blood spilling down his chin.

"I've got you now," he said, grabbing her head with his flaming hand. The jinni yelped as the fire engulfed it.

"Long live Maymun!" she screamed with her last breath. "Long live Maymun!"

And with that, the jinni turned to ash. Mishal crumbled to his knees, coughing up blood onto the sidewalk. In the next moment, he found himself in Asaad's arms.

"Ow," Mishal mumbled, with a wince. "Thanks, boss."

"Quiet!" Asaad said angrily. "You need to be taken care of. See? This is why you need Salwa with you. She could've healed you."

"It's not a big deal," Mishal said, looking up at the sky. The moon was still mighty in the velvet backdrop of the starry night. They'd taken care of the jinni, and that was all that mattered. No-one was hurt. "Did you hear what the jinni said, in the last moment?"

"She knew about me being an intended vessel," Asaad said. "Something is stirring in the night. I think we finally know which jinni is trying to possess me."

"The last name she said…"

"I think that's the jinni after my soul," Asaad said. "We at least have a name now. Maymun."

Chapter Twenty-Two

Weeks later, Mishal was out to buy clothes at the Seeb City Center. Men in ruler-straight dishdashas and women in color-trimmed abayas poured in and out from every store. His eyes fell upon a figure he recognized in the distance. Their eyes met and the man in the long dark hair smiled at him and waved, then turned back to admire some watches. Mishal walked up to the man, politely greeting him.

"And how are you, young one?" the raven-haired man asked.

"Well, trying to balance work and school is a handful, and my… team is training on their own for now," Mishal said. "It feels like the world is stuck, waiting for something to happen. Oh, and my first performance appraisal is coming up," Mishal added nervously. Of course, he didn't mention the jinni aiming for Asaad.

The man laughed, "So melodramatic, at sixteen years old. You need to relax."

"It's a little hard to relax at the moment," Mishal replied defensively. To lighten the mood, he pointed at his midsection, where his ribs weren't yet fully healed. "I need to keep up the pressure." Salwa was still too angry to agree to help, and the other healers could only partially close the wound.

The man chuckled again. "Nonesense. What's the point of a world where you don't enjoy yourself? Especially when it's this interesting," he said, waving at the mall around them. "You'll do fine, so take a break for now. Anyhow, I'll go in see if there are any watches I want."

"Are you buying one now?"

The man shook his head and said, "Just evaluating my options for the moment. The luxuries of life will have to wait for a few months still. Regardless, window shopping is good fun. And you?"

"Clothes for my little sister."

The man tutted. "When have I ever seen a teenager buying clothes for his sister? You must be the most stressed out sixteen-year-old boy in Muscat! Buy something for yourself, I'm sure your sister will do just fine."

Somewhere in the back of his mind, Mishal awkwardly realized that he was oversharing with this friendly man. He said, "I need to help my family out. What kind of son would I be, if I don't?"

The man nodded. "A noble notion." He bent down to look closer at a bronze-encrusted watch. "Oh, I think I want to take a closer look at that one!" With that, the two split into their separate ways. As simple as the conversation was, Mishal found himself feeling better after having it. That day, he bought three shirts for Safaa - instead of two.

And so, the days went by, split between hazy mornings at school, flurries of paperwork, and the occasional mission. Soon, December arrived.

Chapter Twenty-Three

On December 6th, news began to trickle through the Omani population like rain through a rocky river: Sultan Qaboos bin Said was traveling to Belgium, for a medical reason. The news of the monarch's illness collected in the minds of people, captured by terrified imaginations. Parents discussed it during family dinners, and Mishal's family was no different.

That day, his mother had cooked parathas - to be enjoyed with a mixture of hotdogs and nuggets. Simple, greasy comfort food for their worried souls. Mishal's father sat on an armchair, flicking through WhatsApp, Twitter, and the occasional news network.

"I can't tell if it's true or not," he muttered.

"Of course it's true," Mishal replied. "He did go to Germany a few years ago, didn't he?"

"But he isn't that sick," Mishal's mother replied, moving aside the bottom of her green laiso and raising her hands to the air in prayer. "He can't be that sick. We just celebrated the National Day."

His Majesty Qaboos bin Said was the Sultan of Oman, having ascended to the throne in July of 1970. When he first took the mantle, he urged Omanis living outside the country to return back to their homeland and rebuild it. His famous speech contained words that some Omani schoolchildren had learnt by heart and which were often found on websites or National Day videos:

"My people, I will proceed as quickly as possible to transform your life into a prosperous one with a bright future. Every one of you must play his part towards this goal."

He'd built schools, roads, and a full-fledged university in Oman. Over the years, love for him had swelled into a non-material type of adoration.

And now he was sick. Mishal's father scrolled through Twitter, desparate for news. His hands were shaking.

"Dad, are you alright?" Mishal asked.

"I'm sure he'll be safe," his father said. He pushed his reading glasses back onto his face. The façade cracked for an instant, and Mishal saw his father's fear peeking from behind the mask. Mishal's dad had been ten when His Majesty became sultan. His generation had been shaped by the sultan's ideas. *It's normal for him to feel this way,* Mishal thought. However, then his father shook his head. "I'm sure he'll be safe," he repeated.

The next day at school, Mishal's Islamic teacher stood up before class began. He moved in front of the whiteboard, wiping it deliberately until it sparkled clean. "Alright," he announced, then began writing on the board with his most artistic calligraphy, swirling the Arabic letters and precisely adding indents, the tashkeel markers which indicated how letters should be pronounced.

Prayer for His Majesty. The letters popped out on the whiteboard, as if they had been carved with a knife.

"Let's start," the teacher said, starting to pray for the Sultan to be safe, thousands of miles away. The students looked at one another, then joined in. The teacher's prayer flowed for five full minutes, interspersed with the thrumming *Amin* of the students.

Later at work, Mishal walked into the cafeteria to find the atmosphere tainted with sullen worry. Few people spoke, and those who dared did so in strangled whispers. The gloom appeared to cram down on them, enforcing their quiet.

Mishal grabbed a portable meal and walked out, unable to cope. He'd always been a sensitive youth, and seeing so many people in this state pricked at his heart.

"Mishal Al Balushi?" someone asked. Mishal turned to see a girl he didn't recognize. She wore a permanently sad expression on her face.

"Yes," he replied.

"You're requested with Ustath Assim," she said. Then, in front of Mishal's face, the girl dissipated into mist and disappeared.

Mishal shrugged, then made his way up one floor. The floors closer to the surface of Sarim were increasingly more modern than the ones inthe depths. As Mishal went up, the white fluorescent lighting gave the walls a clinical look. Finally, Mishal knocked against a door which read 'Human Resources'.

"Come on in," a female voice called out from the other side. Mishal opened the door to see the receptionist. The tired-looking woman had been here on Mishal's very first day at Sarim, when he first met Ahlam and Eman. Her bored expression brightened slightly when she saw him. "Mishal, you're here," she said. "Good thing Fatma found you."

"Ah, yes," Mishal said, noticing that the sad-looking girl he'd seen before was also here. She sat on a smaller, overloaded desk to the side in front of a PC. This meant that she'd sent a magical clone to search for him. "Ma'am, am I in trouble?"

The receptionist frowned. "No, no, of course not! HR has that bad of a reputation, does it?"

"That's not what I meant!" Mishal protested. "It's just... Well, the last time I came here didn't end all too well." His words drew a knowing smile from the receptionist. The sad-looking girl just nodded politely.

The receptionist rummaged in her desk, knocking over a lamp, then appeared with a piece of paper triumphantly held in her hand. She said, "Here's something for you to sign. Since you've officially completed nine months at Sarim, you're an employee now. This is for the paperwork. Also, I assume you're having trouble with your parents letting you come here?"

"I wouldn't say trouble," Mishal said, "but they do wonder, sometimes, where I am."

"Well, this'll help take care of it," the woman said, swivling her chair slightly. "Fatma, if you didn't know, a good number of employees start early at Sarim. And some, rarely, are still in contact with their family - like Mishal is."

"Yes, ma'am," Fatma dutily said.

"So, we needed to come up with a way to get parental permission without making Sarim public knowledge," the woman said.

Mishal couldn't remember the receptionist's name and truly hoped he didn't need to utter it now. *Ugh, what was it with me and names?* He thought to himself, then suddenly realized where the conversation was headed. "Wait, you're talking about something like that paper we gave Dad, before I left with Ustaath Ismael for training!"

"Exactly like it. It says you'll be enrolled with a government cooperation program for gifted school students. Also," she added matter-of-factly as she handed a large, brown, inconspicious-looking envelope to Mishal's hands, "it says that you'll be paid a monthly salary."

Mishal's mouth gaped as he looked at the package. He'd always wanted to help his family with finances. So far, he'd resorted to leaving money at the house and pretending his father had dropped it, since he couldn't explain his salary. Starting from now, he could just *hand* them the money. "T-this fixes everything," Mishal said, not believing his ears.

"The paper is charmed to be more convincing, so you don't need to worry about talking too much. Just give it to everyone at the house to see it once." The woman said. She pulled out a small black token. "And this is something to replace you, when you're away. You need to calibrate it, so do that at home. You need to put ruh into the coin, then turn the dial when you're alone in your room and give it a few sentences to repeat. That's all you need to do."

Mishal took the token in hesitant fingers and thanked the woman, whose name he dared not ask for. He signed a few papers and left the room, surprised by the bounce in his step. *Now, I can finally support Mom and Dad at the house.*

"Tamathur, Fatma," Mishal overheard Assim, say as he walked out the door. "Did anybody see the latest headcount folder?"

Tamathur, was that the woman's name? Mishal couldn't believe he'd forgotten such an unusual name. A small laugh escaped him.

On December 20th, Mishal sat through his classes at school with a mortified sense of distraction. He didn't care about the few sumr trees lining the grounds outside, nor the schoolkids leaping out of a window on the front floor to escape a particularly nasty teacher, and not even the solitary sobs around him from some of the kids whose parents were in the military.

Rumors had come that His Majesty Sultan Qaboos bin Said had passed away. Mishal had seen it that morning, as he scrolled Instagram on his way to school. It felt more powerful than he'd imagined. Mishal's heart had been stabbed through. Those around him looked as if someone had kidnapped the expression right from their faces. Others discussed with one another, wondering if it was true and, if so, who the next sultan would be.

The teacher slammed his hand on the table, making them all jump. Mishal looked to see open tears streaming down the man's face and into his beard. "We do *not* accept rumors for these things!" the teacher announced to the stunned crowd. He turned around and began scribbling on the board. "Rumors are for the little nothings you kids obsess with. For who married whom, what somebody wore. But if you'll take rumors about the life of His Majesty, may he be in good health, then," he said with a final flourish, pointing at the board behind him. "That's what you are."

Not a patriot.

"Ustath, but what if-" one student began.

"I'll hear none of it," the teacher said, sitting down at his desk. "You go on and do whatever you wish for the rest of the class. I've lost my appetite for teaching you lot."

Back at home, Mishal found his parents in a state. WhatsApp was a den of festering rumors and hushed conversations, apparently. They drooped over chairs at separate corners of the room, reading messages and praying softly under their breaths. His father, in particular, appeared to be in physical pain. Safaa, his thirteen-year-old sister , was nowhere to be found in the living room. Mishal sighed to himself, heading up the stairs to his room. He'd just given his parents the new contract this week, and yet he couldn't rejoice. His head was filled with unfortunate possibilities.

What if?

The sentence hung over everything, bathing the world in heavy melancholy. The world almost looked gray. Mishal didn't know what would happen if the Sultan died. He didn't want to think about it, really.

The sunrays reflected on the white walls appeared half-hearted today. Mishal showered, then went over to his desk. He grabbed the small black disk he had been given by Ustath Assim's assistant. The disk looked like a serrated coin. Cool to the touch and easy to carry, it was created to be ignored by most people if they ever accidentally found it. Next, Mishal tried to remember the instructions given to him by the IT department.

Mishal turned the dial going around the coin, so that it read 'seven hours', then sent ruh to his eyes and measured how much power was still in the coin.

Under Mishal's enhanced vision, he saw spiritual energy leaving the coin in small, dancing figures of various colors, which pranced over his fingers and across his wrist. Good, there was plenty of power in the coin.

"I'm sorry," he said clearly towards the coin, "I can't come out, I'm studying."

Mishal put the coin down and waited. Almost immediately, the black coin opened outwards, oozing a pink goo.

Mishal fell over his bed in fright, crashing his head to the marble. He rolled over on the ground, then rose up with his fire engulfing his fist. A strangled yelp escaped his fist, heart racing.

The goo rose higher, exuding arms, legs, a head. It shifted in color to match Mishal's brown skin, and after some seconds, Mishal watched an exact replica of himself - albeit with an uncharacteristically cheery expression.

"I'm sorry," the figure exclaimed, head swiveling to regard Mishal. "I can't come out, I'm studying!"

"Oh," Mishal said, horrified. Was this the distraction Tamathur was talking about? "Um, are you, uh, real?"

"I'm sorry, I can't come out, I'm studying!"

“I…see,” Mishal replied, feeling aghast. The ruh in Mishal’s eyes showed that the thing in front of him was a construct made out of power and goo. It was probably more like a doll than anything else. He slowly walked out, careful not to show the creature his back lest it attack him.

Mishal locked the door on the way out. His family tended to avoid his room to begin with - a habit which had begun with the dawning horror, five years ago, that they were living with a boy who housed a jinni inside his head. Now, Mishal could feel his relationship with his parents and sister changing. If they tried to barge into his room, it was better for the decoy to answer them from behind a locked room.

Forty-five minutes later, Mishal walked the white marble corridors of Sarim. Most of Asaad’s pending paperwork had been completed, but Mishal had still come here - in the hopes that he would see Shayib Asaad Al Nabhani. Mishal’s Shayib had been particularly elusive this month, ducking in and out of Sarim with barely a hint of his passing. Along the side of one passageway he found a bearded IT employee, speaking to someone from the Jinn Imprisonment Division, who worked deep underground. With them, stood the dark-haired man Mishal kept bumping into, who smiled politely at Mishal.

“Hey there, Mishal,” the Jinn Imprisonment guy said, waving him over. “Where’s that Shayib of yours?”

“I don’t know,” Mishal said, eliciting laughs from all three men.

“He’s always been like that,” the Jinn Imprisonment employee said, between two guffaws. “Don’t worry about it. Man goes off and takes care of threats we can’t even dream about. Hey, if you do see him, tell him there’s a jinni he imprisoned, four years ago, that’s about to break free of the pebble he put it in. What does he want us to do with it?”

Mishal nodded, bidding the three men farewell and moving down the stairs. As Mishal passed through a shadowy corridor, outside the first floor training halls, a hand poked him on the right shoulder. Mishal spun on the spot, only to be confronted by a well-shaved and cocky-looking Asaad.

"Asaad, you almost scared the life out of me," Mishal hissed, putting a hand over his chest to silence his beating heart.

Asaad grinned. "Good. Because I'm about ready to climb out of my skin too. Come with me."

"Wait, but-"

"No buts; let's go," Asaad said with a happy tone. Despite his cheery voice, the man's face looked wary, and when Mishal gave him an inquisitive look, Asaad just smiled again, more forcefully, and slowly raised a finger to his lips.

Mishal stopped in place. Something was wrong. Worry climbed up his feet, towards his midsection, and settled in his stomach like a weight. If Asaad was worried, then something was terribly wrong. Mishal asked, "What's happening?"

"Come with me," Asaad told him with a plastic grin, walking up the stairs, down the white marble corridor, and outside of Sarim. Asaad climbed into his car wordlessly and motioned for Mishal to get in.

Mishal hesitated in place outside the car, saying, "Are you not going to tell me what's going on?"

"Not yet," Asaad said. "Be quiet and get in." Mishal narrowed his eyes at that and the Shayib's expressions softened somewhat. "Please, Mishal."

Mishal tutted in annoyance and opened the door of the Dodge harder than he'd intended. Asaad chuckled to himself, though the noise was layered with apprehension. "Soon," he said.

Asaad drove with Mishal down the main highway, going completely silent. Every so often he looked behind him in the rearview mirror as if searching for something. Arabic music poured out from Shabiba FM, tapping drums in rhythmic beats mixed with the sad lyrics most common in the GCC, but apart from that the car was silent.

Finally, Asaad turned right - near the Al Khoudh bridge - heading into the cramped confines of Al Seeb Souq. A long circular road wound around the area, lined on both sides with small shops fighting for space. Jewelers, perfumers, and furniture craftsmen stood in attention on both sides of the road. Mishal could hear vegetables vendors and perfumers haggling, along with passersby shouting at cars and Al Seeb residents laughing with one another.

At the far edge of Al Seeb, the road turned around and went back in the other direction, framed by wedding-chair rental places and carpet sellers, as well as tailors. Here too, people's voices rang out like drums. Asaad stopped the car next to one of the tailors. The air smelled of tires and salt and hidden perfumes, as well as an odd mixture of odors coming from all the cloth and sweat. Al Seeb Souq was far from glamorous, but it had soul in a way that malls never could.

Finally, they parked the car, chased by honks from three separate cars which had been fighting for the parking spot. Asaad rolled down the window and shouted, "Shut up!" to the other cars, then turned to face Mishal and said, "They don't get it unless you're aggressive, wallah."

"They looked like they weren't shouting," Mishal replied. "You sure you're not just in one of those moods where you lash out at basically every single person in the country?"

Asaad growled, then got out of the car, motioning for Mishal to do the same. They approached a tiny single-room extension to a building. Mishal could see white light spilling from under a battered-looking door, as well as a carpet thrown out on the road like a welcome mat. The carpet had probably been blue once, but now that color had faded. Asaad pulled out a fat key from his pocket and inserted it into the door, then turned the handle and walked in.

"In here," he said.

"Asaad, I'm tired of all the mystery; where are w-" Mishal began, but cut off as soon as he entered through the doorway. In that second, three things happened. Firstly, an electric shock started at his foot when he crossed the threshold and spread through his entire body. Secondly, the noises of the souq, all the shouting and haggling, faded away to nothing; as if the apartment was soundproofed. Thirdly, Mishal found himself looking out into a massive, orange-lit apartment, walls lined with intricate scrolls with symbols on them, a dalla of Omani coffee waiting on a rich wooden table, and scattered perfumes on a shelf on the side.

"Finally," Asaad said, swooping over the coffee and pouring himself a cardamom-infused cup, sipping it loudly. "Now, we can talk. I've found out something huge, Mishal."

Chapter Twenty-Four

Asaad's eyes gleamed with an inexplicable light. Within the strange room, with its warm yellow light coming from peaceful-looking lighbulbs sitting within ornate holders, with the smell of cardamom-spiced coffee dancing alongside frankincense smoke, Mishal felt a creeping sense of anticipation. "What do you mean?" he asked.

Asaad smiled at him, "The demon, Maymun: I've cracked the code - or at least part of it. Come, let me show you."

Mishal asked, "How?"

The youthful Shayib didn't answer him. Instead, Mishal stood up and walked to one corner of the warm room. This corner was covered in a long piece of parchment, painted along the seams of the room so that one side was covered in white, the other side in a murky red. The white side was covered in scrawls in red which looped and connected with one another in fits of apparent frustration. The red side was empty barring for one word. *Ahasees.* Senses.

"See, when I first began searching for Maymun, just a couple of months ago," Asaad explained, pointing at the filled white parchment. "I treated him like just another jinni. I went searching for clues, for informants, for literature. All of those things led me to a grand conclusion: the demon is sealed in another plane. We knew this already."

"An obsidian palace, described by humans as a black and gold structure in the clouds," Mishal recounted, from some of the earliest readings he'd done in Sarim's library as soon as they heard of Maymun.

"Good, you know that part already. But here is the thing: Maymun is undoubtedly still sealed. So, how is it the jinni knows of me?"

"A cult," Mishal reasoned as he sat down on the sofa, leaning forward to look at Asaad properly.

"There is no cult," Asaad hissed. "Trust me: If there was, I'd know of them by now. That is a lie told by my mother, whether knowingly or not."

Mishal glanced around filled parchment, then looked at the other one. "Then, what's the other explanation?"

"This is a creature of terrifying power," Asaad said. "Capable of drawing death in its wake, of carrying a curtain of melancholy over entire lands. It's so powerful, humans were forced to band together and seal it in a far-off pocket of the world. And, there, it gathered even more strength. If you believe me and there is no cult trying to summon Maymun, then wouldn't it mean that the creature sensed me itself?" he asked.

"Maybe a singular sorcerer was able to find Maymun and tell it about you," Mishal reasoned.

"A sorcerer capable of getting its attention?" Asaad asked in disbelief. "I would have known if a sorcerer that strong lived in Oman. Even if it was a long-lived, that wouldn't explain it."

Mishal paused for a moment, wondering again what a long-lived was. He brushed that aside, for now. "Then, how is Maymun aware of you?" Mishal asked, exasperated. "Stop dancing around the issue and just tell me."

"Fine. I think that Maymun simply split off a part of itself. It can't slip through the cage, if it's whole, but it *can* slip through the cage if it is weakened. I believe that Maymun shattered itself into a smaller part, then sent that part of itself off into our world."

Mishal felt the blood drain from his face. "Wait, but if that's true…"

"It's been watching me," Asaad confirmed.

"How?"

Asaad frowned. "Possession of an object, most likely; although, I suppose it could take a form and move about like a ghost. It must be possessing an object or location. I think the jinni found an object which could hold enough of its power, in a weakened state, and so used that to hold on to our world. And if I were a jinni, and wanted to spy on someone, you know where I'd go?"

Mishal considered the question,as he watched Asaad sip coffee from his small fingan. Just then, he heard a snapping sound, like static electricity, and spun around to see the source. Something was stuck on the outside of one of the windows.

"Don't worry," Asaad said, waving a hand away. "That's just a minor spirit. They've been getting more attracted to my presence lately. That's why I took over this place and filled it with spells of warding. Nothing could get in here without me knowing it. So, do you have an answer?"

Mishal did. He began to understand Asaad's hesitancy in going to the base, how often he'd been leaving Sarim on random missions. His insistence on Mishal staying quiet about Maymun.

"Sarim," he reasoned. Asaad gave a grim nod. "Maymun is haunting the Public Authority of Anti-Jinn Operations to keep an eye on you. It's trying to learn more about its potential host. After all, if it fails the possession then the both of you may die."

"Exactly right," Asaad replied. He plucked out a book from a shelf and turned it around to show the page to Mishal. The page had an archaic drawing on it - depicting an ebony-winged figure, with swooping horns. The creature's expression looked grim, as if it was preparing for war. "It has a few other options, such as attaching itself to a human or making a form out of energy, but my money is on Maymun latching on to Sarim. If it stays there, I'm bound to enter sooner or later. Maymun is in Sarim, gathering intel on me. Luckily, I'm trying to learn more about it too. And while I'm here, in this apartment," he added, pointing towards the wide apartment's red corner, with the spell of warding against malicious senses. "Maymun will have no idea what I'm doing."

Mishal let the information swirl around inside of his head. It swam like a drop of ink in a glass of water, mixing in with all the information he already had. Mishal sat back in his comfortable armchair, glancing around the messy room. "But *why*, Asaad? It's an incredibly powerful jinni. The records I read about it are terrifying. Why weaken itself, just to come here?"

"It's like the CEO said," Asaad replied, leaning back in his own chair. "Something that powerful absolutely cannot enter this world unless it can find an object that could hold its power. Worse still, if it manages to enter but fails the possession, it could lose its life."

"So, why not possess you immediately? Does it mean you're still too weak?" Mishal asked, then immediately regretted the question when he caught the prideful glint in Asaad's eyes, sparkling like the pinpoint point of a dagger.

"I hope you didn't seriously suggest that I'm *weak*."

"I didn't mean it that way," Mishal assured him quickly, feeling embarrassed.

Asaad sighed and sipped his coffee again."I think you'd be right. Well, sort of. I don't like the thought, but I might be in a precarious situation." He drained his small cup, then stood up. "Regardless; we're here now, and no one can watch us. How about you update me on the work you've been doing in Sarim? Your performance appraisal is in a few weeks," he added with a wolfish grin, and Mishal felt another pang of regret for hurting Asaad's pride. Asaad wouldn't give him a bad performance score because of a slur, would he?

Mishal spent the rest of that evening recounting his paperwork, hoping to impress his boss. They also spent a long time discussing the reports about Salim and Salwa's training.

"I think it's about time that you apologize to them," Asaad said matter-of-factly. "I heard that when you leave apologies in the air for too long, you're liable to lose your chance."

Mishal gave Asaad a teasing smile. "You're talking like you're experienced with apologies."

Asaad's eyes widned in mock surprise and he threw the papers in his hands up in the air, letting them float through the space around him. "Heaven forbid, no! That's why I said I *heard* this advice. I've never needed to apologize to anyone!"

Finally, Mishal returned home, and only when he saw his father staying up late watching the news did Mishal remember that the entire country was in a state of unease. The rest of that week went by in a gloomy haze, which was cut by throat-grabbing horror every time a rumor appeared saying that the Sultan had died.

Chapter Twenty-Five

Friday , January 9 of 2020 was a rather calm day. The sun had lost some of its bite, and the sparrows and owls had relaxed and they hid under the trees.

Then, noon arrived and Mishal received a call - just after returning from the Jumaa prayers and having lunch with his family.

"Mishal," came Asaad's voice, panicked. For a moment, Mishal thought the Shayib had been possessed. "Get ready, right now."

"What?"

"Just get ready, find a way to sneak out, and get your body double ready. Meet me by the crossroads and don't let *anyone* know you're leaving the house."

Asaad hung up. Mishal's heart began to beat faster. What reason was there for him to be called off so urgently from his home, right at the end of the morning? Mishal's mind immediately went to Salim and Salwa. Had one of them been hurt on a mission?

The entire house smelled like fish and spices at that time, a pleasant odor Mishal associated with lazy afternoons, scrolling Instagram, and working out. The smell came from the small kitchen, where his mothered labored on her Kuttan: a balushi rice gruel, made with a metric ton of mixed spices and turmeric. Mishal looked out into the kitchen, regretting the fact that he had to leave, then said, "Mom, I need to study for something - can you leave my lunch here, in the kitchen?"

His mother frowned from under her wrinkles. Worrying over a possessed son for five years had left her drained and weary. Mishal knew she half-expected him to break out in a fit or start spouting fire at any moment. However, his relationship with her had improved over the past year, thanks in part to his distance. "Alright then," she said crossly. "You suit yourself."

"Mom, I have something to study for," he said. "It's part of the program with the government, remember? We have a test next week."

Her frown softened then, and Mishal went upstairs into his well-lit room. Over the past months, his mother had consented to him giving a percentage of his 'allowance' to them. It felt good to take care of them, and to secretly save money for his sister, Safaa, to eventually go to college - if she didn't get a government scholarship.

She'll make a good college student, Mishal thought. *I can already imagine her sitting in a café, complaining about classes to her friends.*

With the door closed, Mishal headed straight for the black coin, which he re-calibrated and then pressed. The goo slid out from within the coin and solidified into a body wearing his exact same clothes, saying, "Sorry, I'm studying! I'll be out later!"

Next, Mishal went for his bag, but then hesitated. In the middle of the afternoon, he'd find it difficult to sneak out of the house with a bag. He remembered that he'd kept a number of possessions in his locker in Sarim - including enough clothes to last him three days, if need be. Therefore, Mishal only extracted from his bag a single medallion: shaped like a sword, it was something he'd bought in the hopes of giving it to Ahlam as a present. She had died before she could receive the small, yellow sword, but Mishal knew she would've liked it.

Mishal stepped down the steps as quietly as he could, keeping his eyes peeled for any sign of the adults, relying on half a year of anti-jinn operations and brutal battle to sneak past his mother's sharp ears. Finally, he was out in the Friday afternoon.

Outside, the sun's furious beams were dulled by pillow-like clouds, floating lazily across the sky. Mishal turned right, outside the house, and walked along the road until the crossroads. Unsurprisingly, Asaad had not arrived yet, and so Mishal squatted down on the pebbles and began to scroll through his phone, feeling the heat which reflected off the tarmac.

Soon, Mishal began to hear an angry roar. Mishal looked up in surprise to see Asaad's Dodge racing towards him, its driver holding out an arm out of the window. Asaad wore shades across his eyes and appeared to be cursing quietly. The car screeched to a halt, just barely avoiding Mishal's feet as the youth jumped back.

"What in the world?" Mishal asked.

"Get in!" Asaad urged. He took off his stylish bronze-rimmed sunglasses and squinted. "We're on emergency call."

"What?"

"In!"

Mishal jumped at Asaad's tone, then hurriedly opened the door and got in. He barely managed to strap on his seatbelt before the car roared forward, kicking up pebbles and dust in a mad dash towards Sarim.

"Alright, so," Asaad said, cutting off the music in the car. The vehicle's roar filled Mishal's ears. His heart beat fast, as Asaad's Dodge Charger flew over the street, weaving through traffic. Mishal thought that the police would arrest them, but strangely he didn't see any patrol cars. "We're on emergency standby for now."

"What does that even mean? Isn't emergency standby for cases when we're practically at war with a sorcerer sect? Al Nasr and the others wouldn't dare make a move against us now!" Mishal argued. "Did someone summon anS-level jinni or something?"

"No, no," Asaad said, "nothing like that. It's, well… Damn…" Asaad said, starting to drum his fingers against the steering wheel in agitation. "Alright, look. I'll tell you what I can, but you sure as hell didn't hear it from me. The military has been called out too. Across Oman, Navy, Army, and Air Force personnel have been called out. They're in the exact same situation we're in right now."

"The- the *normal* military?" Mishal asked, incredulous. "We have nothing to do with them."

"Right," Asaad said. "Last thing my friends in the Army said is that they'll be going onto high alert, and they'll lose phone privileges. The police too. If it was just them, I'd think Oman was about to go into war or something. But as you said, Sarim has nothing to do with human bloodshed."

Mishal felt a pain creeping up his chest like vines through breaking soil. His throat constricted ever so gently and he cleared it, then asked, "This is about the Sultan, isn't it?" Asaad's drumming on the steering wheel intensified, but he didn't answer. "Has he already passed away?"

"I don't know," Asaad replied. The strongest exorcist looked fragile in that moment, just another scared Omani youth. "For now, we need to be at the base and see what orders come through."

"What happens if he does pass away, Asaad?" Mishal asked, barely audible over the roar of the car. "Not to the succession," he added, when the Shayib opened his mouth to answer. "To us."

Asaad's expression slowly morphed into a determined frown. "The Sultan spent his life building up this country to be our land of prosperity. I'll be damned if we stop now. We'll make it the best place in the world."

Despite himself, Mishal chuckled. That was exactly the kind of answer he'd expected from Asaad Al Nabhani. "I like that," he said, trying to keep up a calm façade, despite the fact that his heart was slowly breaking.

In Sarim, the mood was somber at best. Mishal looked through the winding metal staircase, where people mulled about in muted terror. Fear and sadness radiated from the very walls, and it could be seen reflected on the faces of every person silently roaming the corridors. The crystal at the top of the abyss was glowing with the color of tears, so faint it was almost translucent. Mishal and Asaad walked down to one of the offices, where they found Salim Al Ghafri sitting at the meeting table with his fists clenched and his jaw tight.

Mishal paused. For the past months, Salim had been avoiding him. Mishal had not yet found the right way to apologize. For a moment, he wondered if it might be better to let the man be. *Why bother him?* he thought to himself.

Asaad held on to Mishal's hand, stopping him before Mishal could move. He leaned in, to whisper in his ears. "Be careful; the ex-military agents will be a bit more emotional today. They spent their lives serving the Sultan."

"Yes, okay," Mishal replied, feeling terrified. He'd always been shy around people. Now, seeing Salim sitting like a statue at the desk, Mishal's heart went out to his ex-teammember. Mishal wanted to comfort him, to say anything that could make the man feel better, even if Salim didn't want to hear it from him.

I need to help him, Mishal thought. *If he gets angry, then... Well, I'd have earned it.* "Salim, are you okay?"

Salim immediately started. His eyes were wild, his fingers twitching as he pulled out his chair from under him and stood up. He stood in a stance with shoulders sharp enough to cut. "Sir, I'm sorry!" he said, as if he was in a trance.

Mishal stopped in place. It was like the man didn't even recognize him. In his fear, Salim had reverted to the training received during his old military days. "It's just me," he cautioned, moving forward slowly as if towards a shy streetcat. "There's no need for 'Sir's, right?"

"I, well- right... right, team leader," Salim said, relaxing marginally, his shoulders drooping ever so slightly even though he remained stiff. "I'm sorry."

Mishal could tell the man needed someone to be strong for him. He decided to ignore the apology for now. Instead, he squared his shoulders. "There's no need to feel sorry," Mishal said. He amplified his voice and sat down stiffly, taking on the mantle of a military commander. "What is happening?"

"We don't know," Salim began, his tone halting with each word. "We were told to go into emergency mode, and the milita-"

"Not that," Mishal interrupted. *Don't ask about emotions, he might see that as a sign of weakness. Focus on the tangible.* He tapped his own head softly. "In here. What are you thinking?"

"Sir, the entire military is at standby and we don't know a thing! Everyone's worried about H-His Majesty," he added, bringing his hand up to cough loudly. He was obviously trying to mask a break in his voice.

"The military will take care of itself," Mishal said, taking on a confidence he didn't feel. His own heart fluttered at the thought of the Sultan passing away. The sultan, who'd spent almost fifty years working tirelessly for the nation. Who'd given them schools to study in. Mishal's own school hadn't existed before Sultan Qaboos. It felt like as if the man had built up the entire country, stone by hope-filled stone.

Mishal shook the cold sense of dread building up inside. He needed to be there for Salim now. "The military will take care of itself," he said again. "I want to make sure that you'll be alright. You matter, irrespective of all else. I need you to get some rest."

"But, Mishal, how am I meant to rest now?"

"Do I need to make this an order, Salim?" Mishal asked with a soft smile. Salim, however, stiffened in place as if the words were a physical blow. He gave a curt nod, greeted Asaad, and walked off.

"I'm going to rest!" he said at the doorway, then muttered under his breath, "As much as I can, anyhow."

And, with that, Salim was gone through the white corridor. Asaad and Mishal were left alone in the meeting room.

"You handled that well," Asaad said, coming forward and taking the seat across from the youth. "And how are *you* feeling?"

"Doesn't matter," Mishal replied with a dry mouth.

"The hypocrisy is palpable," Asaad said with a raise of his eyebrow. "You know? I asked Shayib Ghalib for his advice about listening to people and talking to them properly. He said I should start by talking about *my* feelings first, so others could feel more comfortable expressing theirs."

Mishal snickered. "I bet you liked that."

"Hated it," Asaad said with a grin. "So how about, instead of talking about our feelings, you and I can get some coffee and just sit right here until we think of something good to say? We can be quiet together."

Mishal could now feel a mixture of heat and adrenalin rushing through his system, bolstered by a fear which gave him pins and needles. But Asaad's words stole some of the sting away. Mishal took a deep breath. "I'd like that," he said.

Mishal and his Shayib walked down the corridor to an old electric kettle, filled two fragile black mugs with cheap instant coffee and, a few minutes later, they sat back in the office. The steam from the mugs cut a cloudy path through the room.

"Hey," Mishal said, when his nerves had recovered enough to speak. "Maybe it's a magical war or something."

"That's better?" Asaad replied incredulously.

"At least that would be something *we* can deal with. You'd take care of the boss," Mishal added, while pointing right between Asaad's eyes, "and I'd burn some jinn, and we'd be done with it."

Asaad sipped his coffee. "And Salim and Salwa?"

Mishal hesitated. He'd been watching Salim and Salwa's reports and noting their accomplishments. Apparently, the two had done well on some missions, and had even gone together once. "They can help," he said. "The two of them have grown." He left the rest of the sentence unsaid. *And I've grown as well. It's almost time for me to be by their side again.* Mishal saw Asaad nod slowly, and knew that his Shayib understood.

The steam from the mugs had almost faded now. Mishal sent a small hint of fire to his hands, just enough to slowly heat the coffee until the clouds returned. Asaad snickered, shook his head in disbelief, and then offered his own mug so Mishal could do the same for *his* coffee.

"If the Sultan dies," Asaad said afterwards, cradling a steaming mug once more, "A council of the Royal family has to sit and decide on a successor. If they can't come up with one, they open a secret letter he has placed in the Dhofar palace. On that letter, it'll say who Sultan Qaboos thought would be the best fit."

"And… this'll happen easily?" Mishal asked. The entire conversation had an otherworldly feel to it. A secret letter? A council? How could Asaad be discussing this so quietly?

"I don't know," Asaad said with another slurp. The steam from the cup swirled around his face, like wisps of smoke. He wasn't wearing his dishdasha today. Instead, Asaad was dressed for battle - in loose, black, cotton trousers and a top. Somehow, he made even *that* uniform look good. "I don't have the faintest clue what'll happen. But I hope for the best. Our country was built by people who wanted the best for us all. It's not perfect, but we have to believe that we all have goodness in our hearts."

Mishal and Asaad sat together, each lost in frigid thoughts. Occasionally, a Sarim employee came towards them and spoke a few terse words, then walked away with barely contained grief.

At one point, a Shayib walked past. It was an older gentleman with a pointed beard and beady eyed. Mishal knew him as Shayib Basil. He glanced at Asaad and tutted. "Still wasting your time? You should've quit and become a driver years ago," he said.

Asaad glared back. "At least I still have time to drive my car; you're two minutes away from the grave, you Mughayab."

"One day, you'll realize that there's more to life than showing off. Besides, you look like a goat," the old man added with a smug chuckle.

"Oh ho, at least I don't look older than a corpse," Asaad said, standing up to square off with Shayib Basil. Mishal nervously monitored Asaad's ruh, to see if he'd actually leap out and attack the man. "I think the Angel of Death missed you!"

"I will send you to him myself, you egotistical freak!" the old man shouted.

"Oh, come at me, you bag of dust!"

Mishal stared from one man to the other while they exchanged choice insults. Finally, Shayib Basil walked off, hurling a final slur. "Donkey face!"

Asaad glared, then sat down angrily.

"So… he's a friend?" Mishal asked.

"He's alright, I guess. He's actually the one taking care of Salim these days. Says Salim can fight an E-level on his own, now."

Slowly, Sarim filled up with agents. Mishal began to see faces he'd never seen before as the corridors grew more crowded. Men and women arrived, summoned from across the country by the emergency call. They poured in through the main entrance, slipped in through the walls, and some even arrived by transportation magic - appearing in a glow of ruh, atop carefully-inscribed calligraphy. One man, wearing a patch over his right eye, was greeted warmly by the older employees and clapped on his shoulder. Asaad informed him that the man was part of the Covert Operations team, and that he had been away on secret assignment for the past seven years.

“It’s the same faction Eman learned spying from,” he added quietly.

The mood in Sarim remained somber and terror-gripped, despite the flood of powerful exorcists. Mishal could almost feel the fear radiating from the bodies around him, as more and more agents gathered at HQ.

Suddenly, Mishal remembered something. Asaad had recently told him that Maymun the jinni was haunting Sarim, hoping to get information on him. "Asaad," he asked quietly, "do you, erm, feel anything? A mutual *friend*, maybe?"

At first, Asaad looked confused. Then, however, he shook his head. "But regardless," he said, raising a solemn finger to his lips. Mishal took the warning and clamped his mouth shut. If the jinni was listening to them, he didn't want to be the one to give it any more information.

The HQ began to buzz with muted conversations. Agents sat, stood, and milled about Sarim. Every time Mishal and Asaad left the meeting room, where they were waiting, Mishal could smell the agents’ mixture of powerful perfumes, mixing with the sweat of so many frightened people. Agents began to come into the meeting room, running out of space elsewhere. Mishal and Asaad gave them coffee and remained quiet.

At around eight-thirty PM, footsteps sounded outside the meeting room, which now housed five agents. A loosely-turbaned head peeked in, revealing Salim Al Ghafri looking disheveled. "You should all rest," he told the group at large. When voices rang out in protest, he barked, "Rest! We'll know more tomorrow. You're no good to Sarim exhausted."

Quiet fell over the room. In that quiet, Eman Al Lawati walked in behind Salim "He's right," she cooed in that soothing tone of hers. "For all we know, it might be a jinn invasion and we could be fighting for our lives tomorrow."

"It would be better if it was an invasion," a woman Mishal didn't recognize said. Shocked eyes regarded her, yet the woman's expression remained unfazed and she shrugged.

One by one, the agents filed out of the room. Some embraced each other; more whispered prayers. Mishal arrived at one of the Sarim rooms; a bare room, with simple furniture consisting of a small bed, a short table, and a restroom. He could hear people arguing outside in the corridor but thankfully, as part of the team under the supervision of Asaad Al Nabhani, Mishal and Salim had been given accommodations with little fuss.

Now, all alone, Mishal found himself drained. He dropped facedown onto the bed, with his eyes open, observing the smallest stretch of white blanket beneath his face.

"Please don't let it be true," he murmured to himself. "I - just, please. God, don't let it be true."

Mishal drifted off to sleep.

Chapter Twenty-Six

At 4:03 AM, Mishal awoke to loud sobs coming from outside the corridor.

His first thought was that it was an attack - jinn swooping down on Sarim, sorcerers killing his fellow agents. He pushed off the soft bed and got to his feet, ready to fight.

Mishal opened the corridor to see a group of exorcists gathered outside, all talking over one another. Some of them wore shocked expressions, others openly wept. He could see no magic, not a single bolt of lightning or magic circle in sight. Mishal's mouth hung open as he stepped outside into the corridor. Someone tried to talk to him in the crowded corridor, but Mishal couldn't hear them properly. He walked into one of the meeting rooms

The room was dark, with the only light coming from a singular television showing Oman T.V. The Quran was playing. Muted light spilled out from the television and onto the exorcists sitting in the meeting room, giving their faces an otherworldly feel. Some had their heads in their hands, others cast their gazes wildly. Eman was here, crying softly. She'd always been brave in showing her emotions. Mishal, on the other hand, felt a cold terror gripping his stomach, as well as a pained numbness spreading across his body.

Suddenly, a news anchor appeared on the television. He cleared his throat, swallowed, and began to read.

"Oh, peaceful and fully satisfied soul, return to your lord. You are well pleased in your good destiny, and well pleased in the sight of your lord. Join my righteous servants and enter my paradise," he read, reciting from the Quran first. Mishal recognized the verse which traditionally preceded obituaries. "To the people of the beloved homeland with all its districts, to the Arab and Islamic nations and to the world at large: it is with hearts filled with faith in Allah and his providence, and with great sorrow and deep sadness, yet with complete satisfaction and submission to the will of Allah, that the Diwan of the Royal Court mourns the passing of his majesty Sultan Qaboos Bin Said on the Friday of–"

Screams rang through the corridors as every television set in Sarim aired the exact same news to the agents. Outside, Mishal knew that the same was happening in living rooms across the country.

"-who passed on 14 of Jamaad Al Oula, 10th of January 2020, after establishing comprehensive renaissance over the past fifty years after he assumed power on 23rd July, 1970 and a prudent march - abundant with bounty - that prevailed all over Oman from corner to corner, and even spread to the neighboring nations, the Arab and Islamic countries, and the rest of the world."

Mishal's legs buckled under him and he fell onto a chair, not believing his eyes. Something swayed inside his chest, liquid like a wave, and broke against his throat. "W-what?" he asked. Eman said nothing. Mishal could tell she was lost for words.

Just then, a figure staggered into the room. Mishal turned to see Asaad holding up Salim, who was openly weeping like a child. "Mishal, let's go," he said.

"G-go?"

"The funeral," Asaad said, patting Salim's back. As soon as he said the word, Salim sobbed once more, his face a shattered mess.

"I can't, I c-can't," he argued.

"You can and you want to," Asaad firmly replied. "Mishal, are you coming?"

Mishal's head spun. This was too fast. He stepped past Asaad and walked back the corridor to his room in a daze. He stepped into the shower, just going through the motions, with his heart vacant. The droplets simply slid off his skin in the cramped glass enclosure. Water pooled around his legs, and he watched the ceramic square panels in front of him, through the transparent sheen of water. Mishal's hand closed around the tap and he turned it, hoping that colder water could somehow snap him out of it. Everything felt like a dream, even the coarse towel he grabbed, to dry his hair, even the smell of the blankets on his bed, even the sound of his dry sobs as he dressed in a dishdasha and wore his

Kumma. He hesitated, looking at a Msar in the wardrobe. It was a Sarim Msar, white with an almost golden embroidery going around the fabric in swirls which, if looked at closer, would show simple magical inscriptions and symbols designed to keep the Msar neat for longer.

"Should've learned how to tie a Msar properly," he murmured, leaving it and stepping out of the room. There he found Asaad, standing with his hand poised to knock, as well as Salim Al Ghafri.

"Salim is ready," Asaad said, pointing behind him at the ex-corporal, who nodded shakily. "How about you, team leader?"

Mishal's fingers shook, but that was fine. He stuffed them into his pocket. "Let's go," he said.

The climbed the staircase and left Sarim through the single white corridor, where they were met with the pre-dawn twilight. The dark parking lot was overcrowded with the cars of agents, all of whom were avoiding each other's eyes. They got into Asaad's car and Mishal's mind began to replay every moment in his mind associated with Sultan Qaboos. Seeing him on TV, saying his name while singing the national anthem at school, looking at old pictures of the Sultan visiting schools.

Mishal couldn't understand what was happening, even as Asaad's Dodge charged down the mostly empty highway towards Adhaiba. Mishal looked at the sky, a relatively cloudy display. He could glimpse glimmers of stars, as the sun and the moon stared at one another from different corners of the heavens. It felt like each of the celestial bodies was present, as if in mourning. Mishal let his face slide against the windowpane, feeling the cold of the morning and wishing that it would wake him up.

Asaad checked his phone, trying to keep an eye on the road. "The burial will be at a special spot in Ansab, but first they'll do a-ah, I see."

Salim, who sat in the back and was containing his tears for the past few minutes, looked at Asaad. "What?" he croaked.

"We're going to The Grand Mosque," he said.

"Why wo- oh," Salim replied, his face hanging in a stunned expression. Mishal perked up from where he sat in the front passenger seat. "I see."

As the car neared the mosque, Mishal began to understand. He could see hundreds upon hundreds of cars. The cars were crowded together, spilling out into the streets and neighborhoods surrounding the mosque. A river of white-clothed people flooded the neighborhoods in morose silence, distractedly greeting one another as they headed for the mosque proper.

One of the most important parts of a funeral was *Salat Al Mait*: the prayer for the dead. This was a unique prayer, said just before burying a person. Customarily, the prayer would be carried out in a small room within the cemetery. However, Mishal could now see the crowd, marching towards the massive mosque which towered in the distance, its marble the color of cream and its domes shining with golden paint, accented with reflected sunbeams. The gardens were a deep, sorrow-filled green.

The Sultan's *Salat Al Mait* would take place in the giant Grand Mosque bearing his name, with its five minarats and main hall fit for six thousand people. Mishal stood shocked in place next to the car.

A man came walking from mosque's direction, holding a phone in his hand. "Brother, you can't bring these in," he said, pointing at the phone. His voice sounded defeated.

Asaad nodded in somber thanks, then instructed Mishal and Salim to leave their phones inside his vehicle. "If we lose each other in the crowd, let's meet back here."

"Y-yes sir," said Salim. His stern mustache quivered, but he stopped the motion by scrunching up his face. Salim trembled like a fragile glass bottle, filled with pressure. Mishal worried Salim would explode at some point. Being a military man meant keeping a unique depth of loyalty in one's heart. Today would strike Salim the hardest out of the three of them, Mishal feared, and he didn't know what he could do to help.

Mishal himself kept gulping, leading to his throat going dry. His heart trembled as they walked down the paved side road to the

Grand Mosque, where military vehicles stood in attendance and Army men carrying rifles politely asked Mishal and his group if they had brought their phones with them.

"No, we did not," Asaad replied, seeming completely at ease - despite the weapons. Mishal stared at the military men as he joined the massive throng of people, making their way - slowly but surely - towards one of the marble bridges leading to the mosque. A wide queue had formed there, and Mishal could see temporary silver metal detector gates waiting between the mosque's bronze gates. People in police uniforms, reading 'Royal Oman Police Media', came here and there, walking atop the massive handrails, taking photographic and video evidence.

At around seven AM, the police began allowing people through the gates in batches. When Mishal's turn came, he felt nervous walking through the silent detector gates. After that, the realization hit him that he was walking towards the funeral. Mishal took heavy jolting steps, each one threatening to smash his heart into pieces.

As Mishal entered into the mosque, he was struck by the sheer crowd inside. He'd been at the Grand Mosque a handful of times before. Normally, the mosque was so large that it was difficult to complete even one neat line of people. Today, however, the massive chamber was full to the edges. People sat on the floor in neat rows, waiting with a tense air. Despite the cool January chill, the room felt hot. Mishal found an empty spot between two older gentlemen and sat down, his heart pounding. "A-Al Salam Alaikum," he muttered.

More and more people poured in through the open wooden portals behind. With every entrant, the silence in the room intensified, becoming harder and more taut. It was like a rubber band stretched right to the brink of snapping.

Mishal thought about Sultan Qaboos, wondering how a single man could have spent so much of his life trying to improve a country. How hard must it have been for the Sultan? What did it feel like to have the expectations of an entire country on your shoulders? Had he been happy? Had he slept well? Did he have someone to talk to about his own concerns? Had… had he been proud of them?

If he had met Mishal, would the Sultan have liked him?

Mishal wiped a stray tear from his eyes, trying his hardest to stay quiet.

"He was a good man. May Allah keep his soul safe," someone said from the side. Mishal turned to see the older man next to him, doodling idly on the carpet with his finger. Someone sobbed.

"Allah *will* keep him safe," someone replied, voice full of molten iron. "Nobody is more deserving."

The wait lasted at least an hour. During this time, the occupants of the mosque had to stand up, to allow more people to pour into the room, before sitting back down again. Each time, Mishal's stomach dropped, thinking that the time had come.

Finally, it happened.

A door on the left side of the hall opened. Instantly, thousands of shouts rose out. Some were prayers, others were religious salutations, more still were simply sobs turned into roars, as a large platform was carried from the side of the hall into the front of the crowd.

"Our Sultan!"

"Qaboos!" others shouted, over and over as if saying the Sultan's name would bring him back.

"Takbeer!" someone roared over the din.

"Allah Akbar!" the crowd replied, half crying, half cheering, the deceased monarch lying on the platform, covered in a white cloth, as human as could be. Mishal joined them, awed, his chest thrumming with the deafening noise. The people screamed their prayers and praised Allah all at once. Mishal's eyes began streaming tears, but his heart was quiet with the simple truth of death. Every soul must one day go for the Long Wait.

One man, from the right of the crowd, raised his voice above all the others. "May Allah have mercy on you!" he screamed. "May you find paradise, may you find peace, may you be taken care of - like you took care of us!"

The screams continued, on and on. Mishal's voice joined them, going on long after his throat had gone hoarse. The screams filled the room, shook the pillars, rose out to the world. They continued shouting and praying out loud until the platform rose up again and was carried out of the room to the left, where more men took its occupant to be buried in the ground.

Sooner or later, the people began to file out of the room. Mishal followed them, feeling drained, knowing that he had just participated in honoring their leader. As he reached the middle of the massive hall with its ornate carpets, he stumbled onto Salim Al Ghafri, who was busy comforting a sobbing man.

"How can we carry on?" the man said.

"We will," Salim promised him. "But for now, it's alright to weep."

A surge of pride tore its way through Mishal's body as he heard Salim's words.

Tomorrow the world would mend, but today, they were left with the shock and the sadness.

And so, it was over.

Chapter Twenty-Seven

Mishal returned home in the afternoon, exhausted to his deepest core. Inside the living room, he heard his parents talking to one another in hushed tones. Mishal went up to his room unnoticed, opened the door, and found his slime replica melting away in the sun.

"I'm sorry, I'll come out later!" the replica said, with a cheerful expression plastered onto its half-mangled face. It appeared to be trying hard to keep its shape, but Mishal realized that it must have run out of ruh during Mishal's long absence. He rushed forward in horror, holding the replica in his hands. The slime slid off his fingers and puddled onto the floor.

"Oh no, I'm so sorry," he said with a gasp. He knew the replica had no emotions, but Mishal still felt as if someone had punched him in the gut. "I didn't know this is what happened when you ran out of power!"

"I'm sorry, I'll come out later!" the replica said. Mishal took out the black coin with the Sarim logo emblazoned on it and clicked the button. Immediately the coin began to buzz with a sound like a vacuum cleaner. With a powerful sucking sound, the replica was pulled into the coin, leaving nothing in Mishal's hands. He knelt there in place for a few seconds, worried, then sat at his simple desk and held his head in one hand while checking the news.

Oman had chosen a new ruler relatively quickly. The Royal family had chosen to open Sultan Qaboos's letter, which had named Sultan Haitham Bin Tariq Al Said as the new ruler.

Now, Mishal watched the Sultan's first speech. He felt apprehensive, worried. However, as the speech continued, Mishal felt his mind easing. The speech was not about power, nor affirmations. Instead, the new Sultan called his predecessor 'the best of men'. Mishal focused on the Sultan's face as he said:

"Dear people of Oman, words fall short of articulating a eulogy for a Sultan as great as him, or describe his good deeds and

accomplishments. Our only relief - the best with which we can eternalize his achievements - is to pursue his rightful legacy and derivce impetus for the brilliant steps that he treaded in full confidence and determination, to preserve the gains that he made and to build upon them."

And just like that, Mishal was sold. His bones filled with strength, his ruh swelled. He would help the new Sultan, in any way he could.

A period of mourning was declared, and now the general TV channel and all radio channels were playing the Quran. Mishal could hear the sound of the Quran drifting in from the living room downstairs, pulling in comfort and loss altogether into one, unavoidable package.

Salim had stayed in Sarim, seeking the comfort of his fellow agents, but Asaad had quickly dropped Mishal off at his house and drove off. As he did so, Asaad said, "I constantly feel like something is watching me in that building." He'd not offered an explanation of where he was going. Mishal still didn't know what Asaad would do about the jinni, Maymun.

The youth went down for lunch, seeing his mother stare at him oddly. "You didn't come out at all yesterday," she told him.

"I'm sorry, Mom," he replied, hanging down his face in real guilt. He'd rarely ever left the house for a full day, even when accompanying Asaad on missions. The last time, he'd gone away on a two-week excursion - to be trained with a hermit called Ustath Ismail, where he fought against demons on the cliffs of Qurayat. On that occasion, Mishal had given his parents an excuse. This time, however, Mishal had simply pretended to be in his room for an entire day. *She must have been worried sick,* he thought to himself. *What is it with me and making people worry?* "I needed some time alone."

"Well, I suppose we all did," she replied with a tut. "You've missed some meals. Not that I mind, seeing as how you've gotten it into your head to get all muscular and gross."

“I’m sorry, Mom,” Mishal replied, his voice now edged with annoyance, even as he sat at the floral-covered table to eat. He *needed* the muscles, to fight jinn.

His mother harrumphed, “I can tell you don’t like me saying that, but it’s the truth. All of these muscles,” she added, smacking his bicep as she walked past and then pulling her purple laisu over one shoulder. “It’s unnatural.”

“It’ll help when you need furniture moved,” Mishal replied, a slow grin appearing on his face. She smacked him again, harder this time.

Days later, Mishal was sitting in the living room, where his father grumbled about the stores being closed. “I went all the way to Maasa to get a new vaccuum cleaner. Only the supermarkets and grocery stores are open! What would we do if the vaccuum cleaner broke?”

“The vaccuum cleaner’s faulty?” Mishal asked.

“No, but what if?” his father replied, hands up, his brows creased.

Mishal smiled a polite smile, wondering if he got his anxiousness from his father.

Just then, Mishal received a notification from the Sarim app. “*Level-D jinni in Qurum, near the new library. Please acknowledge message.*”

Mishal moved to click the bright ‘Accept’ button. However, his finger hovered over it for a long time.

Instead of clicking accept, Mishal navigated away from the app. “Dad?” he asked.

His father looked away from the TV. “Yeah?”

Mishal hesitated. He had been about to ask his father a question about friendships, and apologies, and taking responsibility for your mistakes. But he stopped himself. *I can’t speak with him about any of that*, he thought to himself in a burst of realization. *The only thing he really ever concerned himself with is whether I ate, and whether a jinni possessed me or not.*

“It’s nothing,” Mishal said.

Later, Mishal sat on his blue bed, meditating. This was something he did sometimes, to regulate the flow of ruh from his core to the rest of his body. Meditation was a way to relax his body, as well as to make sure the flow of his ruh was aligned, making it easier for him to summon his fire.

He remembered when he had first learned to meditate. It had been months earlier, when Shayib Ghalib relegated Mishal's training to Ahlam. Mishal remembered sitting in the large training hall, on the second floor of Sarim, feeling frustrated. With practice came clarity, and he'd gained the ability to use his fire to strengthen his body, and to see ruh in the world.

Mishal began to time his breathing. Four seconds to inhale, a two-second wait, and then four seconds to exhale. He did this over and over, letting his body relax, focusing only on the count.

Slowly, Mishal's conciousness faded, and the darkness behind his eyelids grew deeper, until he was in somewhere like a cave. He almost gasped when he felt water rising up his thighs as he sat cross-legged. *This feeling…*

He remembered this feeling. Mishal opened his eyes.

Water rose to his ankles. This, Mishal suspected, was what his subconciousness was like. He'd never discussed this with anyone in Sarim. However, he'd seen this place twice in the past. The first time, the water had boiled as Mishal ran away from the jinni which had possessed him, finally gaining the confidence to confront and fight it. On the second occasion, Mishal had unlocked his fire of hatred.

Mishal walked around the cavern, feeling the water ripple around him. As he walked, he saw a figure - crouched down on the water - with its arms around its knees. Mishal walked up to it.

"Hi," Mishal said.

This time, the figure wasn't crying. It looked up, and Mishal saw his own face looking up at him. "Why are you here?"

"I just wanted to talk," Mishal said.

The figure frowned. "I know I messed up; I don't need you to blame me."

"Nobody's going to blame you," Mishal said, not unkindly. The figure here was scrawny: all skin and bones. It shivered in the cold. It was, frankly, an unflattering way to see himself. But Mishal didn't blame the figure for its weakness. "Aren't you cold here?"

"Nobody built a light for me here."

"I'm sorry about that," Mishal said. "You… Do you know what you want?"

The figure huddled a bit tighter. "No,"

"Well… how do I put this? I think I'm starting to understand. I think you want to trust people."

The figure's eyes turned frightful as it understood what Mishal meant. "No, they'll only get hurt!"

Mishal went down on his knees, despite the figure's struggling, and he held its hands. It fought against him, but the figure was weak.

"I know it's scary," Mishal said to the figure.

"You want to take Salwa and Salim back. I'm just going to disappoint them again!"

"They need you."

"They need someone better than me."

"They need *you.* You, Mishal. Not Asaad, not Eman, not Shayib Basil. They need *you*. More importantly, they need the space to get stronger. You need to be there, and you need to let them make their own choices."

The figure began trembling, and Mishal realized he was trembling too. "Will you keep them safe if something goes wrong?" it asked.

"I'll do my best."

The figure gave the smallest nod, and Mishal opened his eyes to find himself back in his room, with his legs crossed on the bed and his hands on his lap, palms up.

Well, that was the easy part, Mishal said to himself with a small laugh. Now, he needed to talk to a real person, not just a figment of his subconciousness. Mishal went into his contacts and called Salim Al Ghafri.

"Hi," he said. "Can we talk?"

Chapter Twenty-Eight

Coffee shops were closed - on account of the mourning period - so Mishal found himself, half an hour later, standing against a wall in an alleyway in Al Khoudh, waiting for Salim.

Mishal smiled to himself as he looked up and down the alley's dirt and rocks. About a year ago, Shayib Ghalib had stood here and given him a business card. That day, he had said there was something strange about Mishal.

Allah knows, he was right, Mishal thought to himself, with a grimace. *I think I might be the most indecisive, most un-leaderlike team leader in Sarim.*

Just then, he heard a crunch. Mishal turned, to see Salim standing in the alley. He had his backpack slung over both shoulders, with the fishing line dangling from one of the pockets. "Assalam Alaikum," Salim said in a gruff voice.

"Wa Alaikum Issalam," Mishal replied. He shifted uncomfortably in place. Strangely, his mind was beating fast, and his head fumbled around, but Mishal's voice was clear and quiet.

And there, his tongue was tied. Mishal wanted to speak, but when he opened his mouth, he couldn't say anything.

After about a minute, Salim's expression soured. "This was a waste of time," he said.

"Wait," Mishal blurted out.

"Why? Did you call me out here just to stand there?"

"I called you out here because I-" Mishal felt his throat tighten and his stomach clench. What if Salim didn't take it well? What if he thought Mishal wasn't serious? "Because I made a mistake - because I'm a coward, okay?"

Salim froze in place with his mouth open. "No!" he finally snapped, walking forward as if he was about to punch Mishal.

Mishal backed up, feeling scared. "What do you mean, no?"

"You don't get to call yourself bad names!" Salim raged. "That's *my* job; I'm the one who's angry! Don't you *dare* pretend that you feel bad enough, so we have to forgive you!"

"I-"

"First of all, this isn't all about you!" Salim continued, wagging his fingers. "Do you know what Salwa and I thought, when they suddenly threw us out of your team? We thought that you would come to us, and that we would fight it together. But you *didn't*! You left us!"

Mishal's stomach dropped as he watched Salim rage. He felt like a child, being properly chided, and so he did the only thing he could: he looked down at his feet.

"You made us feel like you didn't want us around," Salim continued. "Even on missions, you'd just push us aside and fight on your own. Do you know what it's like to do *all* that you can, to ignore *everyone* who said you couldn't do it, and then to finally get put on a team, and the *one* guy who was supposed to have your back instead pushes you to the sidelines?"

Mishal shook his head.

"Answer me!"

Mishal jumped in place. "No," he said quickly. *Oh my god, this is so much worse than I thought it was going to be*, he thought to himself, tears pricking his eyes.

Salim's toes, the only part of him which Mishal could bear to look at, fidgeted. "Of course not. *Ya Allah*, you make me so angry with you." The voice went quiet. "Salwa wanted to quit Sarim, that first week, you know?"

Mishal looked up in shock. "Not to join the healers?"

"She said if you didn't believe in her, then she *must* be weak!"

"She's not weak," Mishal murmured.

"What did you say?!"

"She's not weak!" Mishal said, louder this time. He felt terrified.

"Damn right she's not!" Salim practically bellowed. Mishal looked up for a moment. Salim's face was tomato-red, with eyes so wide Mishal could see the veins. He looked down towards Salim's feet again. "We deserved better than to feel that way."

"I… it wasn't that you were weak, it was that I didn't feel like I could make you safe."

"Why would you even be scared for us? Mishal, we want to be able to take care of ourselves. We want to *help,* not be a cause for worry!"

"I understand this now!"

"Do you? Because it seems like you're still worried about us! Sir, it really hurt."

Mishal shut up. It seemed like whatever he said just made things worse.

Salim struck the wall next to him with the palm of his hands. "We're going to get stronger, and we'll make it so that we -Salwa and I- can take care of a jinni together, *without* your help."

Mishal's heart thrummed. *They're leaving me, aren't they?* "Does this mean…?" He couldn't bear to look up, so he kept his eyes glued to Salim's brown sandals. "Do you not want to come on this mission with me? I- I hate doing this alone."

Strong hands gripped either of Mishal's arms. "Look at me," Salim hissed.

Mishal finally looked up and was surprised to see Salim's face looking only mildly annoyed. "Wallah, you make me furious. You need me for this mission anyway, Sir! Of course I want to come."

Mishal didn't know how to reply. Finally, he started to laugh as he realized something.

"What?" Salim asked, letting go of Mishal. The youth stepped out through the alleyway. He wondered if the neighborhood had heard all that screaming.

"Nothing, nothing," he said. "There's someone who needs to hear this."

As they walked, Mishal chuckled. *Salim called me sir again.*

Chapter Twenty-Nine

An hour later, Mishal and Salim stood next to each other in an office - with a floor of metal, interlaced with carmic panels. Four windows overlooked the Sarim pit, letting in bluish light to illuminate the hard lines of Assim's clean-shaven face.

"Rejected," he said quite simply.

Salim froze, but Mishal stepped forward. "What do you mean?"

"I mean your proposal is rejected, and you are *not* allowed to become a team again."

Mishal and Salim exchanged looks. *What does this mean? He was the one who said that I needed to mature.*

Assim seemed to read Mishal's mind because he said, "I don't see someone who's matured. I see someone who threw his teammates aside and still hasn't figured out a way to be a dependable captain. You haven't proven anything."

"Sir, but with all due respect, we'll be able to serve better if we do it in Team 14," Salim stammered, still standing at attention.

Assim's eyes switched over to Salim. "I heard that you don't talk back to your superiors. Was that a lie?"

Salim went quiet.

Mishal tried to process Assim's words. What did the man want? He felt as if he was standing in front of a stern teacher - what with Assim's cold gaze, the way he held himself as straight as a ruler. Assim spoke quietly, which wasn't like him.

He's furious with us, Mishal realized. He saw Assim's eyes turn towards the door.

"What can we do to prove ourselves?" Mishal asked quickly, before Assim could tell them to get out of the office. He let go of his attachment, his willingness to argue. Instead, Mishal relinquished control. "We want to become a team again. What can we do, to prove that we are able to work together?"

For a long time, Assim said nothing. Mishal felt the man's eyes comb them over, searching their faces for something. Finally, he grumbled. "Bah, you're the exact opposite of him," he said, leaving Mishal to wonder *whom* he meant. "It's no fun arguing with someone so flexible. Fine; I think there's a mission you can try together. But don't get me wrong," he added quickly with a raised finger of warning. "You are *not* a team yet."

Chapter Thirty

The Dodge Charger came grumbling over the road, and Mishal and Salim climbed in. Asaad looked tired, but he forced out a smile when he saw the two of them together. "Are you ready?" he asked.

"As ready as I'll ever be," Mishal replied, and they drove out, heading in the direction of Qurum Natural Park: a sprawling expanse of forestry and brick pathways that almost looked like it existed in another country. "What sort of jinni is it?" Mishal asked.

"A darkness fiend," Asaad replied. "It's been hiding in the shadows of the children's library. So far, the kids had only been reporting feeling tired or sick after entering the museum. But last night, a cleaner was found."

"Dead?" Mishal asked, worried.

"Passed out," Asaad replied, turning on the radio. Instead of the customary Khaleeji music, with its drums and pipes, Mishal heard a Quran recital. He raised an eyebrow at Asaad.

"All the channels have this on now," Asaad replied.

Behind them, Salim sniffed quietly. "Forty days of mourning."

Mishal went quiet, listening to the Quran recital. It was a recorded recital, going by the order of Surah in the Quran. The goal, it seemed, was to replay the entire Quran as many times as possible during the mourning period. Mishal found himself listening solemnly, hoping that Sultan Qaboos found peace.

It was cloudy over Qurum Natural Park that morning. The small hill next to it appeared immersed in the clouds. The parking lot lay empty. To the side, a large, rectangular building waited with an ominous air over it.

Mishal and Salim walked together to the public children's library, with Asaad waiting far behind them. "Good luck out there!" he said. "Salim, remember your training. Mishal, don't help him too much; he needs to be able to fight a D-level on his own."

Mishal waved behind him before looking forward towards the massive structure, his face set in determination. He would see for himself how much Salim had grown. *I won't push him to the side this time.*

Today was a test for Mishal, just as it was a test for Salim.

The Public Children's Library was a six-storey off-white building, flanked on both sides by sky-blue glass panels so that it looked like an open book. Nobody was there that day, of course, but Sarim's support staff had left the door unlocked for Mishal and Salim to walk in. They stumbled into the eerily-quiet building, bathed as it was with splashes of filtered sunlight. Every step sounded like thunder, every squeak of their shoes deafening.

"How do you want to approach this, Mishal?" Salim asked in a breathy whisper. He'd removed his backpack from his shoulders and now held it in one hand.

"You're in charge today," Mishal replied.

Salim's eyebrows rose. "Really?"

Mishal smiled at the gasping surprise in Salim's voice. "What do you recommend?"

"Well…" Salim paused. "It's D-level so I can't pull it to us. I could use a scry to find out where it is exactly, then I'll lead us to it."

Mishal nodded. "Let's do that, then. And when we find it?"

"Asaad said I need to take charge, so please put up a fire shield to protect us and I'll try a few of my new tools of destruction."

Salim sat down on the clean marble floor, removing a small piece of parchment from his backpack. On it, he'd drawn an intricate design which looked vaguely like a map, textured and showing swooping mountains alongside oceans made of a thousand curves, with seven directions marked on the map, instead of the customary four. Next, he removed a small brass orb from another pocket and said something. Mishal could see wisps of ruh leaving the man's fingers and attaching themselves to the orb. The pieces of ruh were golden symbols, dancing and twirling like stars.

Salim released the orb but, instead of falling, it hovered above the piece of paper as if repelled by magnets. Slowly, the orb moved to one of the directions on the map, then rose up slightly.

"Forty meters to the right, around… twenty-five meters up," Salim said. "Third floor, I think."

"Your tools are getting more accurate," Mishal whispered. "Impressive."

"Especially since I don't have a small supply of ruh?" Salim asked with a smirk.

Mishal froze in place. "I'm sorry," he said.

Salim chuckled. It seemed like the shouting earlier really had beengood for him. Gone was the cloud of melancholy Mishal could feel over him earlier. "Have you never heard of Sufyan, the exorcist?" he asked.

"Sufyan? No."

Salim stood up and pointed, leading Mishal forward. "It's a story Eman Al Lawati told me, one of the times she came to visit Shayib Basil. In the seventies, Sufyan was introduced to Sarim - via a family friend. He failed the practical test three times because he had a weak supply of ruh."

"So, he was basically an average human?" Mishal asked, warming up to the story.

"Exactly," Salim said as they walked. His hands moved excitedly as he told the story "No store of ruh, no supernatural recovery, no convenient inborn ability. What he did have, however, was control and hard work. He learned to manipulate his ruh. They say he could make it dance so well that even the Shayibs would be entranced. Hell, he even ended up becoming one of the top exorcists at Sarim and beat Shayiba Siham in a one-on-one."

"Oof, she must've hated that," Mishal said. Shayiba Siham was known to be aggressive in nature. She was in charge of a terrifying team of exorcists with anti-jinn sentiments.

"She still gets angry when anybody mentions his name. I made the mistake of asking her about him once," Salim said, forcing a laugh out of Mishal.

Now, they were up on the third floor of the library. A long corridor ran through the building, separating it into open chambers filled with books. Mishal could glimpse small tables and chairs inside the chambers. With no windows here, and the lights off, the white interior was splashed in shadows that seemed deep and uninviting. Mishal shivered in the winter cold. “This is the right place?” he asked Salim.

Before the corporal could answer, a second voice, high-pitched and cracking at the fringes, answered. "The right place? Hmmm, mayhaps.”

Chapter Thirty-One

Mishal stopped in place, staring at the spot he thought the voice had come from. "Salim?" he said.

"Yes, sir?"

Without looking around, Mishal said, "Don't call me 'sir'. I have a bad feeling about this. You'll be in charge, but I'm supporting you. Bring out your strongest tool."

"Noted," Salim said.

Mishal sent ruh to his eyes, strengthening his sight as he stepped forward. However, there was no need. From one of the rooms ahead, he saw darkness spilling out of the doorway like mist, drifting slowly upwards so that it obscured his vision. "Weapons so early?" the voice teased.

"What have you been doing here?" he asked loudly. While he spoke, Mishal put his hand behind him, sparking a low, blood-red fire in his palm. He spun it over and over again, building velocity.

"Waiting for the agents of Sarim," the jinni replied, from inside the room. As Mishal watched, a purple foot came through the doorway, clinking from anklets wrapped around it. The jinni appeared slowly. When it fully appeared, they saw a man with long, dirty hair and green, white-less eyes. The jinni held a long flute in one hand. As it noticed Mishal watching it, the jinni dragged the flute against the white wall next to it, producing a low, musical hum. "Nothing makes me happier than killing those with *power*. My lord always demanded it, long ago…"

Slowly, confidently, the jinni kicked out with its feet, sending out that cursed cloud of darkness surging up through the corridor. Mishal stepped in front of Salim, pushing the corporal back. Then Mishal leaned down and slapped his burning hand on the ground. His fire spread from his palm and sprang up from the floor, spinning violently. The jinni hissed and took a step back. Mishal's fire created a wall between them and the jinni, burning the darkness away.

"Salim, now! Your weapon!" he called. His fire was powerful, but it wasn't made to be stable. The wall would flicker, and once that happened, the jinni would pounce.

"Roger!" Salim said, pulling out a tool that looked like a children's slingshot. He murmured something under his breath and pulled back, then released. Something white and small shot out from the slingshot, passing through Mishal's fire and striking the purple jinni in the shoulder. It smashed into the wall with a shriek.

Salim whooped in excitement, inexperienced as he was, but Mishal kept his heart cautious. His eye stayed on the jinni, which was left bleeding leaning against the corridor. Just as Salim turned to give Mishal a high-five, the jinni lifted its hand and brought the flute to its mouth. Mishal glimpsed a thin, pained smile on its face.

"Salim, careful!" Mishal said, running towards the jinni.

A song rang out through the corridors. Soothing and smooth, it drifted through the air like darkness. Mishal felt his strength bleed from his body, his knees buckling to the floor. Salim stumbled behind Mishal, though he did not fall.

This didn't make sense. Did the jinni have two special abilities? It had used the darkness earlier. And now it used magical music? That was too much for a D-level mission.

Mishal could feel the song seeping into his mind, wrapping around his soul. There was sorrow in the song, a promise that the world was a dark and bothersome place. Perhaps he should close his eyes to it? Maybe it might be better to simply sleep… Wasn't he lonely? Didn't he *want* to just let everything pass him by?

Nonsense, Mishal thought to himself, gritting his teeth. *There are people who need me here.* Certainly, he was brooding at heart. He had a darkness that wrestled with him relentlessly. But that was why he knew, more than anyone, how important it was to hold on to whatever spark of life he had. He needed to live enough for both himself and Ahlam. He deserved to be happy.

Let the dark world be damned.

"Salim!" he shouted. He felt more awake now, but the music still had a grip on his legs. The jinni was playing its wailing flute, its eyes closed, sure it had won.

“Y-yes?” Salim replied, sounding bleary.

“I am going to punch a hole in that demon. So help me God, you’d *better* have a tool with you to free up my legs!” As soon as Mishal said the words, embarrassment flushed over him. How could he speak that way to a man who was his elder? Mishal could feel his face heating up with shame.

Salim laughed long and hard, a manic sound that came right from the battlefield. “Yes, sir!” Salim answered, in pure joy, and immediately Mishal heard the sound of a metallic bell ringing out. The sound was imbued with ruh, amplified so that Mishal felt his ears pop. The magic from Salim’s bell sprang out sharply, drowning out the handsome jinni’s song. The jinni recoiled from the noise, falling back down. Before it could get up, Mishal sent fire through his legs, leaping in the air and landing upside down against the room’s ceiling. The room was flipped, and he could see the entire battlefield splayed out ahead of him: fire licked through the floor, fighting against the darkness. On one side, Salim knelt on the ground with a copper bell in his hands. On the other side, the purple jinni leaned against the wall, bringing the flute back to its lips, cursing them angrily and with utter fear.

Another jump sent Mishal crashing into the jinni, sending the flute falling out of its hand and down to the floor.

Mishal stood over the jinni, fire in his hands. It looked up at him in pure terror, starting to shout gibberish.

“The chieftain will rise!” the jinni promised. “Maymun Abu Nuh, Maymun Thu Jinah, Maymun Al Sahaabi! Help me!”

Mishal felt his heart lurch at the call. The jinni sounded desperate, almost like a child calling for a loving father. It raised its hand to the side and, to his horror, Mishal saw the darkness respond. The shadows leapt from the far wall, going to lick the jinni’s fingers as if trying to help it.

Before anything else could happen, Mishal punched down, bringing his white flame to bear. The jinni burned away instantly, breaking into a thousand glimmering pieces, leaving behind a single flute.

Chapter Thirty-Two

Fifteen minutes later, the recovery van from Sarim arrived. Mishal and Salim stood together with Asaad near the car, watching Sarim support staff bringing out victims of the jinni. Luckily, all of them were still alive.

"It looks like the jinni was holding them captive to siphon off their life slowly," Asaad said, putting a hand on Mishal's shoulder. "You did well out there," he added.

"Most of it was Salim," Mishal replied, looking over at Salim. The ex-corporal held the jinni's strange flute in his hand, examining it. "You might want to be careful with that thing."

Salim turned around, smiling. "It's just a tool, Mishal. A tool is only as dangerous as those who have it in their grasp."

"Poetic," Asaad commented with a raised eyebrow.

"Then again, it is creepy having this thing with me. I can feel the malice coming off it." Salim hastily put the flute in his bag, then zipped it closed.

Mishal paused as they stood in the parking lot. *Did Salim just call me by my first name?* He looked to Asaad, who gave him a surprised look. Salim frowned. "What's wrong?" he asked hesitantly.

Asaad began to laugh, removing his hand from Mishal's shoulder and clapping him on the back, hard. "You've finally done it, kid!"

"Ow! Thanks," Mishal replied with a grin as he tried to defend himself from Asaad's slaps. "But it's a little weird."

Salim raised his eyebrows. "What's a little weird?" he asked.

Asaad and Mishal only laughed.

Later, Mishal snuck glances at Salim, who stood tall with his backpack slung across his shoulders as he walked to the car.

"He looks better," Asaad commented, coming to stand next to Mishal. "He was heartbroken about the Sultan's death."

“It’s momentary,” Mishal told him. He was surprised at the softness in his voice. “Grief hides sometimes, but he’ll feel it again soon. I just wish I could tell him that it gets better with time.”

“It doesn’t?”

“It does, but no one wants to hear about that.” Mishal held Asaad by the elbow, shifting him to the side. “At least we went on a mission together. We can take it step by step. Anyhow, there’s something else I need to tell you about.”

Asaad stood quietly in place as Mishal recounted the details of his mission. When Mishal spoke about the jinni’s appearance and speech style, Asaad’s lips pursed. When Mishal arrived at the part with the magical blackness, the shayib’s eyebrows rose. “*Two* magical abilities?” He asked in surprise. “That’s not a D-level jinni.”

“I don’t think it was two magical abilities. At least, not really. Asaad, I had the jinni beaten; then it began to shout things about a-a patron, I suppose. An almighty jinni of darkness.”

Asaad hissed between his teeth. “Maymun.”

“Maymun,” Mishal agreed. Asaad Al Nabhani shrunk in that moment; he seemed like just a man. Mishal noticed the dark circles under his eyes. “He called Maymun for aid, and I saw the darkness respond. Asaad, Maymun shouldn’t be able to affect the world. What does this mean?”

Asaad tried to grin, but the expression only barely touched his eyes. “It means that we don’t have as much time as we thought. I can’t afford to go to Sarim anymore, Mishal.”

“What? Because Maymun is going to be spying on you?”

“Partly. But, also, because I’ll need to train. As I am now, I’m not strong enough to withstand the possession. Actually,” he added with a montone laugh. “Maybe I’m better off not training at all.”

Mishal gave Asaad a confused look. Did Asaad think he already had the power to withstand Maymun’s power after all? “What are you talking about?”

Asaad began walking towards the car. “It doesn’t matter. Come on, I’ll drive you to Sarim for the paperwork.”

An hour later, Mishal and Salim stood alone in the Sarim building, with its long white corridors, the massive pit in the middle, and the glowing crystal floating near the top. *Welcome, Mishal Al Balushi*, the crystal announced. "Can you please take care of the paperwork this time, Salim?" Mishal asked. "I think I need a shower; I'm getting an itch from where I touched that jinni."

Salim fidgeted in place, rubbing dust off his standard Sarim-issue black fatigues. He looked up at the ceiling, down at his feet, then rubbed the back of his head and said, "That place smells like death. The woman scares me."

Mishal stifled a stunned laugh. "Salim, you're ex-military! Nothing scares you."

"Every time I look up from the papers, she's giving me this look like an owl. Every. Single. *Time,* Mishal!"

Mishal gave Salim a light smack on the shoulder, adopting Asaad's demeanor as well as he could. "Come on now, it can't be that bad."

Salim grumbled, then he pleaded, and finally nodded in acceptance before going down the stairs to the first floor. Mishal watched him go. He wasn't lying about the itch - he could feel his right hand buzzing, as if he'd stuck it in a wasp nest. However, Mishal had another reason for sending Salim ahead: Asaad Al Nabhani had asked Mishal to ask the CEO something on his behalf.

Mishal walked downstairs, hearing his feet clang against the metal stairs. The building materials of each floor changed, becoming older as he went down. Not for the first time, Mishal wondered why the insides of Sarim looked so old, when the organization had only been formed in the 1970s.

Downstairs, Mishal found the man with the long, black hair. "Ah, young Mishal," the man said, appearing relieved. "You're looking like a thunderstorm today."

"Hi," Mishal said, smiling politely. "It's good that I found you. Do you know where to find the office of the CEO's assistant?"

"I…" the man appeared conflicted. He thought for a long moment. "Well, yes, I do."

"Wonderful?" Mishal asked. For a moment, he cracked under the exhaustion of the past few months. The missions, the paperwork, and worrying about Asaad and his teammates all piled up. "Could you take me there?"

The man fidgeted. "Normally, a Shayib accompanies team leaders there."

"Oh," Mishal said. His cheeks grew hot, and he could tell he was turning bright pink under the orange gas lamps above them. "Forget I said anything."

Mishal had taken two steps away from the man when he heard a voice behind him. "Wait, I'll take you there." The man said, still looking slightly upset.

"There's no need if you're busy," Mishal replied.

"Nonesense, it's no trouble," the man replied, leading Mishal further down the stairs. "What would I be, if I ignored someone who wanted help?"

Down and down the two went into the darkness, with the man in front and Mishal behind him. The man was dressed all in black, with his beard and hair matching his clothing, leaving only his light brown skin so that he looked almost like a patch in the darkness. Mishal began to rehearse how he was going to talk to the CEO's secretary. After all, Asaad's request was an odd one.

Finally, they reached the fifth floor, where brick began to slowly give way to old cave stones. He passed through the moss-covered corridors, walking from place to place until he heard the sound of birdsong, loud and insistent. Here, he found the office of the CEO's secretary. "Hello?" Mishal asked, peeking his head into the office with his companion behind him.

It was a mess. Books lay scattered across the floor, some opened, many thrown aside in apparent frustration. Birdcages wrought of simple blue metal hung from the ceiling, three-quarters of which held an assortment species of birds, all squawking manically. Mishal looked more closely. One of the cages held not a bird, but a lizard. The lizard was shouting in a human voice.

"Let me *down,*" the lizard screamed, at a man who sat at a large hexagonal desk below him.

"You'll just bite me, Sohail," the man said, in a long, slow drawl. He looked to be in his forties, with slight silver lining his fringes from beneath his Kumma. The man was writing on a piece of paper.

"I'd be right to bite you," the lizard protested. "A *lizard?* You turned me into a *lizard?*"

"Hey, I didn't do anything," the man replied. "The *CEO* turned you into a lizard. And you had it coming, using your powers to show off."

"I never hurt anyone, so why not?"

"Because civilians aren't meant to know about what we do. The more people believe in powers and jinn, the stronger the spiritual residue coming off them is, which then leads to more jinn forming!" the man snapped. He then glanced up and locked eyes with Mishal. "Ah, the fire boy." His eyes refused to look at the dark-haired man standing next to Mishal, passing over him as if he weren't there. Mishal wondered if the two disliked each other.

"Um, Al Salam Alaikum, sir," Mishal said. He looked nervously at the lizard. "I hope I'm not interrupting anything. Do you want me to come back later?"

The lizard glared at him. "Never tell anyone you saw me here," it threatened. "I'll know it was you."

Mishal glanced at the dark-haired man next to him, who snickered but ignored the lizard. He looked like he was about to walk out, but stopped when he noticed Mishal watching him. Was the lizard talking to the man, or to him? Mishal turned back to the lizard and put a peaceful palm, saying, "Hey, I don't even know you too well, Soheil."

"Good - and keep it that way!" the lizard replied, sitting back on its haunches like a human. It crossed its little arms over the strewn mess of hay in its cage.

Mishal felt bad for the lizard. "Your water bowl looks dirty. How about I come back later and clean it for you?"

The lizard's eyes twitched. "Oh. Yeah, I'd like that. Thanks a lot!"

The secretary cleared his throat, catching Mishal's attention. "Your business here?" he asked.

"I have some information that the CEO needs to know," Mishal said.

The man seemed to think for a time, but then he nodded amicably. He snapped his fingers, causing all the animals in the room, the lizard included, to instantly slump to the floor in deep sleep. "This is about the demon, Maymun, I suppose?" he asked.

Mishal started, turning quickly to look at the man with the dark hair, who sighed sadly. "S-sir, do you think it's wise to discuss it here?" Mishal asked.

"Of course he does," the dark-haired man said in an exhausted voice.

The man's eyebrows furrowed. "We all know about it, so why not? Soheil's sound asleep, and if you'd like I can wipe his memory tomorrow just in case he hears anything while tossing and turning. Anyhow, the CEO is out at the moment, so would you like to leave a message for him?" He appeared steadfast on ignoring the dark-haired man.

Mishal paused to consider. He hadn't known that the dark-haired man had a high enough rank to know about Maymun. Anway, this was too important to wait until the CEO came back. "At our mission today, a jinni appeared to communicate with the shadows. It talked about Maymun coming soon," he added. "Asaad believes it won't be long now, so he's decided not to come to Sarim anymore."

The secretary squinted. "A Shayib, abandoning his post?"

"He said it was important for him to be away."

"I see," the secretary said, his expression cold now. "He thinks he can run away from Sarim, does he? If you ask me, that rogue Shayib be placed under protective custody. It's for his own good. It's a good chance to remind that arrogant man that *he* works for Sarim, not the opposite."

Mishal felt his face flush with anger in defence of his Shayib, but he kept his mouth shut. *Do so many people hate Asaad in Sarim?* Either way, the CEO had promised to protect Asaad's freedom, so these people couldn't do anything. "I see. What has Sarim being doing, to ensure that Maymun won't be able to possess Asaad?" he asked, keeping his voice calm even as his palms grew clammy.

The secretary squinted dangerously, and the dark-haired man sighed almost simultaneously. "The organization has prepared all sorts of safeguards," the secretary said, thumping the table softly. "We've been putting barriers between this world and the one Maymun is locked within. We've also been calling Sarim agents to put out feelers and crack down on any scent of a sorcerer sect, which might be behind the jinni. Worst comes to worst, we've been asking the CEO to put… precautions in place. In case Asaad Al Nabhani is successfully possessed."

"None of it will work," the dark-haired man said sadly. He leaned over to inspect one of the bird cages.

"What do you mean?" Mishal said, turning to stare at the man's back.

The secretary, on the other side of the table, clicked his pen in annoyance. "It's nothing, just precautions to make sure Asaad can't hurt anyone. And look at me when we talk, that bird isn't going anywhere!"

Mishal swung his head to regard the secretary in confusion. "No, I was talking to…" he began, then stopped suddenly as ice filled his heart.

He'd been talking to the dark-haired man. The man whom the secretary and the lizard refused to acknowledge even once during this conversation.

Come to think of it, Mishal had never seen anyone speak directly to the dark-haired man except for him. The man had always simply stood there, making remarks, and nobody answered him.

Everyone has been acting as if the only person who could see him was me.

The dark-haired man's eyes glimmered from where he stood, on the other side of the room.

"I'm sorry, sir," Mishal replied, smiling despite the sick feeling in his stomach. "Well, now that you have the message from Asaad, I think I'll head out." He hastily bid the man goodbye, feeling his head buzz with confusion, his heart thick with fear.

The dark-haired man walked out with Mishal, keeping pace with him easily. They went from floor to floor, with Mishal seeking an empty chamber.

Finally, Mishal found an empty library chamber on the second floor. He walked in, furious, terrified, horrified. The room was dimly lit with lanterns which scattered and distorted the amber light, casting the library shelves in a haze of half-truth.

Mishal immediately whirled on the dark-haired stranger, who only sat at a chair and watched him with a curious expression on his face.

"Who are you?" Mishal stammered, even though he already knew the answer.

Possession of an object or location, Asaad had told Mishal. *Although I suppose the jinni could have taken a ghost-form to move about physically.*

"I'm sorry, first of all," the stranger said, his large eyes appearing sincere. "For all of it, but especially for tricking you. My name is Maymun Abu Nuha."

Mishal felt the room spin around him at this sudden revelation. His legs buckled, and he barely had time to sit down on a chair to avoid falling on the floor.

The dark-haired man continued talking. "I'm the one you and yours have been terrified of for months now. I'm the jinni who's hoping to possess your friend. And, to make a long story short, I would like your help."

Chapter Thirty-Three

Terror.

The chair flipped as Mishal jumped backwards, landing in a crouch with his hands out like claws. He jumped one further step back, anticipating an attack. When none came, ruh ran through his body in intricate pattenrs. Flames immediately burst around Mishal's fingers and he jumped forward towards the dark-haired man, swiping across his face.

The hand passed through the man's face as if he wasn't even there.

Mishal looked around, waiting for Maymun's magic, his disciples. *Something.*

Anger.

This jinni had been haunting them for months. It wanted to destroy Asaad. Mishal attacked once, twice, three times. His hand brushed the chair, singing it, but the jinni didn't move.

Finally, Mishal cursed at the man in front of him. He cursed long and hard, and his voice grew harsher and louder by the word. For *months* he and Asaad had been stressing about the jinni, Maymun. And it had the nerve to be sitting in front of their noses all this time?

Maymun had the decency to look properly chastised. Mishal continued cursing, switching to Balushi when Arabic curse words weren't enough. Finally, when Mishal finished shouting, Maymun crossed his legs, looking uncomfortable. "Well, that was colorful. This realm has really changed in the past millennia. I expected you to come swinging at me, but I didn't expect *that.*"

Mishal finally sat down.

Confusion.

Thoughts crashed through Mishal's head in thick waves, but he knew that the man in front of him wasn't lying about what he'd said. "You're not really here yet, are you?"

The man - the jinni, Mishal reminded himself - smiled widely. “Very good. I knew it was a good move to reach out to you. You’re thoughtful. Well, I also thought you polite, but that’s that.”

“Excuse me for not being *polite*,” Mishal hissed angrily. “One of your jinn just tried to kill me.”

Maymun bit his lips. “I am sorry about that. I hadn’t been aware my followers would go that far. They must’ve thought killing Sarim agents was one of my goals.”

Mishal paused. “It’s not?” he asked.

“Heavens no!” Maymun said with an incredulous look. “I just want to be free of my prison. Asaad Al Nabhani happens to be the only vessel capable of containing my ruh, that’s all. Well, he *might* be able to contain my ruh.”

It took all of Mishal’s self-discipline not to reach across the room and try to burn Maymun’s face off, regardless of whether it worked or not. However, he kept himself quiet. The jinni had come to him willingly. Moreover, Maymun was providing much-needed information. *That’s good, keep going.*

“What are you talking about?” Mishal said.

“I’m saying,” Maymun explained, “that your *strongest exorcist* might just barely be at the threshold needed to contain my power. Ruh is like water, it can flow into a vessel if channeled properly. However,” he added, raising a finger, “it does not overflow. The vessel is tied to the ruh. In the case that I channel my ruh into something which cannot withstand me? It would shatter. This is the fate likely awaiting your friend, as he is now. However, I’m definitely going to give it a try soon.”

Mishal’s heart began to beat louder. Asaad was the strongest. The idea of him not being able to handle Maymun’s ruh was ridiculous. “So Asaad’s options are…either die or be taken over? That’s it?”

“That’s it,” Maymun said, appearing slightly saddened. Mishal observed the jinni, so unlike anything he’d ever seen before. He’d heard of the jinni, Maymun, bringing blights, casting the region in darkness. He’d read of Maymun Al Sahabi as a massive creature of black skin and crimson wings - so large that its wings were like the clouds. A terror unlike any other. *This man feels nothing like that. He talked to me about buying clothes, for God's sake.*

"Why do it, then?" Mishal asked. A small sliver in him tried to appeal to Maymun's better nature. "If he'd die either way, why not just stay in your realm? You don't even have any goals he-"

Maymun began to fidget in his chair. "My prison… it is…Well, how should I say it? It is agony incarnate, Mishal." Pain flitted across his eyes, and Mishal found himself stuck looking at them. He could see something floating within the demon's honest irises. With shock, Mishal realized Maymun was about to cry. "It is pain, followed by numbness, then even more pain. I cannot bear to be there anymore. I will do *anything* to leave. I only want to feel the wind against my skin, to let the sunlight warm me. It's still warm, isn't it? The sun?"

Mishal didn't know what to say. "It's still warm," he murmured. Yes, Maymun was different from the jinni of terror he'd read about, the story he heard with Asaad, the great tyrant the jinni with the flute had called for. Now, Maymun was… just a man, really, with dark hair and kind eyes and worries. He'd given Mishal advice, even encouragement at times.

But none of that changed the fact that this dark-haired, kind man wanted to either take over Asaad Al Nabhani or destroy him in the process.

Sometimes, people became hellbent on their intended future - despite any damage that this future could bring to others. Maymun was like that now. He would not be dissuaded.

"I won't help you possess Asaad. What you've gone through is dreadful, but…"

To his surprise, Maymun laughed. "Oh, I don't want you to help me posess him, young Mishal." He stood up, walking forward to the rich, honey-brown table to the side. He moved to lean against it, but his hand went right through. "You heard the secretary earlier, yes?"

"Yes," Mishal replied, feeling confused again. Where was this conversation going? "He spoke about precautions."

“The barriers and exorcists don’t matter,” Maymun said with a wave of his hand. “I’m in the process of thoroughly dismantling one of the mightiest barriers man has ever created. One country’s exorcists won’t stop me. I’ll simply make them all go to sleep and teleport elsewhere. They can’t even sense me as I am now. However, you realize what their last precaution was, don’t you?” He turned around, cracking his knuckles. “They’re aiming to kill Asaad Al Nabhani before he could be possessed.”

Mishal’s eyes widened. He’d guessed as much, from the secretary’s guarded demeanor. But hearing it spoken in such simple tones felt like a blow from a blade. “The CEO wouldn’t,” he argued.

“But some factions in Sarim *would.* I’ve heard them discuss it. And, I’ve noticed Asaad’s own hesitation. The boy is a proud fool. One of his noblest traits, I believe. But even he is considering taking his own life, or else crippling his magic power enough that he would shatter the moment I touch him.”

The room remained quiet, with the only light coming from the amber lanterns, which seemed to flicker in time with Mishal’s breath. He felt as if the earth was being pulled from beneath him. “Now you’re lying,” he said. “Asaad is the cockiest man in the country. There’s no way he thinks he’ll lose it.”

Maymun shrugged. “I don’t think I need to tell you otherwise. He’s shown it himself, hasn’t he?”

A memory from just that afternoon surfaced unbidden to Mishal’s mind. *Maybe I’m better off not training at all.*

Asaad was considering throwing away this fight. Asaad, selfish, infuriating Asaad, was thinking of sacrificing himself to stop Maymun from possessing him. “You want me to convince him to fight you instead of giving up.”

“He has a chance to beat me,” Maymun urged, leaning forward. “I *am* going to possess him. There are only three ways this could end: either I take over him; or he overpowers me; or he shatters. I’m confident that I will beat his soul to the ground and feel the sun again. If he’s the Asaad I’ve admired, he will meet my challenge, with the pride of a Shayib and the strength of a beast.

On March twelfth, two months from now, I will come for him at sunset. Support him, encourage him, be the friend he needs… and make sure he comes prepared to fight for his life."

Mishal blinked, and suddenly Maymun was nowhere to be found. The youth stood up, his heart beating louder than it had even during the fight to the death earlier that day.

Two months.

Chapter Thirty-Four

Mishal knew that the first thing he needed to do was find Eman Al Lawati. Of all the agents in Sarim, she was undoubtedly the most human - one of the kindest and most sensible people he had ever met. In this moment of uncertainty, Mishal needed the steadiness of someone who knew just what to say.

Mishal found himself drifting down towards her team's office, only to find it empty - save for the quiet, constantly terror-stricken woman who was a part of Eman's team. She was in the midst of filing paperwork, presumably cataloging this week's accomplishments for Team 10. Eman's team had risen through the ranks unreasonably quickly, during the months since they had staged the joint team training sessions. During those sessions, Team 10 had uncovered its own weaknesses. However, Eman's team seemed to progress better than Mishal's had. They'd been completing mission after mission, all C- and B-rank tasks.

It's not the time to feel jealous, Mishal told himself. Team 14 was almost on the right path. A strange competitiveness burned in Mishal's belly.

He knocked on the doorframe, causing the woman to startle. "Hi," he said. "Is Eman nearby?"

"She's at the cafeteria," the woman replied. "I hope you're, er, feeling better?"

Mishal felt shameful heat go through his face, taking root in his hair like sparks in a forest. The last time he had seen the woman, Mishal had gone berserk. "Yes, thank you. I'll go find Eman."

The cafeteria was cloaked in relative silence. It had none of the joyous bustle of the months before, but neither did it exhibit the crypt-like silence Mishal had noted in the weeks preceding the death of Sultan Qaboos Bin Said. Instead, it was quiet; almost comfortably so. The few people inside were talking about a variety of topics, ranging from any major administrative changes they expect the new Sultan to implement, to rumors of a mysterious illness which had first appeared in China.

The cafeteria smelled like Qabooli, and grilled chicken sandwiches. Mishal felt a rumble begin deep inside of his stomach, but he ignored it as he saw Eman Al Lawati sitting at a table, eating quietly. She was dressed in a navy-blue outfit, coupled with a similarly colored hijab which caused her blue-green eyes to sparkle like gemstones. Mishal approached her. "Eman, hi!"

"Mishal!" she said with a gasp. "It's been so long! You, know, you can do more than just 'like' my Tiktoks."

"I'm sorry," he said with a fake laugh. "It's been busy. Oh, by the way, let's go for some coffee." He kept his smile cheerful, his tone neutral, but with his eyes, Mishal tried to send a message. *Unsafe here. Come with me.*

It went completely over Eman's head. She smiled brightly and said, "Sure, let's do it. Just let me gather my team! It's been way too long." She made to stand up from her chair.

Panicking, Mishal put a hand on Eman's chair, stopping her with a jolt. He winced, but injected the cheer back in his voice. He was keenly aware that if Sarim's upper echelon was considering killing Asaad Al Nabhani to keep him out of Maymun's grasp, then they would be listening to Mishal. "Oh, I *think everyone's busy,*" he hissed, trying to get her see the point. Eman had trained as a spy last year, so he hoped she would get the message from his expression.

Eman stared at him, then nodded quietly. "Sure, no problem."

The two of them walked upstairs. Eman was only a year or two older than Mishal and still learning to drive, so the two called in at the reception for someone to drive them into Muttrah.

"So," Eman said. "Is this just because you miss me?" she asked. "I know Salim and Salwa are doing their own thing, but I didn't think you'd want to leave them behind."

Mishal coughed, feeling genuinely guilty.

"How have you been?" Mishal asked. He put something in his voice when he asked the question, a hint that he was *truly* asking her, not just to pass the time.

"It's been…" Eman paused. "It's been alright. Tough sometimes, happy at others. I miss Ahlam terribly."

"I hear you," Mishal said. No other words escaped him. He wondered if Eman had known of the little outline of a plan he and Ahlam had held together. How they enjoyed each other's company and hoped, someday, to maybe be together - if those feelings persisted into adulthood. How, even now, he could imagine Ahlam in a wedding dress. "Some days can be harder than others," he added, dismissing the thought. He'd come to terms with his grief, even if it still lingered in the corners of his heart.

"And some days are happy," she said. "Despite the stress of managing a team."

"Oh, God! How did Ahlam manage it?" Mishal said jokingly.

"Poorly - that's how!" Eman said. "What with Shayib Ghalib overseeing her? Must've been a nightmare, and she was *just* like him. Do you know, she never even once completed a performance appraisal for me?"

"You're joking," Mishal replied, aghast.

"Nope. She just told us we did okay then gave it to Shayib Ghalib, who obviously wouldn't do a thing until Ustath Assim came running after the paperwork." They laughed.

Muttrah Corniche was a long strip of road and walkway which outlined the North-Easternmost coast of Oman. The air smelled of salt. The sky found itself filled by long, warm blankets of clouds, and the bustle was limited. The car stopped just shy of the walkway itself, and the woman pointed towards a small coffee shop which, helpfully, had a sign which only read *Coffee Shop.*

"This is the place?" Mishal asked in surprise. Below him were red and grey bricks, a welcome change to the usual dust. To the right, he could see the walkway in all its beautiful glory, as well as the far-off gate of Muttrah Souq - a traditional marketplace.

Mishal threw a skeptical glance across to the coffee shop. Three of its outer walls were all glass. The interior was a one-room affair with three tables, and he could see only one employee inside. It looked like a cheap teahouse. "I'm surprised you chose this place. You're usually all about… Well-" he rubbed his fingers together, the universal sign for *expensive*.

"Hey, my life isn't centered around fancy things. Besides, they do have good juice, and it's close to Sarim." Eman walked in, throwing the employee a greeting as bright as the sun itself. She then chose a seat around one of the ceramic tables, which were painted with images of oranges and apples. "Besides, most teahouses aren't used to women," Eman added with a small scowl.

"Oh… sorry about that," Mishal said, unsure of what else to say. "Anyway, what do you want to drink?"

"Friend!" Eman said, a little louder to catch the employee's eyes. "Can I please have one lemon-mint? Mishal? I remember you have a sweet tooth. Maybe strawberry?"

A few minutes later, two juices in large glass pitchers were brought forth by the smiling employee, and Eman took care of the bill. She and Mishal sat together in the bright coffee shop, chatting about hobbies, how the library always ran out of the popular magic books, nothing serious.

"I've been trying to get stronger recently," Mishal said eventually, remembering something. "One of my weaknesses when I fight is that my fire isn't condensed enough."

"Right, but it does make you stronger," she replied. "You know what I think? I think you need a way to hit enemies from afar."

"I throw objects sometimes, but it's not good enough," Mishal said. He remembered the jinni by the ocean a few months back. If he had been able to attack it from far away, it would have made the mission far simpler.

"Right. Maybe you'll need Salim to fill that gap for you."

"I want to get stronger before he and I start going on missions regularly," Mishal replied. He thought of Asaad's overwhelming force, and how the Shayib still let him fight alone. *If I was that strong, it'd be easier to trust Salim.*

And still, even Asaad wasn't safe.

Mishal took a long, deep breath to steady himself. He felt guilty about not telling Eman about Asaad and Maymun earlier. However, now he recognized that he needed her help.

Eman put her juice down, interrupting her tirade about rising prices in coffeeshops, and eyed Mishal thoughtfully. "I'm not going to ask you if you're okay," she said quietly.

Mishal's thoughts ground to a halt inside of his head. "Huh?"

"You have a habit of saying you're okay, even if it isn't true," Eman explained, pointing towards. "You collect burdens like they're keepsakes, Mishal. I can tell you have more on your back than you can handle right now. So, tell me."

Mishal's heart beat faster as he put his hands on the table. He'd come here wanting to tell Eman everything and ask for her help. However, now his throat went dry like parched dirt, his fingers quivered. The youth swallowed. "I'm sorry, I should have told you earlier."

"If you didn't tell me before, I'm sure you had good reasons," Eman replied with a soft smile. She adjusted her hijab of the deepest blue, deeper than the ocean, then put her palms on the table.

Mishal took a deep breath. "There's an ancient jinni which will try to possess Asaad in exactly two months, and we need to tell him."

The patient smile slid off Eman's face. "Excuse me?"

Mishal launched into the story, starting with the CEO inviting him and Asaad to his office and divulging the information. He talked about them discovering the jinni was called Maymun while out on a mission. Researching the jinni extensively. Asaad's precautions and all the subsequent discoveries, including the mission with Salim in Qurum. Mishal ended the story with today's events, him finally discovering that the stranger he'd been speaking to occasionally was Maymun himself, and what the jinni told him.

By the time Mishal was done, Eman's hands had risen from the table, and she was now massaging her temples. "Let me get this straight… Ancient jinni. Extremely powerful."

"Yes," Mishal replied apprehensively.

"It's been preparing to possess Asaad for months."

"Possibly longer, we only found out a few months ago."

Eman's blue eyes, now ice-cold, shifted towards him. "Asaad might actually let himself die, rather than risk being taken over, and some factions at Sarim are considering killing him just to stop Maymun."

"Uh huh."

Eman sighed. "I take it back, you dolt. You should have told me this *ages* ago." She stood up. "Right, let's go find him."

Chapter Thirty-Five

Two days later, Mishal and Eman, along with Salim and the sad-looking woman from Eman's team, were standing on the outskirts of the city. None of them wore their Sarim uniforms, based on Eman's insistence. Instead, Mishal wore a light-grey shirt and black trousers; Salim scrounged himself a sweat suit which looked long past its sell-by date, and Eman had dressed in dark blue abaya and turquoise hijab.

The sky was a beautiful velvet. Stars glittered and winked far above, in an ancient light show. To the side, the moon watched on in apparent approval.

They were only a few kilometers away from the old airport building in Muscat. If Mishal strained himself, he could see a long line of lights behind the hills, to indicate the Muscat Expressway. However, Oman was filled with pockets of unexplored, rocky wilderness just like this one.

In between two hills, a small building sat in solitude, as if hiding away from civilization. It had been made completely out of clay, and from far away would have been mistaken for a large boulder. However, as soon as Salim had seen it, earlier that day, the man had laughed.

"What is it?" Eman's team member asked him.

"So cleverly hidden," Salim said, pointing at the building. "Did you check it out with ruh yet?"

The woman leaned forward, shielding her eyes with her hands as if to ward away the cool moonlight. "Um, I don't see much," she said.

Mishal leaned forward, sending ruh to his eyes. "It's painted with invisible paint. Bright yellow background with deep purple lavenders drawn across the wall," he commented. "There's text too. It says *Enter with your left foot.*"

The woman frowned. "E-Eman, is this place really alright?"

Eman took a moment to think before replying. "No, not really. It's a den of violence. But," she added when the woman's eyes went wide. “You don’t need to worry, Rawya. I’m here. The owner knows me and - worst comes to worst - I’ll take care of you.”

The woman immediately relaxed under Eman’s reassuring words. Mishal watched on, then looked at Salim, who was shouldering his backpack with apparent excitement at being out on a mission. Mishal didn’t think the ex-corporal would appreciate it if Mishal promised to take care of him.

Mishal clapped Salim on the shoulder. “Come on, let’s go.”

The man gave Mishal a grateful look.

The four exorcists were here to follow the rumor mill. Eman had a contact here: a friendly jinni who happened to hear more than most other people in Oman and who had often helped her with spying. Salim and Rawya didn’t know *why* they were here, only that Eman was following a lead.

The truth was that Asaad had gone off the map. Soon after Mishal’s discussion with Eman, they’d waited for Asaad at Sarim, then gone to his Seeb apartment, only to find it empty. Neither Sarim’s IT department nor the scouts’ magical search teams could find him anymore. They’d told Mishal that if Asaad didn’t want to be found, they had no way of breaching his defenses.

Mishal wasn’t about to give up that easily, however. This would become a game of chase.

“Are you ready?” Eman said, walking ahead. Mishal followed, feeling the soft crunch of gravel under his feet.

The one-storey building looked odd. Standing this close, Mishal could make out wisps of ruh coming out from the doorway, and could almost see the yellow-purple building warping slowly. “This door isn’t a portal,” he said. “It’s a cloaking technique.”

“Correct,” Eman said, coming forward to stand right in front of the house. “Are you all ready?” she asked.

They all nodded, and Eman took a step into the house with her left foot. She popped out of existence with a loud popping sound. Mishal followed immediately afterwards, taking a deep breath and then taking one step.

He felt pressure in his ear, causing him to blink, and Mishal was immediately assaulted with a variety of sights, smells, and sounds. He could hear laughing everywhere, as well as a well-meaning argument coming from two figures in the corner. He could smell food, fried meat of some kind as well as spices and rose water. Mishal stared.

The building was wider on the inside than it appeared from the outside. It had been partitioned into eighteen-seating booths inlaid with soft velvet seating mats. They were all rimmed with rich brown wood, polished so that they shone in the magical white light floating in small orbs near the ceiling. Each orb shone brightly, encasing a small colored symbol inside. The cooking smell came from a raised counter taken over one side of the building, where a multi-armed green jinni was cooking various different meals at the same time. His thick corded muscles seemed more suited for battle than cooking.

The jinni looked up, spotted Eman, and smiled. "Welcome back," he said. The jinni gave Mishal a quick nod. "He one of yours?"

Eman laughed. "He and two others. I told you I'd get you more human customers."

"And you did. Just as long as none of them come brandishing ruh, all are welcome!" The jinni said, flipping a leg of lamb onto a pan with his lower right arm. "And don't tell *that* faction at Sarim about this place. They don't care whether we're peaceful or not."

Eman gave the jinni a mock salute and booked a seating area. By that time, Salim and Rawya had walked in and were staring around them in wonder. Mishal looked back with a smile, enjoying their sense of wonder.

Music began playing hesitantly. The beats seemed to think about where they wanted to go - then, as they grew more confidant, a jinni flute player in the corner of the room picked up her instrument and blew out a slow melody, guiding the song along towards its sweet conclusion. Mishal felt the stress of the past few days vanishing, causing him to relax. The song, though wordless, brought to his mind an unbidden story of mistakes, of trouble and strife threatening a land of long grass fields. Of apologies which came late, but which were welcome. Of friendships restored and lovers reunited.

With a start, Mishal realized that the flute player, a jinni with long hair to her feet and lips larger than fingers, was casting a spell on him. Wasn't this similar to the jinni he and Salim had destroyed, less than a week ago? Mishal glanced at Eman, who now sat on the floor on a soft crimson mat under the lights. She smiled at him. "It's alright," she told him. "It's just for the mood, not to actually disarm you."

Mishal gulped, then walked forward and sat across from her. Salim and Rawya came in hesitantly and picked their spot on the floor, sitting far apart to maintain modesty. In minutes, the jinni had whipped them up a pot of strong Arabic coffee with cardamom, and they sipped on it.

"This is good stuff," Salim said, sliding into a more relaxed position on the floor, different from the attentive seating posture he usually assumed. The man looked as if he had lost three years off his age. His stern demeanor had disappeared. Even Rawya smiled, showing white teeth for the first time since Mishal had met her.

Eman nodded, giving them a small laugh. Just then, however, her head turned and she stiffened. "Alright, you two - enjoy yourselves. Mishal, if you please?"

Mishal felt relief. For a moment he'd wondered if Eman had made a mistake, bringing them so far into this place of whimsy. "You guys have fun," he said. Salim's face showed open dismay, but Mishal gave him a reassuring nod and followed after Eman. "We're just going out to talk, I'll call for you if anything happens."

The woman had reached a particular jinni, who was chatting with a number of friends. The sight of the jinni gave Mishal pause. It was about four feet tall, two feet of which belonged to a massive nose that sprouted upwards like a mountain. Each nostril was larger than a plate, and Mishal shuddered as he noticed long hairs protruding from the jinni's cavelike nostrils. He looked away, feeling slightly sick.

“Alright, Tanshiq?” Eman said brightly, approaching the jinni from behind. Immediately its eyes widened as it noticed her, and one of the other jinn around it frowned.

“Tanshiq?” the second jinni asked. This jinni looked human enough, save for long tusks and the muscles of a long-time boxer. The jinni looked confused, its eyes moving stupidly from Eman to Tanshiq. “I thought you didn’t like humans. This one of your friends?”

Tanshiq sniffed, a massive huff which actually ruffled Mishal’s hair. “W-w-why no, of course not!” the jinni said, gesturing wildly. “I would *never* be friends with these humans, bah!”

“No?” Eman asked, appearing genuinely surprised. The jinn around Tanshiq fidgeted, casting eyes at him. “Even though last month, you s-”

“Alright you, I’ve had enough of you slandering my honor!” Tanshiq said, eyes wild. He grabbed Eman by the shoulder and pulled her towards the door.

Understanding, Mishal smirked and followed the two of them. “Oh no,” he said loudly. “It’s a huge argument. Whatever will we do?”

The jinn around Tanshiq gave each other worried glances. One of them took a step a step forward. “Uh, should we help you out?” The big, muscular one asked. “We could back you up outside.”

“No need,” Tanshiq wheezed. “I’ll be back in a minute once I’m done!”

Eman and Mishal followed the large-nosed jinni out of the lounge. As soon as they stepped through the threshold, the lights dimmed, the scents and sounds of the resthouse disappeared, and the three of them found themselves once again out in the middle of nowhere, on the outskirts of Muscat.

Tanshiq stomped furiously, saying, “Damn humans, thinking you would dare to be my friends! I’m a powerful jinni, I am the one you fleshlings fear! The great performer of pain! I am the only thing that brings terror to melancholic hearts, I am- Eman, what the *hell* did you think you were doing?" The jinni added in a more hushed tone, as soon as the three of them were out of earshot.

"Sorry, Tanshiq, but I'm kind of in a rush today," Eman said.

"You could have blown my *cover,*" Tanshiq said with another massive sniff, pointing towards the building. Mishal was sure the jinn from earlier were watching them from the windows, trying to figure out how well the 'argument' was going for their jinni friend. "By the way," Tanshiq said, waving a dismissive hand at Mishal, "Don't worry, I'm not actually going to fight her."

"Uh, good to hear," Mishal said. He turned around so that he was facing the building.

"Why, yes. My acting was magnificent, after all," Tanshiq added from behind him.

"Uh huh."

"Eman Al Lawati is my savior."

This piqued Mishal's interest and he glanced back. "Is that so?" he asked. He'd always known Eman had a soft spot for harmless jinn, but he'd never heard this story.

"Indeed," Tanshiq said, his voice growing wistful. He sat down upon a black rock and smiled softly, looking up at the stars. "A few years back, in my days of ignorant rampage, when I was at my lowest moments - with red splattered at my feet, she found me."

"The red was from flowers," Eman explained. "He was caught stealing roses from flower shops to make an acting stage."

"Terrible days of crime," Tanshiq said, sniffling.

Mishal rolled his eyes. He should've seen that coming. However, it did warm him somewhat that Tanshiq wasn't exorcised over something so trivial. Eman had a good heart.

"Tanshiq, enough about that. I need to know something, and nobody's better at sniffing out secrets than you are."

Tanshiq leaned back, eyeing Eman suspiciously. His eyes glinted in the moonlight. "I have a feeling this isn't going to be enjoyable."

For a moment, neither of them spoke. The wind whistled between them. Mishal watched as Eman took a deep breath. “I need to find Asaad,” she said.

Immediately, Tanshiq’s face drained of all color and he stood up. The jinni threw his hands in the air and walked away. “No, no way.”

“You promised to help!” Eman said.

“Wherever I can!” he responded. “Girl, this is not something I can *do*. Asaad Al Nabhani is currently one of the most terrifying things to us jinn. You want me to *spy* on him?”

Tanshiq made to walk away, but Eman stopped him. "Tanshiq, this is important!"

Tanshiq whirled towards her, so angry that his massive nose turned red. "That man is powerful beyond belief. Do you understand what could happen to me if I even attempted to spy on him?"

"Then don't spy on him! I just need to know where he is!" Eman snapped, plopping herself down on the rock Tanshiq had occupied just seconds earlier. "There's something more to this, isn't there?" she gave Tanshiq a long look, making the jinni fidget in his place.

Reluctantly, Tanshiq turned around to face her. He cast his eyes to the left and right. “Eman, the shadows are stirring. There are whispers in the darkness of something dangerous coming. Something that has, in its hands, the power of ancient breakers. Something even the long-lived fear. The blackness comes, it swirls around, and Asaad Al Nabhani is right in the middle of it. The more powerful darkness jinn are in ecstasy, even the small-timers are strolling like they own the place. Can’t you reach out to that jinni friend of yours? Old Man Musafir?” he said desperately. “He can travel freely.”

Mishal frowned at that. Old Man Musafir was an ancient jinni who could run across its own pocket in timespace. He’d met the small jinni on one occasion, but… “Only Shayib Ghalib knows how to summon the Musafir,” Mishal said. It was the first time he'd spoken during the exchange. "Besides, Old Man Musafir wouldn't be able to find Asaad based on his ruh."

"Are you in a rush?" Tanshiq asked.

"You could say that," Mishal replied, with a grimace. Tanshiq had spoken of shadows gathering. Mishal knew that feeling all too well, from his experience during his last mission. A jinni had called for Maymun, and the darkness had answered. "You can help us, Tanshiq. I can feel it."

"Please, leave me out of this," Tanshiq replied, trembling. "The darkness is coming. When it arrives, I don't want to be one of its enemies. I'm scared."

Suddenly, a green light blazed. Mishal shielded his eyes as the green bead bracelet around Eman's arm glowed with inner power. Her ruh shifted to it, just a tad, and Mishal saw a massive ethereal paw coming out of it. The semi-translucent paw glowed as it rested on Eman's shoulder. Her blond hair was wreathed with blue-green power, lighting up her stern gaze. The abaya opened slightly, and Mishal saw that Eman had worn a metallica t-shirt under it. Just like Ahlam's t-shirt.

"Tanshiq," she said, a small smile peeking out of the corner of his eyes. "I want you to listen to me carefully."

Tanshiq took a step back. "You're leaning on threats now?" he asked with a sniff.

"Reassurances," the girl corrected. Eman stood taller, her ruh flaring to reveal a white lion's paw on her shoulder. "The darkness might be coalescing, my jinni friend, but you have nothing to be afraid of. We are the ones whom the darkness fears. We are the ones who took down Bani Safi, last year. We are the light in the darkness, and - as long as we are here - no harm will come to you. We are Sarim."

Mishal felt chills coming down his spine, watching Eman speak with such confidence. He longed to one day sound so sure.

Tanshiq stirred. "You'll protect me? Sarim protects humans, not jinn."

"We'll protect you. I swear it."

Tanshiq said nothing at first, but then he nodded. “Then there might be one way for me to help you.” Surprisingly, he reached into a pocket and pulled out a phone. “I’m sending you a contact right now.”

Eman’s ruh halted. The paw on her shoulder disappeared, as a puzzled expression crossed her face. “A phone number?” A ding sounded and she pulled out her phone, then looked at it. In the light the phone cast on her face, Mishal noticed her eyebrows rising higher and higher. “Inter-dimensional taxi service?”

“Indeed. The man driving that taxi should be able to find anyone, anywhere... If you get him to agree. And I doubt Asaad Al Nabhani would have had the presence of mind to take precautions against him.”

“It’s a jinni who drives a taxi?” Mishal asked.

“Not exactly, though I wouldn’t call the driver human either,” the jinni said, turning aside. “He’s the second long-lived which lives in Oman. He has made it so that memories of him slide off your mind like oil on water. That’s probably why you’ve never heard of him. If not for the phone number, I’d probably have forgotten too.” The jinni walked off back to the building where the jinn were busy chatting and laughing, and where Salim and Rawya would undoubtedly be worried. “I’ll tell my friends I gave you a stern talking to. Good luck finding Asaad Al Nabhani, agents of Sarim.”

Chapter Thirty-Five

The next day, Mishal lay on his bed, scrolling through Instagram. He couldn't be bothered to actually follow the news accounts, but he followed some other accounts which reposted short updates. That day, he saw a post about a virus called COVID. Most countries thought the virus would simply die out on its own, and he paid it no heed.

Eman? He typed on WhatsApp, sending the message to his friend. *Any news yet?*

I was just about to message you, came a quick reply from the girl. *Give me about two hours, then meet me near Mazoon Street.*

Mishal frowned. He knew the area well. Mazoon Street was nearby and led towards Mazoon mosque - a massive white structure in which he'd prayed upon occasion. A good chunk of the street was lined with cafes and stores which appeared rather trendy from the outside.

Mishal sent an affirmative to Eman and leaned back on the bed. His ceiling fan greeted him, spinning lazily as the sun fluttered through the window. A part of Mishal wanted to just stay here until the end of time. He didn't want to face the outside, with its traffic and smiling employees. He felt perpetually annoyed these days.

Still, he had burdens to shoulder. They needed to find Asaad, beat Maymun, and he needed to win back Salim and Salwa.

Life marches on regardless of people's feelings, and so the wise man learns to keep pace or get left behind.

Mishal stood up and felt the cold marble under his feet, letting it push him further towards alertness.

Shops had opened, but the Sultan's mourning period was continuing. Mishal's father had started tending his jasmine plants again yesterday. Safaa, his sister, was studying.

Mishal took out the small black coin, issued by Sarim, and pressed it. The goo oozed out, forming into the shape of a tired-looking boy who'd been frequenting the gym.

"Give me a minute, I'll be right down," he told the body-double, feeling guilty as he remembered the last time he'd used it.

"Give me a minute, I'll be right down!" the thing replied, more enthusiastically than Mishal wanted. However, it'd do.

The youth opened the black door and peeked out, looking on both sides to make sure Safaa was nowhere to be seen. He walked downstairs, only to find no one in the house. In the kitchen, he found a falafel sandwich, as well as a note which read, '*We wanted to go to the park*' scribbled in Safaa's careful handwriting.

An hour and a half later, Mishal was near Mazoon Street. In front of him he could see the blue sign of an Oman Oil Station, which appeared to also feature a Papa John's pizza. Midlly, Mishal wondered if their pizza was any good. His family had always leaned towards Pizza Hut, and he reminded himself to buy everyone pizza this Thursday. Now that his parents knew he could afford it, Mishal had started delivering dinner once a week. A smile touched his lips at the thought.

Off to the side, Mishal glimpsed a tall building with a yellow sign over it. He frowned. Seriously? A hotel *here* of all places?

He shrugged, then looked around. He could see a small cafe on the left side of the gas station. *Let's meet at the café at the start of the street, where the Oman Oil station is.* Part of him felt guilty at picking this café, but he knew he could afford it. Mishal's job in Sarim meant a ridiculously good salary for a sixteen-year-old. He was already leaving a small part of his salary with his parents, to help out at home. Mishal wished he could give more to them. However, he didn't want them wondering why a government 'gifted student' program was paying their son such a large sum.

The youth opened the cafe door, to be blasted by air conditioning and overly loud music. A Filipina employee leaned against the counter, appearing bored. She was singing aloud, her beautiful voice leaping in and out of the music blaring from the speakers. The employee practically leaped out of her skin as soon as Mishal arrived, the woman's lips parting in a greeting. She frowned as she noticed how young Mishal was.

“What can I do for you?” she asked, not unkindly, but with a general lack of interest. People tend to always think of teenagers that way, Mishal thought to himself as he smiled. He’d rather have casual familiarity than forced respect. “Can I please have a, uh…” his words trailed off. He’d forgotten the name of that drink Eman and Asaad usually ordered for him. “Something hot, with a lot of milk and some caramel. A little sweet.”

The employee turned around, tipping her green cap upwards. Mishal and she stood next to each other for a solid second, staring up at the green plastic sign painted to imitate wood. White scribbles filled the sign, and Mishal began to internally panic. None of the drinks on the sign had explanations. Oh no, how was he going to order a drink now? Mishal began to prepare himself for the inevitability of looking stupid in front of the woman. It was bound to happen, he guessed.

The woman turned back to him. “A caramel Macchiato?”

Mishal nodded enthusiastically. “Yeah, that’s the one!” He had no idea if it was.

A few minutes later, Mishal relaxed with his beverage at a table. It was good - better than he'd expected. Something about the unholy heat outside, mixed with obscene amount of sugar in this Macchiato thing, made him feel better about the prospects of the day.

The door swung opened hesitantly and Eman's head peaked in. Her expression perked up as she noticed Mishal sitting by the edge of the cafe.

"Hi," Eman told the employee. "How are you?"

The woman's eyes were wide open now, seeing two customers coming into the cafe at the same time. "Good, ma'am, how are you?" she replied, practically bouncing on her heels. "What can I get you?"

Eman took a long, hard look at the large green sign board behind the woman. Finally, she said, "Oh, just a latte please." She stood there to wait for her drink and motioned to Mishal that she'd be with him soon. "Business is going good?" Eman asked the employee.

The woman's eyes darted left, then right. Finally, she said, "Yes, thank you ma'am, very good." Her voice was weak with the lie.

Eman sat at Mishal's table. She was dressed in a black abaya, made out of a special Sarim material which made it easier to move in. The sleeves were outlined in thin white strips of string, and the blue of her hijab was darker than normal. Practical black sneakers hugged her feet. "Not exactly sure where we're going today," she said to Mishal, when he raised an eyebrow.

"I thought you planned this," he said.

"I did, but... Well, you'll see when he gets here."

They looked again at Eman's phone.

Inter-dimensional Taxi Service

"I don't understand," Mishal said. "Why would this person know where to find Asad? Inter-dimensional? I didn't even know this was a thing."

Eman shrugged. "Me neither. I guess it's part of what makes the service special. But Tanshiq sounded confident. The guy is going to meet us here, and I guess I'll just ask him where Asaad is."

The music in the background rose as the employee turned the volume up. Mishal frowned slightly, looking back at the employee, who was softly singing in tune with the music. "Tanshiq called him a long-lived," he said to Eman, raising his voice slightly. "I, er, I don't know what that is. It's been coming up lately."

Eman's sigh carried with it a warm, affectionate tone. "I constantly forget that, despite how capable you are, your training in Sarim was rushed because of that prophecy last year. You must have come across the term, 'long-lived' while reading?"

"Yes," Mishal admitted. "But it was never explained. I guess whoever wrote those texts assumed the reader already knew what a long-lived was."

Eman nodded, taking a short sip of her coffee. "Something about sugar and milk just makes a coffee ten times better," she said, with a smack of her lips.

"We're just hiding the coffee," Mishal replied. "Might as well get a milkshake." The girl chuckled.

"So, do you remember that mission we went on last year? When Old Man Musafir took us to a jinni that wanted to be exorcised?"

Mishal nodded. That jinni, which had a donkey's feet but a man' s body, had grown too powerful. It had exchanged most of its power for immortality. Now, whenever it built up its strength, it would call in Sarim agents to conduct an exorcism on it. "It'll reform in a few years," he said. "It's immortal, basically."

"Correct. This is a common way for powerful but peaceful jinn to manage their lives and stay out of conflict. Now, a long-lived is the human equivalent of that."

Mishal frowned. "Humans can't become immortal."

"No, but they can use up some of their power to increase their lifespans," Eman said, leaning forward. "It's extremely rare. The amount of power needed to even initiate the spell is enormous. Currently, as far as anyone knew, there was only one long-lived human in Oman. The CEO," she added when Mishal opened his mouth to ask a question. "He's currently in his third century."

Mishal's mouth hung open. "You're telling me the CEO is over three hundred years old?"

"Exactly," Eman said. "He kept some of his power, of course, but he's far weaker than he was before he became a long-lived. Shayib Ghalib told me the CEO also gained one particular power. It's a unique spell he can use only once. It's the threat of this spell which stops Al Nasr from directly declaring war on Sarim, by the way. If they ever try, the CEO could wipe them out singlehandedly, with that one spell."

Mishal didn't know how to process all of the information coming to him. "Wait," he finally said as if grasping onto something. "You said he's the only long-lived in Oman. A long-lived is something special, right?"

"Becoming a long-lived is the highest level of ruh possible for a single human," Eman replied with a nod and another sip. She looked out of the windowpane towards the few cars passing outside. "Nothing surpasses becoming a long-lived. No power can reach the unique spells they may unlock when they make that transformation."

"And Tanshiq said the *taxi driver* is a long-lived? How could there possibly be a long-lived no one knows about?" Mishal asked.

The door opened.

Chapter Thirty-Six

Mishal looked up as the coffee shop door opened, seeing a man in a white dishdasha with a strange red pattern crawling across its sleeves and down the front. It was an outrageous pattern, one which Mishal had never seen on a dishdasha before, but for some reason Mishal couldn't care about it. Mishal looked to Eman, hoping to continue their conversation. She smiled and opened her mouth.

"Hi," said the man who'd just entered the shop. He was trying to catch their attention, but his voice was emotionless. Mishal and Eman heard him and nodded, then turned back to each other, now slightly confused. Mishal could feel a haze clouding over his mind. His ruh triggered, unbidden. It grew hot, then sparked and burned, giving him the intense suspicion that he had forgotten something important.

"What were we talking about?" Mishal asked Eman. She gave him a confused look.

"Silly, it was about the, erm..." she rubbed her green bead bracelet absentmindedly. "Actually, I forgot too," she added.

"You were talking about me," a grey voice added, causing the both of them to jump. The man from earlier was sitting next to them at the table, already sipping from a cup of coffee - as if he'd arrived five minutes ago. "Terrible stuff," he said with a half-hearted roll of his eyes. The man's monotone made it seem like he couldn't care less if people heard him or not. His face was.. It was...

The haze grew inside of Mishal's mind, creating confusing mazes and leaving his thoughts wandering aimlessly. Mishal looked at Eman, not remembering what he had been thinking about. "So, we need to find a way of finding Asaad," he said.

"Ya Allah," the man next to them said with muted annoyance. He snapped his fingers. "There, can you remember me now?"

Mishal blinked. "Wait, who are you?" he said as his mind slogged along in an attempt to recover far-off memories.

"I'm the taxi driver you were just talking about," the man said. "Now, where do you want me to take you?"

Eman and Mishal stared at one another, stunned at how the man had been able to manipulate their perceptions so cleanly. Mishal shivered. Eventually, Eman began to explain. "We're looking for Asaad Al Nabhani," she said.

"Oh, *him*." the man said. "He's in trouble, I guess?"

"How'd you know?"

"That kid was always going to have a hard life," the man said softly.

When they finished explaining, the man stood up and walked away, gesturing for them to come along. By that point, the coffee shop employee was humming to herself, having completely forgotten that she'd received three customers that day.

"Where are we going?" Mishal asked the man.

"Interdimensional taxi service," the man replied with what could have been either a laugh or a cough.

Chapter Thirty-Seven

When Mishal heard the phrase 'interdimensional taxi service', a multitude of possibilities sprang to his mind. He imagined, for example, a car that hid within shadows. He'd considered the chance that the service would consist of portals drawn upon the ground. He'd even entertained the notion that the taxi was a living creature, perhaps a mighty Rukh which sprouted wings and carried jinn from one world to the other.

What he had *not* thought about, however, was that it might be a normal taxi.

The vehicle was square in nature, with one of its front lights blinking, the other long since dead. Its orange and white paint job was marred with scratches and rust spots. On the front, a Toyota emblem was held together by tape.

The man who'd led Mishal and Eman here now walked over to the car and slapped its hood. "Well, let's get in," he said.

Mishal and Eman shared a horrified look, then immediately turned around and began whispering to each other.

"Are we sure this is safe?" Eman asked.

"I don't know!" Mishal replied, his stomach knotting up with nerves. The car looked like a death trap, and the man had been easily able to entrap the two of them in his strange power. Even seconds after speaking with him, both Mishal and Eman had barely been able to remember the man.

If the man with the elaborate dishdasha meant them harm, there was likely no way to escape his grasp. Not if Mishal and Eman entered his rickety vehicle. Mishal considered this. He let the fear suffuse his body starting from his stomach, then rising like a chill wind going up his chest and freezing his mind.

Mishal was no stranger to terror. He had felt its black grasp before. However, over the last year he'd learned to embrace his fear and to wrestle it down when things needed to be done. Now, he nodded to himself.

“Eman,” he said to the girl. “Do we have any other way of reaching Asaad?"

Eman shook her head, casting a look back at the man. He was leaning against the car, watching them with subtle disinterest. The man wore a white dishdasha with a crimson pattern spreading like red smoke on the front and at the sleeves. Mishal had seen such a thing before on an Omani dishdasha: Starting from the man’s wrist, dark red swirls and patterns traveled across the white fabric, wrapping over one another until they trailed off at the elbows. His Kumma was a matching color, paired with a slight beard and vacant, hazy eyes. Mishal marveled at the fact that he’d missed a man with such striking clothing. Mishal could sense nothing from the man. Neither malice, nor kindness. The man stood there as if he could wait all day for them and not bat an eye.

“We need to find Asaad,” Mishal finally said to Eman. “If this man is the way to do it, I say we jump in. But hey, mister,” Mishal said, drawing the man’s attention. “Things won’t go well for you if this is a trap.”

The man smiled. “You think?”

Mishal nodded. “Nothing will stop us, and I’ll burn your car down if I have to. We need to find our friend.” He splayed his hands, wreathing them in a solemn, white flame, which he rarely displayed. It disappeared instantly, but it did the trick. The man pursed his lips, then nodded.

Five minutes later, Mishal and Eman sat in the taxi. Its interior was a mess, strewn with long-forgotten pieces of paper and plastic bottles under the seat. The seating must’ve been crimson at some point, but now dust had seeped into the fabric, and it swirled upwards each time Mishal moved. He tried to hold himself still as Eman sat behind him, moving to be in the middle of the car. She coughed as dust found its way up her nose.

“Sorry about that,” the driver said, his voice entirely vacant of remorse.

“Mess happens over time; it’s alright,” Mishal said, trying to keep the disgust out of his voice.

“Oh no, I had the car deep-cleaned last month. Unfortunately, yesterday’s customer was a desert ifrit. You know how they can be.”

Eman’s color drained from her face as she appeared to process the driver’s statement. Mishal himself felt a short shiver. Desert Ifrit were A-rank jinn, maybe B-rank for the hatchlings. The idea of this man giving one a *ride* felt ridiculous. “Um, I see.” He finally said.

“Are you ready to move?” The man said. When Mishal and Eman nodded, he turned on the radio, which blasted out some old-school Mihad Hamad music. The oud leapt out with melancholy, the drums marched to an irregular beat, and the driver hummed quietly to himself. He began to drive softly, slowly, changing gears as he went. Mishal began to notice that the man was driving down a lonely road. There were no cars on either side, no one to watch… and the man was heading straight towards a fork.

“Mr?” Mishal asked, fasting on his seatbelt.

The man hit fourth gear.

“Uhhh, I think that might be dangerous,” Eman said.

The man reached fifth gear, then sixth. “Now this is where it gets fun,” he said, his voice still empty as a winter breeze.

Just then, Mishal noticed that the man’s car had one more gear. Next to sixth gear, a slot only read ‘Interdimensional’.

As the man neared the fork, Mishal noticed a speeding vehicle coming towards them. They were about to crash into it. Mishal threw up his hands to protect himself.

The driver hit the last gear and, with a muted boom, the car flashed.

When Mishal opened his eyes, the world had transformed into a bizarre shadow of its former self.

Inside the taxi, things remained as Mishal remembered them. The crimson car seats were still dusty, he could see the air freshener hanging from the driver's mirror - Eman still sat behind him.

Outside the taxi, he could see a kaleidoscope of space. The taxi appeared to be flying across a tornado of colors, some of which Mishal had never seen before.

Up ahead, three suns hurtled around one another. A storm raged across a frozen lake far, far below the taxi's tires. Mishal's head spun from an intense sense of vertigo.

"What in the world is going on?" he shouted.

The taxi driver turned to him, his eyes empty with the boredom of a man who'd lived too long for his own good. "I said this was an interdimensional taxi service, didn't I?" Mishal could see comets flashing behind the driver, spinning off into space beyond the taxi. Without looking, the man swerved to avoid a whirlpool which had appeared out of nowhere. Still keeping his eyes affixed on Mishal, he added, "Now, you said Asaad Al Nabhani, correct?"

Mishal nodded. The driver closed his eyes for a moment, murmuring numbers to himself. His mouth began to move faster and faster as he calculated. Suddenly his eyes snapped open, with the light of multiple supernovas glinting off them, and said, "It was hard, but I found him. Brace yourselves." The driver veered with the steering wheel, his crimson hem getting stuck on the turn-signal indicator. The car whirled around, causing Mishal and Eman to both jump in their seats, and then the car turned *downwards*, swooping down out of the spiraling tunnel of lights. Mishal's stomach flipped, his heart leaped to his chest, and then with a satisfying pop, the car stopped.

They were in the middle of nowhere. Clouds hung in small marshmallow poofs in the noon sky, complacent in their stillness. Eman and Mishal paused, gathering their wits after the excitement of the past minute. "W-where are we?" Eman asked.

"Al Wusta," the driver replied in a dry sort of resignation. "It's my favorite, out of all the governorates. Unending wastelands, crowned in silence and loneliness. Even the jinn don't venture out much here," he added. "Anyhow, we've arrived. I'll get into contact with you once it's time to pay." He now turned to regard Eman, the darkness of his gaze expanding until Mishal felt a chill.

"Remember, one favor," he said, his voice sounding like wind over dead trees. "Now, go do your business, so I can take you back to Al Khoudh."

"One favor," Eman promised him. "Thank you." With that, Mishal and Eman left the car. They looked to the distance.

Around a hundred meters ahead of them, Mishal saw a figure - engulfed completely in massive storms of ruh. The figure had its hands up, as if to ward off the world around it. The storm of ruh was made out of figures, Mishal noticed. Figures in infinite shades of colors which spun around and around the figure. As Mishal watched, he decided that the storm was growing smaller, narrower in scope, as if it threatened to clamp down on the figure and strangle all life from Asaad.

"What is he doing?" he asked.

Eman shook her head. "Some of the symbols are vaguely familiar, but I don't quite understand," she said. "It's almost a sealing chant of some sort."

"It is," the driver said from his seat in the car. Mishal and Eman turned to look at him. He pointed one, solitary finger towards the storm. "He's trying to seal himself away from the world so that nothing can reach him, and so that he can never leave. An impenetrable barrier, in theory. I'd hurry if I was you, otherwise you won't be able to get to him anymore."

Mishal looked forwards to the figure, which was frozen in place. No, not frozen. As Mishal watched, he noticed that Asaad *was* moving, only with such miniscule motions that he seemed as still as an eternal statue. Mishal began walking towards him, with Eman at his side.

The first steps were easy. However, as Mishal made his way, he could feel a force warding him, pushing against him with increasing determination until he couldn't take another step. The feeling was akin to pushing against a mountain.

"This is his barrier?" Mishal asked.

"Looks like it," Eman said, with a grunt. Her limbs were trembling from the physical exertion, so powerful that Mishal could barely believe it.

“Asaad!” Mishal shouted. The figure in the distance started. Slowly, over the span of many seconds, the head turned to face him.

Asaad had not shaved in days, with outgrowths of bristles growing from his hollowed cheeks. The bags under his eyes had ballooned outwards, turning into massive grooves for a tired gaze. “You shouldn’t have come here,” Asaad said, voice laden with effort. “Our time is limited.”

“For what?” Mishal growled. Asaad shook his head sadly. “You’re not actually giving up, are you?”

“Mishal, I’m not sure I can handle this jinni,” Asaad said. “It’s my duty to the country to put myself in a situation where it cannot possibly have me and then escape. If it possesses me while I’m in the normal world, it’d be the worst magical disaster of the last thousand years. At least, this way, it won’t be able to escape. I’ll use the last flicker of my life to seal us both in a pocket world.”

Mishal’s mind spun. At the very least, Asaad wasn’t immediately destroing himself. However, this was hardly a solution.

“You don’t believe that!” Eman pleaded. In her anger, her jinni began to crawl out of the girl’s green bracelet. “The Asaad I know would just grin and promise he’d *never* let a jinni possess him. You know you can win!”

“Eman, you’re kinder than most,” Asaad said. “Would you bet everyone’s life on my skills?” At those words, Eman paused. Her strength waned for an instant and the invisible force pushed her like a leaf before a hurricane. She screamed as she blew away, back past Mishal and towards the taxi.

“Asaad!” Mishal shouted. “You can’t know for certain that you’ll fail!”

“I can’t know that I’ll succeed either.”

“Even if you fail, there are other ways to get around this, but you need to have people around to support you! To fight the jinni!” Mishal couldn’t believe the droop in Asaad’s shoulder, the hesitation Mishal could see on his face.

Asaad snickered. "Sarim won't help me. They'd rather that I die or be locked in by *them*. And they are optimistic in thinking they can seal me away so well that Maymun cannot reach me. Better that I prepare a perfect seal for the both of us. His presence and ruh will flow in, then be stolen to power the seal as we fight. The barrier will become an escapable prison, fueled by Maymun's own strength. Regardless of what happens, no power can leak out."

"You don't *need* to be sealed! We still have time to search for a way out, with your help! There are so many ruins we haven't yet searched! What happened to the Asaad who never backed down from a fight?"

Asaad frowned. "You're right," he said, giving Mishal hope. Then he added, "He doesn't exist anymore. He grew up and learned that when push comes to shove, the world matters more than he does. What would you do if you were in my place?"

As Mishal watched, Asaad turned around slowly. The force against Mishal redoubled. Mishal sent out his red fire, burning with anger, but it could make no headway against Asaad's wind. The force exploded against Mishal's chest in a sudden burst, throwing him head over heels and out of the barrier's area. He crashed to the ground next to Eman and the taxi.

With his back towards them, the strongest exorcist drooped once more, working to lock himself away from the world, all in an effort to save it. Win or fail, Asaad would never be able to leave this prison. Even now, Mishal could see glimmers in the ruh around Asaad. Runes locked together like intricate bricks, separating into a glowing prison.

Mishal stared, shaking with helpless anger. He couldn't say for certain that Asaad was wrong.

Chapter Thirty-Eight

The taxi ride away from Asaad Al Nabhani's realm of self-imposed exile was a quiet one. The air inside the taxi had taken on a heavy quality, becoming as cold and sharp as winter-wrought steel. Mishal refused to look outside the vehicle, instead keeping his eyes on his wringing hands as flashes of magic cast cold light on them. Even when a winged jinni knocked on the glass windows of the taxi to ask for directions to 'realm number twelve', Mishal barely spared the enormous bird a glance.

Mishal could feel Eman's depression looming behind him. It rose over his shoulder from where she sat in the back seat. He dreaded speaking to her. A strange feeling had come over him during the pride-crushing walk away from Asaad. Mishal knew this feeling well, from the painful knots inside of his stomach to the crushing agony building up in his chest. Mishal had grown up with it, had locked eyes with it in the mirror over and over again. He could name the feeling well. He'd been able to see it in Asaad's face as well, during that brief moment when he politely asked Mishal and Eman to leave him be.

Helplessness.

It was the lonely realization that your best efforts were doomed to crumble away, like sandcastles in the waves. It broke Mishal's heart to see Asaad in that state. Asaad, who'd always been the paragon of ego, with a sure-cock grin for every occasion, now felt as if the best thing he could do for the world was to lock himself away and accept death. Asaad could possibly still fight Maymun, but he had resolved to conduct their fight in an arena neither could escape. Even if he won, Asaad would never come back.

And Mishal didn't know what he could do to alleviate that feeling. Neither could Eman, evidently, based on her stillness in the taxi. The taxi driver, of course, offered no advice. He was here to drive them around, not solve their problems.

When the taxi finally screeched out from the magic portal and stopped in the dirt in Al Khoudh, the taxi driver sighed. "I took you there and back," he said. "Eman, the payment will be a single favor, as agreed. I will WhatsApp the request to you later."

Eman nodded, silently opening the door and stepping out. Mishal followed suit, his shoulders hunched to ward off the terrible feeling in his chest. Maybe he was trying to keep it choked inside of him.

"What now?" he asked.

Eman shrugged. "There's not a single exorcist in Sarim that could break the spell Asaad's spinning. They have no opportunity to find him, so long as he's locked in there…"

"He'd be safe from them, you mean," Mishal said. "In case they try to kill him."

"Yes," Eman said in a croak. "And he won't listen to us either. I wish I could force my way in, but I can't."

"If you could force your way in, what would you do?" Mishal asked.

"I'd punch him," Eman confessed, with a small laugh. Mishal saw the glimmer of a tear streaking down her face. "I'd punch him so hard he'd turn back into the cocky Asaad I know."

Mishal smiled but it was a pathetic thing, and when it vanished it took with it the last fleeting ray of hope that Eman could fix things. "So that's it?" he asked. "We give up on him?"

"We won't give up on him," Eman said, her hands clenched into fists. "I just don't know what do, and he won't listen to us. I don't know what to do."

Mishal shook his head. "There has to be something," he murmured. "Someone who could get through it him."

"Ahlam," Eman said with a sad smile. "He'd listen to her, if she was still alive."

Mishal stopped in his tracks. A memory had come, unbidden, to his mind. A memory he and Asaad had shared, shortly after Mishal was chosen to be the leader of eam 14. Asaad had been frustrated at the disagreements between him and Mishal, and said that he hated being a Shayib.

“Eman,” Mishal said suddenly, catching Eman’s attention. “I know who can knock some sense into Asaad.”

Chapter Thirty-Nine

On a later day, Mishal set up his clone at the house, murmuring an apology to it. Something about the clone made him feel massively, unbelievably sad.

"I wish you could have a life as well," he said to the clone, which now looked exactly like him - down to the blue, button-up shirt he was wearing.

The substitute looked up towards Mishal, its empty gaze sinking deep into him. "Life?" It asked, with hollow eyes.

Mishal grimaced. "I'm sorry, I'll be down later," he said.

"I'm sorry, I'll be down later," the substitute mimicked.

Mishal walked downstairs, pushing the creature out of his mind for now. He had no idea how the magical devices department had come up with the substitute coins, but they had assured him that the creature within lacked awareness. It could not be hurt, nor annoyed. Its only purpose in life was to look like him and to mimic a single phrase.

Downstairs, Mishal found Safaa arguing with his mother about school. Her grades had apparently been less than satisfactory in the previous semester. Their voices ricocheted back and forth inside the kitchen like missiles, and Mishal sprinted out the door before either of them could call upon him to mediate the discussion. Minutes later, he stood by the crossroads under the sun, waiting for Salim Al Ghafri to come pick him up.

Salim's car rounded the corner with its customary hesitant politeness. Salim always drove in slow deliberation, careful about disturbing passersby. The 2008 Mitsubishi Lancer reached Mishal and ground to a halt, before its windows slid down to reveal Salim, already mid-salute.

"Sir," he barked. "I'm happy to help. Let's do all we can to bring back our Shayib." He seemed to mean it. More than anything, Salim wanted to prove himself as worthy. He was competitive, deep inside.

Mishal had been mid-chide, something about how Salim shouldn't call him 'sir'. However, Mishal bit his response back. "Alright," he said. "Eman told you where to take us, right?"

"Right," Salim said, driving out towards the Sultan Qaboos street. Mishal glanced at the radio. Eman had spent the last few days spying through Sarim's records, trying to get information without Sarim management knowing she'd requested it. The forty-day mourning period over Sultan Qaboos's death had passed, which meant that radio stations had resumed their scheduled programming. However, something within him still cringed at the idea of turning music on. Mishal sighed. "Eman lives in Qurum," he said. "I can't remember the exact house, but she gave me a location via WhatsApp."

Salim frowned. "Turn that thing off, boss."

"How come?"

"I know the city well enough. Just tell me where it is," Salim replied with a grimace, before veering sharply to avoid a car. Mishal stifled a laugh, realizing that Salim was one of those stereotypical Omani men who hated asking for directions. It fit him, somehow.

After forty-five minutes, and around six wrong turns, Salim finally agreed to turn on the Google Maps link. "Qurum is a confusing area - it doesn't have solid urban planning!" he complained. Mishal nodded in supplication.

"Sure it is," he said.

"Wallah!"

Five minutes later, they pulled over next to Eman's house, a wide white building with marble-esque columns holding up a tiered roof. The girl stood outside the building, waving at them in a black abaya. Her green bracelet glowed in the sunlight as she opened the door and lumbered into the vehicle. "Did we think about lunch?" she grumbled.

"I, er, thought we could consider it later." Mishal said.

Salim laughed, pointing a thumb back at Eman. "Team Leader Eman's got her priorities all figured out. Anyhow, where are we going? Mishal hasn't said yet."

Eman made a face, then instructed Salim to drive towards Al Dakhilyah. As Salim took off on the expressway, through mountains and wadis, above cliffs which overlooked vast farmlands nestled between the rocky lands of Oman, Eman picked up her phone. "Hello?" she said, then paused for a few moments. "Um, we are…" she glanced out from the window. "I have no idea where we are."

"We passed Bidbid," Salim interjected.

"Bidbid's gone," Eman told their target, who was on the other side of the phone. "Yeah. Oh no, uncle," she added, her voice going sickly sweet. "We couldn't *possibly* stay for lunch at your house. Oh, well, if you insist then."

Mishal stifled a laugh at that. Eman was using the ancient Omani art of Mujamalah. Even if someone offers something you want, you must refuse it at first, just in case their offer had been insincere. Mishal had seen Sarim agents go back and forth for almost ten minutes, offering each other meals they obviously couldn't provide. The practice had always made him chuckle.

During the drive, Mishal took the time to explain more about Asaad's situation to Salim. At first, confusion clouded Salim's features. However, slowly, the confusion cleared into the embers of anger.

Finally, Salim sighed. "Why is everyone so selfish?" he asked. "First you push us away to make yourself feel better about keeping us safe-"

"That's not what I was trying to-"

"- then Shayib Asaad tries to lock himself in with a literal multidimensional, all-powerful jinni to try and protect Oman from the fallout *if* he loses the fight. Is everyone around me just determined to never ask for help?" he asked.

"Sure feels like it!" Eman exclaimed, from where she sat in the back seat. Mishal had the good sense to not try and contradict Salim.

"Well, I told you now, and I think we'll need your help," he said, then hesitated. "If you're comfortable with it, I mean."

"I'd be furious if you didn't ask me for help," Salim said, even though his eyes still sparkled with pent-up anger.

As the sun rose higher in the sky, Salim's Mitsubishi Lancer curved towards a road, lined on the left side by a low wall of brick. Mishal could see date palms, weeds, and other vegetation lining those farmlands. Salim turned left, deeper into Samail. Now the mud walls stood on both sides, mere inches away from the car as it navigated the tight turnways. Finally, Eman pointed towards an apparent dead end. "That way," she said.

"There's nothing there," Salim protested.

"A little trick our old Shayib had always been fond of," Eman said. "Head that way and a hidden path will make itself known to you."

Salim complied, forcing his car into the bumpy turn, where it trudged along, then dipped downwards suddenly. The vegetation took on a greener hue, and the very air seemed to shift, becoming more pleasant. Mishal's eyes widened as they reached the end of the road and came onto a farm, which had been previously invisible.

Date palms towered in all directions, looking like spiked brown towers with overgrown green crowns. Jasmine and lavender competed for their place, alongside ripe tomatoes and Sidr fruits. Bees hopped from tree to tree in a lazy dance, and a butterfly landed on the hood of the car.

Eman opened her window, letting in a waft of lavender, more potent than a whiff of perfume. She raised her hand in greeting. "Shayib Ghalib!" she shouted in delight. "How's retirement been?"

A hundred meters ahead of them, a small brick building sat, overshadowed by a massive outdoors seating area with sofas and cushions. An old man sat on one of the sofas, with a white cane in his hands. A grin sat on his mischievous face as he waved.

"Ah, boring in the best way possible, but I'm always here for my kids," Shayib Ghalib said. His smile passed over Mishal then, filling him with warmth.

They'd found Shayib Ghalib. Mishal could practically feel the weight lifting off his shoulders. Things would be alright.

Chapter Forty

A few minutes later, Mishal was sipping a cup of steaming sulaimani tea, spiked with an unholy amount of cinnamon and sugar. He sat in a sofa chair in front of Shayib Ghalib's hut, watching the birds flutter from tree branch to tree branch around him. Eman sat two chairs away. She'd taken charge of the conversation, but for now had steered it in whimsical directions. Eman had the kind of tact that politicians dreamed of, it seemed.

After seven blissful sips of cinnamon-laden tea, Mishal's glass lightened and he could see through the amber fluid to the farm. He turned to Eman, gesturing to let her know it was time to move on to the important part of their discussion. *We need his cooperation. And, more importantly, his commitment to siding with us - rather than with Sarim.* She responded by nodding and adjusting her seating position.

Shayib Ghalib, seeing their shared look, sighed. "I should have known you wouldn't be here just to visit an old man," he said. "Nor to talk about this new virus everyone's been hearing about. No, my cute little students have some sort of problem."

"It's not a problem," Eman said weakly.

"More like a disaster," Mishal added, feeling his spirits dampen at the upcoming conversation. Salim kept quiet, as he himself had only heard the bare outline of the story earlier.

"Out with it, then," Shayib Ghalib said, leaning forward. "I can tell this is going to upset me."

Eman frowned, then launched into the story, beginning with the Witch of Calamity's warning to Sarim's CEO months ago. When they mentioned the name of Maymun the demon, a soft hissing noise escaped from between Shayib Ghalib's teeth. "Oh, that's serious," he remarked.

A few minutes later, he stopped hissing and began growling instead. "Absolutely not!" he exclaimed. "Asaad cannot be thinking of just giving up!"

Shayib Ghalib's cup of tea sat forgotten on a small coffee table, now cold instead of steaming. The old man had grabbed onto his white cane, which was slightly burnt at the top. The cane shook in his knuckles. Ruh spread off of Shayib Ghalib in roiling strings of power, like smoke.

"We need to do something," Eman concluded.

"Absolutely," Shayib Ghalib said, but then he took a deep breath and sat down. "Oh, Asaad, why would you do this to yourself? You were such a strong boy. Cocky, yes - but who wouldn't be, in your position?"

Mishal sensed the hesitance in Shayib Ghalib's voice, and it filled him with worry. "You're going to help us, aren't you?" he asked, his voice pleading more than anything else.

"He's all grown up now," Shayib Ghalib said, covering his face with one hand. "If he thinks locking himself away from the world is the only way to save it… shouldn't we at least seriously consider that he might be right?"

Shayib Ghalib's words fell like a stone in the bottom of Mishal's stomach, making his fears ripple and echo. Asaad had spent months researching the ever-elusive truths of Maymun Al Sahabi, starting from the dark jinni's rise to power, then his fall and subsequent imprisonment at the hands of ancient scholars. Asaad knew Maymun's capabilities more than anyone, and he'd decided that fighting this jinni in the open was too risky.

Eman looked aghast. "Shayib Ghalib, Asaad has never failed before. He's one of us," she pleaded, trying to catch the old man's face.

"Eman, our job as exorcists is to protect others," Shayib Ghalib said. "Asaad is not a child. He has a right to decide for himself. If he has balanced the scales and thinks that it's best to take precautions, then who are we to force him to-?"

Shayib Ghalib had no chance to finish his sentence, because just then the sky flickered black. It was almost as if someone had flipped a light switch in the sky, covering the world with gloom.

An ominous power filled the farm, sending a chill down Mishal's back. He heard growls. Mishal turned from his seat and saw jinn staggering out from the trees.

Chapter Forty-One

It was a beautiful February afternoon, with the sun shining pleasantly warm… or at least it had been, just a few moments ago. The sky flickered, then a wide, dome-like shadow began to expand from the top of the sky like a curtain. The curtain cascaded down the sky, obstructing and dimming the sun. Jinn walked through the farm, shadows streaming from their limbs like smoke. Their eyes glowed with broken yellow light, like cracked lightbulbs.

"Enemy," the jinni in the lead whispered, sounding almost worried. "They want to stop the vessel from its chosen path. They intend to lead Asaad Al Nabhani astray. They are roadblocks to the master's return."

"What are these?" Salim asked, glancing from Shayib Ghalib to Mishal.

"I don't know," Mishal replied. "They look like some sort of shadow mughayabs. But how could they make *that*?" he asked, pointing towards the curtain blocking out the sun. Not a single ray could pierce the blockade, and its presence gave him a slight chill.

"Something else is behind these jinn," Shayib Ghalib said. "I can feel it somewhere out there." He paused, stroking the bottom of his beard in thought. His eyes shone black. "I suppose that's mine, then." The old man stood, brandishing his white cane. "You can take care of the small fries for me."

As Shayib Ghalib walked away from the outdoor majlis, one of the shadow-clothed jinn growled at him. The old man paid it no heed, instead focusing on wearing his brown sandals. He walked out across the uneven ground in a leisurely fashion, as if heading out to the store.

The jinni growled again, then took a step forward. It said, "You seek to stop Asaad Al Nabhani from accepting his fate as the vehicle for our master's return."

The jinni attacked, using the shadows to propel itself forward out of the trees and towards Shayib Ghalib, aiming for the old man's head.

"Old man!" Salim cried, but it was too late.

Shayib Ghalib turned his neck suddenly, staring directly at the jinni. His face was a visage of destruction. “Back off!” he snapped.

The jinni was catapulted away, thrown as if shot out of the end of a cannon. This was Shayib Ghayib’s power, the voice of kings, which took control over ruh directly and bent the world according to Shayib Ghalib’s words. The jinni flew away, crashed through the trees and disappeared into the farm, backing off just as Shayib Ghalib had instructed. Mishal saw Salim pull up his Al Sharqiyah-style Khanjar.

Shayib Ghalib waved a hand behind him as he left. “Like I said, I’ll take care of their boss. You make sure none of these small ones damage my house; I’m not done paying it off yet.”

Mishal nodded, feeling his spirit lift. Eman laughed and brandished her green bracelet. Poor Salim, who hadn’t been warned about Shayib Ghalib’s abilities, was left with his mouth hanging open.

Eman’s green bead bracelet glowed like the sun passing through spring leaves, and out of it climbed her beast, Sahib. The half lion, half snake growled at Mishal as it pawed at the ground, but he took it as a friendly gesture. Mishal charged up his own ruh, feeling a blue flame flaring up from between his fingers.

Mishal turned to look at Salim. A part of him wanted to tell Salim to run away. This wasn’t a mission. Salim could get hurt, or worse. Maybe he wasn’t ready.

However, Mishal shook himself. *Stop being such an idiot and trust your friends*, he chided silently. Salim had just proven himself in the Children’s Library.

Besides, Salim would kill Mishal if he knew about these thoughts.

"Are you with us?" Mishal asked Salim. “I think it’s time to test you.”

Salim's face settled into a sort of dumbfounded expression. However, as the jinn took a step forward towards them, Salim caught himself and saluted sharply. "Yes, Mishal!"

Mishal dodged the first swipe of a clawed jinni, frowning. At least Salim hadn't called him ‘sir’ again.

"Support, please!" he yelped, rolling beneath the jinni's fist. Trails of darkness spilled from its knuckles, eating away at Mishal's black, standard-issue Sarim fatigues. Mishal wished he could shoot fire at it from a distance, but the flames would dissipate before reaching the jinni.

The jinni grinned at him, its teeth jagged like the rocks of a thousand-year cave. "You are the one our master had relied on. However, we ought to be the ones who serve him. You cannot be allowed to hinder his plans. You *cannot* be allowed to grant confidence to the vessel."

"Asaad's my friend, not just your vessel!" Mishal argued, then spun around, trying to elbow the jinni in the face. Quick as a serpent, it shoved him from behind, sending him to the floor with uncanny savagery. Mishal's face slammed into the floor before he tucked himself into a roll and stood back up.

"Humans do not grant hope, they do not give confidence," the jinni said to him. "The fate of small beings is to feel small, to shrink before the size of an aimless future. Your hopes are *lies*," it hissed, then smiled, once again revealing those sharp teeth. "Every human ends up climbing into a lonely grave, built out of the built-up disappointments of existence. Why the bravado?"

Mishal growled, his hate rising, sending sickly black fire to his legs. The fire burst out from beneath his feet, burning twin trails of twisting fire around the jinni. It cowered from the heat, but Mishal still had more up his sleeve. He ran forward and smashed his fist into the jinni's shark-like mouth, causing it to stagger out through the fire behind it and fall to the floor.

"Salim?" Mishal asked, extinguishing the fire with a snap of his fingers. "Are you there?"

"Could use a little support, boss!" Salim replied. Mishal could see him holding his own against a lumbering jinni with massive legs. The jinni stomped its feet on the ground, causing a pop of black smoke, which appeared to magically suck Salim closer towards the jinni's waiting claws.

Suddenly, Sahib, the massive white and green lion, leaped through the farm, with Eman *riding him*. She waved her hands in the air, whooping with excitement, and her spirit beast opened its mouth wide. It snapped up a chunk of the jinni which had been attacking Salim.

"*Ya Rabbi*!" Salim screamed.

"Eman, too close!" Mishal shouted at her, before he could calm his nerves. "You almost crushed Salim!"

"Hey, it worked, didn't it?" she retorted as Sahib gulped the jinni up and swallowed once, then burped out a small poof of black smoke.

Mishal opened his mouth to compliment Eman. However, a growl behind him drew his attention. The jinni he'd been fighting was back on its feet. Moreover, he could see no flames clinging to it. Mishal frowned. His black flames were not supposed to be extinguished, once they began.

Then he saw that the jinni was missing its right arm. The arm lay on the ground behind it, burning furiously with savage crackles.

"You're insane," Mishal whispered to himself, realizing that the jinni had cut off its own arm to escape his fire.

"An insignificant price to pay for the release of our lord," the jinni remarked with a tut. "Come, let it be over with." Without another word, the jinni growled and slashed at the ground, sending a cloud of dust up through the air. Mishal heard another sound, and a slash of darkness emerged from the dust, flying through the air towards him.

Mishal immediately sent ruh to his forearms, igniting them in a giant wave of fire, then used the explosive power to repel the slash away from him. He immediately countered, sending fire crackling through the earth back into the dust cloud, where he believed the jinni was hiding. A satisfying yelp came from behind the dust, and he heard something drop onto the floor. Mishal turned to where Salim and Eman were working together to stop the last remaining jinni. Sahib, Eman's lion, was circling the jinni, taking small strikes here and there, while Salim used one of his many tools to confuse the enemy's senses. Finally, the jinni fell to its knees.

A scream rang through the farm. It sounded guttural, like the death throes of a beast, and above them, Mishal saw the black dome cracking. Massive black shards rained down from the sky, thankfully dissipating before they could hit the floor.

Eman's beast took the moment to strike the final jinni, dropping it, and Salim panted in exhaustion. "Is it over?" he asked.

"It's over," came Shayib Ghalib's voice from behind a bush. He emerged, looking none the worse for wear, and cleaning his walking stick with a napkin. The old man looked thoughtful. "And I believe these jinn actually did what you couldn't, Mishal."

"Which is?" Mishal asked, feeling hopeful.

"They convinced me," Shayib Ghalib replied. "These jinn were desparate to kill you, for fear you would cause Asaad to rebel. This tells me that they were afraid of…" He left the sentence unfulfilled.

"They were scared of us convincing Asaad to fight," Mishal said, following his train of thought.

Salim leaned closer to Eman. "I think I'm missing something."

"The jinn, Maymun's followers, think Asaad has enough ruh and willpower to win. They want Asaad to give in to Maymun willingly."

Shayib Ghalib laughed, "Our young friend *could* overcome his possession, if he tried hard enough. He *can* defeat Maymun and come back unscathed after all. Which means that I need to go knock some sense into him to stop him from giving up," he said.

"You'll help us?" Eman asked, appearing like she couldn't believe her ears.

"Just lead the way," Shayib Ghalib said. "Even if he tries to push me away, I'm sure my voice can reach him."

Chapter Forty-One

Half an hour after the battle with the jinn of darkness, Mishal, Eman, and Salim were sitting back at Shayib Ghalib's outdoor majlis. Eman had a piece of paper out, and was connecting the relationship between different factions in the current struggle, for Salim's benefit.

"This, on the bottom right of the chart, is us," she said, drawing a circle around their names. "There's not much that we can do, but we care deeply about Asaad's wellbeing. We don't want him possessed by the great jinni, but we don't want him to lock himself away from the world and die in order to keep it out."

"So far, so good," Salim said.

"Sarim has more say than us in this struggle," Eman continued, playing with her green bracelet. That day, she had chosen to wear a t-shirt under her open abaya. The t-shirt read 'Looking Out Ahead'. "I used some of my spying skills over the past days, and it turns out that over half of the Council of Shayibs has decided that Maymun is just too dangerous. Asaad has reluctant allies in Sarim, but the organization at large thinks it could lock Asaad inside a specific kind of chamber - thereby protecting him from possession."

Salim frowned. "That doesn't solve anything. Wouldn't he be susceptible to possession as soon as he leaves?"

"The thing is, he isn't supposed to leave," Mishal said angrily. "They're hoping to keep him there forever. Well-fed but trapped, just like a bird with its wings clipped. And I'm not about to let my friend go through that."

"Agreed," Eman said, giving Mishal a sympathetic look, before returning to her piece of paper. "So, Sarim is over here. We're part of Sarim, but we're currently out on our own." She drew a line connecting the first circle and the second, but then scratched out the line with a sense of finality. "The other side, our enemies, seem to also have two sides: Maymun and his followers aren't seeing eye to eye, for some reason."

Shayib Ghalib inched closer, sipping his tea. He'd overused his ruh in the past battle – signs of old age, he called it – and needed to recover before the group could go talk some sense into Asaad. "Ah, a bad guy map?" he asked, looking over at Eman's piece of paper. "I guess you learned admin work as well as spying, last year."

Salim asked, "What's a bad guy map?"

"It's a way to find out how to act without enraging all opposing factions at once," Eman said. "You draw out the different factions, then list out what they want and how they are related to one another, as well as what actions would make them immediately hostile against you."

"I don'tunderstand," Salim said. "What's the point?"

"The point is to show you which of your actions would be the most dangerous. For example, right now if Asaad appeared on full display in Muscat, he might get attacked by hoth Sarim and Maymun's jinn at the same time. So," he said, drawing an X in the air, "best that he not do that."

Salim tapped his finger against his backpack of magical tools, which was placed on his lap. "Why are Maymun and his followers not on the same page?"

"Maymun told me that he openly invites Asaad to fight back against him. However, Maymun's *followers* are trying to kill us to stop us from encouraging Asaad in this fight," Mishal said, shaking his head. "It's almost as if they don't have the same goal. Doesn't make sense."

"It does, if you consider what Maymun told you in the past," Eman interjected. She drew two more circles. "This is Maymun, and these are his followers. I think Maymun is confident he can possess Asaad. His only concern is the vessel breaking too early because the vessel hasn't gathered enough ruh. The followers, however, have the exact opposite view: they've heard of Asaad from other jinn and factions in Oman, and they're worried about him overwhelming Asaad. Remember what these last jinn were mumbling?"

Mishal felt a shiver, remembering the jinni which had cut off its own arm to keep fighting him. "They were talking about hope being less than worthless," he said. "They wanted Asaad to just give in to the possession."

"There," Eman said, adjusting the circles on the piece of paper. Shayib Ghalib began to mumble, causing lines of ruh to lift up off the page. Now, Mishal could see the circles orbiting one another like celestial bodies atop the piece of paper. "They have the same final goal, which is to possess Asaad. But they haven't agreed on the *how*. It's the same as our side. We've agreed to stop Maymun, but *one* of the sides has chosen a wrong approach. I won't say which," she added sarcastically.

Mishal was distracted, looking at the circles of ruh floating in the air. Thanks to him and Eman being instinct-type exorcists with inherent abilities, they couldn't manipulate ruh other than to use the powers they were born with. Only external types, like Shayib Ghalib and Salim, could. Mishal felt a pang of jealousy, even though he knew that Salim, and even Shayib Ghalib, had less overall power in their cores, which was why they couldn't manifest inherent abilities. Even Shayib Ghalib's *Sout Il Mulk,* the Voice of Kings, the seemingly impossible ability to compel things to his will using his voice, was just a skilled application of spells any agent could use.

Mishal shook his head to clear it and said, "The jinn and Maymun have opposing goals. This is something we can use to our advantage. Maymun himself will not interfere to kill Asaad early. He's likely to even make it more difficult for his followers to locate Asaad, especially if they're borrowing his ruh."

Shayib Ghalib added, "But on our side, children, there's much more to lose. Sarim wants to hide Asaad from Maymun. Knowing their capabilities, the only way they could do that is by a barrier which stunts Asaad's current, and possibly future capabilities. Maymun's jinn want to kill us and to force Asaad into accepting Maymun, and Asaad himself is aiming to trap Maymun, holding them both within a prison for all time. Seeing these jinn, I can't believe I even considered letting Asaad choose such a foolish escape. No, he *must* not give up hope. I know of Maymun's power quite well. But I know Asaad Al Nabhani even better."

The golden circles in the air shifted, reflecting Shayib Ghalib's words. A new faction now existed. It was simply called *Amal*. It had a singular goal: make sure Asaad beats Maymun and returns safe.

The old man stood up, giving Mishal and Eman a look of pride. He began to chant slowly, then wave his fingers in motions Mishal vaguely understood. He could see the ruh coming off Shayib Ghalib in waves, transforming into clouds and windows, methods of transportation in ancient Omani legend. Shayib Ghalib was channeling spatial power, one of the great powers of exorcists. Furthermore, he was summoning something. No - not summoning. Mishal understood as he saw the gentelness with which Shayib Ghalib moved. This was a friendly invitation.

A door opened in the air, and from it stepped out a small, furry creature, holding a yellow cane. The creature squeaked, then bowed to Shayib Ghalib.

"Old Man Musafir!" Mishal exclaimed in delight.

"Thank you for coming, old friend," Shayib Ghalib said, then turned to Mishal and Eman. "I have hope. If there ever was an exorcist that could live up to this challenge, it is Asaad. And he needs to know that. I'm proud of you, young ones, for sticking to your beliefs. Especially you, Mishal. Now, let's go knock some sense into Asaad." He grabbed his white cane. "Describe to me where you last saw him."

Chapter Forty-Two

Mishal walked across a glowing road which looked as if it had been stitched together from a thousand different brown bridges. He could see cold concrete mixing together with tired cobbles, as well as vibrant wood and bright-colored marble. In the spaces where he saw no physical manifestation of a bridge, Mishal saw something even stranger: roads of glistening colors, stretching out beneath his feet. The entire bridge was suspended in a horizon darker than night. Beyond the road, there was nothing.

Ahead of Mishal, the ancient Old Man Musafir led the way. It was a small jinni, with brown fur covering most of its body - save for a white, leathery face with yellow dimples and round black eyes. Mishal had only been on Tareeq Al Khayal once before, when the jinni Musafir had taken him, Ahlam and Eman with Shayib Ghalib to exorcise a long-lived jinni waiting to die. This time, Mishal and Eman were giving Old Man Musafir directions, based on their memories of the last time they visited Asaad.

"Yes, it was in Al Wusta-"

"Definitely, I couldn't see any mountains anywhere, and it was windy!" Eman interjected.

"Exactly!" Mishal added.

The Musafir walked between the two young exorcists, nodding its head politely or squeaking in recognition when they described something it could identify. The Musafir was unable to speak Arabic, but it could understand humans just fine. In return, they had no idea what it was saying to them. Mishal trusted that the Musafir was a good jinni with all the right intentions, but he wondered if it would actually get them where they needed to go. Luckily, Eman was there.

"You're really good at describing places," he told her, as they walked.

"It's something you pick up while spying, I guess," Eman replied. "You learn to take note of all sorts of odd details, because there's really no telling what might be important." She turned her attention to the Musafir, trying to tell it about a group of seven trees she had noticed near where Asaad had been. The Musafir nodded sagely, seeming to understand Eman's descriptions.

Shayib Ghalib and Salim walked four steps behind Mishal's group, discussing things quietly. Salim appeared to be absolutely smitten with Shayib Ghalib, or so Mishal thought. He had opened his massive backpack and retrieved a notebook, in which he was writing down things the old man told him. Shayib Ghalib, for his part, was talking with an air of self-indulgence, like an old general imparting wisdom on a starry-eyed new recruit. Mishal was glad to see the two talking. Maybe Salim could pick up some tips on how to use his ruh more efficiently.

The Musafir stopped suddenly and turned left, where the bridge stopped. It began waving its cane in the air in magical gestures. Bits of brick blew in from all around, gathering at the Musafir's feet. With a shattering sound, a crack appeared in thin air in front of the Musafir small body. Through the crack, Mishal glimpsed wastelands illuminated by moonlight. The Musafir squeaked something, something that sounded like a question.

"Is that the spot?" Shayib Ghalib translated from behind them, and Eman shook her head. She offered a few more suggestions, and the Musafir led them five more steps before stopping once more. This time, when the portal opened, Eman gasped.

"That's it!" she said, not waiting for the query this time. "Seven trees in a 'C' shape, that's it! Asaad is close to here!"

The Musafir bowed and they thanked it. Mishal led the way out of the portal, with the rest of his companions trailing behind him. As soon as his feet touched the rocks of the wastelands in the middle of Al Wusta, Mishal knew something had gone wrong.

The storm, which had coalesced around Asaad a few days ago, had grown massive now. He could feel enormous ruh spinning, whirling around a figure in the distance. The power pulsed in fewer colors now, growing faded, more solemn. The trees in the distance had knelt before the force of the wind, looking like sentinels watching Asaad's act of sacrifice.

Mishal, Eman, and Salim looked onto the scene with horror. "Is it almost over?" Salim asked, shielding his eyes from the turbulent wind.

"I can't tell," Mishal replied. He could see Asaad's ruh, which looked like nebulae swirling within an infinite galaxy in confusing patterns. The ruh seemed to be folding within itself, in a threat of vanishing completely.

"I can," Eman said, her voice quiet. Suddenly, she shouted. "Asaad! Don't do it!"

"Asaad!" Mishal echoed, adding his voice to hers in an attempt to snap Asaad out of whatever desperation had grasped him. Ruh filled his throat, strengthening his vocal chords. "Asaad, fight with us!" his voice cracked from the sheer force of the shout, and his throat grew parched. He attempted to take a step forward, but a sudden gust pushed him stumbling back. Mishal stood there, barely able to keep his ground against the onslaught of power. "Asaad, you don't need to be alone!"

The figure in the distance appeared not to hear them. Mishal imagined Asaad all alone for the past few weeks. His stubble would have gotten overgrown by now. He'd look terrible, but focused on the final spell designed to protect the world around him. This spell would lie in wait. As soon as Maymun attempted to enter, the jinni's power would add to Asaad's, sealing them in together. Forever.

But that wasn't who Asaad was, Mishal knew. Mishal had come here determined to save Asaad, no matter what. "Shayib Ghalib!" Mishal begged.

"I've got it from here," a gruff voice said. The voice sounded like a furious torrent, flowing under a seemingly calm river. Mishal turned to see Shayib Ghalib standing there. Except it barely looked like Shayib Ghalib. In his anger, the old man appeared taller than a palm tree, harder than a rock, and more dangerous than an unsheathed dagger. Shayib Ghalib's ruh, which took the shape of a mouth, flickered atop his turban-wrapped head. His hands were shaking.

"Boy, you will listen!" Shayib Ghalib said, unleashing his power called *Sout Il Mulk* - The Voice of Kings. His words echoed like thunder, traveling farther than should be possible, ripping through Asaad's ruh barrier.

The figure in the distance turned, cocking its head painfully as it tried its hardest to resist the gesture. It had no choice but to comply.

"Come here!" Shayib Ghalib commanded, in that terrifying voice. The figure shook violently as it was dragged towards them, step by painful step, leaving the storm of ruh roaring behind him even as it the winds weakened. Soon, the figure got close enough to be seen.

Asaad appeared in terrible shape. His beard had indeed taken over his face in large, scraggly black patches. His eyes were wild and defiant, and he'd lost most of his lean weight. Eman clapped a hand against her mouth, and Mishal shook his head in disbelief as the figure slowly, but surely, traveled distance which separated it from them. When it got close, Asaad sat down forcefully on the rocks in front of Shayib Ghalib. The storm was far behind, roiling furiously.

Shayib Ghalib sighed, no longer sounding angry. "I leave for less than a year, and this is what happens?"

Asaad chuckled, sounding as if his mouth was filled with sand. *I don't think he has had anything to eat or drink for the past weeks,* Mishal thought to himself.

Asaad said, "Bad time to leave, I guess."

"I admit that I had my doubts before," Shayib Ghalib said. "When the children came to get me, I thought to myself that Maymun was a jinni like no other. That you must've done your homework about him. That you were a grown man, and knew when to make a painful choice for the sake of others. That it was your choice if you wanted to lock yourself away from the world, just to keep Maymun from harming it."

For a long time, neither of them said anything. Asaad was shaking. "You sound as if you changed your mind."

"And if I have?"

“If I lose, everyone in a thousand kilometers could die. Maymun has enough time to do that before his power overspills and turns me to dust. What do you say now?"

"I say that I'm sorry," Shayib Ghalib replied. "I'm sorry for not believing in you before. Now, I do. Asaad, you will *not* lose. You are the ultimate exorcist. Maymun should be afraid of you, not the other way around."

"And *if* I lose?" Asaad asked, insistent. He seemed to want reassurance. Mishal realized this with a dawning sense of horror. Asaad wanted to know that if the worst happened, someone would end it.

Mishal refused. "I am selfish," he said quietly, before Shayib Ghalib could speak. "I want to make it so that everyone is ok."

"We all want that," Asaad said, not meeting Mishal's eyes. He looked hopeless. "We all want to protect Oman from jinn."

"Asaad, *everyone* includes you too," Mishal said softly. Asaad's eyes widened. All this time, Mishal had simply relied on him to be invulnerable, to be strong and cocky. However, Asaad was only a man. And now, Asaad was in over his head. Mishal wanted to worry about him, to save him. "You matter just as much as everyone else. You're my dear friend."

"We've lost too many loved ones, Asaad," Eman added, her eyes a little wet. "In wars, on beds, across the country. It doesn't have to be that way for you too. We care about you, ok?"

Shayib Ghalib cleared his throat, then said, "I raised Ahlam and you like you were my own born. I've lost one baby, Asaad. I don't want to lose another."

Asaad looked as if he'd been slapped. "Me? But I'm a monster. A deformity of ruh. My own mother cast me away when she realized how much power I was capable of.”

Shayib Ghalib shook his head and dropped his cane, which clattered to the rocks. The old man brought his palms down. He leaned down and embraced Asaad. "No, you're my pride," he said, his tears dropping from his cheeks and onto Asaad's shoulder.

"Once, you told me that Shayib Ghalib was better at listening than anyone else," Mishal urged. "How about you talk to us? You don't have to carry this burden alone, you know."

Hesitantly, Asaad raised his own arms and put them around Shayib Ghalib's back. As he sighed long and hard, the storm behind him cleared into small wisps of ruh.

Asaad began to speak.

Chapter Forty-Three

"My life has been easier than many others," Asaad said. "After Mom tried sacrificing me and failed, I mean. I've been blessed with power from infancy. Jinn bowed to me, mere months after my birth. I lived with them for a while. And after that, I had old Man Ghalib and Ahlam to keep me company. It's been a good run," he said with a small laugh. "It didn't seem like too much of a sacrifice to lock myself in with Maymun in a construct."

Shayib Ghalib looked upset at this phrasing, but he kept quiet. Mishal struggled to do the same. He knew that Asaad's mother was the Witch of Calamity, and that she had done *something* to give him his signature ruh. However, Asaad had never been forthcoming with the details. Seeing Shayib Ghalib's expression now, Mishal thought Asaad's childhood hadn't been as pleasant as he put it.

The five of them sat in the middle of the wastelands. A fire crackled in the middle, made by Salim using one of his odd tools. Shayib Ghalib and Asaad were across from each other, the fire licking up flames in the space between their faces. Mishal could see Eman sitting on the other side of the fire. Her expression held a pent-up tension. "But Asaad, we've seen you do the impossible again and again. What made you think *this* would be your limit?"

"You've seen how powerful I am, haven't you?" Asaad asked with a smile. Eman nodded. "Well, Maymun told Mishal a few weeks ago that I *just* became a viable vessel for him. Just barely," he said, bringing two fingers close together.

Eman's face turned to one of disbelief. Mishal remembered that horrifying day, when Maymun had revealed himself in the hidden library within Sarim's pit. "He visited you, didn't he?" Mishal asked

"He showed up right to my Seeb apartment. All of those barriers, and he just traipsed through. Nothing I tried had any effect."

"What did he say?" Salim said.

"That he was sorry," Asaad said. "That scared me more than anything. I'd read of his terrors, of his power. In his prime, he'd done unspeakable things in this realm. But now? He just looked at me with pity. That was worse than anything I'd imagined."

Mishal shivered, conjuring the image of Maymun with his trimmed beard and black eyes standing in front of Asaad's sitting form, looking sad. "Did he tell you about his intentions?"

"The same thing he told you," Asaad said. "That he just wanted to feel the sun on his skin. That he wouldn't hurt anyone except me, his vessel. That I would last a few days at the most. He wants me to grow stronger so that I can sustain him longer."

"And his followers are scared of you, so now that you've reached the baseline of power needed to become Maymun's vessel, they would rather have you give up on growing stronger," Mishal reasoned. He mulled this over in his head while the silence grew more intense. "Asaad, I think what you need to do is clear."

"Hm?" Asaad asked, leaning forward to listen. Shayib Ghalib and the others looked troubled, but Mishal felt the truth resonate in his heart, clearer than ever before. "What do you mean, Mishal?"

"Now that you've become a viable vessel for Maymun, there's no going back," Mishal said, putting his hands out, palms up. "I know this single fact: You are the best. You always have been. If anyone has a chance of overcoming Maymun's possession, it's you."

"Would you say the same thing, if it was you?" Asaad asked with a sly smile creeping through his expression. It was the first smile Mishal had seen from him in weeks, and it felt truly refreshing.

Mishal crossed a hand over his heart. He could feel the attention of those around him. It caused wrenching anxiety to course through him, but Mishal didn't care. "Asaad, you are different from me. I absolutely, truly believe that you can do this."

Asaad raised an eyebrow. "What happened to the worrywart? I thought you'd be agonizing over a barrier to stop Maymun from reaching me."

Mishal hesitated. In his small room in Sarim, he'd gathered tome upon tome explaining the intricate details of setting up barriers. Some would even be compatible with his white flame, which had the property of extinguishing attacks. But the more research he conducted, the more he realized than none of these proposed barriers could hold Maymun in check. Mishal said, "Recently I've learned how to trust people to take care of themselves. Even though it's scary, I know you can handle this."

Eman cleared her throat loudly, and everyone turned to her. "But…?" She prompted.

Mishal remembered himself. "B-but you don't need to be on your own!" he hastily added. "Let us support you. I don't want you to hurt yourself in the hopes of protecting Oman."

Asaad tutted. "You sound like a mother. Are you going to ask me about my dinners?"

Mishal ignored the comment. "Stay here, if you need to minimize the risk, but spend the coming weeks strengthening yourself. You *can* overcome Maymun. I believe it, and so do Maymun's followers," he added with added confidence. "They wouldn't be so scared otherwise."

"I agree," Shayib Ghalib said. "I could feel their terror when we fought. Maymun's power is unfathomable, but so is Asaad's. My boy, the rules have never applied to you. Use *Abbath* to overcome this obstacle."

"When I was training," Salim put in hesitantly. "There was one name that I heard constantly from the other exorcists. Asaad Al Nabhani. They all had different things to say."

"Something bad?" Asaad asked with a wry smile.

"A lot of it was bad," Salim agreed with a teasing laugh. "But everyone agreed on one thing: there has not been a single jinni born that could defeat you."

Asaad seemed to grow with every comment from his comrades. However, he now looked at Eman. Mishal also looked towards her, hoping she would also encourage Asaad.

Eman gave Asaad one of her smiles crafted out of kindness and concern. "Asaad, what do *you* think? Let go of your concerns for a moment. Imagine you were put in a vacuum. What would you want to do, if you could ensure nobody else was put in harm's way, and you could leave unharmed?"

Asaad paused. "If there was no chance of Maymun attacking Oman?" he asked.

"Yes."

Suddenly, a feral grin spread across Asaad's face. "I would want to face off against him. I would try to tear him to shreds, no matter the cost."

"Wonderful," Eman said, standing up and dusting herself off. "So that's what we'll try to do."

Without a single word more, the woman turned from them and walked away from the fire. She pulled out her phone and began to type furiously. Mishal and the others stared in confusion. As they watched her become increasingly animated, a mental image suddenly returned to Mishal's mind: An old white and orange taxi.

That was it, he realized. There *was* a way to isolate Asaad with without permanently sealing him. The thoughts whirred faster now. Mishal understood Asaad's needs, and he could see a path towards fulfilling them. Maybe they could even find a pocket space which weakened Maymun.

"Hey, Eman!" he shouted in glee, running behind her.

Chapter Forty-Four

"Absolutely not," the strange man said. "I will *not* come with you to negotiate with that elder of yours." Just like the last time they met him, he was dressed in the white dishdasha, which had a strange red pattern which swirled from his wrist and traveled all the way to his neckline, then down to his waist. This time, the man had driven to Al Wusta, but he'd declined to accompany Mishal and Eman to where Shayib Ghalib waited. Instead, he'd instructed Eman and Mishal to come alone behind a cliff, where they found his simple taxi waiting.

Right now, the man was giving them a hard time. He wanted nothing to do with either Asaad Al Nabhani or Shayib Ghalib. "I've already helped you enough," he insisted.

"But this is crucial!" Eman replied to him. "If we give Asaad a separate place to train and fight in peace, he can grow that much stronger to save everyone."

In a dead voice, the man said, "You think I can't sense him from here?" Even now, Mishal could barely feel any emotion from the man. The taxi driver's eyes held the stillness of a hallow rock. "Asaad is shining like a bonfire. And yes, he *can* get stronger. But why does it have to be me?"

"Do you know anyone else who could take Asaad to a completely un-inhabited dimension, leave him there, then return?" Mishal asked, starting to get annoyed.

"Well, no," the man replied. Apparently anticipating a long argument, he opened his car trunk. Immediately, a dark purple light began to shine from inside the trunk, and the man deftly pulled out a bisat, then slammed the trunk shut. "Can't the Musafir take him to the top of a mountain or something?"

"How do you know about Old Man Musafir?" Mishal asked.

"Heh, Old Man indeed," the man said sarcastically. "Regardless, can't it take him somewhere remote?"

Mishal turned to look at Eman, but she shook her head. "You saw the look on Asaad's face. He's ready to give a lion's fight, but only if we eliminate any chance of other people getting hurt. A mountain, a different country - none of that's any good to him." She turned to the man, who was sitting down on the rug giving them a dead stare. "What do you say?"

"I say that's just his whim," the man said. "I know a thing or two about whims."

"I considered something else," Mishal said. "You've said you can access different dimensions. If one of those is filled with light ruh, or has other properties to weaken darkness jinn, then it might even make Asaad's fight easier."

At this point, the man leaned forward in interest. "You come up with good solutions," he said. Mishal shrugged, trying not to feel too proud of himself.

"There's no point in trying to dissuade us from this," Eman told the man with a level stare. "You're not gone yet, which means you're willing to consider it. What do I need, if I want to convince you?"

The man sighed. "A favor. You owe me one already, so I'll simply change what I want from you. I'll tell you about it once it's time. Remember: No matter what I ask, you'll need to do it without question."

Mishal opened his mouth to reject the suggestion, but Eman stopped him with a raised hand. "Deal."

"Eman!" Mishal protested. What if the man asked her to do something sinister, or dangerous?

"Are you sure?" the man said. "You have no idea what I'll ask. Besides, what you're doing here is useless. If Maymun is set on having the exorcist, no amount of training will protect him. Don't underestimate the jinni, child."

"Don't underestimate my *friends*," Eman shot right back at him. "I'll do what you ask. Just make sure that Asaad's somewhere no one could ever find him."

The man sighed. He pulled out his phone and dialed a number. "Yes," he said. "It's a job. I want you to take my taxi to *the exact place* I'll tell you about," he said.

"You're getting someone else to do it?" Mishal asked.

“I told you I don’t want Sarim agents seeing me,” the man replied to Mishal, then turned back to his phone, staring at it as if he thought the phone was stupid. “No, boy, I wasn’t talking to you,” he said into the phone. “Well, *now* I’m talking to you. Yes, the exact coordinates. And after you finish, come to me so I can erase your memories about this job. Yes, trust me, you don’t want to remember this one.”

The man hopped into his car, then disappeared. A few minutes later, the vehicle popped back into existence, dislodging pebbles from its path. Now a teenager, just a year older than Mishal, sat next to the taxi driver in the vehicle. The boy rolled down his windows and gave Mishal a wide smile. “Hi,” he said. “I’m Qais, nice to work with you. Wow, you’re pretty young to be an exorcist!” he added, whistling for emphasis. “Do you know, I have a cousin who’s about your age. All he does is play football, and he’s not even good at it. Good to see someone working his way through life, hahah! How old are you, anyway?”

“Er, hello,” Mishal said, shocked by the barrage of words coming his way. Even Eman wasn’t this talkative. “Er, sixteen and a half.”

“Wow, wow, even younger than I thought, man! Good for you, make sure you enjoy your school years, even though we might all get -”

“Shut up,” the taxi driver said, in that misty monotone of his. He got out of the car and the new driver got in, then beckoned at Mishal to climb in, along with Eman.

Now the new driver had the wheel, and he gave a wide grin to Mishal and Eman. “Thanks for coming. I gotta have someone to prove what I’m doing,” he said, “seeing as how I won’t remember any of this in five minutes’ time. You know, it’s nice to forget something for once.”

Mishal got into the car, smelling again its dusty scent. “Yeah?” he asked, uncertain about how to deal with someone who enjoyed speaking so much. Maybe he should just let the guy go on. It might lead to some good information.

"Oh yeah. Most of the time it's people forgetting about me and the boss. The other day we were delivering something in the UK, we ran into this guy whose life we saved a couple of months ago, and he didn't even know who I was!" The young man rambled enthusiastically as he drove away, towards Shayib Ghalib and Asaad. In the rear window, Mishal could see Eman raising her eyebrows. "It happens all the time, I might actually have to completely step out of human life if I work for the boss long enough."

"So, why do you do it?" Eman asked.

"Oh goodness, sis," the young man said, turning around to face her while still keeping his hands on the steering wheel. Eman began squeaking. "Do you have any idea how bad the job market is nowadays? Besides," he added, his voice going softer, "there are some other perks. Anyhow, we're here." The car wheeled across the wastelands, throwing dust and pebbles in the air. Shayib Ghalib and Asaad stood there with their hands up to ward the dust, eyes wide in surprise. "Oi, bro, are you the legendary exorcist?" he said, shouting out of the window at Asaad and Shayib Ghalib. "Get in, we're going to take you off the map."

"Hey, wait, but-"

"Get in, Asaad!" Eman urged.

"Yeah, Asaad, get in and shut up!" Qais added enthusisastically, giving her a thumbs up, which she returned enthusiastically. Apparently, Eman had simply accepted the young taxi driver. Mishal decided to keep quiet as Asaad was bullied into getting into the car.

"I don't even know where we're go-"

"Stop it, Asaad," Eman said.

"Asaad, you're always like this!" Qais said, rolling his eyes.

"Do I even know you?"

"Did I lie, sis?" Qais asked Eman, who shook her head. "Now, let's get going, the sooner I can finish up putting Asaad into *that* dimension, the quicker I can go get lunch and sanitize my hands."

"What are you even talking about?" Asaad asked, flustered.

“Oh, sanitizing is the most important thing nowadays,” Qais said, motioning with his hands. “Oh, and not shaking hands. Don’t worry, it’ll catch on soon enough!”

Now the car was speeding up, rumbling and tumbling over the badland rocks. Qais began to mutter to himself, pulling the occasional lever. Mishal didn’t like the confusion evident in the young man’s face. “Hey, you know how to work this thing, don’t you?” he asked.

“I know how to drive just fine,” Qais replied, his voice rising in a panic. “Thing is - and I’m putting a lot of trust in you to say this - it’s just that I’ve never really driven this particular car alone so far. Let’s hope we get to the right dimension.”

“Excuse me?” Mishal asked. Eman made a strangled voice behind him, and Asaad looked about ready to hurl his power at them, destroying everything in sight.

“It’ll be fine!” Qais said. “Anyhow, about the pandemic. Really, it’s way worse than you think. Nature’s been reclaiming everything, which is pretty nice, but on the other hand people in a number of countries are–”

Just then, they hit the correct speed. Floating runes began to appear around the car’s outside, and the world shattered ahead of them. The car barreled through the void, going into that strange pathway the taxi took towards other worlds. A storm brewed all around them, with beams of light passing through the darkness. However, the road seemed bumpier this time, with the taxi hopping up and down in midair. Mishal began to see figures floating outside. They appeared to be massive bats, or perhaps birds with leathery wings and long, crooked claws.

“Hey, Qais?” Eman asked calmly.

“Yeah, sis?” Qais asked. He was still fiddling with the dials on the radio, which switched from Oman Radio, to Al Wisal, and then to a strange, black language which rolled in guttural noises.

“These things outside…those are just illusions, right?”

“Um…” Qais’s eyes flickered to the rear window. Mishal saw him flinch.

Just then, one of the creatures reached out. One of its claws screeched against the metal of the taxi. Mishal recoiled, but Eman rolled down the window. She murmured something beneath her breath, and her green bracelet glowed with a blinding light. The creature hissed, its grasp on the metal loosening, sending it screaming out into the void.

"Great! Thanks, sis!" Qais said, then shouted out of the window. "No hitchhiking! The boss'll be back soon and I'll tell him about you!"

"These things, they're scared of your boss?" Mishal asked. He could hear Eman in the backseat explaining to Asaad what was happening.

"Oh, everything's scared of the boss," Qais said.

Mishal took a few moments to consider, then nodded in acceptance. *Good.*

A few minutes later, the car came to a rolling stop and Qais asked them all to leave the vehicle. They stood outside in the blackness, which continued being blistered with whipping winds. Mishal could see a shattering in the world in front of him. Bits of the world fell away like glass, revealing a massive, serene lake on the other side. No, not a lake Mishal realized, a perfect ocean. The water reflected a pure sky marbled blue and yellow. Sand spread around the water in all directions. The sun above shone brighter than normal. It was a world of perfect summer.

"There you go," Qais said, waving a hand towards the lake. "You'll be as safe there as in any place we can think of. The jinni will definitely be able to get in, but it'd be draining for him. As far as the boss explained, this is the best place for you to fight the enemy." For a moment, his jovial tone fell away, revealing a caring gaze. "I know we didn't talk much, and I'm liable to forget all about this experience in a few minutes, but I wish you luck, Asaad."

Asaad nodded, then turned his eyes to Mishal and Eman. "You're actually helping out," he said, then grinned ferociously.

Eman's expression flitted between worry and determination in quick succession. Finally, she grimaced and said, "We got you what you wanted." She stepped forward and reached out a fist. "Now, you need to give us what we want."

Asaad struck Eman's fist lightly with his own. "Victory?"

"You. Back. Safe. We weren't joking when we said that your life is precious."

Mishal watched this exchange. Eman and Asaad had spent little time together on an actual team. Initially, it had been Asaad and Ahlam, supervised by Shayib Ghalib. Just them against the world. Eman joined for a short time, but then Asaad had been designated as an S-class exorcist and moved to work independently. Now, Ahlam was dead and Asaad was a Shayib, with his own teams and worries.

Worrying about loved ones is a seed of constant terror. For the past month, Mishal had let that seedling grow and bloom in his heart. He'd been terrified of what might happen. Now, with one simple action, the worry was kept at bay. He was going to support Asaad with all he could, but he would trust Asaad to win.

"Be safe," he said. "We'll hold things down on this side, make sure no external parties interfere. On the twelfth of March you'll come out victorious, and we'll be here waiting for you."

Asaad raised an eyebrow. "Look at you, all grown up," he said. "Thanks for the care, kid. I've got it from here."

Without another word, Asaad turned and disappeared through the shattered portal. Mishal, Eman, and Qais watched on silently, resolutely.

"Come on, let's go," Qais finally said. As they got back into the car, he babbled about how he was about to get his memory wiped.

"But that friend of yours sure is cool," Qais remarked as they drove out into the wastelands again. The sun was setting, and Shayib Ghalib stood like a palm tree, with his hands on his hips. Mishal and Eman had some explaining to do.

"He sure is cool," Mishal agreed. He felt at peace now, knowing that his Shayib had chosen to fight for his life. He blew a long breath, letting some of his concern fade away.

Chapter Forty-Five

Over the next week, a group of new words entered the Omani dictionary. Three phrases in particular stood out: Social distancing, Corona, and Pandemic.

Mishal had heard of the COVID-19 pandemic before, of course. News had broken out a few weeks after Sultan Qaboos Bin Said passed away. However, the first news had been about a new virus in China. As the pandemic traveled across the world, rumors on Instagram and TikTok had been full of contradictions. On the one hand, he'd seen posts which said the virus was harmless. Other sources had said that Muslims were mostly safe, since washing your hands and nose would keep the virus at bay. Other sources claimed that the virus would eventually wipe out all human life. Posts sprang out across the world, especially posts about 'nature healing'. Mishal hadn't known what to believe.

On the twenty-fourth of February, the first cases in Oman were registered. Over the coming days, more cases appeared. Mishal's parents were nervous, especially considering Mishal was in eleventh grade, just one year away from his final year in school. However, he'd maintained good grades, and so his father waved aside the fears. "If you're good enough to get a special scholarship from the government, I'm sure you'll do just fine," he said.

"But he needs to be careful!" his mother replied angrily from the kitchen. Mishal could hear her brewing tea for that afternoon.

Later in the day, Mishal headed out by bus to Sarim. He was meant to meet Eman there to continue researching Maymun the jinni. The ride was wholly uneventful, but Mishal felt hunger clawing at his stomach. When he arrived at Sarim, passing through the mechanical wall and the white corridors towards Sarim's top floor, he saw an announcement flickering onto the massive blue crystal which illuminated the pit.

The following agents are to report to meeting room three:

Mishal Al Balushi

Eman Al Lawati

Mishal frowned as his phone dinged. He'd gotten a notification on the Sarim app, containing the same summons he'd just seen on the crystal. He began to feel unease spreading across his body, even as people walked back and forth around him, some of them making jokes with one another about not shaking hands anymore.

Was the summons regarding Asaad? Nobody in Sarim should be aware that Mishal and Eman had made contact with Shayib Asaad. Mishal looked to the left, where some of the meeting rooms were, then made his way in that direction. He didn't know what was happening - but if it was about Asaad, Mishal was determined to play stupid.

The meeting rooms here, on the top level of Sarim, had a slick, modern feel that exacerbated Mishal's discomfort. His heart raced as he saw two figures already seated around a long, polished table: The first was a Shayib he'd glimpsed around the building recently. It was Shayib Jamal, known to be one of the more heartless within the Council of Shayibs. Mishal had personally met the man only once before, when he'd been summoned to the council to speak with the CEO. Shayib Jamal had broad beard and, instead of a cane, he wore a scimitar around his waist. The old man exuded confidence, even as he sat at the table with his arms crossed. He was the head of the Jinn Imprisonment Division, and Asaad hated him.

The second person was Eman, and she was in the middle of asking a furious question as Mishal walked in. She turned towards him and raised a pointing finger. "It's not enough that he's lost his Shayib, who went God knows where, now you're dragging him out for questions?"

Mishal paused, one foot inside of the room. As Shayib Jamal turned to look at him, Mishal glimpsed Eman giving him an almost imperceptible nod. He realized that her last sentence was a coded message for his sake: T*hey're here to ask us about where Asaad is, pretend to know nothing.*

I will be the dumbest, most amicable boy this man has ever seen, Mishal thought determinedly to himself, then nodded to

Shayib Jamal. “S-sir?” he asked, only half-feigning his nervousness. Mishal had never been a good liar. Instead of weaving a tall tale, it was best to be polite and avoid answering anything at all.

“Good, you’re here. Rather late for an employee. Do you have an evening shift?” Shayib Jamal asked.

“I come here after school, sir.”

The man’s posture softened at Mishal’s polite response. “Pfsh, school,” Shayib Jamal said, leaning back. “What good is school to an exorcist? So, you were at this school of yours today?” he added, giving Mishal an appraising look.

“Yes, sir,” Mishal replied truthfully.

Shayib Jamal leaned forward. Mishal sent ruh to his eyes, revealing the old man’s power once more. It manifested in a red scorpion which scuttled in increasingly erratic directions across his clothes and over his face, finally settling over his Msar. Mishal had no idea what this image meant but, coupled with the menacing sword hanging from the old man’s waist, the teenager felt a sense of foreboding.

“Sir, what is happening?” Mishal asked.

“A jinni called Maymun is attempting to come back from its ancient seal. It has set its eyes on Asaad Al Nabhani, who is - and always has been - a notorious troublemaker at Sarim.” His eyes scanned both Mishal and Eman, gauging their reactions to his words. Mishal couldn’t tell why the man was revealing this information. Didn’t he know that Mishal was *with* Asaad when the CEO had first told him of the jinni? “Where is Asaad?” he asked suddenly.

Mishal paused, but a sigh from Eman cut him off completely. She leaned forward smoothly. “Sir, I don’t have the slightest clue where Asaad could be.”

“Defending him won’t do you any good. I know how close you were to him,” Shayib Jamal said, leaning forward again.

“I’m not here to defend Asaad al Nabhani. He’s been an *excellent* boon to Sarim, but that’s neither here nor there. The fact is, I don’t know where he is.”

“And you?” the old man said, turning to Mishal. The youth only nodded towards Eman, hinting that he only knew as much as she did. He didn’t trust his voice to lie. “I see,” the old man said, standing up as if to leave. “You know, if the jinni Maymun actually gets to Al Nabhani, we could be seeing the birth of the worst human-jinn monstrosity in the history of our country. The losses could be in the thousands. You might not know this, but Asaad’s history is in question. We, at Sarim, are only trying to minimize the risk.”

Mishal opened his mouth, then closed it. Was this man suggesting that Asaad might be in *league* with the demon? Mishal could feel anger flooding through his heart. Heat flushed his cheeks. Asaad had gone through so much more than this man understood.

“If I remember right from when *my* powers first awakened,” Eman said with a smile, “your version of helping usually involves either a sword in the heart or an eternal prison.” The old man began to bluster, at which Eman waved a hand. “No need to be angry. You’re all righteousness, blade of justice, and all that. But you know what? It doesn’t mean you’re right.”

Shayib Jamal’s eyes grew grim. “Anyone in league with demons will be subjected to the same fate of Asaad Al Nabhani,” he said, pronouncing every word carefully.

“So, you’re going to kill him?” Eman challenged.

Shayib Jamal shook his head vehemently. “There’s minimal danger to him: all we need to do is…” he mimicked a scissor with his hands. Mishal noticed that even then, the man kept a grip on the hilt of his sword and his khaizranah. “…snip out most of his ruh. It would make it impossible for the jinni to possess him, since he’d be too weak. It *also* minimizes any other risks Asaad could pose to Oman.”

Mishal couldn’t take it anymore. This man was already treating Asaad like a traitor. Mishal closed his eyes, controlling his breath, imagining how he would like to respond.

In his mind’s eyes, Mishal put his palms on the table, making every word count. “Then, for our sake and the sake of everyone in

Oman," he would say, gritting his teeth. "I hope you *never* find Asaad, sir."

In Mishal's imagination, the man would lash out then. Mishal and and Eman would restrain Shayib Jamal, then break out in a burst of fire and claws. They would ride out into the sunset, then hide out until Asaad beat Maymun.

Mishal savored the scene in his mind, then he let it disappear. *It's time to be dependable. Keep a good head on your shoulders, team leader. Asaad still needs you free and away from trouble.*

"As agents, our first priority should be protecting Oman," he said. "How can we reach you, in case we find any information?"

The man's eyes narrowed into slits, but he gave them a phone number. Mishal kept his tone cordial as he recorded the number, then tried calling the Shayib. By the end of the interaction, Shayib Jamal looked from Mishal to Eman. "You can learn a lesson from him in *true* Omani manner," Shayib Jamal told her.

Eman only gave him an icy smile.

Mishal walked away. Eman followed, and Mishal felt her putting a hand on his shoulder. "We should go research," she said softly, "but I think this might not be the safest place to speak at the moment. How do you feel about ice- cream?"

Chapter Forty-Six

An hour later, Mishal and Eman were sitting with Salim Al Ghafri outside one of Oman's oldest ice-cream parlors. *Softy* had been in the country since 1975, with its glowing neon ice-cream sign welcoming everyone inside. The employee was a grizzled Indian man with a thick mustache, who smiled when he saw Eman. "I come here all the time," she told Mishal.

After sitting down with their ice-creams – vanilla for Mishal and strawberry for Eman, while Salim had declined to have any – the three exorcists brought their heads closer to whisper.

"I don't think it's a good idea to hide things from command," Salim said quietly.

Eman glared at Salim. "Do you want Asaad dead?" she asked flatly.

"Of course not. But are we really sure Sarim would hurt him?"

"Yes - because the people Sarim has appointed onto his case are that kind of people," Eman said. "You weren't with us, Salim, but I promise you: Shayib Jamal's lazer-focused on this. I know Shayib Jamal's cruelty firsthand. He's *tried* to kill Asaad in the past. He's tried to kill *me* in the past. I don't know about you, but I'm not keen on giving him another chance."

Mishal nodded. This was the first he'd heard of Eman's history with Shayib Jamal. However, she'd divulged a long time ago that when Sahib first manifested, multiple factions in Sarim had advocated for the beast to be destroyed, along with its young owner. Eman had been nine at the time. "What I don't understand is why the CEO is letting this happen," Mishal said.

"I did a little snooping through the Sarim records while, uh, taking care of some business for someone," Eman said, ignoring Mishal's surprised look. "The CEO has been rather reclusive this year. A lot of the decision-making has been going directly to the Council of Shayibs, with the CEO's secretary as liaison." Her phone dinged just then, and she checked it casually while attacking her ice-cream. Mishal and Salim shared a look. Mishal pictured Eman slinking through Sarim's corrdidors and looking through their documents. *I need to remember to be very careful the next time I keep secrets from her,* he thought to himself.

Finally, Eman looked up. "So, what's our current situation?"

Mishal sighed. "I spoke to the IT and HR departments. Basically, none of the non-magical departments can help."

"Shayibs of teams eleven through seventeen are all on Shayib Jamal's side," Eman complained. "The rest seem to be too worried about seeming pro-jinni to help. They still remember what happened to Shayib Faisal."

Salim leaned forward, curious. "What happened to him?"

Mishal winced. "He betrayed Sarim. Got Ahlam killed. And then Asaad, well…" he remembered walking into a room and seeing Shayib Faisal bisected into many parts, floating in the air, like a shattered mirror, still alive and shouting at Asaad. "Asaad took care of him."

Eman finished her ice-cream. "So, the Shayibs aren't going to help, and they might be sore about Asaad destroying one of them. Can't let that get to us."

Salim raised a shaky hand. "Does he still need help?" he asked.

Mishal felt dumbfounded. "What?"

"Does Asaad still need help?" Salim asked again. Eman and Mishal looked at each other. "You said yourself that Asaad could beat Maymun, so long as he believes and gives himself a way out. Now he's in a different dimension, and can return after the battle. What more do you want to do?"

"There's a *lot* to do," Mishal argued. "We need to keep the bad factions in Sarim from interfering or finding out where Asaad's going to appear." Mishal said. He noticed Eman tapping her lips thoughtfully. "You look like you have an idea," he commented. He knew that look.

Eman smiled.

***

Three hours later, just before the evening prayer, Mishal sat in the library - three floors down in Sarim's pit. The walls were lined with ancient manuscripts. Mishal was reading an old manuscript, which detailed some of the unspeakable atrocities committed by Maymun in the centuries before he was successfully sealed.

The jinni's greatest sin was not cruelty, the book read. *As far as most scholars agree, Maymun Al Sahabi had little interest in vain cruelty. The demon's greatest sin was his callousness. He kidnapped mortals in an attempt to strengthen them, but his power left them bedridden, with their skin blackened by sheer ruh. He let them leave his realm, hoping they would live. He often mourned them afterwards.*

Mishal shuddered as he read the passage. The room felt colder now, as if he was not alone.

"This is a part of my past that I wish to forget," a kind voice said, startling him. Mishal looked up to see Maymun, in a black dishdasha, standing in the glow of a light crystal.

"You dare come here again?" Mishal hissed, fury rushing through his body. Mishal burst forward and swung a fist of hate-filled black flame at the jinni, only for it to pass through Maymun's body.

"I dare," Maymun said. "Sarim poses no threat to me. Other than Asaad and your CEO, exorcists nowadays are a pale imitation of the magi I fought during my youth."

"You're going to fail," Mishal said. "Asaad won't submit to you."

"I should hope not," Maymun replied. "The stronger his body, the more time I'll have to bask in the glory of the sun before my vessel fails me."

Mishal didn't know how to reply. His anger was getting the better of him, and he hated it. Hatred was a corruption onto the mind. "What did you come here for?" he asked.

"To thank you for convincing Asaad to not lock himself away," Maymun said. He smiled. "It would have been a problem to take over his body, only to find myself with no way out. No matter what happens, know that I'm touched by your care for those you count among your tribe. And," he added, with a raised finger, "I want to warn you."

“So, warn me and leave,” Mishal snapped, feeling suddenly drained. This was too much for him to take. “I’m sorry to say this, but you’re wrong to think you can win against Asaad. He’ll never be shaken by anything now.”

“My followers have turned rather overzealous, if you take my meaning,” Maymun said. He sat at the table opposite of Mishal, already fading away. “I worry they might try to kill you. They would rather have Asaad weakened than strong, despite my wishes. You defied their intent with your well-executed scheme. Stay safe, Mishal. I look forward to thanking you in person before Asaad breaks.”

And with that, the jinn broke off into a mist that scattered across the room. Mishal continued to research. He had agreed to receive something from Eman here, and he knew that Sarim agents were watching him. He only hoped that they’d heard his words and would take them as confirmation that Asaad wasn’t in league with any jinn.

Soon, a door creaked in the corner of the library. Eman stepped behind him, quietly, not saying anything. She walked towards the bookshelves, past woven circles of painted date palm leaves which decorated the walls, and left a piece of paper on a shelf behind Mishal before leaving.

Mishal took the paper from the shelf, trying to appear as nervous as possible. He read the piece of paper, nodded, then ripped it once and threw it in the trash can, then left. As he stepped away from the library, Mishal heard the quiet padding of well-trained feet going into the library behind him. He smiled to himself.

The piece of paper read *Dvddg Zloo eh vdih lq Qlczd,* written in a simple cypher for Shayib Jamal’s agents to decipher. After they deciphered the text, it would read *Asaad Will be Safe in Nizwa.*

Even though Mishal had ripped the message, the Sarim agents would be able to retrace its form. They would believe that the paper was a hidden message between Eman and Mishal. They would spend the next two weeks scouring Nizwa, a wild chase following a number of clues 'accidentally' dropped by Eman. By the time they realized their mistakes, Asaad would have defeated Maymun, and all would be well.

Mishal shuddered, realizing how a few months of spy training had absolutely transformed Eman. She was becoming a terrifying exorcist.

Chapter Forty-Seven

The days passed with an impending feeling of anxiety. COVID-19 had become a real part of Oman's zeitgeist. Employees in Sarim and elsewhere were slowly coming to the realization that this was not a joke. Mishal worried every time he sneezed, or when he accidentally rubbed his eyes due to exhaustion, exhaustion caused by a lack of sleep, sleep that refused to come because he was constantly worried about the fate of Asaad Al Nabhani.

Stop it, Mishal told himself, shaking his head to clear it. He had decided to trust Asaad to fight Maymun on his own, then return to them. What was the point of trusting someone if you couldn't do it unwaveringly? So Mishal resolved himself to wait, and to only visit Al Dhahirah on the promised day.

The few promised weeks had passed, and it was now the eleventh of March. In just one more day, the jinni Maymun would attempt to enter Asaad's realm of training and attack him, just as he'd promised. The two would interlock in battle, and only one would leave that realm, appearing in Al Dhahirah.

Mishal had done all he could to help Asaad, and now faith was his only remaining weapon. Thankfully, Sarim hadn't gotten wind of Asaad's real location, yet that wasn't for a lack of trying. Mishal had glimpsed Shayib Jamal's scowling face twice that week alone. The man walked through Sarim's buildings,casting hateful glares at everyone.

Just as Mishal thought this, he noticed a figure watching him from Al Khoudh's evening streets. The figure was well-concealed. In fact, the man had taken the form of a swaying tree, with its leaves hanging over the street. However, Mishal's eyesight caught faint glimmers of ruh coming from the tree.

Mishal snorted to himself, looking at his phone. Today's mission appeared simple enough: a C-level jinni had been terrorizing a house in Al Ansab for three months. At night, it scoured the corridors, reacting to loud sounds. It had caused increasing injuries, and the family had reached out for help. Mishal's work was to destroy the jinni, along with Salim.

Mishal waited by Al Barakat roundabout. In the blanket of darkness between streetlights, worries grew cold and suffocating. It was better to stand under a streetlamp.

Fifteen minutes passed by.

Mishal's eyes popped up when he heard a horn. He saw Salim's car, with its driver looking quite agitated, and with Salwa sitting behind him. Salim stopped on the side of the road just after the roundabout, allowing Mishal to climb into the passenger seat.

"Are you alright?" he asked.

"Yeah, why would you think otherwise, boss?" Salim asked, appearing more annoyed than before.

Mishal refused to be cowed. "You look like you're in physical pain right now."

Salim pulled out onto the road, then turned the next roundabout to head out onto the Muscat Expressway. "Well, boss, I just don't know what to do with myself, what with Asaad-" Salim cut himself, glancing at Salwa. She frowned at him. They hadn't told her the details of Mishal's disappearance, since she was still a child, but she knew something was off.

"I know the feeling," Mishal replied. "Tell me about it."

Salim sniffed. "Really?"

"Really."

They passed a turn and went left to enter the Muscat Expressway proper. Mishal liked this road. It had an aloof feel to it. The expressway had no buildings on either side of it. Instead, the road was hewn out of sheer mountainous rock. The yellow lights from the road sought purchase in the darkness, illuminating cliffs and crags. On a lonely road, it was easy to forget the world and embrace solitude.

"Boss, I wish we'd done more for Asaad," Salim said quietly. Salwa leaned in to listen.

"You're the one who said that we've done all we could for him," Mishal remarked, looking out through the window. Lights flickered across his face.

"And I meant it!" Salim snapped, slapping the steering wheel. "It's just that I, I…"

"Feeling helpless can be a pain unto itself," Mishal finished for him. This was a feeling he'd had often across his life.

"Maybe."

Perhaps Salim had more experience than Mishal in the ways of the world. Perhaps he knew how to pick car exhausts, and to fix air conditioners or to use ruh to imbue tools with power. But Mishal knew helplessness, and this was a lesson he was happy to impart. "Sometimes, it can help just to accept that you're helpless. Pray for him, Salim, and trust in him."

"What are you talking about?" Salwa asked from the back seat. "Why won't you tell me where Asaad is?"

"Asaad is on an important mission," Salim said loudly, glancing at Salwa in the rearview mirror. Mishal saw the man's expression contort into a playful frown. "You're with us today because you've been a good girl."

"I'm really strong now," Salwa's voice retorted, Mishal looked and was surprised to see that she was talking to him. "You can bring me along now."

Mishal nodded. "You're right. If this mission goes well, I think we can all go together more often." Her astonished expression was mirrored by Salim, but then they both beamed.

"I need you to destroy the jinni to prove it to him!" Salim said, freeing one hand to high-five Salwa.

"I'll punch it!" she promised, even though Mishal knew she would do no such thing.

The drove the rest of the way in silence. Mishal looked at the GPS and informed Salim about turns in the road, until they reached a normal house in the middle of a neighborhood in Al Ansab.

"We can't help Asaad, but we can help this family," Mishal said. "Let's focus on that for now. Besides, Salwa's been doing exceptionally in her training, so let's see how far she's come."

Salim smiled at the thought. "So, which house is it?" he asked. The three of them got out of the car and turned. The houses all looked similar, with white walls and smatterings of interspersed stones to add flavor. One house, in particular, stood out. Light shone from all of the windows, even though Mishal could clearly see that most of the rooms were empty.

“That’s the one,” Mishal said, then moved through the gate to the porch.

The house was as ordinary as could be. A swing stood in the porch; not brand new, but in rather good condition. A narjas tree brightened the otherwise pristine porch. This place was cared for, Mishal decided. He looked through his phone.

"We're looking for... a mother and four children," Mishl instructed, surveying his team members. "The father died three years ago." He saw Salim's brows furrowing as soon as he heard about the children. As gruff as he looked, Salim always had a soft spot for children. "Don't worry, nobody's going to get hurt tonight," Mishal added.

"Of course not. What do we really know about the jinni?"

"It inhabits the house itself. Has it out for the family. It started with a scratch, about three months ago," Mishal said, then paused for Salwa’s sake. He didn’t want to scare her, but the girl was an exorcist after all. Mishal looked through the phone again. "The jinni always attacks in the corridors. Never in their rooms," he said. He scanned the house. "All the lights are on," he said.

"The jinni hides in the darkness," Salim remarked, then took a long breath. "They chose the worst night for us to fight against a follower of Maymun."

"Actually, tonight's perfect," Mishal said as he opened the front door and peered in. "There's something I haven't told you about feeling helpless yet.”

“And that is?”

“Punching something usually makes you feel better."

The front door opened into a narrow corridor, with all the lights burned out. Mishal could make out a shoe rack, as well as a decorative brown table. Claw marks marred the surface of the table.

“Stay close to me,” Salim said to Salwa, taking her hand. Mishal motioned for Salim to be quiet, then moved into the house, doing his best to be silent. They stepped through quietly, then turned left into the well-lit living room, with its smooth leather sofas. There were no claw marks in this room.

Salim looked through some of the corners, then motioned towards the second floor. Mishal nodded, and they went up the wide, brown stairs. Light spilled into the area through a stained-glass window. Atop the stairs, they found another mangled corridor, this time with broken table legs and claw marks running along the walls. Mishal found a light switch, but he quickly moved through the corridor. He could hear something, a faint sobbing coming the room at the end of the corridor. Light slipped under the doorframe, illuminating its edges in a bright yellow rectangle. Mishal hurriedly hopped over the broken table in the corridor, but his foot suddenly tripped over something suddenly, and he came crashing to the ground.

That was soft, he thought to himself, then horror dawned upon him as he heard a groan. He'd tripped over someone's leg. He could see the shadow of someone injured on the floor. The figure groaned again.

"There you are," an airy voice said, from the other side of the corridor. A creature materialized in the shadows right next to Mishal. Long, metallic claws reached out, grazing the youth's shoulder as he rolled away.

"Mishal!" Salim shouted, holding out a pen as he tugged Salwa closer to himself. He muttered something under his breath and light blazed out from the end of his pen. Immediately the jinni fled, slipping back into the shadows and behind Salim.

"Time to die, exorcists!" it shouted, its metallic claws coming out once more.

Quickly, Mishal rolled around on the floor. He slammed his palm against the wall, exuding bright white fire from his hand and through the wall's plaster. The flames traveled on the wall's surface quickly, faster than the demon could slash. The jinni recoiled, pulling back once more until it reached the stairs and went down them.

Wasting no time, Mishal went to the groaning figure on the floor. The blood looked almost black in the darkness. "Are you still there?" he asked, almost shouting.

"My…children," the woman croaked weakly. Salim leapt over the body, slamming a door open to reveal three children huddled together, crying and covered in cuts. The oldest, a girl who was about twelve, tried to keep her younger siblings calm as Salwa reassured them that help had arrived.

Mishal turned back to the woman in relief. "They're safe," he reassured her, almost choking.

"Thank God," she said with a thick tongue. "Oh, Allah is merciful. That *thing,* it was playing with us. It said it we'd make good starters until the-" a sudden weakness came over her, and she passed out in Mishal's arms.

Mishal pointed towards Salwa, and she walked forward quickly, making arcane hand gestures with her hand. A green ruh began to spread from her fingers to the woman, whose wounds began to slowly close. "Until what?" Salwa asked.

"Until the main course came," a slithering voice said. Mishal turned to see the jinni again. "Even with two of you, we knew we just had to hit both places. Today you die, human. And tomorrow, the master rises again."

The jinni was now revealed in its full form. It appeared almost liquid, with bright silver eyes and metallic claws coming out from an angular shadowy body. Slick like a drop of ink, the jinni's face promised pain.

Two of us? Mishal thought blankly. There were three exorcists here, including Salwa. What was the jinni talking about?

Suddenly, a figure appeared in thin air next to the jinni. Its dark dishdasha mingled with the shadows, as did its jet black, kind eyes.

"You," Mishal hissed at Maymun. Maymun had tricked him after all. His followers were attacking.

"Mishal, I'm so sorry!" Maymun said, stopping Mishal in his tracks. He looked *earnest* in his apology. "They're refusing to listen to me, they said they'd kill you at all costs. My followers are coming for you…" The jinni's voice went fuzzy, as if Maymun were speaking from behind a thick wall.

"What are you talking about?"

"I need to go to Asaad - the promised moment has come," Maymun said. "His time is over; he and I must do battle. But I still want you to be safe." He struck out with his hand, causing a thick, black portal to appear in the wall. It was like a cave of ink, dripping darkness and shadow. "Go, save your people! My followers think there's two of you!"

"Master?" the jinni next to Maymun said, stepping forward. It appeared not to see him. "Why do you hide from us?" it asked in a cracking voice. "What is this strange path you make for the human?"

Maymun's eyes turned to the jinni coldly. "How can you call yourself my follower, when you stray from my path?" he said to the oblivious creature. With that, Maymun disappeared, leaving Mishal, Salim and Salwa alone with the dark jinni and the portal. Salim and Mishal stared at the spot where Maymun had stood. Suddenly, however, Mishal understood and his blood ran cold.

Two of you.

He'd assumed the jinni had meant Salim and him. However, it had clearly ignored the ex-corporal.

Every time Mishal went on a mission, Mishal left another 'him' behind to act as a decoy. A decoy meant to fool only his parents…

The strange being he summoned, using the black Sarim coin. But what if the jinn, which hated Mishal for interfering with their plans, thought that there were two of him?

We had to split up to hit both places.

"There's another one of those jinn at my house," Mishal said, horror dawning upon him. He looked at Salim and Salwa, who stood to his side.

"Master!" the jinni wailed in anguish. "You must rise at all costs, even if you destroy us in retribution!"

The jinni turned to Mishal and Salim, grimacing. Its teeth were jagged, made to rip out throats. “It’s you,” the jinni said. “The two of you need to die!”

Chapter Forty-Eight

Mishal felt anger burst through him, but he forcefully pushed it down. This was not the time for rage. He needed to be there for his family.

"Why would there be a jinni at your *house*?" Salim asked, going pale in the darkness.

"They know where I live," Mishal said quickly, "and they're confused by the decoy I leave at the house to trick my parents." White fire burst from the teenager's hand. When the jinni flew forward, Mishal's thoughts were clear. He threw out a wall of white fire to separate the jinni from Salim and Salwa. Once more, the jinni recoiled from the light. It appeared to be a natural defense from light. If he used his fire like this, the jinni would forever slip away from the flames.

"What are you going to do now?" Salwa asked, still healing the woman they'd found here. Salim stood guard next to the room where the children hid.

Mishal gritted his teeth in mounting frustration. Salwa's question was the exact one thundering through his head. "It's just me here," he told the jinni, trying to reason with it. "There's no need to attack my house."

"Oh, no tricks from you this time!" the jinni replied, giggling with glee. Its insanity was more pronounced than the last jinni, the one Salim and Mishal had confronted in the library. Years of waiting had turned the jinni's fervent devotion to Maymun into thick insanity. It laughed as it struck. "We'll kill the both of you, just in case. Mishal Al Balushi should die!" It tried to attack again, but disappeared when it got too close to the light of Mishal's flame.

Mishal extinguished the fire. Immediately, the jinni returned with a scream of joy.

Too many worries clouded Mishal's mind. On the one hand, he needed to protect the innocents here. On the other, a different jinni was on its way to his *home*, where his family was.

In his mind's eye, Mishal could see the two jinn in the two houses, each of them grinning wicked grins, their metal claws slicing the walls. There was only one way to protect both places.

"Mishal!" Salim said, stepping forward. "I can handle this with Salwa. You go through that portal."

Mishal looked to Salwa, who gave him a strong nod. She'd just finished healing the woman and sent her to her children. Salwa walked up to Salim, her arms crossed. "I can do it. We won't let these people die!"

Mishal found himself coming face to face with a choice he'd dreaded for a year- should he allow Salim and Salwa to come in harm's way? Salim, with his overly serious demeanor and weak ruh; Salwa, a ten-year-old with a healer's temperament. What if they got hurt?

Mishal took a breath. To love people was to trust them, even when you're filled with fear. Salim had proven himself again and again, and Salwa was already a great healer. They had grown beyond the irrational fears he'd had a few months ago, and now were ready to stand shoulder and shoulder as true exorcists. He felt his heart settle with peace.

Mishal reached deep into his soul, and he pulled out the biggest, most reassuring smile he could manage. "Of course, you can handle it!" he said, louder than he'd intended. Before he could hesitate, Mishal ran forward through the inky portal, leaving Salim and Salwa to a fight a C-rank jinni all on their own.

Chapter Forty-Nine

The portal deposited Mishal about four-hundred meters away from the house. The only sounds he could hear were strange flutterings of bird wings through the night air. *I can't hear any shouting,* Mishal thought, with a sudden pang of relief. It appeared like the jinni had gone with the quiet approach, aiming for an assassination from the shadows rather than a full-fledged battle. If he kept equally as quiet, he could be in and out in a few minutes.

Mishal didn't ask for backup. He didn't want Sarim storming into his house. His family's minds were at peace, imagining him free of the jinni that possessed him five years ago.

Mishal began walking, his heart beating loudly in his chest. The cold of dread battled against a deep, seething anger.

His house and family was sacred; it was off-limits, or so he had thought. But now claws were aimed at their throats, and only he could guard them.

Mishal had avoided phoning his parents on purpose. If he was quick enough, he'd be able to stop the jinni before it hurt them and before they were any the wiser. *What if my parents find out that their son willingly dabbles in the astral?* Mishal shivered as he considered their reaction.

Mishal ran forward as quietly as he could. The anger now bubbled in his stomach. He opened the door to see that one of the lights had gone off. He took a step forward, turning left into the living area. Finding nothing there, Mishal ran softly up the stairs into the corridor, and froze in his tracks. The sight before him defied all his expectations.

Safa stood in the corridor, terrified but unharmed. *Alhamdulilah,* Mishal thought, instinctively. On the other side of the corridor stood a shadow jinni, which stood poised with its silver claws out, ready to strike.

Between the two, in the darkness, stood Mishal's doppelganger. It had its arms up, shielding Safa from the jinni, a surprisingly determined expression on its face. Black goo splattered down its shirt.

As Safa glimpsed Mishal, her expression went from horror to confusion. At that moment, the jinni struck again, slicing with its claws through the magical decoy, which immediately fell to the ground like a sack.

Mishal growled in anger and put a flaming hand up. His anger bled through, tinging the fire in red. The light from his flame acted exactly as it had earlier, forcing the jinni away from him. Mishal pushed it back, towards the door which led to the roof. Next to him, Safa was frozen in absolute shock.

"Safa… Safa!" he said to his sister, who stood with a vacant expression on her face. Suddenly she flinched as if seeing him for the first time. "Safa, it's me," he whispered. "Be quiet, run to the light in your room."

"B-but, I saw you fall-"

"It's not real!" Mishal hissed, trying to protect her. "I'll be back in five minutes. Safa, please!"

He didn't wait for her reply. Mishal followed the jinni, pushing it with his light. Thankfully, it stayed silent until they reached the roof of the house. Here, humidity was everywhere, and shadows ruled the world, with lights scant and weak. The jinni grinned. "Did you really think you'd have the advantage here?"

Mishal kept quiet. He worked quietly on his ruh, compressing it. He wasn't trying to get the advantage. All that mattered was getting this monster away from his parents and little sister.

"Why are you so quiet?" the jinni asked. It laughed again. "Today we'll finally set the master free, a-"

"Keep your voice down," Mishal hissed, cutting the jinni off. He took one step forward, trying to keep the hot fury out of his voice. "You thought you could bring my family into this? Do you know what could happen, if they see me destroying you here?"

The jinni's shadow trickled like liquid, taking it from stance to stance. It reached forward with its claws, only for its attack to splatter as it touched Mishal's fire. Mishal struck back, but the jinni dodged beneath his blow and appeared behind him. It fought in a malicious dance, intent on blood.

I can't hit it with my usual fire, Mishal realized. The jinni was faster than he was, even when he sent fire through to his legs.

Mishal kept quiet, focusing on finding a way out of the situation. The problem with his fire is that it was too slow. He dodged and blocked. A claw found its way to his side, nicking him and causing him to gasp.

Mishal remembered Asaad's criticism of him after the mission on the beach. *It's not like you have a long-range attack,* Asaad had said.

Smaller. Faster. I need to attack faster than it can disappear.

Mishal compressed his ruh within his body, condensing it, with the intent of increasing its speed. It turned into a ball, which he then spun, deep inside of his soul, spinning it faster and faster like a tornado. It became difficult to control. Mishal brought the power to his hand. This was dangerous, as he wouldn't be able to use his hand while he prepared the attack.

Three seconds.

The jinni appeared to sense a vulnerability and clawed diagonally, forcing Mishal to turn. With him facing the other side, the beast struck again, its metal claws carving a long gash down Mishal's back. He fell to his knees, panting. His vision grew hazy for a second, but he struggled to keep the ball of ruh spinning with all his strength.

One second.

"It's time for you to die, both of you!" the jinni said.

Mishal put his hand out. All at once, he released the power through the center of his palm. Fire exploded out in a furious jet, almost like a laser. It travelled the distance instantly, blasting a smoldering hole through the jinni's stomach.

The jinni looked down in surprise, then looked back up at Mishal. He was stunned to see that it was crying black tears, even as its body broke away into ash.

"The master will rise," it threatened. "I did my best. By this time tomorrow, Asaad Al Nabhani will be in Maymun Al Sahabi's embrace." With that said, the jinni crumbled onto the roof, its body cracking and breaking apart.

"You should have trusted your master to win fair and square," Mishal said to the empty air. "I'm sorry to say he won't, but at least you'd be alive."

Mishal looked walked back into the hous and stopped in the corridor. He looked right, where he saw Safa in her room, lying on the bed with the light turned on. She shivered, her eyes filled with shock. He could tell she scarcely believed what she'd seen. She looked at him. Mishal waved, drained by the chaos of the past hour. She waved back, looking more like a plastic doll than a human.

Mishal's heart cried out for Safa and his parents. He wanted to explain everything to her, and to ensure his family's safety. However, things were not over yet. Right now, Mishal's family appeared to be safe in their beds.

He climbed down the outside of the wall and walked outside, waiting by the road for Salim and Salwa to come to him. His heart fluttered with fear for them, but Mishal threw trust over his fear and hoped for the best, tuning out the images that popped into his mind, which mainly involved the many injuries Salim and Salwa could have suffered.

Stop it, he told himself.

Mishal stood by the road in Al Khoudh, breathing in the fresh night air. He thought about the night to come.

Three months of fear. Mishal had not rested since the threat of Maymun began circling around Asaad, its claws slowly closing on the ultimate exorcist's neck. Fear, warnings, intrigue, and attacks, culminating in tonight's chaos. His heart had frozen and thawed so many times. Now, all of the past events were coming together.

Suddenly Mishal's phone dinged. He looked down to see a Sarim message. *Jinn are gathering in Al Wusta. All on-duty agents are required to come to the below coordinates.*

The jinn found out where Asaad had vanished? Mishal cursed himself for not seeing this coming. However, after a moment the flickers of his anger disappeated, leaving only anticipation.

Mishal had spent months waiting and training, preparing himself. Worrying about a loved one was a seed of constant terror.

Now, the time of worry was almost over.It was finally time to fight.

Soon, headlights appeared in the road, growing until the glaring lights gave way to Salim's car, which stopped next to Mishal. "Boss?" Salim asked. "Is everyone ok?"

"Yes," Mishal replied, worried when he saw only Salim. "How about you and Salwa?"

"We're safe," a younger voice replied, with a squeak. Salwa appeared from the back seat "I told you we could handle it!"

Mishal laughed. Relief breezed through him even though he'd believed in them. *Alhamdulilah.* "I like this trust thing," he said.

Salim asked, "Did you see the message from Sarim?"

"I did," Mishal said, sitting in the passenger seat. "Salwa, we need to take you home."

"But-" she began to protest.

"Alright Salwa, you've had enough excitement for today. Tomorrow we can go watch a movie!" Salim promised, speeding towards her house in Mabaela. The girl grumbled, but agreed to Salim's suggestion, after seeing what movies were at the Mall of Muscat.

A few minutes later, Salim and Mishal dropped Salwa off at her house, and her father picked her up and took her inside. "Thanks for always taking care of her," the man said.

"No problem, sir," Mishal replied, feeling a little guilty.

"Today Salim and I fought a demon all by ourselves!" Salwa told her father excitedly as they walked away.

Salim laughed, but his expression turned serious as soon as Salwa was through the gate. "The message is clear. Mishal, we need to meet Eman and get there as soon as we could."

Mishal nodded. "Let's go, Salim. It's time to finish this."

Chapter Fifty

Throughout the long drive south, news and updates continued to trickle through the Sarim app in an excruciating torrent of information. Apparently, nearly all of Maymun's forces were capable of traveling long distances faster than cars, via their ability to slip along shadows.

More importantly, it seemed that Maymun's minions were as numerous as motes of dust. More and more of them continued to appear, flitting through the shadows of the night. Where Sarim found them, a battle broke out, but most of the jinn had already arrived at the correct location.

Mishal tried to keep his calm in the car, as Salim drove six hours to Al Wusta, where Asaad would soon appear. Their gambit against Shayib Jamal had backfired, since now most of the jinn were in location, while Sarim's allies were scattered and scrambling to reach Al Wusta.

A thought struck Mishal then. "Salim, do you reckon Sarim is on our side?" he asked.

"What do you mean? Of course they're not," Salim replied, looking confused. Mishal asked him to explain, and he said, "It's the way battle is. The Sarim agents are against the jinn. That's their priority, and - in that sense - we benefit from their righteous fight. But they're not there to help us. If Asaad appears, then suddenly the balance shifts. I have no doubt in my mind that in such a case, Sarim would- oh," he interrupted himself as his phone rang in a short, clear tone. Salim lifted the phone to look, careful to keep at least half his attention on the road, then flipped the phone's glare towards Mishal. The phone read: *All agents to apprehend Asaad Al Nabhani for future questioning.*

"That," Salim said with a disappointed smile. "We might benefit from the two behemoths swinging swords at each other's throat. But, Mishal, neither Sarim nor the jinn want what's best for Asaad. They're just there to destroy each other."

Mishal nodded, thankful to Salim's military expertise. "Then as soon as Asaad appears, we need to get him out of there as soon as we can."

The two drove deeper and deeper south, passing through small villages and long stretches of loneliness narrow roads. Both Mishal and Salim kept quiet. Mishal knew both of them were imagining Asaad inside that shattered world of lakes. They imagined his invisible struggle against Maymun.

Slowly, lights began to appear in the distance. Mishal could see slow flashes of red flames, azure flashes of captured sky, and white lightning. He could also see splashes of shadow, which blocked out some of the light. Clashes began to appear more and more frequently, until finally Mishal and Salim could make out the scene of the fight.

The jinn appeared to have used their early arrival wisely. Long rows of shadow jinn stood on the outskirts of a castle of shadows that wisped and twisted like smoke towards the orange moon. The shadows seemed abyssal, deeper than the night behind them, and very very old. This appeared to be a castle the jinn had constructed, in Al Wusta, out of shadows. In the middle of the castle walls, Mishal could glimpse the first cracks in reality, where Asaad would soon appear.

Outside the castle, scores of exorcists were fighting against the jinn, trying to break into the castle. Eman was already there, riding Sahib through battle, while the young exorcist on her team, Laith, ran from place to place, using the ever-present wind to propel himself, his lavender eyes shining bright. The shy woman was also there, casting protection spells around her colleagues. Mishal smiled grimly, motioning for Salim to stop the car.

"Any good tips for fighting wars?" Mishal asked.

"I never fought in any," Salim replied as they exited the car. However, he immediately went into action, pulling out his enchanted fishing rod. He twirled it once, twice, then caught a shadowy jinni with it, plucking it out of balance just long enough for another exorcist to finish it off.

"Great job!" the exorcist said, panting.

“Of course, this is Salim al Ghafri!” Mishal said in a surge of passion. Immediately, he felt himself flush with embarrassment, but the exorcist only agreed. “Um, Salim, are you going to be alright here?”

“Boss, you go on ahead. I know you’re itching to punch something!”

Mishal ran off without another word. A fire spell shot at around the height of his head, forcing him to slide under it. A jinni was nearby, so Mishal jumped forward, using his white flame to burn it away. He then rolled over a blow and pulled up his hand, sending out that white beam of fire to drop one of the shadow-lurkers, its metal claws snapping on the rocks.

As Mishal fought, he realized there were more jinn here than he had ever expected. None boasted powers formidable enough to bring down a full team of exorcists, but their sheer numbers made them difficult to overcome. Shadows flickered in every corner of Mishal’s gaze. Worse still, the jinn fought with fervor, anticipating the arrival of their hero, Maymun.

Slowly, the crack in the castle was widening, shards of reality spinning out in different directions. One of the jinn flitted through the shadows towards Mishal. The youth dodged, then sent ruh to his legs and jumped high in the air.

Mishal could see the battle spread out below him. So far, the exorcists had the upper hand in skill, the jinn won out in terms of sheer numbers. As he looked, he saw one exorcist, the woman he fought against a few months ago, speeding towards a jinni and biting it, sucking out its shadows. Another sprayed ice across the battlefield. Across the battlefield, Shayib Jamal drew a scimitar and used it to mow down jinni after jinni, growling incantations as he did.

As Mishal landed, he dove into the thick of the battle, heading towards the semi-open portal. He could sense the end coming. Soon the portal would shatter fully, and Asaad would emerge. Fire roared, water bubbled, and people and jinn screamed over one another as the battle raged. Mishal was getting close to the tall, inky wall of the shadow castle, which cast out black smoke into the night.

Suddenly, a hand grabbed Mishal's arm. Mishal whirled, fire in his palms, until her recognized a Sarim agent.

"Let us take care of the rest!" the agent shouted, voice barely audible over the noise. Mishal had to read his lips to make out the words.

Mishal frowned. "It's okay," he shouted back. He moved to brush aside the agents arm, but the man resisted. Mishal gave him a befuddled look.

"We'll take it from here," the agent murmured, avoiding Mishal's gaze. "Thank you for your service so far." He tugged at Mishal a little too hard, yanking Mishal to the floor.

Mishal stared at the agent, standing there with apologies written across his face, even as battles raged all around. This was the moment Salim had mentioned. At this point, Sarim was concerned with stopping Maymun at all costs. Even if it meant killing Asaad…or even destroying the portal before it fully opened.

A group of jinn fell to the ground nearby, struck over by the charge of a group of four exorcists, who pushed into the castle walls. Mishal recognized one of them. This was Team 16, which included Musab and the new member, Ali. The four were running in tandem, their lips moving, gathering ruh for one massive spell. Mishal watched them pushing onwards. The exorcists' gathering ruh swiveled on an axis, over and over again. Mishal could sense its chaos from where he stood. If they hit the portal with that…

"No!" Mishal shouted, sending ruh to his legs and vaulting high over the black castle's walls, dodging flying jinn with bat-like wings and feral teeth. He needed to stop the exorcists. Even though he liked Musab, this wasn't right.

Mishal landed on both legs, immediately striking out with both hands. Two of the exorcists fell, leaving place for a jinni to strike out at Ali, who fell back with a shout. Mishal stopped its black hand, sending fire to his hands to burn the jinni down.

Mishal could feel Ali's wide eyes on him. Not knowing what else to do, Mishal shrugged. "Sorry, but today I guess we're enemies." He spilled white fire from every inch of his body, fighting back jinn and exorcists alike.

A leg popped out from nowhere, striking Mishal in the middle of the chest and dropping him. Seeing their chance, the two remaining exorcists rushed out towards the portal. Out of nowhere, Eman burst onto the scene, riding her white-and-green lion and chanting. The lion slashed at the exorcists, pushing them back. Now, Mishal, Salim, and Eman were in the middle of the dark, shadowy castle's courtyard. They cleared out a circle, stopping jinn and exorcists alike.

Mishal fought onwards, sweating, bleeding, gasping for air. He blocked every strike aimed for his heart, daring to hope that his Shayib would succeed. He would not let anyone close this portal. To do so was to leave Asaad behind, and Mishal had long since decided never to give up on a friend.

He could feel the anger from the exorcists attacking them. They were desparate and confused, following orders to maintain some semblance of righteousness. The tide of society's emotions rose, battering at Mishal's senses. He knew what they expected him to do.

"What you're doing is wrong!" he shouted in the face of his colleague's expectations. "The right thing to do is to keep our hearts strong and march on! Have faith in him!"

A kick came. Mishal dodged, replied with a fiery fist. Darkness roared, he shouted back, throat hoarse, lightheaded from battle, dazed with the sheer odds. He sent a beam of white flame, defying those around him, even as claws cut at his arms and feet, as darkness struck him back.

Eman and Salim were facing the same odds, each fighting as best they could. Salim's fishing rod twirled like a spear, and he used a shield to absorb blows. Eman grappled with a woman, flipping her over with her superior size and weight. She threw a punch, and Sahib's white paw came out of her bracelet to extend the blow.

Slowly, the circle began to shrink, bringing more jinn and exorcists closer to the shattering in the world.

Another fist came down, striking Mishal's face. Blood spattered from his jaw to the dark floor. He raised his head.

There was a portal ahead of him. Now, a hand had appeared, reaching out from the shattered mirror. A light brown hand.

Asaad's hand.

The jinn paused, all at once. Everyone stopped fighting, turning to stare at the hand coming out of the portal. That long hand reaching out of the shattered world, as if it were about to pluck something out of the universe. Salim squinted, with blood pouring down his forehead, his eyes filled with awe. Mishal watched.

The portal shattered.

Chapter Fifty-One

The portal exploded, filling the area with a bright flash akin to a molten star. Pieces of reality shot out of the portal, whizzing by the combatants in all directions. Some crashed to the ground, others flew towards the sky.

Throughout all of this, Mishal was blinded by the pale explosion, which brought with it a resounding sense of finality. For good or ill, the battle had been settled between Asaad Al Nabhani and Maymun al Sahabi.

Finally, the light abated just enough that Mishal could open his eyes.

Jinn and exorcists alike stood with their weapons limp in their hands. The weapons felt…useless, somehow, in the face of the being standing in the middle of the circle. A well-kept, handsome Omani male, around twenty years old, stood with his eyes closed and his hands outstretched. His beard was immaculate, as if he'd had time to shave and get dressed before the battle concluded.

The jinn and exorcists nearest to Asaad stepped backwards, even as the ones in the back leaned forward to take a better look. The crowd rippled with anticipation, looking like a scene out of a fable.

"Asaad?" Mishal asked, his voice cracking with exhaustion. He'd been fighting for hours.

The figure opened its eyes, revealing slick, oil-black eyes which overflowed with power. Darkness flooded out from the figure's feet and hands. "Not quite," the figure said, with a sad smile.

Chapter Fifty-Two

Mishal's throat constricted immediately as he watched the monstrosity before him. Maymun smiled, terrible malice overflowing from its hands. This couldn't be. Asaad - so brave, so strong - could not *possibly* lose. "T-this is a prank, right?" Mishal.

"I'm sorry," the jinni said once more, reminding Mishal of the thousand times Maymun had apologized before. The many times he assured Mishal that taking over Asaad's body was inevitable. His confidence in his overwhelming force. "He fought valiantly. All I want now is-" Maymun stuttered suddenly, and Mishal barely noticed the jinni's eyes shifting from deep black, to a human brown. "What?" The figure said. Mishal recognized Asaad's cadence. "Valiantly? I'm not done yet!"

"Asaad!" Mishal gasped.

"Sorry about that," Asaad said, except it was now Maymun. Mishal could pick the gentle nuance in Maymun's softer, more patient cadence. "It appears he's not done struggling."

All around, the jinn were beginning to cry. The lifted their thousands of arms, chanting with the strength of thunder.

"Maymun Al Sahabi!"

"Maymun Al Sahabi!"

"Maymun Al Sahabi!"

The jinn in the area, bolstered by the arrival of their great leader, led another charge against the exorcists. They surged forward, their shadows leaking along the ground, through the air, and across spirits. The exorcists gritted their teeth in hopeless grimaces and held on, trying their best to quell the unholy charge of jinn.

Maymun, appearing unconcerned with the battle, let the shadows wash over him. The jinni sunk into the ground, traveling through shadows until he stood at a small clearing. The sun was blushing over the black horizon now. Maymun stood in the first sunrays of the day, appearing mesmerized. Behind him, the battle raged on.

Mishal joined the fight, his heart sinking quicker and quicker through his ribcage, until he could almost hear it clattering on the stones between his feet. With Maymun's revival, all hope was lost for Asaad, as well as for Oman.

It was easier to lose everything when nothing had been ventured to begin with. Mishal knew that pessimism was a shield in the cruel face of life. To hope was to invite disaster to your very doorstep. But he *had* hoped. He had bet on Asaad's arrogance, his strength, his life…and Mishal had lost that bet.

Now, Mishal fought in desolation, but he still sent white fire to his hands.

Mishal didn't even have the strength to feel heartbroken, but he kicked back a jinni which aimed its metal claws at an exorcist.

Asaad would likely die, as would most of Oman.

Fine.

Mishal was stupidly fighting to salvage ruins.

So what?

"So what?" Mishal roared at Maymun's back. His voice carried over the rampant beats of death and destruction. "So what?" Mishal screamed again, his voice cracking. "So what, if he's back? Asaad did his *best* to save us, dammit! What are we, if we don't stand up now and show him it wasn't all for nothing?" He was openly crying now, hot tears coming down his face.

He hated this. Mishal detested helplessness, which was funny, because it appeared to be his perpetual state. He cried as he punched a jinni, rolled over a lightning bolt, and laid waste to enemies around him in droves. He wept as he made his way to his Shayib, who was no longer there.

"This can't be the end!" he shouted.

Over the horizon, a light streaked through the night. It was yellow, straight as a ruler, like an arrow from the stars. First, Mishal thought it was his imagination. Then, however, other exorcists and jinn pointed and stared at the light. It was a straight line, appearing to come right for Asaad.

Mishal stared, mouth open, as the light solidified into an ancient man, whose simple clothes contrasted against Maymun's kempt appearance. Who stood there with his beard drooping towards his stomach.

The CEO of Sarim had arrived, and he and Maymun stood for a long time, staring at one another between the first flickers of dawn and the last throes of the night. Then they began to speak.

Chapter Fifty Three

Hello.

Greetings.

I didn't expect this to happen.

It was inevitable in some ways.

What happens now?

I think… why, we're meant to kill each other.

How sad. Is there no way to avoid this?

Not if you insist on having him.

Ah. Well. It was nice seeing you. I think we might have enjoyed speaking, on some other occasion.

You know what? I think we might have.

Chapter Fifty-Four

The CEO and Maymun wrapped their arms around each other, as if they were embracing. Darkness and light filled the air, striking against one another like primordial forces. A blinding flash of light filled the space. In the light, the jinn and exorcists continued to fight, reflecting the battle of their leaders. Mishal summoned white fire, burning up a jinni's chest, then turning and kicking at another jinni with his heel. A strike sent him falling to the ground, but he rolled back up, still fighting the jinn as if he were physically striking at the hopelessness within.

Finally, the flash died down, leaving black charred remains on the wastelands. Now the sun rose in earnest, bringing down the shadow palace with its light. Instead of the castle breaking down, its pieces floated upwards like purple smoke.

The light illuminated Asaad's figure, which swayed in the sunlight. With a gasp, Mishal realized that the CEO was nowhere to be found. Had he failed? Was his body now among the many that littered the ground?

Asaad's figure opened his eyes. Mishal saw that the youth now had alternating eyes, even from this distance. They shifted from color to color.

One moment, the eyes were black, the black of night after the stars had departed. "I just wanted to feel the wind on my skin once more. Being alive is so beautiful…"

A second moment, Asaad's eyes turned almost gray, with a blue halo around them. Eyes like an old man's. "Our boy deserves to live," he said, his voice turning gravely. "He has been through entirely too much heartbreak."

"I have lived three thousand years in a *prison*," he said, voice changing again, eyes turning black. "Do I not deserve reprieve as well?"

"He is our hope!" he murmured, the gray orbs returning.

Mishal didn't know what he was looking at. Was the CEO also inside of Asaad now?

“Stop,” Asaad finally shouted said, raising his arm. Magical power, both light and dark, emerged from his body. The sheer power brought all the jinn and exorcists with a weight of power. Some slammed into the ground face down as if gravity had turned against them. Others fell to their knees. Mishal’s legs buckled but he somehow was able to stand, legs shaking.

And then, without another word, Asaad’s eyes rolled to the back of his head. He swayed once more, as if about to faint. Before he could come crashing down, however, Mishal rushed forward and grabbed his Shayib, holding him up by the back. He cradeled the man’s head.

“You’re safe,” Mishal said, unsure of whether he was talking to Asaad or to himself. “You’ll be alright!” He tried to look at Asaad’s eyes, but he couldn’t be sure of their color.

Mishal looked down at the kneeling crowd. The shadow castle was now more mist than anything else. The sun had pushed the jinn away, so that they dissipated to their hiding spots. Smoke from the battles rose to the air, casting shadows on the many injured and dying exorcists.

All of them, without exception, were looking at Mishal.

Chapter Fifty-Five

Three weeks later.

Mishal groaned. He was sat on the floor of a cave, on the seventh underground floor at Sarim. Manacles kept him chained to the wall, simultaneously holding him and sealing his magic. Every part of him ached.

It was humid here, making it so that the guards stood a few meters away from the cells. Still, Mishal could hear them whispering now.

"It's confirmed," one said to the other, her voice quiet. "The CEO's dead. That last spell took everything he had. They suspect his soul is now inside the traitor's body."

"Oh my God," the second guard replied. Mishal could see his shoulders slumping in defeat. "Sultan Qaboos dying, Corona, and now this?" he asked. "What kind of year is this?"

"Worst of the worst," the first guard replied.

Mishal had been locked in here for the past period, meaning that he had no clue what was happening in the outside world, aside from what these two guards whispered. Mishal knew he was being held here, pending further questioning.

Mishal, Eman, and Asaad were under suspicion of causing the CEO's death. Ridiculous charges, but no one at the organization was on their side anymore. Mishal slumped in his seat, feeling the chains tugging on his shoulder.

It was all over. The CEO was dead, Asaad was locked away in a different place, and Mishal didn't even know if it was Asaad in there, or just Maymun. Apparently, Asaad hadn't awakened since the Ma'rakat Al Dhill, or battle of shadows.

"Did you hear the worst part?" the first guard said to the other.

"Worst?" Mishal said, laughing to himself.

"Shut up, you!" the second guard shouted, then leaned forward. "It's all your fault this is happening!" He leaned towards the first guard, saying, quite plainly. "I heard, all right. Al Nasr is taking advantage of the CEO's death. The Witch of Calamity has declared war on Sarim."

Mishal's eyes widened. Something broke in his spirit as he remembered the sequence of events, starting three months ago. The rift between Asaad and Sarim, the CEO starting to retreat from daily Sarim operations, presumably preparing to cast an unimaginable spell, in the hopes of stopping Maymun.

The CEO had initially been warned by Asaad's mother, the Witch of Calamity. She had warned him about Maymun, then used his absence to declare war on Sarim. Had… had she actually been the one who'd told Maymun about Asaad to begin with?

A bitter laugh escaped Mishal's lips. They had all been led by the nose this entire time. The Witch of Calamity had tricked both exorcists and jinn alike.

Mishal slumped further in his seat. Asaad's mother had been weaving events, right from the start. She had successfully brought everything crumbling down. Sarim had lost, and he didn't know what to do. He didn't even know if Asaad was alive.

Mishal sighed, trying to somehow keep hope alive.

***

Four hundred meters away, in a different cell, a young man lay on his back on a bed of moss and rock. Sunlight flowed from outside, ricocheting from magical mirror to magical mirror within an intricate system of tunnels, ensuring that the young man's face was continually lit up. Chains covered every inch of the figure's four limbs, splaying them even as their owner lay on the floor.

The young man had been asleep for three weeks. He had been the subject of furious discussion both within Sarim and without. Some called him betrayer, others called him hope, and some called for it to be utterly destroyed.

Slowly, the figure opened its eyes.

THE END

Thank you for reading Hazim, the second book in the Sarim Trilogy.

My name is Ammar Al Naaimi. I write books about magic, adventure, and the search for personal freedom.

If you'd like to keep up with what I do, I suggest you follow me on @Naimihero on social media.

You can also check out my website www.ammaralnaaimi.com

www.ingramcontent.com/pod-product-compliance
Lightning Source LLC
LaVergne TN
LVHW091257150826
845673LV00006B/1445

* 9 7 8 9 9 9 6 9 9 9 1 4 7 *